£150
20

PRAISE FOR SIMON BRETT
AND THE FETHERING MYSTERIES

'A new Simon Brett is an event for mystery fans'
P. D. James

'Murder most enjoyable . . . An author who
never takes himself that seriously, and for whom
any fictional murder can frequently form
part of the entertainment industry'
Colin Dexter, *Oldie*

'A crime novel in the traditional style, with
delightful little touches of humour and vignettes
of a small town and its bitchy inhabitants'
Sunday Telegraph

'With a smidge of adultery thrown in,
some wise observations about stagnant marriages,
disillusioned lovers and the importance of friendship,
and, of course, plenty of whiffy red herrings, it all
makes for a highly enjoyable read'
Daily Mail

'This is lovely stuff, as comforting – and
as unputdownable – as a Sussex cream tea.
More please'
Brighton Evening Argus

'Crime writing just like in the good old days,
and perfect entertainment'
Guard

D0255812

DEATH UNDER THE DRYER
&
BLOOD AT THE BOOKIES

Simon Brett worked as a producer in radio and television before taking up writing full time. As well as the Mrs Pargeter novels and the Charles Paris detective series, he is the author of the radio and television series *After Henry*, the radio series *No Commitments* and *Smelling of Roses* and the bestselling *How to Be a Little Sod*. His novel *A Shock to the System* was filmed starring Michael Caine.

Married with three grown-up children, Simon lives in an Agatha Christie-style village on the South Downs.

Death Under the Dryer and *Blood at the Bookies* are the eighth and ninth novels in the Fethering Mysteries series.

SIMON
BRETT

DEATH UNDER THE DRYER

&

BLOOD AT THE BOOKIES

PAN BOOKS

Death Under the Dryer first published 2007 by Macmillan
First published by Pan Books 2008
Blood at the Bookies first published 2008 by Macmillan
First published by Pan Books 2009

This omnibus first published 2011 by Pan Books
an imprint of Pan Macmillan, a division of Macmillan Publishers Limited
Pan Macmillan, 20 New Wharf Road, London N1 9RR
Basingstoke and Oxford
Associated companies throughout the world
www.panmacmillan.com

ISBN 978-0-330-54573-0

1 3 5 7 9 8 6 4 2

A CIP catalogue record for this book is available from
the British Library.

Typeset by Intype Libra Ltd
Printed in the UK by CPI Mackays, Chatham ME5 8TD

DEATH UNDER THE DRYER

To Margaret and Daiva,

with thanks for all those haircuts

Chapter One

If her hairdresser had not been killed, Carole Seddon
would never have become involved in the murder at
Connie's Clip Joint. Though she knew the salon well –
and indeed had to walk past it every time she went
along the High Street to the inadequate local supermarket Allinstore – Carole had never before crossed
its threshold. There was something too public about
actually having her hair done in Fethering. Since she
had moved permanently to West Sussex some ten years
previously, her reclusive instincts had favoured an
anonymous salon in Worthing, where every six weeks
her straight grey hair would be trimmed to helmet-
like neatness by a taciturn man called Graham. The
arrangement had suited her. She and Graham were
polite, but showed no curiosity about each other, and
their haircuts were blissfully silent.

The first time Carole knew anything about his life
outside the salon was when she heard that Graham
had been killed in a motor-cycle accident. This had
happened when she rang to make her latest regular
appointment. The emotion in the voice of the girl who
relayed the sad news decided Carole that she needed to

find another salon. She didn't want the perfect detachment of her relationship with Graham to be spoiled by the maudlin reminiscences of other hairdressers after his death.

So the question then was where should she go. She checked the *Yellow Pages*, but was paralysed into indecision by the sheer number of options available. Carole hated the hidebound nature that made her react like that. About everything. Why did she have to make an issue of things? She ought to have grown out of that kind of introspection by now. She was well into her fifties – about to become a grandmother, for God's sake – and yet, contrary to the appearance she gave the outside world, still vacillated about decisions like a young teenager.

Eventually, as part of her knew she would end up doing, she consulted Jude. Her next-door neighbour's bird's-nest style was probably not the best of advertisements for the art of hairdressing, but she must get it cut somewhere.

Predictably, Jude turned out to be not that bothered where she went. Her haircuts weren't conducted according to a rigid timetable. She would just wake up one morning feeling that her blonde locks were getting a bit shaggy, or be passing a salon and go in on a whim. She did, however, say that Connie, of Connie's Clip Joint on the High Street, was 'absolutely fine'. Also, Fethering rumour had it, the salon wasn't doing that well, and so booking in there would be supporting local industry.

These arguments – together with the unruly state

of her hair – were enough to sway Carole. She seized the phone that very day, a Wednesday, and had a telling lack of difficulty in booking the first, nine o'clock, appointment at Connie's Clip Joint for the following morning.

As she stood waiting outside on the pavement at ten past nine, she regretted her decision. Local people, lightly dressed for the soft September day, were walking past. She knew who they were; they knew who she was; some of them were even people she spoke to. And now they all knew that she was waiting to get her hair cut at Connie's Clip Joint. From when she was a child, Carole Seddon had always wanted to keep an air of secrecy about what she did; she hated having her intentions known.

She tried to look nonchalant, as if she had just stopped outside the salon to check its window display. But the beautifully coiffed women and men whose photographs gazed artfully from behind rubber plants were not objects to retain the interest for long. In spite of her pretences, Carole Seddon looked exactly what she was: a middle-aged woman locked out of the hairdresser's.

Discreetly she drew up the sleeve of her Burberry and looked down at her wristwatch. Although the only other person in sight along Fethering High Street at that moment was a pensioner deep in his own thoughts and a duffel coat, Carole moved as if she was under the scrutiny of a prison camp watchtower.

Twelve minutes past nine. Surely she hadn't got the

time wrong . . . ? Surely the girl who answered the phone hadn't said the first appointment was nine-thirty . . . ? Such doubts were quickly banished. No, she had definitely said 'nine o'clock', and Carole had planned her whole morning around that time. She had taken her Labrador Gulliver out for his walk along Fethering Beach, and after she'd had her hair cut, she was going to do her weekly food shop at Sainsbury's.

Oh, this was stupid, just standing about. Trying to give the oblivious pensioner the impression that moving away from Connie's Clip Joint after precisely seventeen minutes (being Carole, she had of course arrived early) was a long-planned intention, she set off firmly back towards her house, High Tor.

As she took the first step, a silver hatchback screeched to a halt outside the salon, and a small, harassed-looking woman in her forties jumped out. She looked as if she had dressed in a hurry and clutched to her bosom an overflowing leather bag. Her brown eyes were tight with anxiety. No make-up . . . and her red-streaked hair, untidily swept back into a scrunchy, was not a good advertisement for the business she ran.

Because of course Carole recognized her instantly. Connie Rutherford, after whom Connie's Clip Joint was named. Fethering gossip ensured that almost everyone in the village knew who everyone else was, but village protocol demanded that you still didn't speak to them until you had been introduced. So Carole continued her stately progress towards High Tor.

The hairdresser, however, showed no such inhibitions. 'Mrs Seddon!' she called out.

4

Which, Carole supposed, was better than using her first name. She turned graciously. 'Yes?'

'I'm sorry, you're the nine o'clock, aren't you?'

'Well, I thought I was,' came the frosty response.

'Look, I'm so sorry. That idiot girl was meant to be here to open up at quarter to nine.' The woman fumbled in her bag for keys. 'I wonder what on earth's happened to her.' Still getting no reaction from her client, she said, 'I'm Connie. Connie Rutherford. I run the place.'

'Oh.' Carole received the information as though surprised by the identification. 'I'm Carole Seddon.'

'Yes, I know. You live next door to Jude.'

Carole was slightly miffed to think that this was her claim to fame in Fethering. No one knew about her past, her career in the Home Office. Here she was just Jude's neighbour. And Jude hadn't lived in Woodside Cottage nearly as long as Carole had been in High Tor. She shouldn't have been surprised, though. Jude was outgoing. Jude was easy with people. Everyone knew Jude.

Having opened the salon door, Connie Rutherford ushered her client in and went across to switch on the lights, chattering the while. 'This is really bad. Kids these days, they have no sense of time-keeping. You give them a job – and are they grateful? They don't even understand the basics of turning up when they say they will. God, if I ever have any children, I won't let them behave the way most of the youngsters do these days.'

Judging from Connie's age, Carole decided that, if

she was going to have any children, she'd better be quick about it.

But the hairdresser was off into another apology. 'I'm so sorry, Kyra should have opened up and been ready to greet you at nine. I gave her the spare set of keys – I've only got the one – I thought I could trust her. Then she was meant to wash your hair, so that it'd be ready for me to cut when I came in. Oh well, don't worry, I'll wash it. May I take your coat, Mrs Seddon? Now, I can call you "Carole", can't I?'

'Yes,' her client conceded.

'Well, you just take a seat here, and I'll put on some music. You'd like some music, wouldn't you?'

'No, I'm quite happy not to—'

But Connie was already away, fiddling with a CD player. 'I think Abba, don't you?'

'Erm, no, I—'

'Nothing like Abba for clearing away the cobwebs in the morning, is there?' As she spoke, the sounds of 'Dancing Queen' filled the room. 'Now would you like . . . ?' Connie stopped, apparently thinking better of the suggestion.

'Would I like what?'

'Nothing.'

'What I would like, if you don't mind, is for you to do my hair . . . since I already am a bit behind schedule.' Carole hoped that made it sound as if she had a more impressive destination later in the morning than the pasta aisle in Sainsbury's.

'Very well.' Connie turned on a tap above the sink.

'Just give the water a moment to heat up. It's cold first thing in the morning. And let's get this robe on.'

While the water warmed, Carole took a look around the salon. The pine boarding on the walls and the large cheese plants in the windows gave it a slightly dated feel, which was not dispelled by the Greek holiday posters and photos of models with exotic hairstyles. The basic decor probably hadn't changed for a good ten years, and endorsed Jude's suggestion that Connie's Clip Joint was not doing great business.

The stylist flicked her hand under the pouring water. 'Nearly warm enough.' Then she caught an unwelcome glimpse of herself in the mirror. 'Haven't had time to put a face on yet. Oh dear, if Kyra had been here when she was supposed to . . .'

But she decided that going on about the shortcomings of her staff was probably not the best way of recommending her salon to a new client. Instead, she stood behind the chair, rather closer than Carole might have wished, so that their two faces stood one on top of the other in the mirror. Connie ran her hands gently over her client's hair.

'So . . . how would you like it, Carole?'

She got the same reply all hairdressers had got for the past fifteen years – a gruff 'Same shape, but shorter'.

'You haven't thought of giving it a bit of colour?' suggested Connie.

'I have thought of it, but decided against the idea.'

'Not even highlights?'

'No, thank you.'

7

Connie Rutherford was far too practised in her profession to argue with a new client. 'I think you're right, Carole. This style really suits a strong face like yours.' Another test of the water, and a towel was fixed neatly in place around the neck. 'Now may I take your glasses off?'

'I'll do it,' replied Carole, aware of how graceless she sounded. She removed the rectangular rimless spectacles and placed them next to the sink. Her pale blue eyes looked naked, even threatened.

Expertly Connie swivelled the chair round and lowered the back, so that her client's neck slotted neatly into the groove at the front of the basin. Every time she underwent this manoeuvre, Carole could not quite erase the mental image of a guillotine. Even through the protective towel, she could feel the coldness of her ceramic yoke.

By now the temperature of the water was just right and Connie, though long since graduated beyond such menial tasks, had not forgotten the skills of hairwashing. Her strong fingers probed down into the scalp, working in a way that was both sensual and invigorating. Carole began to relax.

And the flow of Connie's talk matched the flow of the water, soothing, rippling away the tensions of her client. She had quickly caught on to Carole's private nature and knew better than to ask for personal information. Instead she kept up a light prattle about the concerns of Fethering: the fact that there had been more visitors than expected that summer; the possibility that English seaside holidays were coming back into fashion; the difficulty of parking in the High Street.

Only at one point was a detail of Carole's personal history mentioned. Connie, who wore no ring on her wedding finger, mentioned in passing that she was divorced, and added, 'Just like you.'

Immediately realizing that she had to cover this lapse, she explained, 'Jude mentioned that when she was in here once.'

Oh yes? And how much else, Carole wondered, has my neighbour been telling all and sundry about me? But she couldn't really make herself cross about it. Jude was by nature discreet, and in a hotbed of gossip like Fethering everyone's marital status was fair game.

'So is Seddon your married name?'

'Yes.' Though Carole wasn't sure what business of the hairdresser that was.

'Yes, I got stuck with mine too. By the time I thought about reverting to my maiden name, the other one was on so many legal documents and what-have-you . . . Of course, the divorce was particularly difficult for me, because Martin was involved in the business too. Yes, we started Connie's Clip Joint together. We'd met when we were both working in a salon in Worthing and . . .' she shrugged ruefully as she looked around, 'I suppose this was our dream. Like most dreams, it fell apart when it came up against reality.'

Recognizing that this was too downbeat a note for her performance as your friendly local hairdresser, she picked herself out of the potential trough. 'Anyway, let me tell you, any divorce is a nightmare, but one where you're also trying to divide up business assets . . . well, I hope yours didn't involve that . . .'

The cue was there to volunteer information about the end of her marriage, had Carole wished to pick it up. Unsurprisingly, she didn't. Connie moved quickly on. 'Still, mustn't grumble. Got a very nice little business here. Having a High Street position . . . well, of course that helps. As they always say, "Location, location, location". All going very well.'

Remembering Jude's words about the precarious state of Connie's Clip Joint, Carole took this assertion with a pinch of salt, and ventured a question of her own. 'And your ex-husband . . . is he still involved in the hairdressing business?'

Connie Rutherford's lips tightened. 'You could say that. Yes, he runs one of the biggest chains of salons along the South Coast.'

There was clearly a lot more information available and Carole felt she had only to issue the smallest prompt to release an avalanche of resentment. She refrained from doing so and fortunately, before Connie could self-start into her diatribe, the salon door opened to admit a slender man in black leather jacket and trousers. A gold chain showed against tanned flesh in the open neck of his shirt. His neat tobacco-coloured hair was highlighted in blonde and his teeth were veneered to a perfect smile. Over brown eyes as dark as coffee beans, he wore tinted glasses with small gold stars at the corners. From a distance he might have passed for twenty-five; close to, he was well into his forties.

'Morning, Theo.'

'Morning, Connie love.' His voice was light, self-consciously camp.

'This is my nine o'clock. Carole Seddon. First time she's been here.'

'Really? I'm Theo.' He gave a little wave; she couldn't have shaken his hand from under the robe, anyway. 'But you do look awfully familiar, Carole.'

'I live right here in Fethering. Just along the High Street.'

'Oh, then I must have seen you around.' A hand flew up to his mouth in mock-amazement. 'With a dog! Yes, I've seen you with a dog. Lovely big Labby.'

'He's called Gulliver.'

'Ooh, I'm such a dog person. I've got a little Westie called Priscilla.'

'Ah.'

'Connie's into cats, aren't you, love. I can never see the point of cats. Nasty, self-obsessed, spiteful little beasts.'

'Takes one to know one,' riposted Connie.

'Ooh, you bitch!'

Their badinage was a well-practised routine, insults batted back and forth without a vestige of malice. Carole Seddon got the feeling that for regulars it was as much a part of the Connie's Clip Joint ambience as the Abba soundtrack.

Theo looked around the salon. 'Where's the human pincushion?'

'Late. She'd got the spare set of keys and was meant to open up at eight forty-five. No sign of her.'

11

'Probably stayed in bed for naughties with that young boyfriend of hers. And actually . . .' he raised an eyebrow towards his boss's mirror image '. . . you look as if you might have been doing something similar.'

His insinuation prompted a rather sharper response. 'Don't be ridiculous!' Embarrassed by her own outburst, Connie looked at her watch. 'I don't know what she's doing, but when she does finally deign to arrive, I may have a thing or two to say to Miss Kyra Bartos.'

Theo slapped his hands to his face in a parody of Munch's *Scream*. 'Oh no! I'll have to wash my nine-thirty's hair myself!'

'Just as I've had to do with my nine o'clock.'

'Yes.' Theo grinned in the mirror at Carole. 'I hope you're appreciative of the quality of service you're getting.' And he flounced off to hang up his leather jacket.

Carole caught Connie's eye and mouthed, 'What did he mean about "the human pincushion"?'

'Ah. Young Kyra's taste for body piercing. It seems to be her ambition to get more perforations than a tea bag.' Another peeved look at her watch. 'Where is the bloody girl? I'll ring her when I've finished with you. Now do you want the cut slightly layered?'

'No,' Carole countered doggedly. 'I want it the same shape, but shorter.'

'Right.' Whatever reservations Connie might have had to this conservative approach, she kept them to herself, and started cutting.

At that moment Theo's nine-thirty skulked into the salon. In spite of the mild September day, she wore a raincoat with the collar turned up, a headscarf and dark glasses.

'Sheeeeeena!' Theo emoted. 'Sheena, my love, how gorgeous to see you.'

'Not gorgeous at all, Theo darling,' his client drawled. 'That's why I'm here. Morning, Connie,' she said as Theo removed her coat.

'Morning, Sheena. This is Carole.'

'Hi. I tell you, Theo, I just need the most total makeover since records began. When I looked at myself in the mirror this morning . . . well, it took great strength of will not to top myself on the spot.'

'Oh, come on,' Theo wheedled, 'we'll soon have you looking your beautiful self again. Now let's take off that scarf and those glasses.'

'No, no. I'm just not fit to be seen!'

'You're amongst friends here, Sheena darling. Nobody'll breathe a word about what you looked like *before* . . . Will you, Carole?'

Though rather unwilling to pander to the woman's vanity, Carole agreed that she wouldn't.

'And when we get to *after*, Sheena . . . *after* I've worked my magic . . . you'll look so gorgeous, men in the street will be falling over each other to get at you.'

'Oh, Theo, you're so full of nonsense.' But it was clearly nonsense his client liked.

After further dramatic delays, Sheena was finally settled into the chair, and there followed the great ceremony of removing her scarf and glasses. Carole, squinting at an angle into the adjacent mirror, wondered what horrors were about to be unveiled. What optical disfigurement lay behind the glasses? What trichological disaster beneath the scarf?

After the build-up, the revelation was a bit of a disappointment. Sheena was a perfectly attractive woman in her late forties – and, what's more, one whose blonded hair appeared to have been cut quite recently.

But she had set up her scenario, and was not going to be deterred from playing it out. 'There, Theo. Now that's going to be a challenge, even for you, isn't it?'

Her stylist, who must have been through the same scene many times before, knew his lines. 'Don't worry, darling. Remember, Theo is a miracle worker. So what are we going to do?'

'We are going to make me so attractive, Theo, that I become a positive man-magnet.'

'Too easy. You're a man-magnet already.'

'I wish. I don't understand.' Sheena let out a long sigh. 'There just don't seem to be any men in Fethering.'

'Ooh, I wouldn't say that,' he said coyly.

'Are you saying you've taken them all, Theo? I bet you never have any problem finding men.'

The stylist let out an enigmatic, silvery laugh.

Throughout Carole's haircut, this archness continued. Connie, who had tried commendably hard to keep conversation going with her client, eventually gave up and joined in the false brightness of Sheena and Theo. Carole found it quite wearing. A little too lively for her taste. She wasn't sure whether Connie's Clip Joint was going to be a long-term replacement for Graham and the anonymous salon in Worthing.

On the other hand, Connie did cut hair very well. Though keeping within Carole's minimal guidelines, she had somehow managed to give a freshness to her client's traditional style. With glasses restored, Carole couldn't help admiring the result she saw in the mirror.

'Excuse me for a moment,' said Connie, 'I must just ring Kyra and find out what on earth's happened to her. Now, I've got her mobile number somewhere.' She crossed to the cash register table and started shuffling through papers.

Carole felt awkward about the business of paying. When booking the appointment, she hadn't asked how much it would cost and now she was worried it might have been very expensive. Prices varied so much. And then there was the big challenge of tipping. Should she tip and, if so, how much? She'd never tipped Graham – that had been an accepted feature of their austere relationship – but she was in a new salon now and she wasn't sure of the protocol.

Connie listened impatiently to the phone. 'Well, she's not answering.'

She was poised to end the call, when suddenly they were all aware of a new noise, cutting through the harmonies of Abba. The insistent jangle of a phone ringing.

Carole and Connie exchanged looks. The hairdresser huffed in exasperation, 'Oh, don't say the bloody girl's left her mobile here.'

As Connie moved towards the source of the sound, Carole, curiosity overcoming her natural reticence, found herself following.

A door led through to the back area, storeroom, kitchenette and lavatory. As Connie opened it, there was a smell of stale alcohol and cigarette smoke. Beer cans and a vodka bottle on its side lay on a low table. On the work surface beside the sink stood a vase containing twelve red roses.

But it wasn't those that prompted the involuntary scream from Connie's lips. It was what she could see – and Carole could see over her shoulder – slumped in a chair over which loomed the dome of a spare dryer.

The girl's clothes were torn. There were scratches on her metal-studded face.

And, tight as a garrotte, around the neck of her slumped body was the lead from the unplugged dryer.

Chapter Two

'Drink this.' Jude placed a large glass of Chilean Chardonnay on the table in front of her neighbour. 'You look
as though you need it.'

The extent of Carole's trauma could be judged from
the fact that she didn't look at her watch and ask, 'Isn't
it a bit early in the day . . . ?' It was in fact only two-
thirty in the afternoon, but a lifetime seemed to have
elapsed since she had entered Connie's Clip Joint
that morning. She hadn't felt it proper to leave until
the police had arrived and, once they were there, she
couldn't leave until she had submitted to some polite,
though persistent, questioning. Her training in the
Home Office told her that they were only doing their
job, and she knew that they were starting from an
empty knowledge base, but she did feel frustrated by
the depth of information they seemed to require.
Though she kept reiterating that it was the first time
she had ever entered the salon, the police still wanted
her to fill in far more of her personal background
than she thought entirely necessary. What business of
theirs was it that she was divorced? Surely, rather than
following up such fruitless blind alleys, they ought to

have been out there finding the murderer. Again she reminded herself of the huge mosaic of facts from which a successful conviction was built up, and managed to endure the questioning with the appearance of co-operation. But she hadn't enjoyed the experience.

And it had all been made considerably worse by the presence of Sheena. Theo's client had taken the discovery of the girl's body as a cue for a full operatic mix of posturing and hysterics. 'Something like this was bound to happen!' she had wailed. 'I knew when I got up, this was an inauspicious day. I shouldn't have left the house. I should have stayed in bed. It's horrible! Though the poor girl may have deserved something, she didn't deserve this!' But through the woman's tears and screams, Carole could detect a real relish for the drama of the situation. Kyra's murder was the most exciting thing that had happened in Sheena's life for a long time.

Eventually Carole had managed to escape. While the Scene of Crime Officers embarked on their painstaking scrutiny of the premises, the detectives told her they were from the Major Crime Branch, and would be working from the Major Crime Unit in Littlehampton police station. They gave her a list of contact numbers, and urged her to get in touch if she thought of or heard anything which might have relevance to the investigation.

'I've done a bacon and avocado salad,' said Jude, and went off to the kitchen to fetch it. That was quick, thought Carole. But then perhaps more time had elapsed from the moment when she had knocked on her neighbour's door at the end of the interrogation and the moment she had come back to Woodside Cottage. Her recollection was a bit hazy. She had gone to High Tor and taken Gulliver out to do his business on the rough ground behind the house. And she had stood for a moment of abstraction, from which his barking had roused her. Maybe it had been a longer moment than she thought. Maybe that too was a measure of the shock she had suffered.

'So . . .' said Jude, finally nestled into one of the shapeless armchairs in her untidy front room, 'tell me exactly what happened.'

And Carole did. Unaware of the speed at which she was sinking the Chilean Chardonnay, or the readiness with which Jude was replenishing her glass, she told everything. Dealing with unpleasant subject matter during her Home Office days had taught her the value of drily marshalling facts and investing a report with the objective anonymity that made its horror containable.

At the end of the narrative Jude let out a long sigh and sat for a moment with her round face cupped in her chubby hands. As ever, she was swathed in many layers of floaty fabric, which blurred the substantial outlines of her welcoming body. Her blonde hair, which had been innocent of the attentions of a hairdresser for some time, was twisted up into an unlikely topknot, held in place by what looked like a pair of knitting needles.

'So you didn't get any insight into who might have killed the girl?'

'For heaven's sake, Jude. This morning was the first time I've even stepped inside that place. I don't know anything about any of the people involved.'

'I wasn't meaning that. I thought perhaps the police might've let something slip about the direction in which their suspicions are moving.'

'So far as I could tell, they're clueless. When they arrived, they had as little information as I had. Besides, you may recall from past experience that even when the police do start having theories about the identity of a murderer, people like us are the last they're going to share them with.'

Jude nodded ruefully. 'True.'

'In fact, you're probably a more useful source than I am.'

'How do you mean?'

'Well, you actually know all the people involved. You're a regular at Connie's Clip Joint.'

'Hardly a regular, but I suppose you're right.'

'And,' Carole went on, unable to keep out of her voice the note of envy that such thoughts usually prompted, 'people always confide in you, so probably you actually know a great deal about Connie Ruther-ford and her set-up.'

'A certain amount, yes.'

'She isn't one of your *patients*, is she?' This word too had a special recurrent intonation for Carole. Jude worked as a healer, which to Carole still meant that she operated in the world of mumbo-jumbo. And the people who believed that such ministrations could do them any good were, to Carole's mind, gullible neurotics.

'You know I prefer to use the word "client",' Jude responded calmly. It wasn't in her nature to take issue about such matters. She knew that healing worked. Some people shared her opinion; some were violently opposed to it. Jude was prepared to have her case made by successful results rather than verbal argument. And she knew that depriving Carole of her scepticism about healing would take away one of the pillars of bluster that supported her prickly, fragile personality. 'But no,' she went on, 'I haven't treated Connie. I just know her from chatting while I've been having my hair done.'

'Well, she volunteered to me that she was divorced – and that the divorce hadn't taken place under the happiest of circumstances . . .'

'What divorce does?'

Carole did not pick up on this. Though some ten years old, her own divorce from David was still an area as sensitive as an infected tooth. And lurking at the back of her mind was a new anxiety. Her son Stephen's wife Gaby was soon to give birth. Grandparenthood might mean that Carole was forced into even more contact with David. Resolutely dispelling such ugly thoughts from her mind, she went on, 'And I gather that she and . . . what was her husband's name? . . . Martin, that's right . . . used to own Connie's Clip Joint together, but now he's got a rather more successful set-up . . .'

'That's an understatement. He owns Martin & Martina. You must have seen their salons.'

'Oh, yes, I have. I'd never particularly paid attention to them, but they've got that big swirly silver logo, haven't they? There's one in Worthing.'

'Worthing, Brighton, Chichester, Horsham, Midhurst, Newhaven, Eastbourne, Hastings. Martin Rutherford seems to have the whole of the South Coast sewn up.'

'So every time Connie sees one of his salons, it must rather rub salt in the wound of the divorce.'

'Yes, Carole. Particularly since the name of the woman he left her for was Martina.'

'Ah. Not so much rubbing salt as rubbing her nose in it.' Carole tapped her chin reflectively. She was relaxing. The Chardonnay and Jude's calming presence were distancing her from the horrors of the morning. 'And has Connie found her equivalent of Martina? Has she got someone else?'

'No one permanent, as far as I know. I think she has had a few tentative encounters, but from what she said, most of them had a lot in common with car crashes. I don't think Connie's a great picker when it comes to men.'

'Pity. Because she seems to have a pleasant personality . . . You know, under the professional hairdresser banter . . .'

'Yes, she's a lovely girl. And very pretty. Always beautifully groomed.'

'Well, she wasn't this morning. No make-up, hair scrunched up any-old-how.'

'Really?' Jude looked thoughtful. 'That's most unlike her. I wonder why . . .'

'No idea. She implied she would have done her make-up in the salon . . . you know if Kyra hadn't been late . . .'

'Unfortunate choice of words in the circumstances, isn't it?'

'Yes, I suppose it is.' The thought brought Carole up short. The screen of her mind was once again filled by the contorted, immobile face, and she felt the reality of what had happened. Someone had deliberately cut short a young girl's life.

'Did you know her? Kyra?'

'She washed my hair last time I was in the salon. Didn't say much. Rather shy, I thought. Or maybe she was concentrating on learning the basics of practical hairdressing before she moved on to the refinements of inane client chatter. So, no, I can't really say I knew her.'

'Theo mentioned there was a boyfriend. Did Kyra say anything about anyone special in her life?'

Jude shook her head. 'Poor boy. I should think the police would be getting very heavy with him.'

'Yes. He'd be the obvious first port of call. And from the look of the back room of the salon, Kyra had been entertaining someone there. Empty bottles, beer cans, you know . . .'

'Adolescent passions are very confusing . . . they can so easily get out of hand,' said Jude, with sympathy.

'Yes,' Carole agreed, without any.

'Hm.' Jude refilled their glasses. Still Carole made no demur. 'So we're back in our usual position when faced with a murder . . . total lack of information.'

23

'And not much likelihood of getting any,' Carole agreed gloomily.

'Oh, there may be ways . . .'

'Like . . . ?'

'Well, obviously Connie's Clip Joint is going to be closed for a few days. It is a Scene of Crime, after all. But, assuming it does reopen . . . I think I should have a haircut.' Jude shook her precarious topknot; it threatened to unravel, but the knitting needles just managed to keep it in place. 'I could certainly do with one.'

Chapter Three

'So what's the word on the street?'

'How should I know?' Ted Crisp replied gruffly 'I never go out on the street if I can help it.'

'All right,' said Jude patiently. 'What's the word in the Crown and Anchor?'

'Ah, that's a different matter entirely.' Irregular teeth showed through the thicket of his beard in a broad grin. 'What happens in the pub I *do* know about. In fact, not a lot goes on in here that I don't know about. And there's not a lot said in here that I don't hear either.'

'Well then,' said Carole with less patience than her neighbour, 'what is being said in here about the strangling in Connie's Clip Joint?'

Deliberately delaying his reply, the landlord took a long swallow from his beer mug. It was near closing time, the only part of the day when he allowed himself any alcohol. He'd watched too many landlords drink away their health and profits to start any earlier. 'There is a general consensus,' Ted began slowly, 'that the girl's boyfriend dunnit.'

'And is that based on anything more substantial than speculation?'

'Well, Carole, speculation is obviously the biggest part of what people are thinking, but there are a few other details that might point in the same direction.'

'Like what?' asked Jude. 'We know nothing about the boyfriend, not even his name.'

'That I can supply. Nathan Locke. Sixteen . . . seventeen. Still at college, somewhere in Chichester. Parents live here in Fethering. I've seen him in the pub.'

'With Kyra?'

'Really can't remember. Those students tend to come in mob-handed, hard to tell which one's which or who belongs to who. And I'm so busy watching out for which ones of them are underage that I'm not concentrating on much else. The photo of the girl they showed on the television news looked vaguely familiar, but whether I'd seen her with anyone particular, I couldn't say. Certainly not as part of a regular couple.'

'She looked rather different from the photo on the news. She'd had some piercing done on her lips and eyebrows,' said Carole, for whom the image was uncomfortably recent. There was always something poignant about photographs of young murder victims – particularly girls – when they appeared in the media. Frequently they were out of date, posed school pictures of children who didn't look old enough to inspire adult passions. Which only seemed to make their fate more painful.

'What was her surname?' asked Ted. 'I must've

26

heard it on the news, but it was in one ear, out the other.'

'Bartos,' Jude supplied.

'Oh yes, I knew it was something foreign. "Bartos" . . . now where do you reckon that would come from? Spain perhaps . . . ? South America . . . ?'

'Originally maybe, but there's such a variety of surnames in this country, it doesn't necessarily mean she's "foreign".'

Ted took Jude's reproof on board. 'Yeah, OK, but it is an unusual name.'

'So's Crisp.'

'Nonsense. There's Crisps everywhere. Behind this bar here I've got salt and vinegar, cheese and onion, barbecue, smoky bacon—'

The two women groaned as one, both aware of the huge blessing the world had received when Ted Crisp gave up being a stand-up comedian.

Carole was quick to put such frivolity in its proper place. 'Bartos still sounds a foreign name to me.'

'Everything sounds foreign to you, Carole.' It was an uncharacteristically sharp response from Jude. Usually she let her neighbour's prejudices pass without comment.

'Well, it's true. Bartos doesn't sound English.'

Jude couldn't resist the tease. 'And does Seddon?'

And Carole couldn't resist the affronted knee-jerk reaction. 'Seddon is very definitely an old English name. It's been around since at least the fourteenth century. And it's common in Lancashire.'

'I thought you thought everything in Lancashire was common.'

'Jude! If you—'

Ted Crisp was forced into the unusual role of peace-maker. 'Don't know what's got into you two tonight. Can we just leave it that "Bartos" is a slightly unusual surname and could possibly be of foreign origin?'

'Very well,' said Carole huffily.

Jude just smiled.

'Anyway, Ted . . .' Carole reasserted her position as a serious investigator. 'You said you knew something about the boyfriend . . . ? Nathan Locke.'

'Only, as I say, that he did come in here sometimes.'

'He must have been quite a regular for you to know his name,' Jude observed.

'No, but one of my regulars does know him fairly well. Lives down the street from his family.'

'Who is the regular?'

Ted Crisp gestured over towards one of the pub's booths, in which an old man mournfully faced the last few centimetres of his beer. 'Les Constantine. Holds the Crown and Anchor All-Comers Record for the longest time making a pint last.'

'Could you introduce him?' asked Jude.

'He may not want to talk to us,' said Carole, her natural distrust of strangers asserting itself.

'You buy him a pint and he'll want to talk to you all right. Buy him a pint and he'll tell you anything you want.'

'Haven't you called "Time", though, Ted? You can't serve him, can you?'

'Listen, Carole, I'm landlord of the Crown and Anchor. I can do what I like.' He lumbered across towards the booth. 'Oy, Les, couple of ladies want to buy you a drink.'

The old man looked up lugubriously. 'They're probably only after my body.'

'Do you find that's what it usually is with women?'

'Oh yes.'

He moved daintily towards them. He was quite short and his long-lasting pints of beer hadn't put any flesh on his thin bones. He wore a dark grey suit which shone here and there from too much ironing, and a broad sixties flowered tie in a neat Windsor knot under a frayed collar. But though the clothes had seen better days, everything was spotlessly clean.

Ted made the introductions and set a full pint in Les's hand. Carole waited for a grateful mouthful to be downed before asking, 'So you actually know Nathan Locke?'

The old man looked disappointed. 'Oh, so you mean it wasn't my body you were after?'

'Just a few questions first, then we'll get on to the sex. What do you fancy – a threesome with the two of us?'

Carole was appalled by the suggestion, but once again was forced to admire Jude's uncanny skill of hitting the right note with people. That kind of outrageous badinage was the response Les Constantine wanted; she had instantly tuned in to his wavelength.

'All right,' he wheezed. 'We'll sort out the fine-tuning later . . . you know, "Your place or mine?" How's that?'

29

'Sounds perfect.'

'Sounds perfect to me too, Jude.' He relished the taste of her name on his lips. 'So what can I do you for? Presumably you're interested in the boy because of what happened down the hairdresser's?'

'Well, yes.'

'You and everyone else in Fethering. Yes, suddenly – just thanks to a geographical accident, living down the road from the boy – I'm very popular.' He took another swig of beer. 'Not the first free pint I've got this evening for my . . . inside knowledge, is it, Ted?'

The landlord guffawed agreement, and for a moment Carole wondered whether they had been seduced into a handy little scam between publican and customer. Then, with a wink, Ted Crisp wandered off to collect up glasses from the slowly emptying tables.

'I live in Marine Villas,' Les went on. 'You know where I mean?'

'Parallel to Beach Road, running down to the Fether.'

'That's it. I been there nearly forty years now. With the wife Iris I was, till she passed away . . . 1999 that was.' The recollection still caused him a pang. 'Anyway, the Lockes moved in about a year after that. Nathan was, I don't know, ten, maybe younger. Nice kid, not one of these that's always causing trouble and nicking your dustbins and throwing McDonald wrappers in your front garden and that. More interested in books and schoolwork, I gather. Whole family's a bit arty-farty, from what I hear.'

'So do you actually know Nathan?'

'Just to say hello to. Not bosom pals, but in a street

like Marine Villas . . . well, you hear a bit about everyone's business. Like, I suppose, most of them know
about everything I get up to . . . that is, except for the
Torture Chamber in the cellar and the Dominatrix,
obviously.'

'Oh, I'd heard rumours about her,' said Jude, again
finding exactly the right level.

'Blimey O'Reilly! You can't keep anything secret in
a place like this, can you?' He shook his head at the
prurience of Fethering residents.

'Anyway,' Carole pressed on, 'do you know anything
about Nathan Locke's relationship with Kyra Bartos?'

'She's the dead girl, isn't she?'

'Yes.'

This time the headshake was more measured and
regretful. 'Heartbreaking, isn't it? Kid like that. Got
everything ahead of her . . . you know, could have been
a mum, had lots of kiddies . . . and this, it kind of all
stops it, doesn't it? I saw that photo of her they had on
the telly . . . just a little girl. Reminded me a bit of my
Iris when I first met her . . . We used to do our courting
in Brighton . . . nice dance hall there was there then . . .'
With a more resolute shake of his head, he jolted himself out of maudlin reminiscence. 'Anyway, what was
the question? Did I know anything about Nathan's
"relationship" with the dead girl? Not really. Just heard
along the old Marine Villas bush telegraph that he'd got
this girlfriend who worked up the hairdresser's . . .
General feeling was that it was good news, because
he'd always had a reputation of being a bit bookish,
you know, coming from an arty-farty family, apparently

hoping to go to university and that . . . and I think everyone thought he deserved a bit of fun, like. "All work and no play" . . . you know what they say.'

'Do you know what he's hoping to read at university?' asked Carole.

'Read? I've no idea. I told you I didn't know him that well, so I don't know what books he reads.'

'Carole meant: what does he want to study at university?' Jude explained.

'Ah. Right. I don't know . . . language or something like that. Not anything useful.'

'What do you mean by "useful"?'

'Well, it's not something that might've, like, taught him a trade. Just all to do with books. That's all any of them seem to learn these days. I mean, when I was young, boys of that age done an apprenticeship. You know, learned something that might be useful in later life.'

'Is that what you did?' asked Jude gently.

'Too right. Couldn't wait to get out of school. My dad worked in boat-building . . . pleasure boats, yachts, you know. Got me an apprenticeship at the yard where he worked in Littlehampton, Collier & Brompton. I loved the work. My dad thought it'd last for ever.'

'You imply that it didn't?'

'No, but at least my old man never knew that. When he passed away, I was . . . what, early twenties? Just met Iris, we was courting, but me old dad never saw us married. Never saw what happened to the leisure boat-building industry either.'

'What did happen?'

'Fibreglass, that's what happened. Started in the fifties, then more and more in the sixties. And suddenly the skills I had . . . you know, woodworking skills, suddenly there's not so much demand from them down the boatyards. Oh, a few keep going with the old methods, some adapt. Collier & Brompton, yard I worked in, they did. They ask me if I want to retrain, but putting fibreglass in moulds, that wasn't my idea of boat-building. And I was in my forties by then . . . old dogs and new tricks, you know. So I give up the boats.'

'And haven't you worked since?'

'Oh, blimey, yes. Got a job putting in fitted kitchens. Bit overqualified I reckoned I was – a trained shipwright trimming edges off MDF shelf units, but . . . well, can't be too choosy when you haven't got no income. Did that till I was sixty-five, but by then the old hands were getting a bit shaky and I wasn't finding it so easy to lug all them units around, so . . . heigh-ho for a happy retirement. Which it was . . . till . . .' He didn't need to complete the sentence.

Carole broke the ensuing silence. 'So you can't tell us any more about Nathan Locke . . . ?'

'Well, no. Except that everyone in Fethering reckons he topped that poor kid.'

'And have they any reason for saying that?' asked Jude.

'He was definitely due to meet up with her the evening before she was found dead.'

'Do you know where they were due to meet?'

'Certainly not her place, I'll tell you that for free. Apparently her old man didn't approve of Nathan . . .

or any other young man who come sniffing round his daughter. No, the Fethering view is that, since Kyra had got the keys to the salon – you know, because she was due to open up the next morning – she entertained her boyfriend there.'

'Ah.' Carole nodded. The theory fitted in with the empty bottles she had seen in the back room of Connie's Clip Joint. And perhaps the red roses. 'Well, presumably, as we speak, the police are questioning Nathan Locke about just that.'

'I'm sure they would be,' said the old man, 'but they can't.'

'Why's that?'

'Because nothing has been seen of the boy since he left his home in Marine Villas at seven o'clock that evening.'

'Oh.'

'Which is another reason why all of Fethering have got him down for the job of murderer.' Wistfully, Les Constantine drained the last dregs of his pint. 'Oh well, I'd better be off.' He lowered his thin limbs gingerly down from his bar stool.

'Aren't we coming with you?' asked Jude, with a look of innocent sultriness.

'What for?'

Carole found herself blushing as her neighbour replied, 'For that threesome.'

'Ooh yes,' said the old man. 'Yes, I'd really like to do that. Trouble is,' he added with an apologetic smile, 'today I've got a bit of a cold.'

Chapter Four

Jude didn't make an appointment. From what she'd heard about the commercial health of Connie's Clip Joint, she didn't think it'd be necessary – even with the added attraction for Fethering people of having their hair cut at a murder scene.

The salon had reopened on the Friday, eight days after the discovery of Kyra Bartos's body. Jude reckoned the first few days would have mopped up the locals booking out of prurient curiosity, and it was the following Tuesday morning when she wandered in.

By then very little more had been heard from the police about their investigations. There had been some televised press conferences in the first few days, at which the detective chief inspector in charge of the case had demonstrated a caginess which could have meant he was within minutes of cracking the case wide open, or alternatively that he hadn't a clue what the hell was going on. Fethering opinion, lavishly expressed in the Crown and Anchor and at church, as well as in Allinstore and the rest of the local shops, continued to cast Nathan Locke as the murderer. There had still been no sign of the boy, and some local

Jeremiahs reckoned it was only a matter of time before he turned up as a 'Fethering Floater'. People who drowned from the seashore or, more frequently, in the fast-running waters of the Fether estuary, tended to be washed up on the beach before too long. But if a remorseful Nathan Locke had committed suicide by jumping into the river on the night of the murder, the sea was slow to return his body. 'Fethering Floaters' usually came back within twenty-four – or at the most forty-eight – hours. Jude felt pretty confident that, somewhere, Nathan Locke was still alive.

When she walked into Connie's Clip Joint, she received a cheery greeting from the owner and a polite nod from Theo. That Tuesday the owner's hair and make-up were immaculately in place. Both stylists were actually occupied, but Connie said she'd be through in ten minutes, so if Jude would like to wait . . . ?

This suited her purposes very well. Her vision enlarged by the description Carole had given her of the tragic scene in the back room, Jude just wanted a few moments to absorb the atmosphere of the salon. Murder, she had found, left a psychic signature on a setting that was at least as informative as a fingerprint or a bloodstain.

That morning there was no music playing, which again was helpful to her. The less distractions, the better. She disguised her intense concentration on the feeling of the place by flicking idly through the pages of a magazine. Hairdressers always offered a wide selection of reading, though – as was appropriate in Fethering – the magazines in Connie's Clip Joint favoured a more mature clientele. Apart from the predictable gossip-mongering of *OK!* and *Hello!*, also present were *Marie Claire*, *Vogue* and even *Country Life*.

Jude chose a *Vogue* and, while the surface of her mind was amused by the void between the stage-managed images on its pages and the reality of living women's looks, at a deeper level she tuned in to the aura of the salon.

There was discord there certainly, and it dated from long before the recent crime. Perhaps the conflict which had soured the atmosphere had been Connie and Martin's deteriorating relationship, its pressures increased by the necessity of maintaining a front of harmony while they worked together.

It certainly had nothing to do with Theo. Jude could detect an almost tangible warmth between the two stylists. They enjoyed working together; there was no discord there. And yet within each of them she could sense depths of personal conflict, directed at people outside the hermetic world of Connie's Clip Joint.

Jude hadn't got far, but she had extracted a sense of the place, a platform on which she could build future conjecture. Since she knew she wasn't going to get any further that morning in the psychic direction, she concentrated instead on the behaviour of the two clients having their hair done. Which, as things turned out, was a cabaret in itself.

Theo was dealing with the woman's hair, Connie with the man's. Theo must have been at work longer, because his client had clearly already gone through a colouring and washing process. Now both had reached the same stage, as though there were a prearranged plan to make the two haircuts finish at the same time.

Theo's client was a small, sharp-featured elderly woman, whose heavy make-up didn't quite coincide with the contours of her features. Her hair was newly red, though not a red that featured anywhere in the natural world. It was the defiant red of a burning oil-spill, and Theo was cutting it into the kind of 'Dutch bob' favoured by the silent-film star Louise Brooks. From the way he was working, this was clearly not a new style, but one he had been assiduously re-creating for some years.

The male client had broad amiable features gathered round a large squashed-in nose. Thinning a little on the crown, his remaining hair was thick and steel grey, with a corrugated effect, as though its natural curl had been subdued by a lifetime of brushing back.

Jude was very soon left in no doubt that the pair were married. The woman seemed much more interested in what was happening to her husband's hair than her own.

'No, shorter over the ears, Connie. You like it shorter over the ears, don't you, Wally?'

Wally, who appeared to have lived a life of listening to rhetorical questions from his wife, did not bother to reply.

'We don't want him walking round Fethering like some beatnik, do we, Theo?'

Theo agreed that that wouldn't be the thing at all.

'Do you know,' the woman went on, 'I can't believe the behaviour of young people these days, the sort of things they're always doing.' She almost dropped the final 'g' from the last word, a little giveaway that perhaps her origins weren't quite as refined as the voice she now used. 'I went into Allinstore only last week, just to buy some kippers . . . because you like a kipper, don't you, Wally?' Again her husband did not feel he had to confirm this self-evident truth. 'And of course it came from the freezer. I'd rather buy kippers, you know, like, fresh, but where'm I to do that since the fishmonger closed? I ask you, we've still got fishermen working out of Fethering, but if you want to buy fresh fish, you got to go all the way to Worthing . . . Not of course that a kipper is strictly fresh, because it's been kippered, but one from the fishmonger does look better than something out of the freezer that comes sealed in a bag with a little flower-shaped dab of butter on it. You say you can tell the difference in the taste, don't you, Wally?' With no pretence at waiting for a response, she went on, 'Anyway, I take the kipper up to the checkout and the girl behind takes it, and I give her the money, and she doesn't say a word. Not one word. It was like I was putting my money in a slot machine. So, as she gives me my change, I say to her, "Aren't you girls taught to say 'Thank you' any more?" And she says, "No, it's printed on the till receipt." Ooh, I was so angry when I got home. I was that angry, wasn't I, Wally? Yes, I was.'

She paused for breath, and her husband ventured,

'Similar thing happened to me as happened to Mim when I went to Tesco's in—'

'Don't talk while she's cutting your hair, Wally.'

He was obediently silent again. But in the few words he had spoken Jude was aware of a long-buried accent. The 'w' of 'went' had contained undertones of a 'v'.

'I don't know what young people are coming to today,' Mim went on. 'Makes me glad Wally and I was never blessed with children . . . well, though I don't think "blessed" is probably the right word. "Cursed" with children might be a better word, the way some of them behave these days. Because, of course, you had that terrible business here, didn't you, Connie?'

'Yes.'

If Mim was surprised by someone actually responding to one of her rhetorical appeals, she didn't show it. 'Drugs at the back of it,' she announced knowingly. 'Drugs at the back of most of this stuff, you know.'

'I don't actually think Kyra ever had anything to do with drugs, Mim,' said Connie.

'No, her old man wouldn't let her do anything like that,' Wally agreed. 'Was very angry when she had her ears and nose pierced. He always had standards, Joe.'

Mim looked a little miffed, as though allowing her husband space to inject three sentences into the conversation was somehow a failing on her part, and quickly resumed her monologue. 'Yes, more parents should have standards, and they don't. What are kids brought up on these days? Fast food, discotheques and video games . . . that's what they're brought up on, aren't they, Wally?'

Her husband, still basking in the glow of his recent conversational triumph, didn't feel the need to respond.

'I think bringing back National Service would do them all a lot of good. Your time in the Army didn't do you any harm, did it, Wally? Then these kids wouldn't go round smoking stuff and sticking needles in themselves and stuffing substances up their noses. Me and Wally worked in the music industry, where there was supposed to be lots of drugs going round, and we never saw any of them, did we, Wally? No . . . whereas these days the kids can buy drugs as easy as ice lollies – and they don't think no more of taking them than they would of eating an ice lolly. No wonder it all ends up with violence and murder.'

'But as I said,' Connie repeated patiently, 'Kyra didn't have anything to do with drugs.'

'I'm not saying she did. But the boy . . . the boy must've done. People don't go round strangling people for no reason. The boy must've been on drugs.'

'We have no means of knowing that,' said Connie, trying to bring a little rationality into the conversation. 'And nor, indeed, do we know that Kyra's boyfriend is the guilty party.'

But Mim's prejudices weren't so easily shifted. 'Oh, come on, if he didn't do it, why's he disappeared? If he's innocent, if he's got an alibi, why doesn't he come forward and tell the police about it? No, I'm sure he was on drugs.'

'Now let's blow it into shape, shall we?' said Theo, and started fluttering around Mim with the hairdryer.

'On drugs,' said Wally, taking advantage of the diversion to continue dramatically, 'or in the grip of a passion that he could not control.'

Mim once again seemed to regret the lapse that had allowed her husband to get a word in. 'Don't talk, Wally. You always move your head when you talk, and that makes it very difficult for Connie to cut your hair. Doesn't it, Connie? You come out of here with a cut on your ear, Wally, and it'll be your fault, not Connie's. Won't it, Connie? Incidentally, Connie, did you know the boy . . . you know, this Nathan, the one who killed the girl?'

Jude, who'd been taking in everything, listened with even greater attention.

'Yes, I had met him,' the hairdresser replied, 'and you really must stop saying that he killed her.'

'That's what everyone else in Fethering is saying.'

'I know, Mim, but in this country everyone is innocent until they're proven guilty.'

'That's nonsense. Was Hitler innocent? He never went to trial, he was never proved guilty, but are you telling me he wasn't?'

'No, I'm not. But that wasn't in this country and—'

'I think it's rubbish, that business about people being innocent until proven guilty. There's some people who should be locked away from birth. Paedophiles, and some of those illegal immigrants.'

Realizing that she wasn't participating in the most rational of arguments, Connie contented herself with saying, 'Well, as I told you, I did meet Nathan a few times. He'd sometimes pick Kyra up after work, and to me he seemed a very nice boy. Shy, not very sure of himself – only sixteen, I think – but I wouldn't have said he had a violent bone in his body.'

'It's the quiet ones you have to watch.' Mim pronounced the words as if they were an incontrovertible truth that clinched her argument.

'There,' said Theo, showing off his handiwork to his client in the mirror. 'That's how we like it, isn't it?'

She responded admiringly. 'Back to my natural look, yes.'

'Just a little whoosh of spray to fix it, and we can unleash you onto the streets of Fethering to break all the men's hearts, eh?'

'Yes.' Mim preened in the mirror. 'I could do with a few compliments. Never get any compliments from you, do I, Wally?'

'There – you're done too.' Connie stood back from her client, the co-ordinated timing of the haircuts having worked to perfection. 'Look all right, does it?'

The question had, inevitably, been put to Mim rather than Wally. She looked appraisingly at her husband's hair. 'Little more off the back. Don't want it trailing over his collar like some errand boy.'

While Theo made a big production of the final primping of his client, Connie duly did as she was told to hers. The couple were pampered into their coats. They paid their money, with Mim duly tipping both stylists. (Jude wondered whether Wally was allowed to carry any money of his own.) Then Connie crossed to the appointments book. 'Usual five weeks, shall we say? The Tuesday again. Same time?'

'Oh yes.'

'So that'll be nine-thirty for you, and the ten forty-five slot for the gentleman.'

'Doesn't matter. We'll come at the same time, and you'll sit and wait, won't you, Wally?'

Once again long experience told her husband that no response was required.

'Grenston's their surname,' said Connie. 'Wally and Mim Grenston. He was quite a successful musician – had his own band and did a lot of arranging, I believe. And she was a singer – also a very good career, but she gave it up when they got married . . . as women often did in those days.'

'But she said they didn't have children.'

'Maybe she didn't need them, the way she treats Wally. They're absolutely devoted to each other, you know.'

'I could see that,' said Jude thoughtfully. 'And Wally implied that he knew Kyra's father . . .'

Chapter Five

Like Carole, Jude had the privilege of having her hair washed by the salon's owner. 'I must get another junior soon,' Connie had said, 'but it seems, I don't know . . . so recent after what happened to Kyra.'

'Yes. Will it be hard to find someone?'

'God, no. Hundreds of girls still want to be hairdressers . . . in spite of the rotten pay. I get a dozen letters a week from kids asking to be a junior here, some with a bit of training, some not even left school yet. But the problem is getting the right one, one who's going to take the job seriously and actually be of some use to me.'

'Was Kyra one of those?'

'I think she could have become quite good. I mean, she was only seventeen. Like most girls of her age, she was easily distracted, mind often away somewhere else, not concentrating on the job in hand. But she was interested in the hairdressing business, and she definitely wanted to make something of herself. Get a bit of independence . . . her home life wasn't that easy.'

'As Wally implied.'

'Yes. Her father's very old. Kyra was the product of

his second marriage, but then her mother died a few years back. If she didn't get something of her own going, Kyra could see the prospect of being stuck here in Fethering as a carer for her old dad.'

'He must have taken it hard . . . you know, what happened to her.'

'I assume so. I don't know. Although he lives only in the next street to me, I've never actually spoken to him. I don't think he goes out much.'

Jude's hair was now towel-dry. Connie appraised it in the mirror. 'You're lucky, you know, not to need colouring . . .'

'At my age.'

'I didn't say that.'

'No, but you thought it. You're right, though. I am lucky. I think I've got the kind of hair where I won't suddenly start finding grey ones. I think it'll just get paler and paler until one day I look at it in the mirror, and it's all white.'

'Maybe.' Connie grinned. 'Now, is today going to be the day?'

'The day I look at it in the mirror and—?'

'No, no.'

'The day for what then?' Jude asked innocently.

'You know perfectly well. The day you decide to do something different with your hair.'

'Are you about to use the dreaded "short" word, Connie?'

'Look, it's lovely hair. It should be shown to advantage. It's funny, Jude, I don't think of you as someone who's afraid to take risks.'

46

'I'm not. And let me tell you, my hair has probably been through more metamorphoses than Madonna's. Back when I was modelling . . . God, it was a new style every couple of days. Which is why I really feel I've done my experimenting. I'm happy with it the way it is.'

'But you could look so much smarter. With it like this you look like . . . I don't know . . .'

Perhaps delicacy prevented Connie from continuing, but Jude provided a suggestion. 'A superannuated hippy?'

'You said it. Come on, Jude, make today the day.'

Firmly, the client shook her head. 'Nope. Don't feel like it. One day I will feel like it, and I promise you, when that happens, I will have the transformation done at Connie's Clip Joint. But today is not the day.'

'Huh.' Connie picked up her scissors without enthusiasm. 'So today it's just like your neighbour's, is it?'

'What do you mean?'

'"Same shape, but shorter."'

The impression wasn't perfect, but it did capture something of Carole's manner, and Jude chuckled. 'That's right.'

Connie started cutting, and her client relaxed into the experience. Theo didn't have an appointment for a while and sat reading a motor-racing magazine, a choice that seemed butchly at odds with his public demeanour. Jude was once again amazed at how people in certain jobs coped with the waiting. Shop assistants, restaurant staff and hairdressers had an ability to slip into a half-life, go inert and yet come immediately to energetic life when a customer entered. That was another part of the job, she reflected, that a salon junior like Kyra might have found hard to cope with.

'Ooh, Jude, something I was going to ask you . . .'

'Yes?'

'You're into alternative therapies and that, aren't you?'

'Well, to some extent,' Jude replied cautiously.

'I'd really like to talk about that at some point.'

'Why? Have you got some problem that you need help with?'

'No, no, it's not for that, not for me. It's just increasingly salons are offering other services, apart from the straight hairdressing. Manicure, ear-piercing, massage, all that stuff. Lot of modern salons are getting more like beauty spas. Sunbeds, detox wraps, you name it. That's certainly the way Martin & Martina are going.' She couldn't keep the resentment out of her voice when she mentioned her ex-husband's business. 'I just wondered if you were into any of that stuff, Jude . . . ?'

'Not really. What I do is therapeutic . . . you know, helping people feel better.'

Connie grinned. 'So you're just like a hairdresser. I tell you, we're very definitely therapists – for all the listening we do, apart from anything else.'

'Yes, I'm sure you are.'

'Well, if there were some service, you know, that I could refer my clients to you for . . . we'd make it a business deal. Look, take one of my cards. That's got my mobile number on it too. And give me a call if you can think of a way we can make it work.'

'I will.' Jude couldn't envisage anything coming of it. She didn't want her healing services to become part of anyone's pampering regime, but discussion of the project might be another way of keeping in touch with the hairdresser and maybe, eventually, finding out more about what had happened at Connie's Clip Joint. In the meantime, the best way of eliciting information remained the direct question.

'Have you had any more contact from the police, Connie, you know, since you reopened?'

'No, thank God. The amount of questioning I had to go through in the first couple of days . . . It was pretty wearing. They wanted to know all kinds of things that I wouldn't have thought could be relevant in a million years . . . asking about my marriage and a whole lot of other private stuff.'

'Did they talk to your ex-husband as well?'

'Yes, I gather Martin went through quite a grilling. But after the first couple of days, they seemed to decide there was nothing more I could tell them.'

'Did they lay off him too?'

She seemed about to make a different answer, but then said brusquely, 'That I wouldn't know. Anyway, the good thing was that quite suddenly they seemed to lose interest in me. Maybe that was when they got more news about Nathan Locke disappearing . . . I don't know. The detectives in charge told me to stay in touch, but – thank God – since then they've left me alone. Oh, they've given me lots of numbers to ring if I remember anything else, or if anything happens that might have a bearing on the crime. But then I can't imagine that anything is going to happen that has a bearing on the crime.'

'Unless Nathan Locke suddenly turned up on your doorstep one day . . . ?'

'I can't think that's very likely.'

'Do you mean you share the general Fethering view that he's committed suicide?'

'It'd be an explanation, wouldn't it?'

'Mmm.' There was a silence, disturbed only by the snipping of Connie's scissors. Eventually Jude broke it. 'You said you hadn't met Kyra's father?'

'That's right.'

'But Wally Grenston knows him. Talked about him as Joe, didn't he?'

'Yes. When Wally was last in he said hello to Kyra like he'd met her somewhere before. Probably seen her round her old man's place. From what he says, he's one of the privileged few who's allowed in there. The Bartos place backs on to my garden, but I've never had so much as a "How do you do?" from the old boy.'

'Mmm.' Jude looked thoughtful. 'Do you still live in the house you did when you were married?'

'Yes. Part of my settlement. That and this place . . .' she smiled ruefully '. . . while Martin went on to greater things.'

After a few moments' silence, Jude said, 'You know, I'd like to talk to Wally Grenston . . .'

She had no inhibitions about saying this. You could tell everything to a hairdresser. Whatever you said, they'd always heard worse. And generally speaking, they were discreet about keeping things to themselves.

'He's in the phone book.'

'Right.'

'Mind you, Jude, if you're going to call him, I'd recommend you do it on a Thursday morning.'

'Oh. Why?'

'That's when Mim goes out to her flower arranging club.'

Chapter Six

'Is that Mrs Seddon?' The voice on the telephone was male, cultured, even slightly academic.

'Yes.'

'You don't know me. My name is Rowley Locke. I am the uncle of Nathan Locke.'

'Ah.'

'And I'm sure I don't need to tell you that my nephew is currently the subject of a lot of local gossip.'

'No. It's hard to escape it.'

'The fact is that, without any evidence, without any trial, Nathan is being spoken of as the murderer of that poor girl in the hairdresser's.'

'I had heard that suggestion, yes.'

'Well, I apologize for troubling you, Mrs Seddon . . .' He was extremely polite in his approach '. . . but, from the perspective of our family, this is very distressing . . .'

'I'm sure it is.'

'And . . . I hesitate to ask you this, but I understand you were at the hairdresser's when the murder victim was discovered . . . ?'

Carole confirmed that she had been.

'Look, you may think this is an awful cheek . . . and I will fully understand if that is your view . . . but I wondered if we could talk to you about what you saw . . . ?' Carole wondered who the 'we' was. 'The fact is, Mrs Seddon, that, apart from constantly questioning us about Nathan's whereabouts, the police are giving us nothing in the way of information about what happened . . . which makes it very difficult for us to build up a defence for the poor boy . . . when he finally does turn up again.'

'You are confident that he will turn up again?'

'Yes, of course.'

He sounded bewildered that the question should have been asked, so, without spelling out the other local rumour that the boy had topped himself, Carole moved quickly on. 'I don't quite understand, Mr Locke. What is it you want me to do for you?'

'Just talk to us about what you saw in the hairdresser's that morning. I realize that you may think this is a police matter and that you shouldn't discuss it with anyone else . . .'

The priorities of her Home Office past made Carole think exactly that, but on the other hand she was being offered the opportunity to garner more information about people involved in what she and Jude were increasingly thinking of as *their* next investigation . . .

'I have telephoned the two hairdressers who were there that morning, and they have both taken the view that they shouldn't talk to us . . . which, as I say, is entirely their prerogative . . . but I was just wondering, Mrs Seddon, whether you felt the same . . . ?'

'I can see their point of view completely,' Carole began. 'On the other hand, I'm also feeling slightly frustrated by the lack of information I'm receiving from the police, so if we were to pool our knowledge, I think it might be mutually beneficial.'

'I am so glad to hear you say that.'

'So what do you want to ask me?'

'Well, if it's not inconvenient, I would rather the conversation were conducted face to face than on the phone.'

'That's fine by me.'

'I don't know how committed your time is . . .' His phrasing was again scrupulously polite.

'I'm retired, so I'm . . .' Carole overstated the truth '. . . relatively free.'

'Good. Because, seeing from the phone book where you live, I was wondering whether it might be possible for us to meet up at the house of my brother and sister-in-law . . . Nathan's parents . . . ?'

Better and better, thought Carole.

As soon as she arrived at Marine Villas that same afternoon, it was clear that, though Arnold Locke owned the house, Rowley was the dominant brother. There was a strong family likeness between them. Both were tall and spare, with thinning straw-coloured hair and large surprised blue eyes, which made them look unworldly almost to the point of vulnerability.

The front room into which Carole was ushered deliberately showed the Lockes to be an artistic family.

At the end away from the window stood an upright piano, and beside it a Victorian wooden music stand, which suggested at least one other instrument was played in the house. Nearby shelves held neatly upright books of sheet music. The same tidiness had been brought to bear on the extensive collection of CDs in parallel racks. Carole felt pretty certain they'd all be of classical music. Some tasteful framed prints on the walls and rigidly marshalled bookshelves re-emphasized the Lockes' rather intense interest in culture.

Also present in the room were Arnold's wife Eithne, and Rowley's daughter Dorcas. The former was a dumpy woman whose ample figure strained against the buttons that ran all the way down her flower-printed cotton dress. She wore her dark grey hair in a generous bun low at the back of her neck. Carole couldn't help being reminded of the figure from a childhood pack of 'Happy Families', Mrs Bun the Baker's Wife.

Dorcas, on the other hand, with honey-coloured eyes, long spun-gold corkscrew curls and a tall slender body, was the kind of girl who would have been earnestly pursued as a model by the Pre-Raphaelites. The clothes she affected, long eau-de-nil top over ankle-length pale green skirt, encouraged the impression. Her speech showed the same academic earnestness as the other Lockes', but with a slight lisp. It made her sound more childish than her age, which Carole estimated at about twenty.

'My wife Bridget would have liked to be here too,' Rowley apologized, 'but sadly she has to work. She's a teacher in Chichester.' Maybe at the college where Nathan was a pupil?

Carole was struck by how relatively calm Arnold and Eithne Locke seemed. If her son Stephen had disappeared under suspicion of having committed a murder, she didn't think she would be behaving with such equanimity. But Nathan's parents appeared to think that everything was in hand and, from the way they looked at him, that Rowley was the one who had it in hand.

'I hope you don't mind meeting us all together, Mrs Seddon.'

'That's no problem. Please call me Carole.'

'Thank you. And I'm Rowley. But this is obviously a family thing we're talking about. And it's quite serious.'

'Particularly because it involves Fimby,' added Dorcas.

In response to Carole's look of puzzlement, Rowley explained, 'Sorry, Fimby's a nickname we have for Nathan.'

'Everyone in the family has a nickname,' said Dorcas.

Carole hoped she wasn't about to be told what they all were, and fortunately Rowley continued, 'I must tell you, Carole, that our starting point is that Nathan did not kill Kyra Bartos.'

'Do you have any evidence to support that?'

'The evidence we have is our knowledge of the boy's personality. We've all watched him grow up. He's only sixteen, and he does not have a violent nature.'

'People's nature can change . . . under provocation.'

'Maybe, but I can't see Nathan's nature changing that much. He's a gentle boy. His main interest is English literature.'

'Rowley . . .' Carole didn't find that the name tripped easily off her tongue, '. . . I'm playing devil's advocate here, but it is quite possible that someone whose main interest is English literature, who is what one could call "bookish", might have great difficulty in adjusting to the realities of the real world and, you know, particularly in an emotional relationship . . .' She left them to fill in the rest of the sentence.

Rowley nodded in acknowledgement of her argument, noting it down as a good debating point. 'I agree that is a possible scenario, but not in the case of Nathan.'

'No, we really can't imagine him doing anything like what he's being publicly accused of,' Arnold contributed, and the 'we' he used seemed to encompass not just himself and his wife but the whole family.

'But you don't have anything handy like an alibi for him at the time when he was supposed to have been with Kyra?'

'No.' After his brother's brief intervention, Rowley once again took up the reins of the conversation. 'And, indeed . . . I'm telling you this, Carole, because I respect the fact that you've agreed to come and talk to us this afternoon, and because I trust you not to spread the information around . . . we are pretty certain that Nathan did actually see Kyra Bartos the evening before she died.'

'You haven't heard that from Nathan himself?'

'We've heard nothing from Nathan himself.'

'And you don't think he's just run off, for reasons which have nothing to do with the murder?'

Rowley was puzzled by the question. 'Why on earth would he do that?'

'Young people do it all the time. You know, if they're unhappy at home . . .'

'Nathan was not unhappy at home,' said Rowley firmly. 'We are a very strong family, and he always enjoyed being part of it.'

This was spoken so much like an article of faith that Carole found herself wondering what it must have been like for any family member who questioned the party line. She knew she'd find such a set-up impossibly claustrophobic. Maybe Nathan did too . . .

Eithne Locke, perhaps because she feared being thought unmaternal, interjected at this point. 'Of course he wouldn't want to run off. Listen, we haven't seen Nathan since he left here early that evening, round seven. Arnold and I are obviously worried sick.' But she didn't sound worried sick. Still, Carole knew that that meant nothing. The woman's surface calm might well be a coping mechanism for her anxiety.

'We are sure he will come home eventually,' the boy's mother went on, 'but he must be aware that he's a suspect and I'm sure he's terrified of the police getting hold of him.'

'Our fine boys in blue,' said Rowley Locke, clearly speaking from a long-held agenda, 'do not have the best reputation in the world for the way they deal with suspects. Human rights tend to cover only what can be seen; they frequently cease at the door of the interrogation room. We don't want Nathan to have to go through that.'

Carole, whose experiences in the Home Office had given her a less cynical attitude to the British police, did not think that this was the moment to take issue. Nor did she think it was the moment to raise the question of suicide with the boy's parents. It seemed to have entered their thoughts no more than it had Rowley's, and Carole was not about to create new anxieties for them.

'Have you any idea how the police's search for Nathan is going?'

Rowley Locke shrugged. 'As I say, we're not very high up the distribution list for police information.' Join the club, thought Carole. 'They've asked us about where he might be, obviously.'

'They even had the nerve,' said Eithne, 'to search this house to see if he was hiding somewhere.'

'Though they did ask our permission first,' her husband pointed out.

'Yes, but only because they would have had to get a search warrant otherwise,' Eithne added.

'And they looked for him in our house as well,' said Rowley. 'We too gave permission. We have nothing to hide. They even searched Treboddick.'

'Treboddick?'

'Oh, sorry, Carole. It's a place we have in Cornwall. They thought Nathan might have hidden himself away down there.'

SIMON BRETT

'Well, I suppose that's a reasonable suspicion, isn't it? If it's a family place?'

'Huh.' Rowley Locke was not temperamentally inclined to listen to any arguments in favour of 'our fine boys in blue'. 'Anyway,' he went on, 'the reason for wanting to talk to you, as I said on the phone, is because the police are telling us nothing. And it's very difficult for us to get a handle on what Nathan might or might not have done, when we don't know exactly what it is he's been accused of.'

'He hasn't been accused of anything yet.'

'All right. What he's suspected of having done. And I just thought . . . because you were actually on the scene when the body was discovered, you might know something . . . well, more than we do, anyway.'

Carole nodded thoughtfully and looked around the room. She felt justified in taking her time. What the Lockes were asking could be considered as a major intrusion into her privacy. They weren't to know she was at least as desperate to find out everything about them as they were about her.

The framed photographs on the mantelpiece and walls corrected an image of the family that she had received. Dorcas's prissiness had suggested to Carole that she was an only child, but the evidence negated that impression. All the pictures showed lots of children, and both sets of parents, in a variety of relaxed holiday settings. Both Nathan and Dorcas had siblings, one of hers being an identical twin. Carole got the strong impression that the Locke cousins did every-

60

thing together. And no doubt, she thought with a mental cringe, they all had nicknames like Fimby.

'I see you're looking at the photographs,' said Rowley. 'That's Nathan.'

The boy he pointed out had darker hair, but the same susceptible pale blue eyes. He was good-looking, probably about thirteen when the photograph had been taken. The massed children were on a boat in a creek that looked Cornish, the Helford River maybe. Presumably the setting was somewhere near Treboddick. The other children were taking up nautical poses for the camera, like something out of *Swallows and Amazons* (a book which Carole suddenly felt certain the Lockes would have read with enormous relish). But Nathan looked detached, almost embarrassed by the play-acting around him. Maybe it had only been a phase, an adolescent grumpiness which had afflicted him that one particular day, but Carole got the impression of the boy as an unwilling outsider in the claustrophobic world of the Locke family.

'Thank you. I haven't met him obviously,' she said. 'And I'm afraid I don't know much about the background or the history at Connie's Clip Joint. That morning was the first time I had been in the salon.'

'It must have been a terrible shock for you. But do you mind telling us what you actually saw?'

'No, not at all.'

'And is it all right if I take notes?'

Carole shrugged permission. Rowley Locke took a small plain leatherbound notebook out of his jacket pocket, and then unscrewed a large fountain pen. He

opened a page on which she could see neat italic writing in brown ink. She had a feeling that everything
Rowley Locke did in his life would be balanced on that
fine line between individuality and pretension.

Her description of what she had seen in the back
room at Connie's Clip Joint was delivered as impassively as she could make it. When she had finished,
Rowley Locke completed his last note with a neat full
stop.

'Thank you so much, Carole. There were quite a lot
of details there we didn't know about.'

'Oh?'

'Well, we knew how the girl had been strangled, and
what had been used to do the deed, but we didn't know
anything about the vodka bottle and beer cans. Or the
red roses.'

'Those all seem to suggest that Kyra had been entertaining someone in the salon that evening. She had the
keys, you see, so that she could open up the following
morning.' Carole remembered something Les Constantine had told her, and could see no harm in passing it
on. 'I gather that Kyra's father was very protective of
her, wouldn't have liked the idea of her having
boyfriends around at home. So I suppose, if the girl
wanted to be alone with Nathan, Connie's Clip Joint
was the obvious place for them to go.'

Eithne Locke, interpreting this as some obscure
slight on her as a parent, insisted that Nathan had
always been welcome to bring Kyra to Marine Villas.
'We made that very clear to him. Arnold and I have
very liberal attitudes to that kind of thing. Diggo had

one girlfriend virtually living here just before he went to university.'

Carole assumed this was another of the ghastly Locke nicknames, probably for Nathan's older brother, but she didn't ask for an explanation. Instead she went on, 'I haven't heard it as a fact from the police, but I had assumed that the vodka bottle and beer cans might have given them a direct link to Nathan. You know, through his DNA or fingerprints.'

'Yes, except that they don't have his DNA or fingerprints on file – and we refused to let them take any samples from the house. We know our rights.' Rowley Locke was mounting another of his human rights hobby horses. 'I am aware that this government would like to have everyone's details on file from birth, but at the moment they can only keep such records for people who have actually been found guilty of a crime. And I am glad to say that my nephew has never fitted into that category.'

'But you're not denying,' asked Carole, 'that it does look likely that Nathan spent some time with Kyra in the salon the evening before she was found dead?'

'No, none of us is denying that. We think it very likely that he did spend time with her. What happened while they were together . . .' For the first time he looked embarrassed. 'Carole, you didn't gather from the police whether there had been any sign of . . . sexual activity . . . on the girl's body?'

'They're no more likely to have told me that than they are you.'

63

'No, I suppose not. I wasn't suggesting rape or . . . I was thinking of consensual sex.'

'Do you know whether Nathan and Kyra were sleeping together?'

Instinctively Rowley looked to the boy's mother to answer this question. 'I can't actually be sure,' said Eithne Locke, 'but I would have thought it likely. According to everything one reads in the newspapers, young people seem to be sexually active from about the age of fourteen these days. And certainly Nathan would have encountered no disapproval of such behaviour in this house, would he Arnold?'

Her husband concurred. 'No, we're not prudish at all.' But he contrived to sound prudish as he said it.

'Had you actually met Kyra?'

Arnold looked to his wife for consent before saying, 'Not really. Well, that is to say, Nathan never brought her back here to introduce us, did he, Eithne?'

'No. Which one might have thought was rather odd.'

Carole didn't find it at all odd. 'You said "Not really", Arnold . . .'

'Yes. Well, Eithne did once meet them together in Fethering High Street, didn't you?'

'Yes. And it was a situation where Nathan couldn't avoid introducing the girl to me. Though he didn't do it with very good grace . . . almost as though he were ashamed of her.'

Much more likely that he was ashamed of you, Carole thought. 'And neither of you ever met Kyra's father?'

'Oh no,' said Arnold.

'Right.' Carole turned back to the dominant – not to say controlling – brother. 'So, Rowley, your view would be that Nathan did spend some time with Kyra in the salon that evening, then, after he'd left, someone else came along and murdered her?'

'That seems to me to be the most likely scenario, yes.'

'Well, it looks as though all such speculations are going to be no more than speculations until the boy reappears and gives an account of himself.'

Rowley Locke agreed.

'And presumably . . . I'm sorry to ask you this, but I feel I have to . . . none of you have any idea where Nathan might have gone?'

They all confirmed that they hadn't. So, with assurances on both sides that they'd get in touch to share any further information that might come up, Carole left the house in Marine Villas and walked back the short way to High Tor – with an uncomfortable feeling that she had just been interrogated.

Chapter Seven

Jude had borne Connie Rutherford's advice in mind, and waited till the Thursday morning to contact Wally Grenston. She had been through various possible excuses for her call, but, not being by nature a devious person, had opted finally for the truth. 'I was in Connie's Clip Joint on Tuesday morning when you and your wife were having your hair done . . .'

'Oh yes. You were waiting. Blonde lady, am I right?'

'You are. Plumpish.'

'Well covered, I would have said.'

'You're a gentleman, Wally.'

'So I like to think.'

'Look, I'm going to be honest with you. I've got rather interested in what happened to Kyra Bartos . . . how she came to be killed . . .'

'You and the rest of Fethering.'

'Yes, and you said something about the girl's father . . . you know, as if you knew him . . .'

'Right.' For the first time there was a note of caution in Wally Grenston's voice.

'I just wanted to follow up on that . . . find out more . . . ask a few questions . . .'

'Are you some kind of journalist, Jude?'

'No, I'm just . . . as I said . . . interested,' she finished lamely.

'Interested in protecting the boy who's supposed to have murdered her . . . or interested in finding out who really did it?'

'Both. But why did you ask that question?'

'I have my reasons. Tell you what – you want to talk, you can come round here. Straight away, though. And you have to be gone by quarter to twelve.'

'Sounds good to me,' said Jude.

'Hello?'

Carole was taken aback. 'Oh, sorry. I wasn't expecting anyone to be there. I was just going to leave a message.' Then, aware of her daughter-in-law's condition, she asked anxiously, 'Are you all right, Gaby?'

'Yes, of course. I'm not ill, I'm just pregnant.'

'I know. But you being home in the middle of the day . . .'

'Just taking a couple of days off to try and get the baby's room sorted. Steve keeps saying he's "going to do it at the weekend", but his weekends seem to be as busy as his weeks at the moment.'

'Yes.' Not for the first time, Carole wished she understood more about her son's high-powered and extremely lucrative job. It was to do with money, and computers came into it too, but whenever Stephen tried to provide more detail on the subject, she found her mind glazing over. 'And how long are you going to keep on working?'

'Plan is to go till the end of the month. That'll give me four weeks till the ETA.'

'Sorry?'

'Estimated Time of Arrival.'

'Oh yes, of course. Twenty-eighth of October.' The date was engraved on Carole's memory.

'That's assuming I can still reach across the desk to pick up my phone, and deal with all those penny-pinching producers.' Gaby worked as a theatrical agent. 'I'm getting absolutely massive. Well, I was no sylph to start with.'

The image of Gaby's chubby body came into her mother-in-law's mind. She hadn't been showing much when they last met. Carole realized that that had been more than two months before. 'It'd be lovely to meet up,' she said, rather guiltily.

'Yes. We were saying that only last night.'

'You and Stephen?'

'Well, and David. He'd come round for supper.'

'Ah.' Carole felt a pang of something that included jealousy. She had always worried about the post-divorce David being closer to Stephen than she was . . . or now being closer to Stephen and Gaby . . . soon perhaps to be the favoured grandparent to the forthcoming baby.

'He was actually saying it was daft we hadn't invited you last night as well. Sorry, we didn't think, but it would have been a great idea.'

No, it wouldn't, was Carole's immediate, but unspoken, reaction.

'I mean, you both managed so well at the wedding.

DEATH UNDER THE DRYER

David was saying how great it was that the two of you could at last be together again without any strain.'

Clearly, thought Carole, his recollection of the wedding was very different from hers. All that the prolonged exposure to her ex-husband had made her think was what a good idea the divorce had been. If she'd had her way, she would have liked a written guarantee that she'd never have to see David again for as long as she lived. But she knew Gaby – and particularly Stephen – were very keen on a rapprochement between the estranged parents. She could see their point of view. With the baby coming, it would be so much nicer to have family harmony, both grandparents coming together every time they visited the new arrival. But if that was Stephen and Gaby's ambition, Carole was afraid they were going to be disappointed.

'Well, it would be nice to meet up,' she said.

'Yes.'

Was she being hypersensitive to detect a lack of enthusiasm in Gaby's tone? Was she regarded as a 'difficult' mother-in-law? In private, did Stephen and his wife giggle about her? Did Gaby groan every time he said that they really ought to see his mother?

'That'd be great,' the girl went on, still with not quite enough enthusiasm for her mother-in-law's taste. 'I'll check with Steve. His diary's always so much busier than mine. And then we'll get back to you and sort out a date.'

'That sounds fine.'

After the phone call had finished, Carole felt restless. Though she had always loved Stephen, she still

69

felt guilt for not being as maternal as she should have been. And now there was the challenge of forming a relationship with the next generation. She didn't feel she'd been a great success with her own child. Would it be different if the baby was a girl? (Though Stephen and Gaby had had the opportunity at various scans to know the gender, they'd chosen not to.) For the millionth time in her life, Carole Seddon wished she could have a personality transplant.

Wally Grenston's old face creased into a grin as he handed Jude the coffee. It was in a bone china cup with a delicate design of shrimp-pink and gold. On the saucer lay a small silver spoon whose thin handle ended in a wooden bead like a coffee bean. The sugar bowl and tongs were similarly decorated.

The grin stayed as he sat back in his chair. 'Let me enjoy this moment.'

'What do you mean?'

'Mim – that's my wife . . .'

'I saw her at the hairdresser's.'

'Yes. Well, she's gone through her life imagining that, the minute her back's turned, I am immediately entertaining some attractive woman . . .'

'Ah.'

'. . . and let me tell you, this is the first time it's happened.'

'Right.'

He leaned forward a little. 'Could you tell me something, Jude? Are you wearing lipstick?'

'No. I very rarely wear any make-up.'

'Oh, dash it,' he said, with mild regret.

'What's the problem?'

'Just, if Mim came back, and she found a second coffee cup here, *with lipstick on it* . . . well, that really would set the cat among her pigeons.'

'Do you want to upset her?'

He was affronted by the suggestion. 'Of course not. I adore the old bat. But it doesn't do her any harm to be kept on her toes.'

This seemed to him disproportionately amusing and, while he chuckled, Jude took in the room around her. The most striking thing was the number of awards it contained. In purpose-built chestnut-framed display cases stood cups, figurines, engraved glassware, abstract sculptures and calligraphed citations, all naming 'Walter Grenston' as their winner. Jude didn't recognize any of the awards, but all their artwork seemed to imply success in the field of music, and this impression was confirmed by the white grand piano at the back of the room. The rest of the decor was busy and fussy; lots of little objects – photographs in elaborate silver frames, statuettes, vases and animals made of swirling coloured glass – were everywhere. Though her own sitting room at Woodside Cottage was equally cluttered, the impression could not have been more different. Every object in the Grenstons' house looked as though it was dusted and had its alignment checked every hour on the hour.

They lived in Shorelands, a large estate on the west side of Fethering, whose denizens had to comply with a daunting number of local regulations, policed by a committee of residents. People had to be extremely rich to live there, so clearly during his musical career Wally Grenston had collected money as well as awards. The house was on one of the Shorelands Estate's prime sites, and its picture windows showed a perfectly maintained garden leading down to the sea. In fact, the openness of the English Channel seemed at odds with the claustrophobia of the overcrowded room, which might have been more suitably set in the depths of a middle-European forest.

Having indulged his laughter to the full, Wally moved on to business. 'So you wanted to know about Joe Bartos?'

'Yes.'

'And just to confirm again . . . you have no professional axe to grind here? This is out of pure curiosity?'

'Murder makes everyone curious, doesn't it?'

'Maybe.' The idea brought a new seriousness to his manner. 'Though for many, murder has been a signal to stop curiosity. Don't ask any questions. Play safe. Do not put your head above the parapet.'

'Are you talking about during the war?'

'A lot of things that were true during the war are still true now. People do not change . . . enough . . . sadly.'

'You weren't born in this country, were you?'

He shook his head, unoffended by the question. As ever, Jude's directness worked its magic.

'No, I came here early in 1939, just before it all happened, but when it was already pretty clear what

72

was going to happen. I was nineteen . . . one of the ones who got away.'

'One of the lucky ones?'

He smiled sadly. 'I didn't say that, did I? But, as things turned out, lucky, yes. I would rather have gone back to the world in which I grew up, but that world very soon ceased to exist, so there was nowhere to go back to.'

'Are you talking about Germany?'

'It was true of Germany as well, but that was not my country. My country – though some would say that a Jew does not really have his own country – is Czechoslovakia. Have you been there?'

Jude nodded. 'A couple of times. Before the . . . what did they call it? . . . "Velvet Revolution"?'

'They always have a new name for changes in my country. And they always have new changes. Once somebody renamed my country "The Protectorate of Bohemia/Moravia". I tell you, Czechoslovakia has had more invasions and occupations than you have had hot dinners.' He chuckled, trying to shift himself out of an encroaching gloom. 'You wanted to know about Joe Bartos . . . So, if you see yourself as an amateur sleuth . . .'

'I didn't say that I did.'

'Then why else are you so interested in this murder?'

'Well . . .'

'Anyway, if you *do* see yourself as an amateur sleuth . . . you will no doubt have worked out how I know Joe Bartos . . . ?'

Jude shook her head. 'I'm sorry. I'm clearly not a very good amateur sleuth.'

'No, you are not. Do you not know where the name "Bartos" comes from?'

'Spain, maybe . . . or . . . ?'

Wally Grenston shook his head and clicked his teeth in exasperation. 'No, no. You think that because everyone here pronounces the name wrong. With an "s" sound at the end. No, it's pronounced "Bartosh". The name is Czech.'

'Ah. So you knew Kyra's father back in Czechoslovakia?'

'No, I met him in England. And not that long ago. In Brighton there is a club for people who originated in my country. I have met Jiri there once or twice.'

'Jiri?'

'His real name. When he comes to England, no one can pronounce it or spell it, so he settles for "Joe". Makes life easier.'

'Ah. And did you meet Kyra at the club too?'

He shook his head. 'Not at the club. I've met her in Connie's salon, and then once or twice when I went to her father's house. But I did not go there very often. Mim did not like me going to Jiri's house.'

Jude's quizzical eyebrow was greeted by a huge laugh. 'Mim does not like me going anywhere without her, remember? Does not like me out of her sight. She is afraid that, if she is not watching me, I am off serenading beautiful women.' With surprising ease for someone his age, he levered himself out of the armchair and crossed to the piano stool. His fingers instantly found the keys and started to play a wistful ballad. In a voice that was not really a singing voice, but which could still find the right weight and value of each word, he sang:

> 'There is no one I have ever wanted by my side.
> Just to have you with me is a source of pride,
> Knowing you're the one in whom I can confide,
> Whenever I want to . . .
> Whenever I want you.
>
> There is nothing I have ever wanted more than this.
> Just to be beside you is the height of bliss,
> Knowing I can lean across and take a kiss,
> Whenever I want to . . .
> Whenever I want you.'

The song spiralled away in a little tinkling of notes.

'Did you write that, Wally?'

'Of course. And Mim sang it. A minor hit. I don't think it would get far now on *Pop Idol*.'

'It's a beautiful tune.'

'Oh yes, of course. All my tunes are beautiful.'

'And sad.'

'All my tunes are sad.' He was silent for a moment, then firmly closed the lid of the white piano and came back to sit opposite her. 'So, what do you really want to know about Jiri Bartos?' He looked at his large old gold wristwatch. 'We must be quick. I am about to lose my . . .' he smiled, '. . . window of opportunity.'

'I really want to know about his relationship with

his daughter. Someone suggested that he was quite a difficult father.'

'Difficult . . . ? Strong . . . ?' The old man opened out his hands in a gesture of helplessness. 'Perhaps they are different words for the same thing. Jiri, like most of my generation who come from Czechoslovakia, has quite a long history. He is an old man, older even than me. He was married when he lived in Czechoslovakia, with children I think. Then the war came and I do not know what happened. He never talks about such things, but when he came to England, he was alone. His first family . . .' Wally gave an expressively hopeless shrug. 'So he was old, seventy perhaps, when he married again. To an English girl . . . well, I say "girl", but she was no chicken either . . . Young enough, though, to give him a child. A little girl, Krystina.'

'So "Kyra" was . . . ?'

'Yes. The young always want to reinvent themselves, don't they? New names, new clothes, new body-piercings . . .'

He sounded contemptuous, so Jude said, in mitigation, 'They're only trying to find their own identities.'

'Of course. And that is something that people like Jiri and me understand all too well. "Grenston" – do you think that is my real name? I think "Grünstein" might be closer to the mark. But who cares? What is a change of name if you feel happier with the result, if you fit in better because of the result? We all find our own ways of survival.' He looked thoughtful, but a glimpse at his watch brought him out of introspection. 'Anyway, "Krystina" is a good Czech name. "Kyra" . . .

I don't know where "Kyra" comes from. The girl only changed her name to annoy her father.'

'It was an adversarial relationship, was it then?'

'It was not an easy relationship. But for reasons that came from outside, the pressure of events. Krystina's mother died when the girl was only twelve. Breast cancer. Not an easy time for a child to lose a parent. So she was left with Jiri, who was . . . not the most natural person to look after a teenage girl.'

'Was he cruel to her?'

'Not deliberately. He did the best he could, did what was right according to his view of things. But his view of things was . . . I suppose you would say old-fashioned. Children, he felt, should always be on their best behaviour, always respectful to their parents. He didn't encourage his daughter to make friends. I don't think she ever invited anyone from school back to the house. And, of course, Jiri had no domestic skills, so after his wife died, Krystina was expected to do everything about the house. He did not want her to leave him. He could not manage without her.'

'Are you saying that in the emotional sense?'

'Jiri would deny it. He would say he only needed the girl to act as housekeeper for him. But Jiri was never one to wear his heart on his sleeve. To show his emotions costs him more than he is prepared to pay.'

'So presumably . . . a man like that . . . he would not have found it easy when his daughter started to lead a life of her own . . . when she got a job . . . when she got a boyfriend . . . ?'

Wally Grenston shrugged. 'I would not have thought

so, but I don't know for sure. Jiri Bartos is an acquaintance, not a close friend. He doesn't unburden his feelings to me. Mind you, I don't imagine he unburdens his feelings to anyone.'

'Do you think he'd agree to talk to me?'

The old musician's mouth narrowed doubtfully. 'It depends what you were offering him. Maybe, if you had some information that would tell him how his daughter came to die . . . ? I don't know. I cannot speak for him.'

'But do you have his phone number?'

'It is in the local phone book. There is no secrecy about where he lives.'

'No.'

Wally Grenston looked uneasily at his watch. Jude realized her window of opportunity was closing. She thanked him for talking to her, and said she must leave.

'Yes. I am sorry it cannot be for longer. I would like to play you some other tunes. I always like playing tunes for a beautiful lady.' But even as he spoke the words of flirtation, he looked worried. From seeing the two of them in Connie's Clip Joint, Jude had got the impression that Wally wasn't genuinely henpecked, that his subservient behaviour to Mim was part of a public double act. But his current anxiety made her question that assumption. Maybe he really was afraid of his wife.

Still he kept up his facade of roguish gallantry. 'It is a pity that you do not wear make-up, that you could not have left the tell-tale trace on the coffee cup . . .'

Jude grinned at him and, reaching down into the

bottom of her capacious African straw basket, produced a battered lipstick. She painted her lips, and then deliberately picked up her cup and pretended to drink. A very satisfactory smudge of pink appeared on the gold rim of the china.

Wally smiled, absolutely delighted. 'Oh, that is good, very good.' But his eyes could not stay long away from his watch. 'I think perhaps though, the time has come . . .'

'Of course.'

'Would you mind,' he asked nervously, 'going down the back way, through the garden? There is a gate at the end that only opens from this side. It leads directly on to the beach path.'

'No, that's fine. It's a nicer walk back.'

So that was the route by which she left, clandestinely, like a spy or a lover. When she reached the gate to the beach, Jude looked back. She could see the huge wide window of the sitting room. Next to it was a smaller one, clearly belonging to the kitchen. In front of this, Wally Grenston, unaware of her scrutiny, was carefully washing both coffee cups.

Chapter Eight

Jude looked up Jiri Bartos's number as soon as she got back to Woodside Cottage. She rang it straight away and he answered. But before she had finished saying, 'Mr Bartos, I wanted to talk to you about your daughter', he had put the phone down.

Carole and Jude had agreed to meet for lunch in the Crown and Anchor that Thursday. They both ordered Ted Crisp's recommendation of Local Pork and Leek Sausages with Mash and Onion Gravy and, while they waited for them to appear, sipped their Chilean Chardonnays and brought each other up to date on their investigations.

What Jude had found out from Wally Grenston seemed pathetically little in the retelling. 'Couldn't be more contrast between the two families,' Carole observed when her friend had finished. 'Joe Bartos is very closed in, just him and his daughter . . . though now of course just him . . . and it doesn't sound as though Kyra had many friends . . . whereas the Lockes seem to do everything as a pack.'

'Did you find out how many children there were there?'

'The way they talked there seemed to be hundreds. Nathan's certainly got at least one brother, and Dorcas has an identical twin sister. Mind you, it's doubly confusing because they've all got nicknames. And they have that quality close families often have, of assuming that everyone knows all about them, so it wasn't easy to work out who was who.'

'Did you discover whether the Lockes had actually met Kyra Bartos?'

'Eithne had, but only by accident. And, given how his parents kept going on about how liberal they are, and how they wouldn't mind him having a girlfriend in his room . . . well, that might suggest the boy deliberately kept them apart.'

'He wouldn't have been the first young man to have done that,' Jude mused. 'A new relationship being seen as a new beginning . . . particularly if it represented getting away from a family where he wasn't happy.'

'The Lockes would have denied stoutly that Nathan wasn't happy. They seemed to have this . . . I'm not quite sure how to explain it . . . pride, I suppose. Pride in themselves as a family unit . . . as if being a Locke was the highest achievement anyone could hope for. And they were at pains to give the impression Nathan subscribed to that view too.'

'And yet from something you've said, Carole . . . or something someone's said . . . I get the feeling Nathan felt differently . . . that he found all that family stuff a bit claustrophobic . . . suffocating even.'

'It's funny. I get that impression very strongly as well.'

They were interrupted by the arrival of their Local Pork and Leek Sausages with Mash and Onion Gravy, which were delicious. Ted Crisp's recommendations always were. Carole looked across to the bar where he stood, a bearded scruff in a colourless T-shirt, regaling late holidaymakers with more of his dreadful jokes. She still felt shock at the knowledge that they had for a time been lovers. But it was not a wholly unpleasant feeling.

The Local Pork and Leek Sausages kept them quiet for some time, and it was only when they were mopping up the last of the Mash and Onion Gravy that Jude returned to the subject of Nathan Locke. 'And you say they didn't seem at all worried about where he was? Or that he might have committed suicide?'

'No, that was really the strangest thing about the whole morning.'

'Well, it would suggest one of two things.'

'Which are?'

'Either they have no imagination at all . . .'

'Unlikely. I got the impression that all of the Lockes lived quite vividly in their imaginations.'

'Then it must mean that they've heard from Nathan since he disappeared. They know where he is.'

Her neighbour wouldn't have done what Jude did that afternoon on her way home from the Crown and Anchor, but Carole had had to hurry back to take

Gulliver out for a walk, so Jude was alone when she found herself passing Connie's Clip Joint. And since she could see through the window that there were no clients, she dropped in to talk to the owner.

Connie was sitting at the small desk, going through a pile of correspondence, but she seemed to welcome the distraction.

'I came in about that massage idea you talked about the other day,' said Jude, offering her hastily prepared cover story.

'Oh yes. Nice to see you.'

'Not stopping you from doing something you should be . . . ?'

'No, just going through some application letters. Like I said, I must appoint another junior soon, but somehow it seems, I don't know, with Kyra only just . . .' Connie shook herself and stood up. 'Would you like a coffee?'

'Lovely, if you're sure it's no—'

'I was just about to have one.' And Connie crossed to the machine in the back room, leaving the door open so that they could continue their conversation.

'You given Theo the afternoon off?'

'He's given himself the afternoon off. He's not an employee.'

'Oh?'

'No, he just works out of here as a freelance. Rents a chair from me. He hasn't got any appointments this afternoon, so he's off home.'

'Ah.' Theo's independent status was perhaps

another indication that business at Connie's Clip Joint was not exactly booming.

Jude wondered whether she should begin by saying something more about her therapies, but since the girl's name had just been mentioned, there did seem to be a natural cue . . . 'Must be strange for you, Connie, being here without Kyra . . .'

'It is. And sort of stranger as time goes on. You know, at the beginning there was the shock, and then I was busy with the police and everyone was talking about it, but now, as things have settled down . . . well, I'm more aware she's not here.'

'How long had she been working with you?'

'Oh, only about four months. And we hadn't always seen eye to eye. I'd had to put her right about a few things. Youngsters starting out at work have often got attitude problems, but Kyra wasn't a bad kid . . . She certainly didn't deserve what happened to her.'

'I don't think anyone would have deserved that.'

'No.' Connie was silent for a moment, then brought her mind back to the coffee. 'Milk or sugar?'

'Just black, please.'

'You know, I think my insides must be totally cof-fee-coloured,' the hairdresser said as she brought the cups across. 'I hate to think how many cups I get through in a day. Live on the stuff.'

'Do you have lunch?'

'No. If I'm busy, there's no time. And if I'm not busy . . . well, I forget about it.' Connie sat cosily beside Jude in one of the leather armchairs for waiting clients.

'Was here Kyra's first job?'

'No, it wasn't actually' The hairdresser's face clouded. 'She'd started at a salon in Worthing. A Martin & Martina.'

'Ah.' Jude was fully aware of the subtext of those words.

'But it only lasted a few weeks.'

'Why?'

'She hadn't got on with the management.' Jude stayed silent, hoping she was going to get more. And she did. 'Well, not the management of the salon, the management of the chain.'

'Are you talking about your ex-husband and his new wife?'

'Yes.'

'You don't think he's got anything to do with her death, do you?'

'What?' Connie looked totally incredulous. 'Martin? But why on earth . . . ?'

'Don't know.'

'Look, he may have done me wrong, but there's no evil in him. He's basically a good man.'

'Are you defending him now?'

'No, no, I—'

'You sound a bit as if you are. Do you still see each other?'

'Only when we can't possibly avoid it,' Connie replied fervently. She looked confused for a moment. Then she seemed to reach some decision and said, 'Martin never comes over this way. The Worthing branch is his base, really. That's where he has his office.' Her bright brown eyes were thoughtful for a moment, assessing how much she should confide. Fortunately, Jude's presence worked its usual magic and Connie decided she could tell everything she wanted to. Her words came out like a prepared speech. 'The fact is, Martin has never behaved very responsibly with the junior staff. I don't think he ever did, even when we were working together. Shows how naive I was, didn't even notice how he was chatting up the girls – and touching them up too. He seemed to think, because he was their boss, it gave him some sort of right to . . . I don't know . . .'

'*Droit de seigneur* . . .' Jude suggested.

'I've never heard of that, but if it means a boss thinking he's got a God-given right to come on to any of his female staff . . .'

'That's exactly what it means.'

'Well, I must remember the expression.' Suddenly Connie felt the need to defend herself. 'Look, I'm not just saying this to badmouth Martin. It is true.'

'I believe you.'

'Well, good, 'cause I know women talking about their ex-husbands aren't always the most reliable witnesses . . . And when I first suspected what he was doing, I thought I must have got it wrong, must be making things up in my mind, but the more it went on . . . and on more than one occasion the girls would complain to me, you know, when Martin wasn't there . . .'

'You mean he used to do it when you were working together in this salon?'

'Oh yes. As I say, at first I didn't believe it, made

excuses for him. Amazing what you'll do when you're in love, isn't it?'

'Yes,' Jude agreed. She'd done some pretty stupid things in her time too. 'But I thought when you two split up, Martin remarried . . . ?'

'To Martina, yes.'

'Well, do you think she'd put up with him coming on to the staff?'

'Martina . . . how can I put this . . . ?' Connie's mouth screwed up with the effort of finding the right words. 'Martina is a businesswoman. The success of the Martin & Martina chain is all down to her. Martin's got a lot of surface charm, he's good front-of-house, but he's got no commercial sense. All that comes from Martina. I think when she took him on, from her point of view, it was purely as a business venture. I don't think there was much love involved there.'

Jude grinned knowingly. 'Now what was it you said . . . ? "Women talking about their ex-husbands aren't always the most reliable witnesses"?'

'Yes, all right. I'm probably not being fair. I certainly don't want to be bloody fair to either of them. Maybe there was some wonderful magical moment of connection between the two of them . . . one day their eyes met across a crowded salon, and in an instant Martin and Martina knew it was the real thing, they were *in lurve* . . . Maybe that's what happened. As you say, I'm probably not the best person to comment on that. From the way it seemed to me, Martina looked at Martin and saw a first-class ticket to a very nice lifestyle, thank you very much. From then on she devoted herself single-mindedly to getting hold of that ticket.'

'And succeeded.'

'Yes.' Connie sighed. Though some years had passed since then, the defeat and humiliation were still with her. She took a savage sip of her coffee.

'And what about Martin coming on to the juniors in all the salons? Are you saying that Martina doesn't know about that?'

'She can't not know about it. She's not as young and naive as I was. She's a tough, hard-bitten foreigner.'

'Oh. Where from?'

'I don't know. Hungary? One of those places like that. Martina's just a gold-digger.'

'But a hard-working gold-digger.'

'Oh yes. Even I – who have great difficulty saying anything nice about the bloody woman – cannot deny that she's a hard worker.'

'So, going back to her husband groping the staff—'

'How charmingly you put it, Jude.'

'You say she must know it goes on . . . ?'

'Must.'

'. . . but is prepared to turn a blind eye?'

'I guess so.'

'I'm surprised.'

'Why?'

'Well, because it's quite a risky thing for a man to do these days. There's so much more legislation about sexual harassment and stuff. And young girls know all about it. Martin could be putting himself at risk of a court case if he goes on behaving like that.'

'Yes.' Connie's agreement contained a degree of satisfaction.

'What? Are you saying someone has registered a complaint about him?'

'Well, yes and no.'

'Sorry?'

'Look, when Kyra approached me about getting a job here . . .'

'Yes?'

'She was very upset. She'd just been unceremoniously asked to leave the Worthing Martin & Martina.'

'Because she'd objected to Martin coming on to her?'

'Basically, yes. He'd denied it obviously, and found some other reason to have her sacked. That was always his strength, you see – will always be the strength of men with power who behave like that. "You tell anyone about what I did to you and you'll lose your job." And who's going to believe the word of a teenager against the boss's? It usually worked for Martin, anyway.'

'And was it just chatting them up, giving them the odd grope . . . or was he trying to get them to go to bed with him?'

'No. It was just the groping.' Disgust twisted Connie's face. Jude couldn't lose the feeling that the hairdresser was somehow play acting . . . or maybe just enjoying her dramatic revelations. 'I think I'd almost feel better about it if it was full sex he was after. Somehow that makes it more acceptable, just good old-fashioned lust. But no, he just liked touching them. And he even used that as a defence when I finally realized what was happening and challenged him about it. "What's your problem," he said. "I'm not being unfaithful to you. I don't go to bed with any of them." As if that somehow justified his behaviour. Yeugh, from my point of view, it seemed to make it worse.'

'Perhaps that argument works for Martina?'

'Maybe it does. I think she just closes her mind to it, concentrates on the business and the lavish lifestyle it's brought her.' Connie could not keep the naked envy out of her voice.

For a moment there was silence. Then Jude pressed on. 'You said someone was going to register a complaint about him. Are you talking about Kyra?'

'Yes. When she came to see me, she was so upset about what had happened—'

'Was that why you took her on?'

'One of the reasons, yes. And also because I thought that shouldn't be allowed to happen to a kid her age. I thought she was in a perfect position to make a complaint against Martin.'

'On the grounds of sexual harassment?'

'Yes.'

'And did Martin know that this was about to happen?'

'Oh yes.' There was no disguising the satisfaction in Connie's reply.

When she'd heard Kyra's story, she'd seen the perfect way of getting some kind of revenge on the man who'd humiliated her.

But that wasn't the dominant thought in Jude's mind. She now knew of another person for whom Kyra Bartos's continuing existence had represented a considerable threat.

Chapter Nine

Carole had just got back with Gulliver from their walk and was towelling the sand off his paws, when Jude dropped by to share what she'd heard at the salon.

At the end, Carole asked, 'Do you think Connie's likely to have told the police about the threat to Martin . . . you know, over the sexual harassment charge?'

'I didn't actually ask, but she must have done, mustn't she?'

'Yes, from what you say about their relationship, she would have volunteered it at the first opportunity. Putting the police on to him as a murder suspect might be a very good form of revenge on an ex-husband.'

'Maybe.'

'Still, even if Connie didn't tell them, the police might have got the information from another source. You don't know whether Kyra had got as far as consulting a solicitor about what happened?'

Jude shook her head, and Carole sighed with exasperation. 'It is frustrating, isn't it, not having a clue what's happening in the official investigation?'

'Not an unusual position for us, though, Carole.'

'You're right. Do we have any means of contacting Martin Rutherford?'

'Well, Connie said the Worthing branch is his head-quarters.' Jude ran her fingers through the knot of her recently trimmed tresses. 'But I guess there's a limit to the number of times one can book in for a haircut. And, also, I doubt whether Martin himself does much of the actual cutting these days. Mind you, it might be worth trying. Get a bit of background . . .'

'Maybe.' Carole wasn't really listening any more; she was tense and restless. 'I do wish there was some-thing else we could do. Somewhere else where we could get more relevant information.'

'Apart from Martin Rutherford, the other person we really need to talk to is Joe Bartos.'

'Who, from what you say, clearly doesn't want to talk to anyone.'

'No.' Jude tapped her teeth thoughtfully. 'I wonder if we can approach him through some different route. I might have another word with Wally Grenston. And maybe you can follow up with the Lockes.'

'How?'

'Come on, Carole. I thought Rowley Locke asked you to keep him up to date with any new informa-tion you got on the case . . .'

'Yes.'

'Well, would you say that Kyra Bartos's threat to bring a charge of sexual harassment against Martin Rutherford constituted new information?'

'Yes. Yes, I suppose I would.'

*

93

The Lockes liked working on their home ground. In some families that might have been from a sense of insecurity, but in their case it was the opposite impulse, a desire to impress visitors with their united-front solidity. That was the impression Carole got as Dorcas Locke led her into her parents' house in Chichester on the Saturday morning. The day before Rowley had said on the phone that meeting at their house would be simplest, 'if you're likely to be in the Chichester area'. Carole had immediately remembered the half-truth that she needed to buy some dog food in bulk for Gulliver, and replied that by chance she did have some shopping to do in the city's Sainsbury's the following morning. Though making no claims to aura-detecting antennae like Jude's, Carole still recognized the value of the information that an environment could impart.

The Lockes' lack of insecurity was emphasized by the fact that Rowley and his wife were not at home when Carole arrived at the agreed hour of eleven-thirty on the Saturday morning. The house was a substantial one – probably five bedrooms – out in Summersdale, beyond the Festival Theatre to the north of the city. It was one of the most sought-after suburbs of Chichester, with house prices to match, so there was money some-where in the Locke family. Or at least there had been money at one time. The weeds poking up through the gravel of the drive, the blistered paint on the fascia boards and sagging window frames suggested that no routine maintenance had been done for some years. Or maybe the priorities of an artistic family like the Lockes lay elsewhere.

'Mummy and Daddy won't be long,' said Dorcas. She was dressed in a long skirt and top of pale coral cotton, which again emphasized the red-gold of her outward-spiralling hair. Although she recognized Carole, her manner was distant, her patent lack of interest just the right side of bad manners. 'Come through.'

The room into which Carole was led was larger and less cluttered than Arnold and Eithne Lockes', but its bookshelves, piano and artlessly abandoned guitar put across the same message: 'You are in the home of cultured people.' Like the exterior of the house, the decor could have done with a bit of attention, and the sofa and armchairs were worn and frayed. Here too the walls were adorned with photographs of the massed Locke family, siblings and cousins mixed together in a variety of settings. Fancy dress featured a lot, and there was more *Swallows and Amazons*-style posturing in boats. Again the background scenery looked Cornish. Mementos of more family holidays at Treboddick.

By a low table on the floor sat two girls, probably about fourteen and twelve. They had the same hair as Dorcas and their clothes, in pale tones of respectively raspberry and blue-grey, made them look as though they had been cloned from her. Had they not been so thin, the three diminishing sizes of sisters could have emerged from the same Russian doll.

The younger girls hardly looked up at the visitor's arrival. They were engrossed with some game laid out on the table. But it was not a commercially manufactured game. The map, which acted as a board, was hand-drawn and painted in coloured inks. The manikins were two-dimensional, cardboard cut-outs on cardboard stands: knights, heraldic beasts, dwarves and goblins. Open exercise books beside the map were covered with densely handwritten text, which swirled around embedded hand-drawn illustrations.

But everything was worn and faded. The map was criss-crossed with parallel lines from much folding. The paint on the figures was smudged and dull, and it was impossible to tell the original colour of the now-beige exercise book covers. On the map the words 'Kingdom of Verendia' and 'Forest of Black Fangdar' could be read. Oh no, thought Carole, we're not into Tolkien country, are we? (Such things did not appeal to her. She was of the view that coping with a single universe was quite enough of a challenge, without creating any parallel ones.)

Indicating an armchair for Carole, Dorcas had made no attempt to introduce her sisters, but instead joined them on the floor and continued with the game, as if there was no one else in the room. When they spoke, the younger girls had a lisp just like hers. Carole wondered idly whether it was caused by a genetic physical abnormality, or had been learned. Maybe the as-yet-unmet Bridget Locke would turn out to have the mother of all lisps, which had been passed down to her daughters . . . ?

Though incomprehensible to an outsider, the rules of the game the girls were playing made sense to them and there was a high level of excitement in their playing. For a few minutes Carole tried to follow what was happening, but soon gave up. After a time she almost got used to cries from the floor of 'I challenge thee to the Ordeal of Furminal, vile Tritchbacker', 'Your Eagrant magic has not power in the Vales of Aspinglad' or 'Let not the valiant offspring of Leomon cross swords with one of the blood of Merkerin.'

She was just sneaking a look at her watch to discover that the Locke parents were nearly a quarter of an hour late, when Dorcas clapped her hands and said, 'One last sortie, girls. Then you must do your music practice.'

Though deeply engrossed in the game, her sisters did not complain. They each had a 'sortie', which so far as Carole could tell was like a roll of the dice in any other game. But there was nothing looking like a dice in evidence and she had no idea what force dictated where on the map one of the figures should move next. When their 'sortie' was finished, both girls obediently rose to their feet. 'Will you leave it out, so's we can have another Grail-search tonight?' asked the younger one.

'No, sorry, Tarnil. Daddy says it must always be put away, so that each Grail-search starts anew.'

'Tarnil!' thought Carole. It must be another of those wretched nicknames, like Fimby and Diggo. But then again, parents who called their eldest daughter 'Dorcas' were quite capable of having another one actually christened 'Tarnil'.

The two smaller girls made no further argument, but left the room. Carole heard their footsteps clumping up the stairs and, later, the sounds of distant music wafting from their bedrooms. One appeared to be learning the oboe, the other the clarinet.

As she gathered up the pieces of the game and placed them, in long-remembered sequence, into an old flat biscuit tin, Dorcas felt no need to apologize for her parents' lateness – or indeed to say anything else.

Carole, inept as ever at making small talk, asked what the girls' names were.

'Their real names are Chloë and Sylvia, but they're called Zebba and Tarnil.'

The assertiveness of Dorcas's tone put Carole off asking the obvious question: Why? Instead she observed that the girls had been playing what looked like an interesting game. Dorcas did not think the comment worthy of response.

'Is it something you're going to develop commercially?'

'What?' The girl stopped packing the game away and for the first time looked directly at her visitor. The eyes, which Carole had previously noted as 'honey-coloured', were, close to, more complex than that, a very pale hazel flecked with black.

'Well,' Carole explained, 'you keep reading in the papers of people who've made huge fortunes from devising computer and—'

'This is not a computer game!' Dorcas snapped. 'It's a board game. Daddy wouldn't have a computer game in the house.'

'No, but hearing you playing it, it sounds very similar to a computer game.'

'It is nothing like a computer game!' The girl's pale face was now red with anger.

'All I'm saying is that that kind of game can be very lucrative. If it's a good idea you've got there, you could—'

'Nobody wants to make money out of the Wheel Quest.'

'But just think about it. You know, when all that fantasy stuff is being so successful . . . *Lord of the Rings*, *Narnia*, *Harry Potter*, there could be quite a demand for—'

Dorcas Locke was deeply affronted by the suggestion. 'We don't want to have other people playing it.'

Her indignation was so strong that she might have said a lot more, had she not heard the sound of a car scrunching to a halt on the weedy gravel outside. Carole turned to the window to see a beat-up Volvo estate, out of which Rowley Locke and his wife were emerging.

Bridget Locke was a good-looking woman, nearly as tall as her husband. Her hair was shoulder-length ash-blonde, with a well-cut fringe. The dark trouser suit gave her an aura of efficiency, separating her from the feyness of her daughters. Indeed, they didn't appear to have inherited any of her genetic make-up. She unloaded Waitrose carrier bags from the back of the estate, while her husband came straight through into the sitting room to greet Carole.

'Good of you to come,' he said, with no apology for his lateness. 'Has Dorcas offered you coffee?'

The girl gave her father a look which implied that was the last thing she'd have done.

'No, but it's fine. I don't want anything, thank you.'

Dorcas put the biscuit tin containing the Wheel Quest in its regular place on the shelf and announced, 'I'm going to read.'

'All right, Doone,' said her father. Oh God, another nickname, thought Carole.

Bridget Locke had by now come in through the front door and was presumably taking her shopping to the kitchen.

'How old is Dorcas?' asked Carole.

'She's twenty-one, just finished at uni.' It was a surprise to hear the abbreviation from a man of Rowley's age.

'Has she got a job lined up?'

He shook his head. 'No, she needs a bit of time to chill out. She's worked hard the last three years.'

'What was she studying?'

'English with drama.' That figures, thought Carole. 'At Reading.'

'So you just have the three girls?'

'No, there's a fourth. Doone – Dorcas – has a twin. Mopsa. She's, erm, working in Cornwall at the moment, arranging holiday lets.'

'Ah.' Mopsa! You wouldn't need a silly nickname if you were called that. Though in the Locke family, Carole would have put money on the fact that Mopsa had one. 'Is that near your own place?'

'Sorry?'

'When we met before, you said you had a family place in Cornwall, called Treboddick.'

'Well remembered, Carole.' His tone was patronizing, the omniscient teacher to the aspiring student. 'Yes, the cottages are in Treboddick. Mopsa's staying down there for the duration.'

'So you have four girls.'

'Yes,' said Rowley with pride. 'I do girls. Arnold and Eithne do boys.'

'How many have they got, apart from Nathan?' She thought it might be intrusive to call him 'Fimby'. And she couldn't have brought herself to do so, anyway.

'Just the one. His older brother Julian.'

Diggo, thought Carole. I'm getting the hang of this.

'Arnold never had my sticking power.' It was delivered as a joke, but Carole got the feeling that there was some truth behind it as well. Seeing the two brothers together, she had been left in no doubt that Rowley was the dominant one. And he, rather than the boy's father, was very definitely leading the family investigation into Nathan's disappearance.

Further revelations of sibling rivalry were prevented by the arrival of Bridget Locke from the kitchen. Carole was immediately impressed by how sensible she seemed, a beacon of sanity in the midst of her flaky family. Maybe, to allow the family to be as flaky as they appeared, someone had to be in touch with the real world.

'I'm sorry I wasn't able to meet you the other day in Fethering,' Bridget apologized. 'One of us has to work, I'm afraid.'

The words weren't spoken viciously, but there was no doubt they represented a dig at her husband. Carole wondered what Rowley Locke did for a living. Not a lot, was the answer implicit in his wife's remark.

'Don't worry. I did seem to meet quite a lot of the family.'

'That's always the case when you mix with the Lockes.' Rowley Locke spoke as if Carole were the recipient of a privilege, but his wife's 'Yes' again suggested less than full-bodied support for his view.

'Have you come here because you know something about Nathan's whereabouts?' Carole realized that this was the first time she had heard anxiety about the boy's fate from any member of the family. Bridget Locke was not the sort to give in to panic, but she was obviously deeply worried about Nathan.

'No, sadly, I don't know anything about that.'

'Don't worry about it, Bridget. The boy's just lying low for a while,' Rowley said.

'And where does a boy of sixteen lie low for more than a fortnight? What does he live on? Eithne says he hasn't drawn any money out of his account.'

Carole felt this gave her an opportunity to mention the unmentionable. 'The gossip around Fethering is that the boy might have committed suicide.'

'Well, that's nonsense!' said Rowley forcibly. 'Like all gossip it's totally unsubstantiated.' His wife was not so sure. 'Oh, come on, Bridget, you've known Nathan for ten years. He's not the kind to harm himself.'

'Not under normal circumstances, no. But who

knows how any of us would react to being the prime suspect in a murder investigation?'

'We'd do what Nathan has done. Go underground until it all blows over.'

'You make it sound so easy, Rowley. You can't just disappear in a country like this. And also the idea that a police investigation is just going to "blow over" is, I would say, at the very least naive.'

Carole did not get the impression that the Lockes normally argued like this. Maybe her presence in connection with Nathan's disappearance was the catalyst that enabled Bridget to unburden herself of what she was really feeling.

'And I wonder whether what Carole calls "Fethering gossip" may not have some truth in it. Particularly if . . .'

'Particularly if what?' asked her husband sharply.

Bridget Locke took a deep breath. She knew he wasn't going to like what she was about to say. 'Look, Nathan's at a difficult age and he was in the throes of his first big love affair. That's confusing enough for anyone. Particularly for someone who's never really engaged with the real world.'

'That's a very unfair description of him.'

'No, it's not. It's accurate. So there's Nathan, facing the conflicting pressures of love and lust and the girl's demands and his parents' disapproval and—'

'Now that's unfair, Bridget. Arnold and Eithne are the most tolerant parents in the world. They wouldn't mind Nathan bringing a girl home and going to bed with her. They didn't mind when Diggo had—'

'No, they wouldn't disapprove of Nathan having sex, but they would disapprove of the girl he was having sex with.'

'They never really met Kyra.'

'I'm not talking about Kyra. They'd disapprove of anyone who Nathan fancied. No girl would be good enough for the Lockes.'

'Now you're just being silly.'

'No, I'm . . .' But she didn't continue. It was an old argument, not worth reviving in the presence of a stranger. 'All I'm saying is that we should at least entertain the possibility that Nathan might have . . . harmed himself.' As her husband snorted disagreement, Bridget Locke chose her next words very carefully. 'Particularly if he was actually responsible for the girl's death.'

Rowley was appalled. 'You can't say that! You're talking about your nephew. You can't say he's a murderer.'

'Until it has been proved otherwise, you must at least acknowledge why the police see him as a major suspect.'

'No. The police have got it wrong,' he insisted, before appealing to Carole. 'Come on, you've got something new to tell us. You said on the phone there was someone else who had a motive to kill Kyra Bartos.'

Carole quickly recapped what Jude had heard from Connie Rutherford about her ex-husband. Rowley Locke seized on the information avidly. 'Well, there you are, you see! This Martin Rutherford, he wanted to stop Kyra Bartos shopping him about the sexual harassment. He must have killed her. It was nothing to do with Nathan.'

Bridget looked at Carole. 'Do the police know about this? Did Connie tell them?'

'I didn't actually ask her, but I think we can safely assume she did.'

'Hmm.'

'If we don't know for certain that they have been told, then we must see to it that they are,' Rowley announced.

'How?' asked his wife.

'I'll tell them.'

'I don't think that's a very good idea.'

'No,' Carole agreed. 'Going round scattering murder accusations at people can get you into serious trouble.'

'I'm not suggesting that I'll tell the police in person. I'll just see that they get the information.'

'What will it be, Rowley? An anonymous letter? A call from a phone box with you holding a handkerchief over the receiver?'

Rowley Locke didn't enjoy his wife sending him up like this. With a rather petulant cry of 'I've got to sort out some stuff,' he left the room, and Carole heard his footsteps stomping upstairs.

'I'm sorry.' Bridget Locke sighed. 'He can be very childish at times.'

'I'm sure you're all under a lot of stress at the moment.'

She nodded agreement, as Carole went on, 'You really think Nathan might have killed the girl?'

'Without further information, what else is there to think?'

'And that he might have killed himself too?'

Bridget Locke sighed. 'Again, there is a logic to the idea. He's certainly disappeared off the face of the earth. If he had somehow killed the girl, I hate to think of the kind of state he'd have been in.'

'But you think he'd be capable of killing himself?'

'Yes. I've got to know Nathan quite well. He has dark moods, and sixteen isn't the easiest age for a boy. He could have done it . . . done both perhaps, I mean. The murder and the suicide.' Carole had a mental image of the photograph she'd seen at his parents' house, of the brooding figure amongst all the extrovert children on the boat.

She nodded, then said, 'You're not Rowley's first wife, are you?'

'No. Sorry. Should have made that clear. His first wife, who was called Joan . . . went off with someone.'

'So the girls . . . ?'

'Are hers. All of them. Not that she's ever in touch. Rowley used to teach at a local girls' school. I met him when I got a job there.'

'But I gather he's no longer teaching . . . ?'

'No.' Bridget Locke chose her words with delicacy. 'Rowley's always had a problem with authority. He's one of those teachers who'd rather make a lasting impression on his students than guide them through the required curriculum.' Her mouth set in a rueful expression. 'Just coming up for our tenth wedding anniversary.' She looked pleadingly at Carole. 'I'm sorry, he doesn't often behave like he did this morning. There's much more to him than he sometimes shows to strangers.'

There would need to be, thought Carole.

'Do you think he will go to the police about what I told him? Because I'm not sure that that would be wise.'

'I'll see to it that he doesn't.' Bridget Locke spoke with assurance. Her husband might never encounter any opposition from the other members of the family, but when necessary his wife could stand up to him. 'The way he's behaving at the moment is because he's really worried about Nathan. It's his way of showing it. Quite exhausting though.' Bridget Locke wrinkled up her nose in wry amusement. 'Being part of the Locke Family Roadshow can sometimes be very wearing.'

Chapter Ten

Jude had been lucky to get an appointment at the Worthing Martin & Martina. When she rang the day before they'd just had a cancellation. Saturday was the busiest day of the week in any provincial hairdresser's, and Jude seemed to be in the town's most popular one. The decor was in marked contrast to that of Connie's Clip Joint. Everything looked gleaming new. There was a lot of black glass with trim in brushed aluminium. And the silver 'Martin & Martina' logo was omnipresent. Looking round the salon, Jude saw a scene of almost manic activity. With all the chairs full, twelve stylists were snipping away, while clients sat under dryers or sipped coffee in the waiting area. There was a buzz about the place, an air of deliberately orchestrated chaos.

Jude introduced herself to the woman at the reception desk and was told that her stylist Kelly-Jane was just finishing with another client and would be ready for her very soon. Would she like a cup of coffee? Jude accepted and took the only free seat in the waiting area, which was adjacent to the reception desk. The woman sent off a junior to get the coffee. She didn't do menial tasks like coffee-making. There was an air of authority about her, and the speed at which the junior moved showed that it didn't do to cross her.

The woman was so smartly dressed and made up that she looked as though she'd just been taken out of her packaging. A slate-grey business suit with a froth of white blouse at the neck. Light brown hair cut immaculately short (maybe similar to the style Connie had had in mind for Jude). Blue eyes above Slavic cheekbones, and full red lips. But the eyes were cold, and the line of the mouth was hard.

Jude flashed a grin at her, and was rewarded by a professional smile in return. 'I am Martina,' the woman said. Her English was immaculate, but still flavoured with an accent from somewhere in central Europe.

'Martina of Martin & Martina?'

'Yes, Martina Rutherford. My husband and I run the chain.'

'Congratulations. It seems to be doing very well.'

'Yes, we have put a lot of work into the business and I am glad to say it is now paying off. We are opening a new salon in Folkestone soon.'

'Moving all the way along the South Coast.'

'We hope in time to go north to some of the big towns nearer London.'

'And then throughout the whole country?'

She took the question at face value. 'Why not? Our standards are higher than most of the opposition. We are very successful.'

'It certainly looks that way.' Jude knew she must take advantage of the situation into which she had so serendipitously arrived. She had come hoping to find out more about Martin & Martina, and here she was being offered one half of the partnership on a plate. 'This is my first time in one of your salons,' she began cautiously.

'I know. I have not seen you before.'

'Do you remember all the clients in all the branches?'

'Pretty well. I move around a lot, but we have our main office here.'

'Previously I've had my hair done at Connie's Clip Joint in Fethering.'

'Ah.' Clearly Martina knew the name, but she responded without a flicker of any other intonation.

'Presumably you heard about the dreadful thing that happened there?'

'Of course.' The phone interrupted them. Martina answered with practised charm, booking someone in for highlights the following Wednesday. When she'd ended the call, she looked across at the row of stylists. 'Kelly-Jane has nearly finished. She will be able to look after you soon.'

'Thank you. So, the death at Connie's Clip Joint . . .'

'Yes.' Martina was too much of a professional to change the subject when a client was talking, but she seemed to have little interest in what had happened at the Fethering salon. No doubt, being so close, the event had already been the subject of a lot of gossip amongst her clients, and she was sick of it.

'I gather that the girl who died had worked here . . .'

'Yes. Very briefly.'

'Oh?' It was the lightest of interrogatives, but it asked for an explanation.

Martina shrugged. 'Not everyone is suited to this business. It takes a special kind of personality to be a hairdresser, a special attitude. A lot of young girls start without having really thought about what the job entails.'

'But in the case of Kyra Bartos—'

'Ah, here is Kelly-Jane.' A lanky girl in her late twenties, with jet black hair rising in little spikes over her head, came across with a welcoming smile. 'This is your client, Jude, is that right?'

'Yes.'

'Nice to see you, Jude. Come with me. We'll get your hair washed first.'

As she moved across to the chair, Jude was aware of the shrewd scrutiny of Martina's blue eyes following her. She wondered if there was anything sinister in the interest, or was it just another manifestation of the woman's control-freak personality?

Jude might have known there would be no problem having another haircut so soon. There is nothing stylists like better than running fingers disdainfully through someone's hair and asking, 'Who on earth did this?' And after she'd had her hair washed by a junior, that was exactly what Kelly-Jane did.

'Oh dear,' she said. 'Bit of a salvage job, is it? I can tell it's only been cut a couple of days ago. Normally I wouldn't mention how badly someone's hair's been cut,' the girl lied, 'but since you've come in here so quickly after, I'm not telling you anything you don't know already.' The stylist trailed despairing fingers through the blonde tresses. 'Dear, oh dear. Now do tell me where this was done.'

'No, I'm sorry, I can't.' Although she'd already mentioned the salon to Martina, Jude had too much loyalty to betray Connie to Kelly-Jane. Besides, she knew that there had been nothing wrong with the haircut she'd got in Fethering. But it was a point of honour amongst all stylists to disparage everything that had been done to a client before she had the good fortune to find them.

'Oh well.' Kelly-Jane didn't pursue the matter. She perhaps thought it better for the perpetrator of the previous haircut to remain anonymous. She didn't want to intrude on private grief. Lifting Jude's hair out to the sides and letting it drop, she said, 'So . . . what are we going to do with it? You know, you'd look smashing with it really short.'

Why is it everyone wants me to have short hair? Jude wondered. Could it be that stylists, like everyone else, like to see a positive effect for their efforts? Yes, there must be some kind of satisfaction in making a total transformation, completely changing the appearance of your client. But Jude, having rejected the 'short' option with Connie, wasn't about to grant the honour to Kelly-Jane. Besides, she thought mischievously, since having my hair cut seems to be my main means of investigation in this case, I'd better proceed slowly, an inch at a time.

'No, thanks,' she said easily. 'I'd just like it tidied up, you know, maybe about an inch shorter all round.'

Kelly-Jane gave a token sigh – she was clearly used

DEATH UNDER THE DRYER

to clients not knowing what was best for them – but
didn't press the point. Instead, she started combing
Jude's hair preparatory to the cutting. 'Haven't seen
you here before. Your first time at a Martin & Martina?'

'Yes.'

'Oh well, now you've found us, you'll never change.
It sounds like boasting, but it's not boasting if something's true. Martin & Martinas are by a long way the
best salons on the South Coast. You'll never want to go
anywhere else.'

Jude wasn't convinced. Guilty for the badmouthing
Connie's skills had just received, she felt defensive. A
new sense of loyalty developed within her. In future
she'd regard Connie's Clip Joint as her regular hairdresser's.

'It's all down to the training, you see. All the staff
at Martin & Martina salons are intensively trained.
Martin – he's the boss – is very hands-on.'

So I've heard, thought Jude wryly. But now his
name had come up, she wasn't going to waste the cue.
'So he's a good person to work for?'

'Oh yes. None of the staff ever want to leave, and if
that's not the measure of a good boss, I'd like to know
what is.'

Kyra Bartos had wanted to leave. For a moment
Jude wondered whether Connie's account of the circumstances of that departure had been entirely accurate, or had it been embroidered by the venom of a
spurned wife?

'And do you actually see a lot of Martin?'

'Oh yes. As I said, he's very hands-on. Goes round

all the branches, but his office is here, so we probably get to see more of him than the others.'

'Is he in today?'

'Always here on a Saturday, yes. I'm surprised he hasn't put in an appearance yet.'

Good, thought Jude. And I've already met Martina. So my investment in a second haircut won't be completely wasted. At the very least I should get to know what Martin Rutherford looks like.

She pretended ignorance for her next question. 'And are he and Martina actually married? Or are they just partners whose names give a nice unisex feeling to the salons?'

'Oh no, they're married. Very much so. I don't think Martin ever does anything Martina doesn't know about.' The warmth with which Kelly-Jane had spoken of Martin Rutherford did not extend to his second wife.

Given that kind of monitoring, thought Jude, Martin must be very discreet in his approaches to the salon's juniors. Maybe Connie had overdone her description of his behaviour, making out her husband was worse than he actually was. Now she thought about it, there had been something false and prepared about what she'd said.

'Yes, I was just talking to Martina.' What she said next didn't reflect her true feelings, but she thought it might prompt some more confidences. 'She seems very nice.'

Kelly-Jane, however, was not about to be drawn into indiscretion. She just said, 'Oh yes. Mind you, I'm surprised she's here today.'

114

'Why?'

'Last weekend of the month she usually flies over to Prague. Her mother's out there and not very well. Oh well, maybe she's not going this weekend, or catching a later flight or something.'

'Does Martina actually cut hair?'

'No. Used to be a stylist, but doesn't do any now.'

'And what about Martin? Does he still do any hairdressing?'

'For a few favoured clients. He'll do a bride's hair for her wedding, something like that. Not very often, though. He's too busy schmoozing.'

Jude took another look at Martina Rutherford. She was very beautiful, but her strength of will was written in every feature. Connie's good-natured fluffiness would not have stood a chance against the force of that personality. And, though she hadn't met Martin Rutherford yet, what Kelly-Jane had hinted at reinforced the feeling that he too would crumble to his wife's every wish.

Nothing was said for a few moments while the haircut began. Then suddenly Kelly-Jane asked, 'Do you want to know a way of making money?'

'What?' Jude was wary; she had expectations of being lured into some pyramid selling operation.

'It's to do with hairdressing.'

'I haven't got any skills as a hairdresser.'

'You don't need any.' Kelly-Jane stopped cutting and put her hands behind her back. 'All you have to do is bet people that they can't tell you which fingers hairdressers use to hold their scissors.'

'Well, it's obvious, isn't it?' Jude looked down at her right hand and found that she was instinctively miming cutting with the two fingers next to the thumb. But that couldn't be right. Fine for a visual shorthand, but you couldn't get enough grip and you couldn't move the scissors like that. 'No, not those.'

'Right, not those,' said Kelly-Jane, biding her time with the confidence of someone who had played the game many times before.

'So let me think . . . Oh, this is daft. Goodness knows how many times in my life I've had my hair cut . . . Do all hairdressers use the same fingers?'

'All,' the girl assured her. 'All over the world.'

'Right, let's be logical here. I think the thumb must be involved . . . Yes, because that would give you a bit of leverage . . .' Jude was fishing for some kind of clue, but the stylist's face in the mirror remained impassive. 'OK, there aren't many options. It can't be the little finger, because that's not strong enough . . .' She looked down at her hands in frustration. 'It must be . . . It must be . . .' She made her decision. Pressing the top of her middle finger against her thumb, she announced, 'It must be those two.'

With gleeful triumph, Kelly-Jane brought her hands round from behind her back. 'Wrong!' She raised her right hand, and showed Jude the unexpected combination of digits that hairdressers have always used for the purpose of holding their scissors.

'Gosh, you're right,' said Jude. 'Yes, I think you could win a few bets that way.' Something to tell Ted Crisp. Another way for him to amuse his customers at the Crown and Anchor. And certainly better than his jokes.

Kelly-Jane grinned as she resumed cutting. She'd done the little party trick she tried out on all her new clients. And once again it had worked. Back to more conventional chat. 'Do you live in Worthing?'

Jude had hardly got out a 'Fethering' before they were interrupted by a whirlwind of bonhomie. 'Good morning, and how are you, Kelly-Jane? Looking lovely, as ever. And a new client – how exciting! What a pleasure to see you in Martin & Martina. I am one half of the salon's name – Martin. And you . . . ?'

'I'm called Jude.'

The first impression was of an attractive man in his early forties, though closer inspection revealed him to be a well-preserved man in his early fifties. Perhaps as much as ten years older than Connie. Jude wondered how they had met. In some salon where she'd been another junior he'd come on to . . . ? He was of average height, and kept himself in shape. He wore a charcoal linen suit over a slate grey shirt, and the blackness of his short hair looked as if it might have been assisted. His teeth too were unnaturally white and even; some expensive veneer work had been done there. But his brown eyes were shrewd.

'And where are you from, Jude?'

'Fethering.'

'Oh, so close. So why haven't you been into a Martin & Martina salon before, you naughty girl?'

She'd actually got him there. She wouldn't get a better chance of raising the subject of Kyra Bartos's murder. So Jude finessed the truth and said, 'I normally have my hair done at Connie's Clip Joint.'

'Ah.' He had been taken by surprise, but was far too cool an operator to let it show. 'And how is dear Connie?'

'Pretty good.' Jude couldn't see any other way of proceeding than the crassly direct. 'I gather she's your ex-wife.'

'Yes. Pity it didn't work out. Lovely girl. But, you know, we were young and . . .'

She may have been young, you weren't that young, Jude thought. 'Have you managed to stay friends?'

'I'm sure we'd be perfectly pleasant to each other if we ever met, but we haven't seen each other for ages.' He was keen to move on. 'So, anyway, Kelly-Jane, what are you going to do to Jude's hair to make sure she never strays from the path of Martin & Martina again?'

'Well, I—'

Jude interrupted. It wasn't her usual style, but they were meeting her for the first time and weren't to know that she wasn't by nature a woman of galumphing tactlessness. 'Of course, you heard about the dreadful thing that happened at Connie's Clip Joint? You know, that girl who was strangled?'

'Yes, of course. It was all over the television news. You couldn't miss it. Apart from the fact that none of the clients in the salon talked about anything else. Horrible for poor Connie. I was going to ring her to offer my sympathy, but, you know, there never seems to be any time for—'

Having taken on the persona of a diplomatic

rhinoceros, Jude stuck with it. 'Connie said that Kyra Bartos used to work for you . . .'

'Yes, yes. She was in this salon briefly.' But he didn't want to be drawn on the subject. 'I really must be checking other clients and—'

Finding new extremes of crassness, Jude announced, 'Connie mentioned that there was something funny about Kyra's dismissal from here . . . that the girl had been consulting a solicitor about the rights and wrongs of it.'

This time there was no mistaking the shock in Martin Rutherford's face, even though he managed quickly to cover it up. 'Well, it's been such a pleasure talking to you, Jude. Welcome once again to Martin & Martina. Now excuse me . . .' And he swanned over to another client. 'Darling, you're looking just too fabulous. Is it for a special occasion or just your natural beauty shining through . . . ?'

Jude was afraid that Kelly-Jane might have thought her conversation with Martin odd, but she needn't have worried. The stylist had gleaned one piece of information though, and that was all she wanted.

'So it was Connie who did your previous haircut, was it?'

Jude felt terribly disloyal.

'I don't know why I behaved like that. It's not my usual style.'

'But did it work?'

'Not really. I didn't get any information out of him.

119

I've probably just forfeited his goodwill and made him very suspicious of me. If any further investigative approaches need to be made to Martin Rutherford, I think you'd better take them on, Carole.'

'Right.' She fingered the steel-grey helmet of her hair. 'I can't really pretend this needs doing again.'

'No, and I think we must find a different sleuthing modus operandi. Having constant haircuts is very expensive, apart from anything else. Martin & Martina was nearly double the price of Connie's Clip Joint.'

'Hmm.' There was a silence. Both sipped their Chilean Chardonnays. They'd agreed to meet in the Crown and Anchor when they returned from their respective Saturday morning expeditions. Just for a drink, they'd said, but Ted Crisp's recommendation of the Cheesy-Topped Fisherman's Pie had proved too tempting.

Carole idly flicked through the Martin & Martina promotional brochure that Jude had brought back from the salon. Expensively produced, it featured news from the branches, ideas for hairstyles, a photograph of the Stylist of the Month, and so on. The publication gloried in the company's achievements. Again Carole was aware of the contrast with the small-scale operation that was Connie's Clip Joint. At the back of the brochure, portraits of the owners framed a message of welcome to their customers. A good-looking couple, glowing in their shared success.

'I think I behaved as I did,' Jude said thoughtfully, 'because I feel we're getting nowhere on this case. We're surrounded by blind alleys. We can't get anywhere on the Locke side of the case until Nathan is found. Getting in touch with Joe Bartos seems to be impossible.'

'Did you talk to Wally Grenston again?'

'I did – gave him a call to thank him for my coffee. He didn't have any ideas. I think he got rather protective of his friend Joe. The old man's mourning the death of his daughter. Wally implied that if he doesn't want to speak to us, that's his right, and his wishes should be respected.'

'Which is of course true.'

'Yes. So I suppose I just wanted to shake things up. I thought maybe being rude to Martin Rutherford, possibly even frightening him with reference to Kyra's proposed legal action might . . . I don't know . . . make something happen.'

'Rather a risky strategy,' said Carole primly.

'Yes.' Jude looked contrite and uncharacteristically down.

Then their attention was drawn by a raucous shout from the bar. 'You owe me a fiver!' roared Ted Crisp. Jude giggled.

'What is it?'

'Before you arrived, I was talking to Ted. I told him this way of making money by betting which fingers hairdressers use to hold their scissors.'

'Really?' Carole looked down at her hand and moved the digits around. 'So which fingers are they?'

'Ah,' said Jude. 'That'd be telling.'

Chapter Eleven

There were a lot of dog owners in Fethering, but Carole Seddon prided herself on usually being on the beach with Gulliver before any of them. Waking early was a habit dinned into her all her life, to be ready for her daily train journey to school, and then her commute to the Home Office. During the relatively brief period she took off work after Stephen's birth, the baby's imperatives had also ensured early rising and, though in retirement the demands on her time were less, the habit was engrained. For Carole, rising late would have been an unacceptable indulgence, on a par with watching breakfast television. And getting up early on a Sunday, when most of the world was having a lie-in, gave her an even greater sense of being on the moral high ground.

Besides, Carole liked to be active as soon as she woke up. Lying in bed, being immobile even for a moment, was dangerous. It was at such moments that she could be ambushed by unwelcome thoughts. Her mind was a pressure cooker, whose lid needed to be firmly tightened down.

Gulliver didn't care when she got him up, so long as

there was a walk involved. He still became puppyishly exuberant at the prospect of being taken out, particularly to Fethering Beach, where the melange of sharp smells and the range of flotsam and jetsam represented a canine nirvana.

That Sunday dog and owner were on the beach before six o'clock. The early morning air was a cold breath of impending winter. It was hardly light when she had left High Tor and, as September gave way to October, she knew she would have to start her walks later, unless she wanted to set off in total darkness. There'd be a brief respite when Summer Time ended, and then winter would once again inexorably put its squeeze on the early mornings.

End of October the clocks changed. Carole always remembered details like that. In retirement she needed more than ever to have her year delineated, to have fixed points in the potentially unstructured void of her life. And also by the end of October, she remembered suddenly, Stephen and Gaby's baby will probably have arrived. I will be a grandmother. The thought filled her with an uneasy mixture of excitement and apprehension.

Gulliver had the personality of all Labradors, which meant that at times he could be exceptionally soppy. But on Fethering Beach he became a hero. Beleaguered on all sides by potential attacks from waves, stones, swathes of bladderwrack, ends of rope, water-smoothed spars and broken plastic bottles, he triumphed over them all, scampering off in sudden sallies, only to return breathless to his mistress's side with the gleam of victory in his eye. King Arthur never had a more gallant knight errant than Gulliver on Fethering Beach.

Carole didn't always take him on the same route. Like all creatures of habit, she hated to be thought of as a creature of habit. Where the road met the beach, she would sometimes turn left towards the Yacht Club and the mouth of the Fether; other times she would go right, where the dunes stretched as far as the eye could see. Coming back, too, there were alternative routes possible. They could either take the High Street directly to High Tor, or they could walk along the bank of the river and cut back along one of the little roads parallel to the sea. Or then again, if she felt like it, having curtailed Gulliver's freedom by putting his lead back on, Carole could take him along the little service road which ran behind the High Street shops.

For no very good reason, this was the route she chose that morning. Though busy with deliveries during the week, the road was virtually unused at weekends because there were no houses there. On one side was an area of scrubland, its surface a mixture of sand and earth, from which the local residents discouraged summer picnickers. And on the other were the backyards of the shops: some double-gated parking bays for major delivery vehicles, others like the ends of gardens, wooden-fenced with small doors. The back of Connie's Clip Joint was of the second kind, and as Carole led Gulliver along the road that Sunday morning, she saw a man come through the door and hurry to a gleaming new Mini. Something about his movement was furtive. Just before he got into the driver's seat, he gave a quick look around, and Carole recognized a face whose photograph she'd seen only the day before.

It was Martin Rutherford.

Chapter Twelve

'Well, what does that suggest? Why was he there, do you think?'

Jude pinched her upper lip between thumb and forefinger for a moment, then said, 'It suggests he's still got keys to the place.'

'Connie's Clip Joint?'

'Yes.'

'But Connie said the only spare keys were the ones she gave to Kyra.'

Jude shrugged. 'Maybe Martin copied a set before he handed them back to her . . . ? Maybe he handed over the keys to the front, but hung on to the one for the back door . . . ?'

'So what would he have been doing there this morning?'

'I don't know, but, given the state of armed conflict between Connie and him, I can't think he was paying a social visit.' A thoughtful smile came over Jude's features. 'Maybe my clumsy approach had some effect . . .'

'How do you mean?'

'Remember I mentioned to him that Kyra had been planning legal action about her dismissal from Martin

& Martina in Worthing. Maybe he was checking out
Connie's Clip Joint to see if any incriminating evidence
had been left there?'

'Pretty unlikely that there would have been. And if
there were, you'd have thought the police would have
found it, and then surely they'd have been on to Martin
pretty sharpish to find out what had been going on . . .
The police must've spoken to him since the murder,
mustn't they?'

'Yes. Connie said they did . . . you know when I
went to have my haircut before last. She said the police
questioned her and Martin quite extensively for the
first couple of days, and then seemed to lose interest in
them . . . well, in her, anyway.'

'Right.' Carole sipped at her coffee. It was nearly
cold. They'd been chatting too much since she arrived
at Woodside Cottage. She'd taken Gulliver back to High
Tor after his walk and then gone straight next door. It
was early, but the news she had to impart couldn't wait.
'Of course,' she went on, 'if Martin Rutherford does
have keys to Connie's Clip Joint . . .'

'Yes?'

'. . . then he could have got in there the night Kyra
Bartos died, couldn't he?'

'He could.'

'Because there was no sign of forced entry, was
there? So far we've been assuming that's because Kyra
invited her killer in to the salon, but if Martin had
keys . . .'

'Yes.' Jude looked at her watch and picked up the

card the hairdresser had given her. 'As soon as it's a reasonable hour, I'm going to ring Connie.'

The hairdresser did not seem particularly surprised when she answered the call just after ten. But she did sound sleepy, and Jude felt guilty that the phone had probably woken her.

'I'm sorry to be calling so early.'

'Don't worry. I should be up. I overslept.' Connie sounded snugly drowsy. 'It's just I . . . you know, always wiped out at the end of the week.'

'Well, as I say, I'm sorry.'

'It's fine.'

'But I thought I ought to ring you, because something's happened that might have a bearing on the case.'

'Case?'

'Kyra's murder.'

'Oh yes. Of course.'

'My friend Carole – you remember her?'

'Certainly. "Same shape, but shorter".' Again the impersonation was spot on.

'Yes, her. Anyway, she was taking her dog for a walk on the beach early this morning, and she came back via the service road . . . you know, behind the shops.'

'Mmm?' Suddenly Connie was alert, the drowsiness gone from her voice.

'And she saw your ex-husband leaving from the back gate of Connie's Clip Joint.'

'Ah.' There was a long silence. When she broke it,

Connie sounded hesitant. 'And what's she going to do about it?'

'Well, tell the police presumably.'

'Why? Is it a police matter?'

'Surely it is? If Martin had keys to the back of Connie's Clip Joint to get in there this morning, then he probably would have had them if he'd wanted to get in on the night Kyra was killed.'

'Right.' Now it made sense to Connie. 'Sorry, I was half-asleep. Yes, of course, I hadn't thought of it that way. The police must be told. But, Jude, can you think of any reason why Martin might have been round to Connie's Clip Joint?'

'Well, if one were to go to the extreme hypothesis that he was actually the murderer . . .'

'Oh, I don't think so.' Instinctive loyalty for her ex-husband prompted Connie. 'I can't imagine Martin ever doing anything like that.'

'He had a motive.'

'Did he? Sorry, I'm being very slow this morning. I'm not properly awake yet.'

'You told me about it. That Kyra was threatening to sue him for constructive dismissal over the sexual harassment business.'

'Oh yes.'

'Well, it could be argued that he therefore had a very good motive to get her out of the way.'

'I suppose so. Maybe I overstated that, anyway. Kyra wasn't *definitely* going to take him to court. It was just an idea we discussed, not entirely serious.'

Why was she backtracking on that? Jude wondered.

She'd sounded fairly definite about it when the subject last came up.

'Anyway,' Connie went on, 'I still can't see Martin killing anyone.'

'All right. Say he didn't kill her, but he still knew about the threat of legal action . . .'

'I'm not sure whether he did know about that.'

'Oh, he did.' And Jude was embarrassed to realize that she would have to own up to what she'd said to Martin Rutherford in the Worthing Martin & Martina the day before. She did so, as quickly as possible, with the minimum of apology.

Connie took the news in slowly. 'And how did he react?'

'He changed the subject and moved on.'

'Yes, I'm not surprised.'

'But what I'm saying, Connie, is that, having heard about the potential legal action against him, Martin might have let himself into Connie's Clip Joint this morning, hoping to find and destroy any evidence . . . you know, papers Kyra might have got together for her case against him.'

'Yes.' Connie seemed very relieved to have a possible explanation for her ex-husband's appearance at the salon. 'Yes, that would make very good sense.'

'But, whatever his reason for being there, I think the police should be told about it. Even if it's not criminal, it is at the very least rather odd behaviour. I mean, that is assuming that you didn't know he was going to be there . . . ?'

'Good heavens, no!' Connie responded vehemently.

'Well, I suppose Carole could talk to the police. She has got a connection with the case, after all, having been there when the body was discovered. They did give her contact numbers, but . . . there's always a danger that the police will treat her as some nosy local crank. Alternatively, you could do it . . .'

'That'd make much more sense,' said Connie firmly. 'It was my premises he was making an illegal entry into, after all. No, leave it with me, Jude. I'll speak to the police.'

And she sounded relieved that that decision had been made.

Chapter Thirteen

'The question is,' said Carole, 'do I share this information with the Lockes?'

'Ah, I hadn't thought of that.'

'Rowley asked me to pass on anything I found out that might be relevant to the case . . .'

'Yes.'

'On the other hand, to tell them I saw Martin Rutherford coming out of Connie's Clip Joint this morning would be tantamount to making an accusation against him.'

'Which I'm sure the Lockes would seize on. Anything which offered a suspect apart from their precious Nathan.'

'Hmm. Again, you know, Jude, it struck me as odd yesterday how little Rowley Locke seemed to be worried about Nathan.'

'Well, I suppose the boy's not his son. He's only his nephew.'

'Yes, but when I met the parents, they were equally unruffled about it.' Even though her own maternal skills might be open to criticism, this still seemed odd to Carole. 'Not natural.'

'People hide their emotions.'

'Of course they do. But I still have a sneaking suspicion that the reason they're so calm about it is that they know Nathan's all right. They're in contact with him. They know where he is.'

Jude grinned ruefully. 'I don't think I can help you much in following up on that. You're the one with an open invitation to the Lockes' camp. Maybe you should tell them about seeing Martin this morning. It'd at least maintain the continuity of contact.'

'Yes.' But Carole felt disinclined to pick up the phone in a hurry. A little of the Lockes, she had found, went a long way. 'I won't do it straight away. See what else develops.'

'Maybe when Connie tells the police about Martin, that'll be the breakthrough they've needed.'

'You think he did it?'

Jude shrugged. 'I've no idea. But what Connie said about Kyra and the sexual harassment thing does at least give him a motive. Though there's still something odd about the way she told me that. I still can't quite put my finger on it. The whole story came out too pat, as though she'd prepared it. I don't know . . . Anyway, Connie's and Martin's does seem to have been a very bitter divorce.' Out of sensitivity towards Carole, she restrained herself from adding 'like most divorces'. 'Maybe there's another motive out there of him trying to sabotage the business prospects of Connie's Clip Joint.'

'I'm not sure that he needed to do that. From what you were saying, the salon's not very healthy, anyway.'

133

'No.' Jude screwed up her face in puzzlement. 'I get the feeling we're missing something.'

'I get the feeling we're missing everything,' said Carole tartly. 'Our investigation can't really be said to be making much headway, can it?'

'But I'm sure there's someone else we should be talking to . . . someone we've forgotten about.'

'Well, there's Joe Bartos. You've tried without success to make contact there.'

Jude screwed up her eyes and shook her head. Even after two haircuts in a week, there was enough left for her topknot to wobble precariously. 'Someone else . . . Someone who had something to do with the day of the murder . . . or the day of the discovery of the murder . . .'

'Well, I can't—'

Jude's brown eyes sprang open. 'The woman! The other woman in Connie's Clip Joint when you had your hair cut. The very dramatic one.'

'Oh, her. Her name was Sheena. That's all I know about her.'

'But there was something you told me she said.'

'I can't remember. She was behaving so hysterically, she said all kinds of things.'

'No, there was one thing . . . Something about Kyra deserving her fate . . . ?'

Carole's memory cleared, and the words came back to her, exactly as she had heard them that morning. 'Yes. "Though the poor girl may have deserved something, she didn't deserve this!"'

134

'Well, wouldn't that suggest to you that this Sheena knew something about Kyra or her background?'

'Yes. Yes, it would.'

'In that case,' said Jude, 'I think we ought to see if we can get in touch with Sheena.'

'And how do you propose to do that?'

'I'll ring Connie back. She'll have a number.'

'Hello?'

'Hello.' The voice was so tense with emotion that at first she didn't recognize it. 'It's Stephen.'

'Stephen. What on earth's the matter?'

'It's Gaby. She's been taken into hospital.'

'What – something wrong with the baby?'

'With the baby, with her, I don't know.' He sounded totally distracted, so unlike himself, not the buttoned-up distant personality he had presented to the world ever since his mother could remember.

'Calm down, Stephen. Tell me what happened.'

'It was in the middle of the night. I don't know, one-thirty, two . . . ? Gaby woke up, feeling pain in her stomach. And, you know, we thought maybe the baby was starting, because it's due in less than four weeks and I suppose it could be premature . . .' He still didn't sound in control of his speech. 'So we rang the hospital and I suggested I should drive her round, but they said, no, they'd send an ambulance . . . and then Gaby was bleeding a bit . . . and they took her in . . . and she's on a drip and . . . I don't know. I don't know what I'd do if anything happened to Gaby.'

'Stephen . . . Is the baby moving all right?'

'What? Oh, yes, yes, apparently so.' In his anxiety about his wife, their unborn baby was an irrelevance. 'Or at least the doctor said it was OK.'

'What else did the doctor say?'

'The one I saw said Gaby'd be fine. But that they wanted to keep her in for observation.'

'Well, if that's what he said, I'm sure that's what he meant.'

'But suppose he only said it to keep me calm? I mean, she's been bleeding and I don't know what—'

'Stephen . . . That kind of thing can happen. There are very few completely straightforward pregnancies. I had a similar scare when I was expecting you.'

'Did you?' He was shocked, partly by the information itself and partly by the fact that he and his mother were talking about such a subject.

'Yes, David and I were scared witless, just as you are now. It was a couple of months before you were born. I was kept in overnight, then sent home and told to take things easy. I did just that and, as you know, everything was fine. As I'm sure it will be with Gaby.'

'Yes.' He didn't sound convinced, but he must have relaxed a bit, because he now became aware of the kind of conversation he was participating in. 'I'm sorry to worry you, Mother.' Not that relaxed, thought Carole wryly. Not relaxed enough for a 'Mum'. He went on, 'I just couldn't think of anyone else to talk to.'

Carole liked that a lot more.

'I mean, Gaby's mother . . . well, I don't think she's strong enough to cope.'

Even better. 'No, probably not. Have you talked to your father?'

Stephen seemed amazed by the suggestion. 'What would be the point of talking to him? He wouldn't know what to do. It'd just make him flap.'

He was right. Just the sort of news to send David into a tailspin of panic. Carole couldn't deny herself a little glow from the fact that she had been Stephen's first port of call in the crisis. Emboldened, she said firmly, 'Stephen, Gaby's going to be absolutely fine. So's your baby.'

What she spoke was what she felt. Though by nature perpetually prone to self-doubt and suspicion, Carole Seddon had never had any misgivings about the safe arrival of her forthcoming grandchild. She had no medical knowledge, she wasn't privy to Gaby's current state of health; she just knew the birth would be all right. The only anxieties she had were about her ability to form a bond with the imminent arrival.

'Would you mind telling her that, Mother?'

'What, telling Gaby?'

'Yes. She's so scared. I've never seen her looking so scared . . . even when, you know, she was worried that someone was trying to murder her. If you could just have a word . . . ?'

'Of course. Can I ring her?'

'No, no mobiles allowed in the hospital. I'm out in the car park talking to you now. Gaby's not allowed out of bed at the moment, but I think they bring a phone trolley round to the wards or something, so she could ring you. Are you going to be about later?'

'I'll have to take Gulliver out for another walk at some point, but basically I'm here.'

'Oh, great. I'll get Gaby to call you. I just hope she's . . .' Once again he sounded lost, like one of those rare moments when he came home from school having got into trouble for transgressing some rule he did not understand.

'Stephen, Gaby and the baby will both be fine.'

'Right. Thank you, Mum.'

He'd never know how much that last word had meant to her.

Gaby rang just before lunch. Carole was very calm and reassuring, and in fact the mother-to-be was also more relaxed. Her panic of the early hours had receded. The bleeding had stopped and she drew comfort from being surrounded by experts in pregnancy and childbirth. Gaby had sent Stephen home to catch up on some sleep, and she thought she'd probably doze through the afternoon herself. She was definitely going to be kept in overnight, but she'd know more after her consultant had done his rounds in the morning.

Carole was surprised how easily she found herself sharing her own comparable experience with Gaby. She'd never really talked about such things, except to a doctor. Carole Seddon had never been part of a group of female friends who discussed their entire gynaecological history. Finding herself talking to her daughter-in-law about these things, building on the bond of their mutual gender, was a novel experience, but a rewarding one. When she put down the phone at the end of their conversation, she felt she had really been of use to Gaby.

And she tried to keep at bay the insidious thoughts that maybe her uncharacteristic confidence was misplaced, that there really was something wrong with the pregnancy.

She contemplated steeling herself to ring David. He was secure in his little flat in Swiss Cottage; maybe he ought to be informed of the family crisis. Oh dear, that would mean talking to him, something she had pretty thoroughly avoided since they'd both put on such a good show of being civilized to each other at the wedding. It would also mean looking up his telephone number. Her photographic memory for figures blanked out that particular piece of information. Still, she supposed she should ring him.

But then she thought: why? As Stephen had said, hearing the news about Gaby's scare would just make him flap. David had always been prone to flapping. When her son needed a rock in his life, it was his mother he turned to, not his father. The knowledge gave Carole a surge of guilty pleasure.

Chapter Fourteen

Jude was a shrewd judge of character and, even though they hadn't met, Carole's description had made her certain Sheena was the kind of woman who would seize any opportunity to talk about herself. So it proved. In response to a phone call from a complete stranger who wanted to talk about what she'd seen at Connie's Clip Joint, Sheena was more than ready to fix a meeting. 'Soon as you like. Friend was going to come down and see me today, but he's cried off. Apparently has to spend the weekend with his *wife*. What a feeble excuse. Bloody men, eh?'

So a rendezvous at the Crown and Anchor when it opened at noon was easily arranged.

Sheena must have been there waiting before Ted Crisp unlocked the doors, because she was well into a large gin and tonic when Jude arrived only a couple of minutes after twelve. 'Oh, I should have got you a drink, Sheena. I set this up.'

'Don't worry, darling. You can get the next one. What're you having?'

Sheena managed to get Ted's attention away from the customer whom he was asking which fingers hairdressers use to hold their scissors, and bought a large Chilean Chardonnay for her interrogator. Jude had instantly recognized the woman from Carole's description. As when she'd made her entrance that morning at Connie's Clip Joint, Sheena was wearing dark glasses and had her hair swathed in a scarf. She was maintaining that illusion of unobtrusiveness so often affected by people who like to be the centre of attraction. Her silk top and linen suit were expensive, showing just enough fussy decoration to be designer garments.

'There you are, darling. Cheers!'

It was still warm enough to sit outside – and that might have been a justification for the dark glasses – but Sheena had selected one of the pub's shady individual booths. Again the attempt at self-effacement had the reverse effect, exacerbated by the loud husky whisper in which she insisted on talking. Any casting director looking for someone to play a spy would have rejected her as too obvious.

'Jude, I'm so glad you got in touch. Because I must confess I'm still traumatized by what I saw that morning at Connie's. I keep wanting to talk about it, but holding back. You know, a shock on that scale is not something you can talk about to just anyone.'

But evidently – and fortunately for Jude – something she could talk about to an unknown woman who'd rung her up out of the blue that morning.

'I mean, let me tell you, mine has been a life not without incident. I've had a few shocks in my time – particularly where men have been concerned – but nothing like this. Actually to have been present at a murder scene – it's the last thing in the world I would have wanted to happen to me.' Even though the opposite was clearly the case, this was spoken with great vehemence. 'And the thought that the perpetrator of this awful crime is still at large . . . well, it's too, too ghastly even to think about. I mean, when I wake up in the middle of the night, I am positively *terrified*. I am currently living on my own and I get these appalling fantasies. Suppose the murderer wants to silence all the people who were witnesses to his crime . . . ?'

She left a pause for this awful thought to sink in, thus giving Jude the opportunity to interject, 'But you weren't strictly a witness to the crime, were you?'

'I was a witness to the effects of the crime. I saw the poor girl with that flex around her neck. I tell you, the image of her face is one that I will keep with me to my dying day.'

She attempted to punctuate this line with a dramatic swallow from her gin and tonic glass, but found it to be empty. Jude went up to the bar for refills. Ted Crisp was betting another customer a fiver that he couldn't say which fingers hairdressers held their scissors in.

When she returned with the drinks, further discussion of Kyra Bartos's murder was delayed by Sheena saying, 'I see you don't wear a wedding ring, Jude. Have you had trouble with men?'

'Yes, sometimes,' came the even reply. 'I have also had more pleasure with men than with anything else in my life.'

'Oh yes, me too,' Sheena hastened to assure her.

'I have known the heights of sexual ecstasy . . . many, many times. But I have also known the hideous free-fall from that ecstasy . . . the moments of betrayal . . . the moment when one realizes one has just been too trusting . . . that one has once again listened to too many lies. It's heartbreaking, but it's the fate which we women are born to.'

This did not coincide exactly with Jude's view of relationships with men, but she didn't want to break the growing mood of complicity, so let it pass with a casual 'Mmm.'

Which Sheena, of course, took as agreement. 'Have you ever been married?'

'Yes,' Jude replied, rightly confident that she would not be asked for any more details. Very few people knew about her marriages – or indeed her divorces. Jude's soothing company drew confidences from people about their own lives rather than questions about hers. Which suited her well. And so it proved in the current situation. It was her own experiences Sheena wanted to discuss, not anyone else's.

'Oh, I was married. For twelve years. I thought we loved each other. I thought he loved me. But suddenly, after twelve years, he said he wanted it to end. Now why would he do that?'

'Emotional exhaustion' was the answer that offered itself to Jude, but she kept it to herself. Anyway, the question turned out to have been only a rhetorical flourish. 'I'll tell you why he did that. Because he had another woman. For seven of the twelve years we had been together, he had been seeing another woman.

143

A stupid girl at his office, hardly out of her teens. She couldn't offer any of the things I could offer him.'

Like bent ears, thought Jude.

'And he's now gone and married her – and serve him bloody well right.'

'You don't know whether they're happy together?'

Sheena let out a derisive laugh. 'I can hardly think they would be. The girl's total number of brain cells is in single figures.'

'There's no logic to who gets on with who.'

'There certainly isn't. Otherwise he'd still be with me. God, the adjustments I've had to make in my lifestyle since the divorce!'

'Were you left very hard up?'

'Well, I got a house down here, but it's not nearly as big as the house we used to live in. Where Miss Pinhead is currently doing her impression of the Lady of the Manor.'

'But have you had to work hard to make ends meet?'

'No, not work as such. But my house has only got four bedrooms, hers has got six. I'm not nearly as well off as she is.'

Jude's sympathy for the divorcee's plight was waning. From what she said – and from the clothes she was wearing – she hadn't done at all badly out of the settlement. Her feelings might not yet have healed, but in material terms she was OK.

Time to move the conversation on. 'Going back to that morning in Connie's Clip Joint—'

Fat chance of getting Sheena off her favourite subject, though. 'Since the divorce,' she went on, 'I've had many attempts to find love again, but they've all ended in disappointment. Men are such bastards, why do we love them so much?'

Jude didn't offer an opinion. She reckoned she'd have to ride out the tide of anti-men hatred before she got back to investigation.

'I mean, this man I was meant to be seeing this weekend . . . usual thing. We meet, it's all magical. The sex is just stunning. He's never met anyone like me. And then it slips out that he's married. OK, I've been there before. But his marriage is a sham, he hasn't made love to his wife for years. And everything's so wonderful with me, he never wants to see his wife again. And I say, OK, divorce is a possibility, you know. People do it. I'm living proof that people do it. And he says, yes, great, he'll talk to his wife. But time passes and he hasn't got round to talking to her. And then I discover they've got children. And, of course, he doesn't want to hurt his precious children. So I say, well, look, you've got to make some choices here, and he says yes he will, because he adores me and he's never known sex could be like that. And still he doesn't do anything. But this week he promises he's going to talk to his wife, and does he? Does he hell? No, instead the bastard rings me and says he still loves me and he can't wait to be with me, but this weekend, no, sorry he can't make it. His wife's ill and he's got to stay at home with her and look after the children. Huh!'

Jude hoped the pause for breath would be an opportunity to get back to the murder, but Sheena hadn't finished yet. 'And how does that leave me? Washed up on the shore once again, like some piece of rubbish that's past its sell-by date. He was younger than me, of course. Men of my own age just don't seem able to keep up with me. And I suppose he was immature. Didn't know when he was well off. Thought opportunities of being with a woman like me would keep cropping up for him. Huh, he'll find out. Serves him bloody well right.' Her hand moved instinctively up to the scarf covering her head. 'I'll go to Theo tomorrow. Get a completely new style. I can't stand the sight of myself in the mirror with this one.'

Jude did the sum. Another restyling so soon after the previous one. If Sheena used a visit to Connie's Clip Joint to resolve all her emotional crises, it could be an expensive business. Mind you, Jude thought, I'm a fine one to be criticizing, me with my two haircuts in five days. But mine, she reassured herself, were in the cause of investigation.

Still, Sheena had at least brought the subject back to the murder scene. Better grab hold of that before she flitted off again. 'The morning Kyra Bartos's body was found . . .' Jude began firmly.

'Yes. Oh, it was terrible! I was just sitting there having my hair done when—'

'I do know everything that happened. My friend Carole told me.'

'Carole?' What Jude had said on the phone that morning, her minimal justification for getting in touch, had already been forgotten. Sheena didn't care about the reason people wanted to talk to her, so long as they did want to talk to her.

'Yes, I've heard all the circumstances of what was actually seen, but I was interested in something you said at the time.'

'How do you know what I said. You weren't there.'

'No, but as I explained, my friend Carole was there and she told me everything that happened.'

'And she actually remembered everything I said?' Sheena was quite impressed.

'She remembered one thing in particular. You said that Kyra Bartos deserved something, but not something as bad as what had happened to her.'

'Did I? I honestly can't remember. I was in such a terrible state. I mean, I'd left home that morning feeling sort of doomy, like it was going to be a bad day, and suddenly I'm at a murder scene and I'm being interviewed by the police and . . . Oh, it's too, too ghastly,' she announced with relish.

'What you said,' Jude persisted, 'implied that you knew Kyra.'

'I'd seen her around in the salon. She'd washed my hair a few times.'

'No, that you knew more about her than that.'

'How do you mean?' Either Sheena was very stupid or she was deliberately prevaricating.

'You said "Though the poor girl may have deserved something, she didn't deserve this." Now to me that implies that you knew something about the girl's past, something about her behaviour, which meant that she deserved some kind of punishment.'

'Oh, I see. Well, I didn't know her well. As I say, she just did my hair. But, you know, you often get chatting to the girls who wash your hair . . .'

'Yes.'

'And we were talking about men . . .' I bet I know who was doing most of the talking, thought Jude. 'And she was saying that she'd got this boyfriend . . .'

'Called Nathan Locke.'

'I don't remember her saying the name at the time, but from what I've heard since that must've been who she was talking about. Anyway, she said she didn't know how serious it was and she didn't want to get involved if it was likely to go pear-shaped. And she didn't want to raise the boy's expectations if the relationship wasn't going to go the distance.'

'That sounds eminently sensible. She didn't deserve punishment for that.'

'No, I agree. But we're only talking about what she told me. You may change your mind when I tell you what I heard from another source.' She held her hands dramatically apart, asking Jude to let her pace her own narrative. 'Anyway, I said to Kyra at the time that the only real test – or at least the first test of a relationship – has to be: is the sex any good? And do you know – she was amazingly reticent about that. I mean, I thought these kids nowadays were screwing everything in sight from the first flicker of puberty, but you wouldn't have believed it from the prim way that girl Kyra talked about sex.'

'Again, nothing wrong with that.'

'Jude, will you please let me tell the story my way!'

'Yes, yes, of course.' Sheena was not a woman used to being crossed. Maybe another reason why her relationships with men hadn't worked out.

'All right, that was how Kyra talked to me, playing the little, shy, butter-wouldn't-melt-between-her-legs girl. I heard a rather different story from Theo.'

'Oh?'

'Well, she was actually out of the salon when he was doing my hair – I was trying strawberry blonde that time – and he said that young Kyra was "a right little cock-teaser".'

'Did he?'

'Yes. Which was quite strong language from Theo. He usually hasn't got a harsh word to say about anyone. But he said Kyra was leading this poor boyfriend of hers a terrible dance. You know, blowing hot and cold ooh, unfortunate turn of phrase there perhaps. Theo said the boy was a really nice boy – yes, Nathan, he did mention the name Nathan – and that he deserved better than being messed around by "a right little cock-teaser".'

She seemed to relish repeating the phrase, and her penetrating whisper of it had prompted some uncomfortable reactions from worthy Fethering pensioners enjoying a Sunday drink at adjacent tables.

'So Theo knew Nathan?'

'Well, he'd at least talked to him. I can't think that Kyra was going to describe herself as "a right little cock-teaser".' The whisper was even louder this time. Old men cleared their throats and tried to avoid the eyes of their wives. 'No, Theo clearly felt sorry for Nathan. He said it was awful how a good-looking boy like that could be messed around by some little . . .' The old men froze in anticipation, but in fact Sheena contented herself with '. . . tart.'

'Hmm.' This did open up a new dimension. Jude was more inclined to accept Kyra's own presentation of herself, as a young girl confused by her first love affair, than the alternative description reported by Sheena. But why should Theo be so violently anti the salon junior? Unless, of course, she was monopolizing the attention of the young man who he himself had his eye on . . . ? It was a thought.

Jude didn't really think she was going to get a lot more useful information out of Sheena, and she was right. But that realization did not allow her to escape another hour of the woman's self-dramatizing moaning. And keeping pace with Sheena's drinking meant that she left the Crown and Anchor with an annoying and unnecessary headache.

As she walked back via the beach to get some air, Jude reflected that she couldn't have asked for a more indiscreet witness. Anything that Sheena knew about the case – however confidential – she would have been happy to blurt out. The trouble was that she didn't know very much.

Still, the thought she had inadvertently planted about Theo having an interest in Nathan . . . that would be worth following up.

Chapter Fifteen

'Hello. Is that Carole Seddon?' The voice was male and unfamiliar. It had a light, almost joshing quality, but with an undercurrent of tension.

She confirmed her identity. It was about ten o'clock on the Monday morning. She had just had a very relieved call from Stephen. Gaby had spent a restful night. There had been no more bleeding and the baby was still moving as it should be. The only small cloud on his sunny horizon was that there were some worries about her blood pressure. The consultant wanted to keep her in for another twenty-four hours.

The news had come as a relief to Carole too, but after she had put the phone down, she felt restless. The day stretched ahead of her without enough to fill it. A bit of housework, a light lunch with the *Times* crossword, another walk with Gulliver. She was a woman who needed things to fill her time. Even after all these years, she missed the imperative of setting off every morning to her job at the Home Office. She didn't dare hope that the arrival of her grandchild would give her much more to do. In spite of their oft-stated intentions to move to West Sussex, Stephen and Gaby still lived in

London. Carole couldn't see herself being used by them for childcare on a frequent basis. When Gaby went back to work at her theatrical agency, they'd get a nanny or a childminder. Which would of course be a blessing. Carole didn't reckon her grandmaternal skills would turn out to be much more instinctive than her maternal skills had been. So her life would remain empty.

Her sleuthing with Jude had helped to fill the void from time to time, but on their current case they didn't seem to be getting anywhere. Once again she wished she was privy to what the police were doing, what was going on at the Major Crime Unit in Littlehampton, how far their enquiries had progressed. She felt isolated in the austere and sensible comfort of High Tor.

'My name,' said the voice on the phone, 'is Martin Rutherford.'

'Ah.' That he should be calling was so unexpected that the monosyllable came out almost as a gasp. Still, she could no longer complain that nothing was happening on the case.

'I'm the ex-husband of—'

'I know who you are.'

'I'm sorry to ring you out of the blue, but I hear that you saw me yesterday morning coming out of the back of Connie's Clip Joint.'

'Yes.' So Connie had done her stuff. The police had already been in touch with him.

'Listen, I'm calling from the salon and it's rather difficult to talk.'

'Maybe we could meet?' Carole wasn't going to let slip any opportunity to pursue the investigation.

'I'd like that.' He sounded relieved. He must have been anticipating resistance. Little did he know how welcome his call had been.

She suggested meeting in the Crown and Anchor, but he didn't have time that day to come so far. If she wouldn't mind coming to see him . . . There was a Caffè Nero just along the road from Martin & Martina.

Carole readily assented and, pausing only to tell her neighbour of this new development, set off for Worthing in her neat little Renault.

Martin Rutherford was again wearing a charcoal linen suit – maybe it was a kind of Martin & Martina livery – but today's shirt was very pale blue. He carried himself with a certain poise, though Carole could tell he was nervous. The fact that he'd arrived early for their eleven o'clock rendezvous was an indication of that, as well as the slight shake of his hand as he brought her cappuccino across to their table.

He got straight down to business. 'I gather you had the misfortune to be there when the poor kid's body was discovered, Mrs Seddon.'

'Yes, I did. And please call me Carole.'

'Thank you.' That seemed to relax him a little. He'd been expecting a more adversarial attitude. 'It must have been terrible for you. And for Connie too, of course,' he added, concern for his ex-wife apparently an afterthought.

Carole didn't say anything. As he was the one who

had made contact, he must have some kind of agenda. She waited to hear what it was.

'And you saw me yesterday morning.'

'Yes. I had been taking my dog for a walk.'

He smiled wryly. 'Early risers in Fethering.' He paused before asking, 'Did you inform the police?'

'No. My friend Jude told Connie about it, and Connie said she would tell the police. Mind you, it could have been me who passed on the information. The detectives did ask me to keep them informed of anything I discovered that might have relevance to the murder case.'

He gave a rueful nod. 'Yes, of course. And you would have been absolutely right to do so. Though, as it happens, what I was doing at Connie's Clip Joint had nothing to do with the murder case.'

'I'm sorry. I could only react to what I saw, and I'm afraid to me it seemed suspicious. I know the state of affairs between you and Connie since the divorce.'

'Do you?' He looked surprised.

'Yes, she talked to me while she was doing my hair. She talked to my friend Jude as well. It sounded as though you are still very much in conflict . . .'

'Well . . .'

'. . . so I couldn't imagine that you'd been at the salon to meet her . . . even assuming that she'd have been there on a Sunday morning.'

'No. All right. I take your point.' He looked relieved, as though he'd been expecting her to say something worse.

'So if you weren't there with Connie's knowledge,

and since I assume you don't still have any legal rights in the property . . . well, I came to the conclusion that you couldn't have been there for any legitimate reason.'

'You're a very logical woman, Carole.'

'I like to think so.'

'All right. I'll tell you why I was there.' And he did. He confirmed exactly the conjecture that Jude had spelled out to his ex-wife the day before. Kyra Bartos's departure from the Worthing Martin & Martina salon had followed her resistance to his advances. He tried to make light of what had happened. 'It was only in fun. Just jokey chatting-up, the kind of thing that goes on in the salon all the time, you know between the men and the girls.'

Carole sat stone-faced during his attempt to laugh it off and, embarrassed, he continued his explanation. Kyra, he said, did not have much of a sense of humour and she took his playfulness more seriously than he had intended. So yes, there had been a bit of awkward ness about her leaving. And though, on one of the rare occasions when he'd spoken to Connie, she'd said something about the girl contemplating legal action, he'd never taken it seriously . . . until he'd heard what Jude had to say to him in Martin & Martina on the Saturday morning.

'That made me think there was a real threat, and so I thought it was just possible that, if Kyra had actually got any information together or approached a solicitor or something, there might be a record of it left at Connie's Clip Joint. I knew she had a fairly tense rela-tionship with her father, so she was more likely to have kept that kind of documentation at the salon than at home.'

He looked pleadingly up at Carole, offering himself to her judgement. 'So that's why I was there yesterday morning. I wasn't thinking very rationally. I just got it into my head that it was worth trying. If the police had found anything which suggested Kyra was contemplating legal action against me . . . well, suddenly that would put me in the frame with a motive to do away with the girl.'

'Yes,' Carole agreed implacably.

'Which, for anyone who knows me, is an absolutely daft idea. If there's any criticism ever made of me, it's that I'm a bit soft. I haven't got it in me to hurt anyone. It would just go against all my instincts.'

'Hmm. Did your wife not think it was odd, you going off early yesterday morning?'

'She would have done, I'm sure. I always give her exact details of where I'm going at any time. It's necessary when you're running a business together. But she's away this weekend. Her mother lives in Prague and she's not well . . . dying in fact, so Martina flies over there roughly once a month. She got a flight on Saturday afternoon and she's coming back tomorrow.'

'I see. So there was nothing to stop you making your illegal entry to Connie's Clip Joint?'

'No.' He sighed. 'In retrospect, it would have been better if Martina had been at home. Then I wouldn't have gone on such an insane wild goose chase. I didn't find anything in the salon, needless to say. But I was in a very manic state, and I thought there was a chance, and I was desperate to do anything that would stop the police wanting to question me any further.'

'Whereas in fact what you did has had exactly the opposite effect. The police now do want to question you about what you were doing at the salon yesterday morning.'

'Yes. I thought at that time of the day I'd be safe. I didn't reckon on you and your dog.'

'Lucky I wasn't taking my dog for a walk when the person who killed Kyra Bartos came out.'

It had been a risk to make the connection so openly, but Martin Rutherford was smart enough to pick up her implication. 'Look, I didn't kill her. I don't know whether any of the local gossip is suggesting that, but it's absolutely untrue.'

'As I'm sure you'll be able to prove to the police.'

'The police?' He sounded bewildered.

'When they question you about your movements.'

'Oh yes, yes, of course. Sorry. Bit slow there. No, it'll be fine when I talk to the police.'

'You mean you have an alibi?'

'Not for when you saw me yesterday morning. But you know that. You saw me. There's no way I can wriggle out of that and say I was somewhere else.'

Carole pressed him. 'But for the night of the murder? Do you have an alibi for then?'

'Of course I do,' he replied confidently. But then he seemed to lose his nerve. 'That is . . .'

'What?'

'Well, I . . . Look, I'm sorry, Carole, but I don't have

157

to tell you. When the police ask me, then of course I'll tell them where I was that night.'

'Fine,' she said, and then dared to add, 'If the answer's embarrassing . . .'

'No, it's not embarrassing.' He made a decision. 'All right, I was at a conference that night. There's a big annual one, the Brighton Hair and Nail Conference. I haven't been there before, but this year I decided I should.'

'Was Martina with you?'

'No, it started on the Wednesday evening. Someone had to be around the salon, in case anything came up in any of the branches. So she stayed and I went to Brighton. Just stayed the one night.'

It was an alibi that could be checked. On the other hand, it was not a totally watertight one. Brighton was not that far from Fethering. A determined murderer could easily slip away from the conference hotel for a couple of hours to do what he had to do. Unless he could produce someone who could vouch for his attendance at the conference all night, the alibi was pretty worthless.

But Carole didn't say any of that. Indeed, she didn't get the chance to. Martin Rutherford had finally got on to the real purpose of their meeting. 'Listen, this whole situation's very unfortunate. I've been stupid and, as a result, I'm going to have what I think could be quite a nasty grilling from the police.'

If he was fishing for sympathy, Carole didn't feel inclined to grant him any. She was surprised by how negative she felt towards Martin Rutherford. Connie was far from being a bosom pal, but Carole still had a lot of fellow feeling for her. The way Martin had behaved in their marriage – and indeed the way he continued to behave with girls like Kyra – was appalling. Carole felt empathy for Connie, the solidarity of divorcees who had been badly treated by men.

'Anyway,' Martin went on, 'that will be my punishment – and it serves me right.'

'It's possible,' said Carole waspishly, 'that that won't be all your punishment.'

'What do you mean?'

'I'd have thought, even if you used your keys to get into Connie's Clip Joint yesterday . . .'

'Which I did. Still got a set to the back door.'

'Even if you did, you could be charged with breaking and entering.'

The idea didn't seem to worry him. 'No, surely that'd only happen if Connie pressed charges. And she'd never do that.'

'Don't underestimate her.' And don't underestimate how much you have hurt her and how vengeful she might be towards you, Carole thought.

Martin still dismissed the idea of a criminal charge. 'Well, that is not currently among my many worries. But look, Carole . . . now this business about my going to Connie's Clip Joint yesterday is known to the police . . . and they'll probably soon know about the reasons for Kyra's dismissal too . . . could you please – you and your friend Jude – not say anything? I mean, don't spread the news to anyone else.'

'I had no intention of doing so,' said Carole sniffily.

'Good. I'm sorry, but I do have a business reputation round here. It's not going to be improved if anyone finds out the police are questioning me again. And I don't want to risk any further damage. So please, will you and Jude keep quiet about it?'

'Yes, of course we will.'

What does he take us for – a couple of local gossips? Carole couldn't help thinking.

'And look . . .' He produced a card from his top pocket. 'That's got my mobile number on it. If you hear anything that you feel's relevant, don't hesitate to ring me.'

'What kind of thing were you thinking of?'

'Anything that points to who might have killed Kyra . . . or . . .'

Or anything that gets me off the hook. Mentally Carole provided the end of the sentence for him.

Chapter Sixteen

There was one thing at least that she could check right away. As soon as she got back to High Tor, Carole got out the Yellow Pages and made a list of the main conference centres and hotels in Brighton. She started to ring round, asking if they had recently hosted a Hair and Nail Conference. On the third call she got lucky. Yes, they'd had some four hundred delegates there just over two weeks ago. The dates tallied with what Martin Rutherford had said. So the conference certainly existed; whether he'd been at it, of course, was another matter.

Carole asked for the name of the organizer of the Brighton Hair and Nail Conference. The girl on Reception couldn't tell her, but put her through to someone in the relevant department who very efficiently provided her with the name and contact numbers of the events company who had staged the conference. Another call confirmed that a Martin Rutherford had indeed been booked in as a delegate. And he had booked in for the dinner on the Wednesday night. What's more, he had been there. By chance, the girl at the end of the line had sat next to him during the dinner. He had been very charming and amusing. No, she didn't know where he'd gone after the meal. Now she really must be getting on with some work.

Carole was digesting this information when her phone rang. It was Stephen. He sounded tense again.

'What's up?' she asked.

'Gaby. They want to keep her in a few more days.'

'Any reason? Has there been more bleeding?'

'No. They just want . . . Something to do with blood pressure. They think she'll be safer there.'

'Then I'm sure they're right.'

'Yes . . .' He didn't sound convinced.

'Listen, Stephen, it's only about a month till she's due. If the baby was born tomorrow, it'd be absolutely fine.'

'Mmm.'

'And the baby's still moving around all right, is it?'

'Yes, yes. It's not the baby they're worried about. It seems to be Gaby.'

'Stephen, lots of women have problems with blood pressure when they're pregnant. The hospital is just observing sensible precautions, that's all. You should be grateful that they're doing so.'

'Yes. Yes, I am.' But he still didn't sound at ease.

'What is it?'

'Mum . . .' She was warmed by the word. 'I'm worried.'

'You wouldn't be human if you weren't. But I'm sure there's no need. Gaby and the baby will both be fine.'

'Yes, but what worries me . . . I'm so concerned

about Gaby that I don't really care what happens to the baby . . .'

The admission cost him a lot. For a moment Carole lost her nerve. She couldn't find the right response to what he had just said. Jude would have done it instinctively, immediately come up with the right formula of words. Carole didn't have those skills. But somehow she managed to swallow her anxiety and found herself saying, 'That's a natural thing to think, Stephen. You shouldn't feel guilty about it. You know Gaby, you love Gaby. If there's any threat to her, you don't care about anything else, so long as she's all right. But you will get to know and love the baby just as much.'

'Will I?' He still sounded uncertain, pleading.

'Yes. You will.'

After the phone call ended, Carole was assailed with doubt. She had had to sound more positive than she really felt. And a tremor of guilt ran through her too. Easy enough for her to tell Stephen about the love he would feel for his child when it was born, but had she ever had that instinctive reaction to him?

There were a lot of things Jude cared about which came under Carole's definition of 'fads'. Her work as a healer headed the list. To Carole's mind that was a fad, or at least the people who indulged in it were faddish. Healing was just a craze, there'd be another one along in a minute. It was Carole's view that if you were so unfortunate as to have something wrong with you, then you should make an appointment at Fethering Surgery and go and see a proper doctor.

She also thought a lot of the decor at Woodside Cottage was faddish. Nobody really needed wind chimes or aromatic candles. And certainly no one needed crystals lying about the place. But Carole couldn't deny the warmth and comfort that her neighbour's home exuded, particularly when contrasted with the almost antiseptic austerity of High Tor.

When it came to food, though, Jude was really faddy. Not faddy in the sense of being picky about what she ate when she was out; she didn't have a portfolio of personal allergies like a lot of the denizens of Fethering. But she was faddy about what she bought. Everything had to be organic. Carole thought such discrimination was an expensive luxury. The food she'd grown up with had kept her pretty healthy, and she couldn't be bothered with checking the source of everything. She didn't like shopping and the less time spent on her weekly trip to Sainsbury's, the better. Besides, the organic stuff was always considerably more expensive than the normal food and, although Carole was economically secure with her Home Office pension, she didn't believe in waste. As for all that nonsense about organic food tasting better . . . well, she could never tell the difference.

For Jude, however, it mattered. At home she liked to know the provenance of everything she ate. But she didn't go for the overpriced supermarket organic option. Instead, she had built up a network of local nurseries, farm shops and farmers' markets to source her supplies and either walked or travelled by train or bus to track down what she wanted.

That Monday afternoon a grudging Carole had agreed to drive her to a nursery outside Littlehampton which specialized in organic vegetables. Carole was not grudging because she resented doing the driving, only because of her innate suspicion of all things organic. In fact, she was still at a loose end and the trip had been her suggestion. At the nursery she was even prevailed upon to buy a bag of potatoes, saying stuffily that she'd 'see if they tasted any different'. Mind you, she couldn't fault the price. They were cheaper than the supermarket's cheapest non-organic offerings.

Their route back to High Tor and Woodside Cottage took them along the High Street and, as they were approaching Connie's Clip Joint, Jude said urgently, 'Slow down.'

'What?'

'Look.'

Carole watched as Theo emerged from the salon. He was dressed in his uniform black shirt and trousers and had his black leather jacket hooked on a finger over his shoulder. His tinted glasses with the gold stars at the corners were in place. He didn't exactly mince, but he sashayed along the High Street away from them, unafraid of looking camp.

'Follow him,' hissed Jude.

'Why? He's just going home, I assume. Must've done his last appointment of the day. So why on earth should I follow him?'

'Do you have other major plans for this afternoon?

Are you going to try out some new organic potato recipes?'

'No,' Carole replied testily. Then, with an 'Oh, very well', she put the car in gear and moved slowly along behind the stylist. 'Though I still don't know why I'm doing this.'

'So that we can see what he does.'

What he did was to click his key remote to unlock a dark green Skoda Fabia, into which he climbed and drove off.

'See, I told you. He's just going home.'

'Follow him,' said Jude mischievously.

Carole sighed at the pointlessness of the exercise, but in the tradition of endless Hollywood movies, followed the car in front. It wasn't very difficult. The prevalence of road bumps and assiduous traffic police, combined with the overwhelming sedateness of Fethering, meant that nobody ever drove fast there. And, unlike a character from a Hollywood film, Theo appeared to have no suspicion that the women in the Renault pootling along behind him had any ulterior motive. He wasn't about to break into a routine of sudden reversing and screeching tyres.

'I don't know why we're doing this,' Carole repeated grumpily.

'Just a hunch. But if you'd rather be making an organic potato salad . . .'

'Huh.'

The route Theo's Fabia was taking led out of Fethering in the direction of Bognor Regis, which was a mild surprise. Because of his gayness, Carole and Jude had expected him to gravitate towards Brighton. But, fair enough, there are gay men in Bognor Regis too.

That wasn't where he was going, though. He suddenly indicated and turned right off the A259 towards Yapton. No reason why he shouldn't. Maybe that was where he lived. There were almost certainly gays in Yapton too.

But his destination was not a private house. The Fabia turned into the impressive drive of Yeomansdyke, a luxury hotel and health spa which Jude had visited when she was investigating the murder of Walter Fleet, owner of a nearby livery stables.

'What shall I do?'

'Drive in. Keep following him.'

With bad grace, Carole did as instructed. By the time they reached the hotel car park, the Fabia was parked and Theo was walking towards the spa entrance. The Renault was neatly guided into a parking bay, but Carole didn't turn off the engine. 'What're we supposed to do now?'

'I don't know.' Jude was almost girlishly irresponsible, knowing that her attitude was irritating her neighbour, but blithely incapable of changing it. 'Odd place for him to come, though, isn't it?'

'It's a free country. People can go where they want to go.'

'Yes, but he's just walked into the spa like he's a regular. The membership for this place is seriously expensive. I can't think he pays for that on what he makes as a hairdresser.'

'He may not be a member. He could just have come here to meet someone.'

'Yes, but you'd have thought, if he was going to do that, he'd go in the main hotel entrance. That's where the bars and places are. Not so likely to meet someone in the leisure centre. I don't think the Yeomansdyke spa is like a New York bathhouse.'

Carole didn't get the reference. 'Well, I don't know,' she said huffily. 'All I do know is that I feel a complete idiot sitting here in the car, like I was some police detective on a stake-out.'

'Well, if you imagine that's what you are . . . does that make it any easier?'

'No.' Carole switched off the ignition. 'Ten minutes we're going to wait here. If he doesn't come out within ten minutes, we're going.'

'But look, if he's come here for a swim, or a work-out in the gym . . . well, that's going to take him more than ten minutes.'

'Ten minutes,' Carole reiterated firmly, and folded her arms behind the steering wheel. She wished she had brought the *Times* crossword with her on this wild goose chase. There were three clues in the top left-hand corner she hadn't managed to complete yet.

They didn't have to wait ten minutes. In just over five Theo emerged from the Yeomansdyke spa entrance, and moved briskly across towards his Fabia.

He was unrecognizable. Gone were the tinted glasses and the black gear. Now he was dressed in beige chinos and a light tweed sports jacket. His whole body language had changed too. There was no longer any feyness, but a firm resolution in his stride.

'What on earth . . . ?' breathed Carole.

'Wait till he gets back into the car, then follow him,' said Jude.

They watched the Fabia parked in front of them for what seemed an inordinately long time. Then their attention was drawn by the gunning of a powerful engine. They turned as one to see a silver BMW sports car speeding past them out of the car park. At the wheel, unaware of their presence, was the new Theo.

By the time they reached the road at the end of the Yeomansdyke drive, the car had disappeared, whether to the right or left they had no idea.

Chapter Seventeen

As the Renault nosed its way back along Fethering High Street, Jude suddenly shouted, 'Park!'

'What?' demanded Carole, obeying nonetheless. She brought the car to a halt behind a muddy Land Rover. The back was sticking out and she began to manoeuvre so that the wheels should be exactly parallel to the kerb.

'Don't bother with that.'

'But I must. I hate messy parking. What is this, Jude?'

'When we went past the salon, I noticed Connie was in there on her own.'

'So?'

'Well, we can go in and ask her about Theo.'

'Just ask her? Just like that?'

'Yes, of course. Why not?'

'It's a bit obvious, isn't it?'

Jude sighed with exasperation. 'And what's wrong with the obvious? We ask Connie about Theo. There's probably nothing sinister in what he's doing. There'll be a perfectly simple explanation. We ask her and she tells us.'

'But we can't just walk in. She'll think it's odd.'

'No, she won't. She owns a hairdressing salon. People walk in and out all the time.'

'But not without an appointment.'

'Carole, are you coming?'

'I should really be getting back to Gulliver . . .'

'Fine. You do that.' There were times, thought Jude as she opened the car door, when being friends with Carole could be quite difficult. 'Do you mind taking my vegetables? I'll drop by and pick them up later.' She was tempted to say she'd drop by 'without an appointment', but restrained herself. Carole agreed she'd take the vegetables.

Jude looked back just before she reached the salon. Carole had straightened up the Renault first, made sure it was exactly parallel to the kerb, before driving it out of the space on the way back to High Tor. Her neighbour shook her head in bewilderment.

As Jude entered Connie's Clip Joint, Barbra Streisand was trembling from the CD, doing one of those misleadingly quiet bits which always presages a full-volume screech. Connie herself was sitting with a cappuccino and a *Hello!* magazine, looking as though she hadn't a care in the world.

'Hi. Good to see you. Like a coffee?'

'Please.' So much for Carole's worries about not having an appointment. Jude wasn't even sure that she needed a cover story, but just to be on the safe side, she produced the one she'd quickly prepared. 'Actually, I wanted to ask you about Theo . . .'

'Yes?' Connie called from the back room by the

coffee machine where she was preparing Jude's cappuccino.

'I was talking to someone who was asking about hairdressers who might come and visit . . . you know, cut their hair at home. I know you told me you don't do that. I was wondering if Theo ever "makes house calls".'

'Don't think he does. He's never mentioned it.'

'I suppose it'd depend a bit where it was . . . you know, if it was near his home . . .'

'Maybe.' Connie came back into the salon and closed the back room door. 'There's your coffee.'

'Thanks.' Jude took a sip and wiped off the moustache of froth before asking, 'Where does he live, actually?'

Connie looked surprised by her own reply. 'Do you know, I don't actually know.'

'Really? But if he's a member of your staff . . .'

'No, I thought I told you.'

'Oh, that's right. He rents the chair.'

'That's right. And he pays me in cash, which is very good news. I've always believed there are some areas of one's life that should be kept a secret from the taxman.'

'I agree,' said Jude. 'So you really don't have an address for Theo?'

'No. I always contact him on his mobile. I mean, I just had a call from one of his clients this afternoon. Wants a cut and highlights tomorrow afternoon. Two o'clock. So I'll put it in the book and call Theo on the mobile so he knows to come in.'

'Is that the only booking he's got tomorrow?'

'Yes. Neither of us doing particularly well at the moment.' But it didn't seem to worry her. 'I haven't got a landline for Theo, so I've no idea whereabouts he lives. But then why should I? I mean, I get on with him fine, but it's purely a business relationship. We don't socialize together outside work.' Connie Rutherford pulled a lugubrious face. 'I may be looking for a man, you know, but Theo wouldn't be highest on my list of possibles.'

'No.'

'He'd be very good for my ego, keep telling me how wonderful I looked, but in other departments . . .' she giggled ruefully, '. . . I think I might be disappointed.'

'I think you might.' Jude took a sip of cappuccino. 'So you don't know whether he's in a relationship?'

'I don't know anything about his private life. Theo's a great one for gossip, he loves earwigging on everything all the women who come into the salon talk about, he really encourages them, they open up to him . . . but, now I come to think of it, he never gives away anything about himself.'

'Good trick if you can do it,' said Jude, who could do it and recognized the technique. She asked a few more questions about Theo, but got similar answers. Connie had no idea about his private life. He didn't volunteer any information, and few of his clients wanted to probe. Many Fethering women got quite a charge out of having their hair cut by a gay man, but they didn't want too much detail. And Connie seemed equally incurious.

One thing Jude felt pretty sure of after she'd finished her questioning was that Connie had no idea about the change of persona that Theo had effected at Yeomansdyke.

'If you like,' the hairdresser concluded, 'I'll ask him in the morning.'

'Ask him what?' asked Jude.

'Whether he does visit people's houses to cut their hair.'

'Oh, yes.' She'd completely forgotten her cover story. 'Don't worry, it's not important. I think my friend has a lead to someone else, anyway.' She looked around the salon. 'So did neither of you have any bookings this afternoon?'

'I had a two o'clock shampoo. One of the old dears who's never washed her own hair in her life. There are still a few of them around.'

'And that was it?'

'Yes. Might get someone else wandering in later . . . After school finishes, quite often get girls in with their mums . . . which is usually quite entertaining.'

'Why?'

'The mums want them to look like innocent little cherubs. The girls want shocking pink colouring and razor cuts.'

'Ah yes, of course. Don't you get frustrated when you're just sitting around?'

Connie shrugged. 'You get used to it. Part of the business.'

'But not a very lucrative part of the business.'

'No. You get used to that too. Business comes and goes. That's just part of being a freelance.'

'I suppose so.' But Jude was surprised how laid-back

Connie seemed about the salon's lack of success. Fethering gossip said that the business was in a dire state, and bets were almost being taken on how long it could survive. But the proprietor seemed unbothered. Indeed, she was as relaxed as Jude had ever seen her. The habitual restlessness that accompanied her every movement was no longer in evidence. Her make-up was perfectly in place, and her hair hung neatly, its red highlights recently done, a fine advertisement for her skills. Around her glowed an aura of fulfilment.

Which made Jude think of a time when Connie had not looked quite so soignée. Gently she moved the conversation back to the morning that Kyra Bartos's body had been discovered in the back room.

'It seems a long time ago,' said Connie.

'You haven't got around to getting another junior yet?'

'No.' She gave the impression that she hadn't thought about the subject for some time. 'No. I must do something about it, but . . .' She shrugged a gesture that took in the empty salon '. . . no great need when business is like this. Saves me a bit of money too.' But she didn't make it sound as though saving money was that important.

'And have you had any more contact with the police?'

'Nothing. Presumably they're still trying to track down that boy Nathan.'

'Maybe. They didn't give you any indication of how far they'd got with the investigation, when you spoke to them yesterday?'

175

Connie Rutherford looked puzzled. 'Sorry?'

'When you spoke to them yesterday? About Carole having seen Martin skulking round the back of this place?'

'Ah yes, of course.' It all came back to her. 'Sorry, I'd forgotten, because it was all over so quickly. I rang through to the number the detective chief inspector had given me, told him my piece, and that was it. Hardly even a thank you, let alone any useful information about how the murder case was proceeding.'

'And you don't know whether they've been in touch with Martin yet?'

'Jude, Martin and I are divorced. We contact each other as little as is humanly possible.'

'Yes, I'm sorry, I wasn't thinking.'

'So unless they suddenly arrest him for Kyra's murder . . . which is very unlikely . . . I can't really think it likely that I'll hear anything about his encounter with the police.'

'No.' Jude felt duly chastened. 'Thinking back to that time, though, Connie . . .'

'Mmm?'

'You know, the morning when Kyra didn't open up the salon as she should have done . . .'

'Yes?' The hairdresser looked wary. She had recovered a degree of equanimity since the tragedy, and apparently didn't want to have the memory brought back.

'Carole Seddon gave me a blow-by-blow account of what happened . . .'

'I'm not surprised,' said Connie with some edge.

DEATH UNDER THE DRYER

'Probably the most exciting thing that had happened in her life for some time. But she at least was quite restrained while it was all happening. Unlike that woman Sheena . . .'

'Yes, I heard.' Not necessary to mention her recent encounter with the drama queen. But it did remind her of something Sheena had suggested. 'Sorry, Connie, going off at a tangent . . . back to Theo . . .'

'Mmm?' The hairdresser sounded more enthusiastic. She hadn't liked reviving the images of discovering Kyra's body. Discussing her fellow stylist was much more appealing.

'I mean, presumably he is gay . . . ?'

'Oh, come on, Jude! Is the Pope Catholic?'

'Yes. OK. Well, you never saw any sign of Theo . . . coming on to anyone, did you?'

'No. As I said, we don't mix socially. What he gets up to in his spare time . . . well, that's not my business, is it?'

'Of course not. I only mentioned it, because . . .' What the hell, time for another indiscretion. 'Someone suggested that Theo might have made a play for Nathan Locke.'

This was a real surprise for Connie. 'I don't know that he even met Nathan. I never saw them together.'

'But could there have been an evening when, say . . . you'd left early and Theo was still here, and Nathan came round to pick up Kyra . . . ?'

'Well, yes, there could have been. Quite possible, but I'm not aware of that ever having happened. And, even if they had met, I really can't see Theo having "made a play", as you put it, for Nathan. He's a very professional stylist. I've met a lot of gay men in this business – it goes with the territory – and they're all very camp with the clients, but I've never met one who came on to anyone in the salon.'

'No.' Jude was being tarred with the brush of homophobia, but it wasn't the moment to correct Connie's misapprehension. 'Sorry, it was just something someone said.'

'Everyone in Fethering's got something to say about Kyra's death, and I wish they'd stop it. Nobody really knows anything . . . except perhaps the police.'

'And they're keeping anything they know very firmly to themselves.'

'Yes.' Their recent conversation had spoiled the serenity of Connie's mood. 'Look, there are some things I've got to sort out, Jude.'

'Yes, of course, I must be on my way.'

'Just a minute.'

Jude stopped on her way to the door. 'What?'

Connie was looking curiously at her hair. 'You haven't had it cut again since I did it, have you?'

'No, of course not,' came the guilty reply.

But Connie was not deceived. Looking closely at the hair, she echoed exactly the words of Kelly-Jane at Martin & Martina, 'Dear, oh dear. Now do tell me where this was done.'

'No, look, I can't. Sorry, I must be on my way.' It took a lot to fluster Jude, but this had achieved the feat. She realized she had overstepped a diplomatic boundary. Having another haircut by another stylist at another salon within a week is probably about the most offensive insult you can give a hairdresser. And Connie's face reflected the affront she had just received.

Jude opened the door, but before she went out, turned back and said, 'There was one other thing I wanted to ask you . . .'

'Oh?' Connie wasn't a natural at being frosty, but the welcome had definitely gone from her voice.

'Something Carole told me. The morning Kyra's body was discovered . . .'

'Yes?' The hairdresser had already had quite enough of that subject.

'Well, I'm sure she must have got it wrong, because you always take such care of your appearance, but Carole said that morning you weren't wearing any make-up, and you hadn't done your hair.'

'No, I hadn't. I sometimes do all that after I've arrived here. Go through to—' She corrected herself. 'Do it in the mirror here.'

The image did not match the picture of the woman that had formed in Jude's mind. Connie had her standards as the owner of the salon; she wouldn't do her make-up in the mirror when she had a client present. She didn't say anything, but Connie seemed to feel she needed further self-justification. 'I just got delayed that morning, that's all.'

'Do you remember what delayed you?'

'The fact that my alarm clock didn't ring. With the result that I overslept.' Jude's welcome was in danger of being outstayed. 'Now, I really do have things to do . . .'

'Of course. Thanks for the coffee. See you.'

As she walked back to Woodside Cottage, Jude felt certain that, whatever had delayed the owner from reaching Connie's Clip Joint on the morning after Kyra Bartos's murder, it wasn't just that she'd overslept.

Chapter Eighteen

'But would you do that, Carole?'

'I'm not sure that I'm the best person to ask. I'm not one of those women who cakes herself in make-up every time I leave the house.'

'I know you're not. But you always look smart when you go out, don't you?'

Carole wasn't sure whether or not what Jude had just said was a compliment. She hadn't had much practice with compliments and did not receive them naturally. 'I don't know,' she conceded. 'I certainly don't like to look a mess.'

'No, none of us do. It's a feminine instinct. You check you look OK before you leave the house.'

Surely *you* don't, Carole was tempted to ask. Jude always looked as though her hair and her clothes had just been thrown together on a whim. But maybe she had to work at that look just as carefully as Carole had to check that the belt of her Burberry wasn't twisted. Anyway, it certainly did the business for Jude. Wherever she went, men drooled.

'Well,' she went on, 'imagine how much stronger that instinct must be for someone in what in the broadest sense can be called the "beauty industry". Connie Rutherford has to be a walking advertisement for what she's selling. If she looks a mess, she's going to discourage customers to Connie's Clip Joint. So we come back to the same point: what made her late that Thursday morning?'

'She didn't give you any answer?'

'Not a detailed one. Just that she'd overslept. I'm afraid once she noticed that I'd had my hair cut somewhere else, I ceased to be a welcome guest. I don't think I'm going to get a lot more information out of her now.'

'Perhaps it's as well that I didn't come in with you then. At least she doesn't have anything against me.'

'Except that you're a friend of mine.'

'Maybe.'

'And a fellow lover of organic vegetables.'

'I only bought these as an experiment. To see if they taste any different.' This was said very sniffily. Carole had low expectations for the results of her taste test.

'I was only teasing.'

'Oh.' From schooldays onwards, Carole had never been very good at recognizing when she was being teased.

'There's another thing, though, Carole . . .'

'What?'

'Well, OK, let's say Connie does sometimes leave the house in a hurry in the morning . . . for whatever reason . . . one of her car crash encounters with a man perhaps . . . and so she gets to the salon and she hasn't done her hair or make-up . . .'

'Like on that Thursday?'

'Yes.

'Well, she couldn't do her make-up then, because I was waiting to have my hair washed and cut.'

'But I'm sure if all had gone to plan . . . if Kyra had opened the salon at eight forty-five as she was meant to and had already been washing your hair when her boss arrived straight from bed . . . there's no way Connie would have done her make-up in the mirror where you could see her.'

'No, I'm sure she wouldn't.'

'So she would have put on her war paint in the back room. She virtually said that to me. She said she'd "go through" – and then she stopped herself and said she'd do it in the mirror at the front.'

'Except that morning she couldn't do what she'd normally do, because I was already there waiting for my appointment.'

'Exactly.' Jude had a hand up in the bird's nest of hair and was tapping her skull reflectively. 'Every time I've gone into that salon, the first thing Connie's done is to offer me a cup of coffee. Did she offer you coffee that morning?'

'No, she didn't. I wouldn't have accepted it, because she was already late and it would have just taken more time and—'

'Are you sure she didn't offer you any coffee?'

'Yes. I remember thinking it was quite odd. Because it sounded as though she was about to offer me something . . . and then she stopped . . .'

'Hmm. You know what the reason for that could be?'

'No.'

'The coffee machine's in the back room. It's possible that Connie didn't offer you coffee because she didn't want to go into the back room . . . because she knew there was something she didn't want you to see back there.'

The following morning, the Tuesday, Jude was on the way down the High Street for a walk on the beach when she saw someone she recognized. Sitting in a parked car, looking patiently out towards the sea, was Wally Grenston. The day was warm and his window was down, so she greeted him as she passed.

After the customary pleasantries, she said, 'So Mim's let you out on your own, has she?'

The grizzled head turned nervously at the suggestion and nodded towards the building outside which he was parked. 'She's in at the chiropodist. A martyr to her feet, Mim. I tell her it's down to all those ridiculous stiletto things she wore when she was a singer. If God had intended women to walk like that He'd have put prongs on their heels. You don't go for shoes like that, do you?'

Jude laughed and lifted up one brown sandaled foot.

'Very sensible. If Mim'd worn shoes like that all her life, she wouldn't have her current trouble.'

'I haven't worn shoes like this all my life, Wally. I've had my time in stilettos.'

'Well, clearly not as much time as Mim.' Again he looked with some anxiety at the chiropodist's door, but he was all right. She hadn't come out yet. 'And are you still doing the amateur sleuthing, Jude?'

'Still trying to work out how Kyra Bartos died, yes.'

He nodded, mulling over an idea, then said, 'I had a call from her father yesterday.'

'Joe?'

'Jiri, yes. There is a meeting of the Czech Club in Brighton tomorrow night. He asked me if I was going.'

'You mean he is?'

He caught the eagerness in her voice. 'Yes, he is going. And no, Jude, there is no chance that you could go there too to meet him. The club is Members Only.'

'Ah,' she said, disappointed. 'And what do you do when you're there?'

'We sit and drink.' He smiled fondly. 'Some drink beer, some slivovitz. I drink Becherovka. And we talk about times . . .' There was a catch in his voice. '. . . about times that will never come back.'

'Does the club have its own premises?'

'No, no. We meet sometimes in a hotel room, a pub, sometimes at the house of one of the members. Two times a year we have big dinners, socials . . . with food from Czechoslovakia. Mmm, carp . . .' He smacked his lips nostalgically. 'Guests come then, to those dinners. They are good evenings.'

'Maybe you'd invite me to one, one day . . . ?' Jude joked.

Wally Grenston chuckled. 'Nothing that I would like more. Nothing, though, that Mim would like less.'

'Ah.'

He smiled and lightly whistled a couple of bars of a lilting but melancholy tune, almost definitely one of his own. Then he announced, 'I think it is good that Jiri rang me . . .'

'In what way?'

'It means perhaps he is coming out of his grief a little. Since Krystina died, so far as I can tell, he has hardly left the house.'

'Bereavement is a terrible thing.' Suddenly Jude had an idea for another approach to the old man. 'I have actually done work with the bereaved.'

'Work? How do you mean?'

'I do healing . . . you know, like counselling. It has proved very effective. Maybe Joe Bartos would—'

But her suggestion was cut short by a wry laugh. 'You couldn't have chosen a worse idea for Jiri. He does not believe in asking help from anyone, and certainly not help of the kind that might be called "psychological". Joe is very much of the old "suffer in silence" school. He has never talked about his emotions to me – or, I'm sure, anyone else. No, he will sort himself out. And, in fact, that he is talking of going to the Czech Club, this I think is good news. He is, as you say, "coming out of himself".'

'Do you think that means he's more likely to talk to me?'

The old man shrugged. 'Who knows? It's quite possible that he doesn't want to talk to anyone about

186

Krystina, that the reason he wants to go to the club is to talk about other things. I will only know when I see him.'

'Well, if he does want to talk . . .'

'Yes, yes. I have your number. I will tell him.' But Wally Grenston didn't sound optimistic.

'I don't want to put pressure on him to—'

But Wally was frantically shaking his head and gesturing for her to leave. He had seen something through the chiropodist's window. Jude moved off just as she heard the door opening. By the time Mim had emerged on to the pavement, Jude was twenty yards away. Once again Wally Grenston had lived danger-ously and survived.

The landline was ringing when she returned to Woodside Cottage after her walk. 'Hello?'

'Is your name Jude?' A woman's voice, cultured, confident.

'Yes.'

'My name's Bridget Locke.'

'Ah.' A coincidence? Except Jude didn't really believe in coincidences. There was an intention and synchronicity to everything that happened. Nor had she any doubt that the Bridget Locke on the phone was the one married to Rowley Locke.

'I was given your name by a friend called Sonia Dalrymple.' A horse-owning client with whom Jude had had some recent dealings. 'She said you do healing and stuff . . .'

'Yes.'

'I've suddenly done something to my back. I don't know if you do backs. Maybe I should be talking to an osteopath?'

'I do backs.'

'Well, mine's suddenly gone and—'

'Gone in what way?'

'Sort of seized up down in the small of my back, but the pain comes all over the place, if I try to turn my head round or lift my legs in a certain way.'

'Mmm. Lower back pain. So you'd like to make an appointment?'

'Please.'

'Well, I live in Fethering, just on the High Street. I'm fairly free at the moment, so if you name a time when—'

'Ah. The trouble is, I can't drive. I mean, I can drive normally, but at the moment I can hardly move off my bed, and even just lying there's terribly painful. I certainly can't bend my body to get into the car. It's agony. Look, I'm sorry, but would it be possible for you to come and see me?'

Jude needed no second invitation. She had heard enough from Carole about the Lockes' set-up to want to see it at first hand. If she could cure Bridget Locke's back pain – and she had a high success rate in such cases – then good. And if she could find out any more about Kyra Bartos's murder and the disappearance of Nathan Locke, then even better.

'Yes, of course I could come to you. Where do you live?' she asked, knowing the answer full well.

Chapter Nineteen

Jude fixed to go to Chichester that afternoon. After four, when the younger girls were back from school and could let her in. She could do the journey by rail. The coastal trains on the Brighton to Portsmouth Harbour line were slow and kept stopping in the middle of the bungaloid sprawl at numerous stations with 'wick' in their names, but they'd get her there eventually. Then a taxi from Chichester Station to Summersdale.

She knew Carole would have driven her, but Jude didn't want that, for a couple of reasons. First, the Lockes were presumably unaware of the connection between the two women. The sight of Carole's Renault outside their house could ruin that. Then again, when she was going to do a healing session, Jude needed some quiet time to build up her concentration and focus her energies. That would be difficult to achieve in a car full of Carole's scepticism.

Anyway, as it turned out, she couldn't have got a lift from her neighbour. The immaculate Renault and its owner were elsewhere.

*

Carole wasn't at home because she was on a mission of her own. An only child of borderline paranoid tendencies, she had never been good at sharing. Her relationship with Jude was one of the easiest and least judgemental of her life, but Carole still sometimes felt the necessity for secrets. Particularly in connection with their murder investigations. She could never quite suppress the pleasing fantasy of her doing something very successful on her own; of her finding the link of logic that brought together two apparently unrelated elements in a case. And the fantasy always concluded with the image of her casually presenting the vital new development as a rich gift to Jude.

For nearly twenty-four hours an idea had been simmering in Carole's mind. A piece of the investigation that she could do completely on her own. Indeed, it made sense that she should do it on her own. She was, after all, the one with the car.

The germ of the idea had come to her on the previous day when she had driven out of the Yeomansdyke car park, only to discover that Theo in his shiny BMW had vanished. When Jude had told her about his two o'clock appointment for the Tuesday afternoon, she knew exactly what she should do.

Carole Seddon's experience of stake-out work was limited. Though there were undoubtedly people connected with the Home Office who had honed such skills by long practice, it was not something that had ever come up in her own professional duties. She had spent most of her time writing and reading interminable reports. So her knowledge of surveillance techniques was based only on what she had seen at the cinema and on television.

The first important prerequisite, she knew, was an unobtrusive vehicle, and here she already scored highly. In Fethering a Renault like hers automatically became part of the landscape. The streets were full of such elderly but beautifully nurtured old cars. Nobody would ever give it a second glance.

The second essential was that the driver should also be unobtrusive, and in this respect she was not so well placed. Though she had few friends in Fethering, everybody in the village knew exactly who she was (just as she knew a great deal about all of the people she never spoke to). Anonymity is only granted to people who live in cities; in the country it is impossible to attain.

Balancing this in her favour was the fact that her quarry didn't know either her or her car well. Theo's behaviour the previous day suggested that he'd been completely unaware of the Renault tailing him.

Fortunately, at the end of Fethering High Street there was a small car park for people using the beach. Carole settled the Renault into a bay from which she had a perfect view of Theo's Fabia, parked more or less exactly where it had been the previous day. Having never undergone the procedure, she didn't know exactly how long a cut and highlights would take, but she reckoned it had to be at least an hour. Theo's appointment, she knew, was for two o'clock. Being, however, a person paranoid about being late, she was in her surveillance position by half-past two.

She hoped she didn't look too obtrusive. It was quite common for people – particularly old people – to sit in their vehicles in that particular car park, but the favoured way was facing the sea. To have one's back to the view was unusual but, to Carole's relief, did not attract any curious looks from passers-by. And she did have the *Times* crossword there as a smokescreen.

It was a particularly recalcitrant puzzle that day. Tuesdays, Carole knew from long experience, could be tricky. Mondays and Fridays were always easy. She felt sure that this was a deliberate policy on behalf of the newspaper. The pains of returning to work after the weekend, like end-of-the-week exhaustion, could be eased by an unchallenging crossword. Completing it quickly could give a disproportionate lift to the spirits of the weary commuter. But midweek was a different matter altogether; then the clues could be much more arduous. And Carole had a feeling *The Times* had taken on a new setter. Over the years she had become skilled at reading the minds of the people devising the cross-words, but some of the clues that had been cropping up recently seemed to express a whole new attitude to the English language. Carole found the newcomer's work both satisfying and frustrating – satisfying when she could get an answer right, frustrating when she couldn't. It would take time to find out precisely how the new mind worked.

That Tuesday's crossword was definitely one of his. Very unusually for her, Carole had to look at the clues for nearly ten minutes before she could get her first solution. Normally, even on a difficult day, she could get a couple straight away and then slowly grind through the others. And there were some magical occasions when the whole crossword opened up like a book and the answers came as quickly as she could write them down. Then, by simply narrowing her eyes, she could instantly pick out the anagram from a jumble of words. At such gilded moments she felt omniscient, there was nothing in the world she could not cope with. Such gilded moments, however, were rare.

Doing the crossword was meant to stave off the advance of Alzheimer's, but that afternoon she could feel it encroaching at a rate of knots. Even as she had the thought, though, she knew what was really to blame was her concentration. Constantly flicking her eyes away from the page towards the immobile green Fabia was not conducive to effective clue-solving.

She had a long wait and filled in very few more answers. A cut and highlights clearly took a lot longer than her estimate. She was beginning to think that Theo must've had some other customers booked in, when finally she saw a woman with newly highlighted hair emerge from Connie's Clip Joint. Only moments later Theo came out, and swanned along the High Street towards his car. It was just after four o'clock.

Once again Theo was dressed in his black livery. Once again his movements were light and mildly effeminate. Once again he got into the Fabia and drove out of Fethering in a westerly direction.

And once again Carole Seddon's Renault tailed him.

The previous day's history repeated itself. The Fabia stopped in the Yeomansdyke car park, and the hairdresser, looking neither left nor right, again went into the hotel's spa entrance.

No swim or workout on the Tuesday either. Within five minutes Theo was out again in his other persona. The day's clothes for this character were jeans and an oatmeal-coloured linen jacket. Without even a look at the Fabia, he got into the BMW and drove off.

This time Carole was ready for him. The Renault's engine was on before he was out of the car park, and she was in time to see him turn right out of the entrance. She followed. He was going north, through Yapton and past Fontwell Racecourse towards the A27, the major road that runs parallel to the South Coast. The BMW turned right, rejecting the delights of Chichester, Portsmouth and Southampton in favour of Arundel, Worthing and Brighton.

On the minor roads, there had been little traffic and Carole had had no difficulty keeping within sight of Theo's car. Indeed, her only worry had been that her trailing him was too obvious. On the A27 the problem was different. There were many more vehicles and an open stretch of road would give a car like the BMW opportunities to let rip and lose the more sedate Renault (not to mention the even more sedate Renault's owner).

But Theo proved to be a very law-abiding driver. He rarely took the car above fifty and Carole had little difficulty in keeping no more than one or two cars away from him. Where the traffic slowed to a crawl through the outskirts of Worthing, she found she was directly behind. Rather belatedly, she put on a pair of

dark glasses from the Renault's neat glove compartment. It was unlikely that Theo would show any
interest in the driver of the car behind – he was probably lost in a radio programme or music CD – but
Carole still thought putting the glasses on was a prudent move. The action also gave her a *frisson*; she was
behaving like a real private investigator.

Worthing left behind, the BMW showed no signs
of stopping. It didn't take long before Carole started to
feel less like a real private investigator and more like
the middle-aged owner of a dog who would soon be
needing a meal and a walk. She had no idea how far
Theo was going. His destination could be anywhere –
London, Canterbury, Folkestone. Yes, he might even be
going through the Channel Tunnel. Paris? Lille? He
could be going to any place in Europe or beyond.

With difficulty, she curbed her imagination and
made a decision. Brighton would be the extent of her
surveillance. If he went beyond Brighton, then that was
it. End of adventure. She'd go back and feed Gulliver.

The possibility of a destination in Brighton or
nearer was boosted by the fact that, after leaving the
magnificence of Lancing College to his left and climb-
ing the steep incline above Shoreham-on-Sea, Theo left
the A27 in favour of the A2770. While the major road
led up through a tunnel to all kinds of distant places,
the one he had selected led through a variety of over-
lapping small towns until it reached Brighton.

The traffic was still heavy and slower on the minor
road, so keeping the BMW in sight was again no problem. The two cars stopped and started through the

suburban sprawl, then took a right turn down towards Hove. Where the road met the sea, Theo turned left, along the magnificent frontage towards Brighton. Carole knew it didn't really make sense, but she seemed to feel a relaxation in his driving now, as if he were on the home straight.

And so it proved. Taking his tail by surprise, Theo's BMW suddenly swung left up into a magnificent Regency square of fine houses frosted like wedding cakes. Carole almost overshot the junction, but, to a chorus of annoyed hooting from behind her, managed to manoeuvre the Renault up the same way.

At the top, on the side facing the sea, Theo bedded the car neatly into a reserved space. The lack of other parking left Carole with no choice but to drive past him. She juddered to a halt on yellow lines beyond the row of residents' cars and looked ahead, trying to find that rarest of phenomena – a parking space in Brighton.

She was so preoccupied with her search that she didn't look behind her. The tap on her window took her completely by surprise. She turned in the seat to see Theo looking down at her. Sheepishly, she lowered the window.

'So, Carole . . .' he asked, 'why have you been following me?'

Chapter Twenty

Jude was let into the Summersdale house by one of the little Locke girls, dressed in a green school jumper and skirt. Whether it was Chloë or Sylvia – or indeed Zebba or Tarnil – she had no means of knowing, and the information wasn't volunteered. All the child did, when the visitor had identified herself, was to say lispingly, 'Oh yes, Mummy's expecting you. She's upstairs.' Then, turning on her heel and announcing, 'I'm playing,' she went back into the sitting room.

As Jude climbed the stairs, she tried to tune in to the atmosphere of the place. Beneath the surface chaos of lovable family life she could feel strong undercurrents of tension and anxiety. Those might be natural, given the Lockes' current situation, but the impression she got was that they pre-dated the disappearance of Nathan from Marine Villas.

At the top of the stairs she paused, and a weak voice said, 'I'm through here.'

Bridget Locke was wearing a plain white nightdress, and was propped up high on pillows in a single bed. But before Jude had a chance to process this information, she was told that this was the spare room. 'I'm so uncomfortable in the night that I can't share a bed with anyone. Rowley wouldn't get any sleep if I was in our own room.'

Jude, as usual with a new client (she preferred that word to 'patient'), began by asking a few general questions about Bridget's medical history. Apparently, back pain was not a recurrent problem for her. This was the first time it had happened, or at least had happened so badly that she needed treatment.

'Why did you come to me? Most people's first port of call would have been their GP.'

'Yes.' The woman seemed slightly confused by the question. 'The fact is, I've always favoured alternative therapy over conventional medicine. My experience of doctors has been that, whatever your complaint is, they reckon a drug prescription will sort it out. I'm rather reluctant to cram my body full of chemicals.'

While Jude entirely agreed with the sentiment, she wasn't convinced that Bridget Locke was telling the truth about her reasons for approaching her. 'You said it was Sonia Dalrymple who suggested you call me . . . ?'

'That's right.'

'How is she?' A bit of general conversation might relax the woman – even, Jude found herself thinking for some reason, put her off her guard.

'She's fine. Well, I say that . . . I think the marriage has broken up. Difficult man, Nicky.'

Jude, whose investigations with Carole into a murder at Long Bamber Stables had found out some interesting secrets about Nicky Dalrymple, might have put it more strongly. But she wasn't about to say more about that. 'So, if this is the first time your back's gone, Bridget, what do you think's caused it?'

'I don't know. Lifting something out of the car perhaps? Standing at a funny angle?'

'Was there any moment when you suddenly felt it go?'

'No, it sort of happened gradually.'

'Hmm. You know, a lot of back pain isn't primarily physical.'

'Are you saying it's psychosomatic?' The reaction was a common one. No one wanted to have their suffering diminished by being told it was 'all in the mind'.

'That's a word you can use, if you want to,' Jude replied soothingly. 'The mind and the body are very deeply interrelated. And whether the cause is something mental or something physical, it doesn't make any difference to how much your back hurts.'

'No.' Bridget Locke sounded mollified.

'What are your normal stress reactions?'

'Sorry?'

'Most of us have some kind of physical response to stress. With some people it's headaches . . . stomach upsets . . . insomnia . . .'

Bridget Locke seized on the last word. 'I don't sleep that well. I suppose that is my normal stress reaction, yes.'

'And presumably, with your back like this, you're sleeping even less?'

The woman nodded. She did look exhausted. Under the neatly cut hair, the skin of her face was tight with tiredness and there were dark hollows beneath her eyes.

'You're worried about Nathan?'

'Oh, you've heard about that?' Again something didn't ring true with Jude. Bridget knew she lived in Fethering, she must have known the level of village gossip that an event like Kyra Bartos's murder would generate in a place like that. Surely she would have assumed that Jude knew about it.

But this was not the moment for a challenge. 'Yes, dreadful business. It must be hard on you . . .'

'Quite tough.'

'. . . and of course the rest of the family.' Though from what Carole had said, Bridget was the only one who seemed worried about the boy.

'Yes.'

'Hmm. I gather, Bridget, you're not Rowland's first wife?'

'No. How did you know that?'

No point in lying. 'A friend of mine told me. Someone you've met. Her name's Carole Seddon.'

'Ah, yes.' Was Jude wrong to detect a note of satisfaction in the response?

'Can I ask you . . . I'm sorry, you may think it's being nosy, but it's a question anyone from Fethering would ask you . . .'

'Because everyone from Fethering has now become an amateur detective?'

'If you like.'

'Including you and your friend Carole?'

'Maybe. We can't help being interested.'

'No, only natural. So what was this question that everyone in Fethering would ask me? Do I know who killed Kyra Bartos?'

'No, not that one. They might be intrigued, but the question they'd ask is one that you might be more likely to have an answer to.'

'Which is?'

Jude looked the woman firmly in the eyes. 'Do you have any idea what has happened to Nathan?'

This time she had no problem in believing the response. A weary shake of the head and, 'No, I wish I did. I feel very close to him.'

'Oh?' As ever the gentle manner promised to elicit confidences. And it did.

'The fact is, this family . . . I mean, when I met Rowley, it was him I fell in love with. I didn't realize to quite what an extent by taking him on, I'd be taking on the rest of the Locke clan too . . .' Jude stayed silent. She knew more would come. 'They are very all-enveloping. They see themselves as a kind of coalition against the world. I think it all started when Rowley and Arnold were boys. They were brought up in Cornwall . . .'

'At Treboddick?'

'Yes. And, you know, they were always playing these fantasy games. There's one in particular called the Wheel Quest.'

'Oh?' Jude responded as if she'd never heard of it. She'd admitted knowing Carole, but didn't want to suggest that they'd discussed the Lockes together.

'It's something Rowley devised. Started off as a

201

role-playing thing the boys acted out, then he turned it into a kind of board game. And a family obsession. I expect Chloë and Sylvia are playing it downstairs right now. Anyway, that stuff was all instigated by Rowley. He was the imaginative one, he invented everything, and Arnold was happy to be his acolyte, to go along with whatever Rowley said. Then, when they got married, the wives became part of the . . . well, it may be overstating it, but you could almost call it "the alternative Locke universe". Eithne was fine about the whole thing, still is, and of course the children love being part of it. Joan – that was Rowley's first wife – well, the impression I get is that she went along with it quite enthusiastically at first. She'd been an only child and suddenly being part of this huge, hermetically sealed comfort zone . . . she loved everything about it. But, as the years went on, I think she got a bit disillusioned with the whole set-up. It can be difficult for an outsider.'

Ignoring the implication about Bridget Locke's own position, Jude asked, 'And was Nathan something of an outsider too?'

She'd got it right. 'Yes. I suppose that's why I bonded with him. Neither of us swallowed the whole Treboddick and Wheel Quest business quite as much as we should have done. We liked it, we loved the individual members of the family, but both of us I guess had a kind of independence in us . . . something that meant occasionally we didn't want to do everything as a pack. At times it could all feel a bit claustrophobic. We both liked some level of solitude, which is very difficult to achieve in this family.'

'And that's the bond between you and Nathan?' Jude was rewarded by a nod. 'So is it worry about him that has got you in this state . . . and probably brought on the back trouble?'

'Maybe. Yes, probably.'

'Hmm.' Here was a slight dilemma. By asking what she wanted to ask next, Jude would be admitting that Carole had reported back every detail of her visit to the Summersdale house, and there were some people who would find that an invasion of privacy. Still, it was worth the risk. 'Another thing my friend said, Bridget . . . was that, having met you and your husband, and Arnold and Eithne . . .'

'Yes?'

'. . . you seemed to be the only one genuinely worried by what might have happened to Nathan.'

There was a silence, and Jude feared she might have made a misjudgement. But Bridget proved to be more concerned about the boy than about having her affairs discussed by total strangers. 'I know what you mean, but that's very much a Locke way of doing things. With their solidarity there also comes a huge confidence, so they really can't imagine that anything dreadful's happened to Nathan. He's a Locke – he'll be all right.'

'I don't suppose you think it's possible . . .' Again Jude was treading on potentially dangerous ground, '. . . that they're confident because they actually know where he is . . . they know he's all right?'

'No. Absolutely not.' But then came a concession. 'I did actually suspect that at first. Not very loyal of me, was it? But straight after the murder was discovered, my immediate thought was that Nathan had taken himself off to Treboddick and was lying low down there. That would have been a very Locke solution to the problem. Whatever goes wrong with anyone in the family, a few days at Treboddick is always reckoned to be what's required. That's the universal panacea. So I was suspicious.

'But the police were also suspicious and they went down to Treboddick . . . searched all the cottages and found nothing.'

'You've got a lot of cottages down there?'

'A sort of terrace of four. Old miners' cottages. Rowley's parents used to own all of them. Now one of them's permanently for the family, the other three are let.'

'During the summer holidays?'

'And any other time of year anyone'll take them. Mopsa lives down there and she's supposedly in charge of organizing the lets.' She didn't sound over-confident of her stepdaughter's organizational skills. 'Anyway, once I knew that the police had searched Treboddick, I stopped being suspicious of the rest of the family. They don't know where Nathan is. They've just convinced themselves that, because he's a Locke, nothing bad can happen to him.'

'It must be rather wonderful to have that kind of confidence.'

Bridget Locke grinned wryly. 'Well, it is . . . and it

isn't Rowley and Arnold feel more secure in the family circle, being judged by family standards, than they do in the real world. So, if something goes wrong, like say when Rowley lost his teaching job, rather than going out into the competitive marketplace trying to get another one, he shrinks into himself. The world of Treboddick and the Wheel Quest is more benign than the real one.'

'Hmm.' Time, Jude decided, to get back to the purported reason for her visit. 'Well, let's have a look at this back, shall we?'

Obediently, Bridget Locke rolled back the duvet and lay on her front. Jude removed the pillows and began very gently to pass her hands up the line of the woman's vertebrae. Not actually touching the skin, she waited to feel the angry energy of pain rising from the body. After the scan, she asked Bridget to perform various movements and tell her which ones hurt. Then, rolling up the nightdress and anointing the shapely back with some aromatic oil she had brought with her, Jude started to do a deep hands-on massage.

The effect was almost immediate. Bridget Locke's body relaxed, and her breathing settled into a slow, regular rhythm. Her limbs twitched and, within minutes, she was fast asleep. She really had been exhausted.

As Jude tiptoed out onto the landing, her mind was full. She'd dealt with a lot of lower back pain, and this was the first sufferer she'd seen who was more comfortable propped up on pillows than lying flat. Nor had she seen many who could shake their heads and throw off duvets with quite such abandon.

Whatever Bridget Locke's reason had been for calling Jude to the house, there certainly was nothing wrong with her back.

Chapter Twenty-one

To leave while a client was asleep would not be the proper professional procedure, and yet to wake her seemed unnecessarily cruel. Bridget Locke's main problem was exhaustion, and the best remedy for that was a large dose of rest. Besides, Jude could hear the excited sounds of the two girls playing in the sitting room. She had been granted more information than she had ever anticipated from their stepmother. Maybe there was more to come from Chloë and Sylvia.

'Your mother's asleep. I'll just wait here until she wakes up.'

The girls hardly reacted to Jude's words as she settled herself into an armchair. They seemed to share the Locke lack of interest in people outside the charmed circle of their own family. And, as their stepmother had predicted, they were deeply absorbed in their game. Jude sat back to watch and listen to the two little, uniformed Pre-Raphaelites. From their conversation she deduced that the one who had let her in was Chloë (aka Zebba) and the smaller one Sylvia (aka Tarnil).

Carole's description left her in no doubt that they

were once again playing the Wheel Quest, and she found the mechanics of the game quite as puzzling as her neighbour had. The action still took place between the Kingdom of Verendia and the Forest of Black Fangdar, but, with more time to look at the board, Jude could now see that the main port of Verendia appeared to be Karmenka, over which loomed an extensive castle called 'Biddet Rock'.

Though she could not possibly understand the detail of what was happening, she did after a while work out that the game concerned a battle between Verendia and Black Fangdar and that the two powers represented – surprise, surprise – Good and Evil. Chloë was playing for Verendia and Sylvia for Black Fangdar. They moved their cardboard figurines around the map with great speed and no discernible logic. And they talked in the incomprehensible language Carole had described. 'The Ordeal of Furminal' was again referred to, as were 'the Vales of Aspinglad' and 'the blood of Merkerin'. And there was a lot more where that came from.

So far as the confused spectator could piece together the action, the forces of Good, in the person of Prince Fimbador, were being pursued by the evil hordes of Gadrath Pezzekan, who of course represented Evil. Prince Fimbador had suffered a heavy defeat at the Battle of Edras Helford, and was now being hounded by the enemy army of gedros, jarks, monitewks and various other monsters. He, cut off from his comrades, had retreated to the stronghold of Biddet Rock. His ghastly opponents were at the gates of the castle and about to break them down.

'Yield, Prince Fimbador!' lisped Sylvia. 'You cannot resist Gadrath Pezzekan and the power of Black Fangdar! Hand over the Grail and your life will be spared!'

'My life is worthless,' Chloë lisped back, 'if the Grail ends up in the evil hands of the Merkerin! I defy you and your false accusations! You have not yet defeated me, Gadrath Pezzekan!'

'Oh no? You are alone. Your army is vanquished. You arc outnumbered by thousands to one. And now you are cornered in the Castle of Biddet Rock like a rat in a trap. There is no possible escape for you, Prince Fimbador. Yield the Grail to me!'

'Never! Biddet Rock still has its secrets. Pursue me if you will, but you will never find me in the labyrinth of the Wheel Path. No one has ever found anyone in the Wheel Path. No one has even found the Key of Clove's Halo nor used it to open Face-Peril Gate, which is the secret entrance to the Wheel Chamber. There I will go, carrying the Grail with me for safe-keeping. And from there I will escape, and come back to vanquish you another day, Gadrath Pezzekan!'

'You're bluffing, Prince Fimbador. Already my jarks have broken through the flimsy gates of—'

Quite how that particular Grail-quest might have ended Jude never found out, because at that moment Bridget Locke, yawning and with a towelling robe wrapped around her, entered the sitting room. As if a switch had been flicked, Chloë and Sylvia were instantly silent.

'Sorry, Jude,' said their stepmother. 'I do hope the girls have been keeping you amused.'

'You could say that.'

'I'm so sorry, though. I just passed out.'

'The best thing that could have happened to you. Lots of sleep, that's what you need, Bridget. How does the back feel?'

'Amazing. I don't know what you did to it, but it feels completely back to normal.' Hardly surprising, since there was never anything wrong with it. 'Now tell me – what do I owe you?'

Jude's charges for her healing services were very flexible. Some people she treated free; those who she thought could afford it, she billed for whatever figure came into her head. Even though the Lockes were not well-heeled, she charged Bridget at something near her highest rate. Jude was very sympathetic to psychosomatic sufferings, but not to non-existent ones.

She called on her mobile for a taxi, and exchanged conversation of little consequence with Bridget until it arrived. The two girls sat silently on the floor, in suspended animation until they could resume their game. A stranger's presence hadn't inhibited them at all; but their stepmother's did. Jude wondered how they'd react had it been Rowley who came into the room. She got the feeling the Wheel Quest would have continued uninterrupted.

When the cab arrived, Bridget Locke escorted her to the door. Her farewell words were: 'Do give my good wishes to Carole.' This possibly answered the question that had been building in Jude's mind since she arrived at the house: why had Bridget summoned her there? Could it be that all the Lockes had wanted to do was confirm that there was a connection between Carole and Jude? Were they aware of the two neighbours' interest in the circumstances of Kyra Bartos's death?

Jude couldn't be sure, but in the taxi back to Chichester Station, she certainly felt more that, rather than investigating at the Summersdale house, she herself had been being investigated.

Chapter Twenty-two

'This is where I live. Since you've come all the way from Fethering, can I invite you in?'

Carole had never felt so foolish in her life. To have failed so dismally at surveillance was bad enough, but to be patronized by the person she was supposedly tailing added insult to injury. Her first instinct was to drive off immediately, to slog shamefacedly back to High Tor and give Gulliver his supper and a nice walk.

But another part of her demanded that, having come so far, she had to see the thing through. She hadn't worked out precisely what she was going to do when Theo reached his destination, but she had prepared herself for the possibility that, if he did see her, he would tell her to get lost. Instead, she was being invited inside his home. Surely, for someone who occasionally dared to think of herself as an investigator, that was too good an invitation to turn down.

On the other hand, what she was investigating was a murder and Theo's odd behaviour suggested that at the very least he had something to hide. He was quite possibly in the frame as a suspect. To go into the house or flat of such a person could be risky to the point of recklessness.

Theo himself interrupted her indecision. 'Make your mind up. I'm going in. You can come with me or not. But I'm not likely to ask you again.'

'I'll come in,' she said with a boldness she didn't feel.

'Fine.' He showed his beautifully veneered teeth in a smile that looked just sardonic, but could easily have been evil.

The BMW turned out to be parked exactly in front of his home. He used a key to let himself in through the heavy black door with fine brass trimmings, and summoned an old brass-gated lift – or, when inspected more closely, a reproduction of an old brass-gated lift. Inside, the control panel was all high-tec and computerized. Politely he gestured Carole to go in before him, and pressed the button for the third floor. Nothing was said as the lift moved smoothly upwards.

The silence continued as he led her out and moved straight ahead to open his flat. There were no other doors on the landing, indicating that Theo owned the whole of one floor. Carole just had time to register that hairdressers must make a lot more money than she had previously thought before he ushered her into the flat itself. There her impression was confirmed. Through the open hall door, she could see that the huge sitting room, its tall windows looking down over the square to the sea, was exquisitely and lavishly appointed. Sunlight glinted on the deep dark patina of fine furniture, and the paintings on the walls looked as if they were the work of artists Carole had heard of. If all of this came from hairdressing, Theo's prices must be absolutely astronomical.

'I hope you don't mind if I close the door,' said Theo. 'I'm not sure what it is you suspect me of, but I don't in fact have any intention of either raping or murdering you.'

His words so closely matched the anxieties running through her head that Carole found herself blushing. Theo indicated an armchair for her and sat down opposite, his bright brown eyes fixed on her pale blue ones. She looked away. She got the unpleasant sensation that he was enjoying her discomfiture.

'So . . . what's this all about? You following me two days running? With your chubby friend yesterday . . . when I managed to give you the slip . . . and today on your own? As they say in the worst kind of thrillers – what's your game?'

Carole decided to brazen it out. 'I've been following you because I think you have a guilty secret.'

His hands flew up to his mouth in a theatrical gesture of shock. For the first time that afternoon, she saw some of the high campness he had demonstrated in Connie's Clip Joint. 'I heard you used to be a civil servant. Don't tell me you're from the Inland Revenue.'

'No, I'm not.'

He did an equally elaborate impression of relief. 'Thank God for that. If you had been, then I might have had to admit to the odd guilty secret, but then I regard it as a point of honour to deceive the taxman in any way possible. If it's not tax, though . . .' he spread his hands wide in a display of innocence, '. . . my conscience is clear.'

'It's nothing to do with tax.' Having started on a course of confrontation, she had to continue. 'It's to do with the murder of Kyra Bartos.'

'Ah.' The small brown eyes narrowed. 'I might have guessed. In a hotbed of gossip like Fethering, I'm sure there are quite a lot of busybodies who have their crackpot theories about that. Yes, I suppose every second pensioner over there sees herself as the reincarnation of Miss Marple.'

Carole's first instinct was to be affronted, until she realized that 'pensioner' was in fact an entirely accurate definition of her status. She tried being a little less combative. 'All right. Everyone is gossiping about the case, I agree. And everyone is making wild conjectures about all the people involved with Connie's Clip Joint . . .'

'Thank you for the "wild conjectures". The use of the expression displays remarkable self-knowledge.'

'So,' she persevered, 'it therefore does become of interest when one of those people turns out to have a guilty secret.'

Theo looked puzzled. 'But I thought we'd established that, apart from a little finessing on my tax returns . . .' Light dawned. 'Ah. You are referring to my habit of changing cars at Yeomansdyke . . .'

'Not just cars. Changing personalities too, I'd say.'

She didn't know how he was going to react to this, and was surprised to see him laugh. 'Well, I can assure you it's quite legitimate. My membership at

Yeomansdyke is fully up to date. And I have special permission to park a car there overnight. I drive to the hotel in the morning, do a work-out in the gym, and then drive on to be a stylist at Connie's Clip Joint. Anything wrong with that?'

'You change clothes.'

'And when you were employed as a civil servant, Carole, didn't you quite frequently change out of your work clothes at the end of the day?'

'Maybe. But I didn't change cars. Changing clothes and cars suggests very definitely to me that you have something to hide.'

'Perhaps.' But the accusation still seemed to amuse rather than annoy him. 'Before we go into that . . . in your Miss Marple role . . .' Carole found herself blushing again. 'In that role, where do you see me fitting into . . . "The Case of Kyra Bartos"?'

She didn't enjoy being sent up and came back with some vigour, 'I see you as a murder suspect.'

'Do you?' This amused him even more.

'Yes, I do. And quite a strong suspect too.'

'I see. And would you be generous enough to tell me why?'

'Very well. First, you work at Connie's Clip Joint, which was the scene of the crime . . .'

He slapped the back of his hand on his forehead in a 'Foiled again!' gesture. 'How on earth did you work that out?'

Carole wasn't to be deterred. 'What's more you presumably have keys to the place, so you could get in and out at any time of the day and night . . .'

'That too I can't deny. God, where did you learn to be so devilishly clever?'

'What is more,' Carole pressed on, 'you had a very strong feeling of dislike for Kyra Bartos.'

'Did I? And where did that come from?'

'It arose, because she was the one who had got Nathan Locke to fall in love with her, and you loved him.'

Her previous statements had tickled his sense of humour, but this one reduced him to uncontrollable hysterics. Carole sat rigidly still and deeply embarrassed until the paroxysms died down.

'Oh, that is wonderful!' said Theo, wiping the tears from his eyes. 'That is so brilliant! Thank you, Carole. We all need a good laugh, and that is the funniest thing anyone has said to me for years and years. "I killed Kyra because she had stolen the affections of the man I love . . ." Too wonderful.' Relishing the idea brought on another spasm of laughter.

When the last ripples had died down, Carole said, 'I don't know that it's such a ridiculous idea. I've seen photographs of Nathan – he's a very attractive young man. Just the sort who would appeal to a . . .' she couldn't bring herself to say 'gay man' '. . . to a homosexual.'

'A homosexual like me, you mean? How many gays – how many *homosexuals* do you actually know, Carole?'

'Erm . . .' Her knowledge wasn't that extensive. There were one or two men in Fethering who everyone said *were*, but she didn't actually know any of them to speak to. 'There were quite a few in the Home Office,' she concluded lamely.

'I'm sure there were. And were they homosexuals just like me?'

'Well . . .'

Her answer was interrupted by the sound of a key in the front door. As soon as it opened, a tornado of two small children and a large Old English Sheepdog thundered into the sitting room and wrapped itself around Theo. Behind them, closing the door, stood a tall slender woman with long black hair. She moved forward and, picking her way between children and dog, planted a large kiss on Theo's lips.

'You haven't lost your sense of timing, Zara.' He grinned across at his guest. 'Carole – my wife Zara. Our children Joey and Mabel. And our dog, Boofle.'

'Ah.'

'I'm actually tied up for a little while, love.'

'Don't worry,' said Zara. 'The horde needs feeding. Come on, kids. Come on, Boofle. Teatime.' And she led them out into the hall, discreetly closing the door behind her.

Carole was lost for words. All she could come up with was, 'That's an Old English Sheepdog. You said you had a little Westie called Priscilla.'

'Ah – discovered! Mea culpa! Yes, I knew I could not keep my guilty secret from you forever. I do not have a little Westie called Priscilla.'

'Look, what is all this, Theo? Am I to gather that you're not . . . homosexual?'

'Once again nothing escapes the eagle eye of Miss Marple. It's uncanny. How does she do it?'

'But you . . . I mean, the way you behave at Connie's Clip Joint . . . Even when I was there, when you were talking to Sheena, you said things that definitely implied you were . . . homosexual.'

'I did. I admit it. So far as Connie's Clip Joint is concerned, I'm as gay as a pair of Elton John's glasses.'

'But I don't understand.'

He dropped into his arch hairdresser's drawl. 'Give the customers what they want, darling. Someone like Sheena positively loves having her hair cut by a gay man. She'd be disappointed if she didn't have a gay man doing it. So, if that's what she wants . . .' He gave a helpless, camp shrug.

'There must be more to it than that.'

'Ooh, there is, yes. It's also self-protection. Let's take Sheena as an example yet again. Imagine what'd happen with someone like her if she thought I was *available*. She'd be flirting, she'd be all over me. I tell you, behaving the way I do saves me a lot of aggravation. I'm much safer appealing to the fag hag in a harpie like Sheena than I would be if she thought I was hetero.'

Having met the woman in question, and having heard Jude's account of a lunch with her, Carole could see Theo's point.

'So did you invent the business for her about fancying Nathan and being jealous of Kyra?'

'I remember hinting at it to Sheena, just as a joke.

But maybe it got embroidered in her rather over-active imagination.'

'All right, that's possible. But it still doesn't explain everything. The changing clothes, the changing cars.'

'In Fethering everyone thinks I'm gay. In Brighton everyone thinks I'm heterosexual. Yeomansdyke is where I change identities, that's all.'

'That's not enough. There's more to it.'

'Oh? Tell me what there is more to it, Miss Marple.'

'Well, it's an incomplete disguise, for a start. Fethering and Brighton aren't that far apart. Maybe you don't see many of your Brighton friends in Fethering, but it must sometimes happen that you meet one of your clients here.'

'Less often than you'd think. And on the few occasions when it does, they see me out of context, with Zara, with the children and they do a sort of take. I can see their minds working. And usually I can see them concluding: I've just seen someone who looks extraordinarily like my hairdresser. I promise you, it's never been a problem.'

'Is that all the explanation I'm getting?'

Still with a glint of mischief in the dark brown eyes, he spread his hands generously wide. 'Why? Isn't that enough?'

'No, Theo. It isn't.'

'Ah, I see.' He gestured round the lovely sitting room. 'You're telling me that *all this* is a bluff. A cleverly constructed front. The Theo of Connie's Clip Joint is the real me. I am a closet gay, who fancied Nathan

Locke so much that I killed his girlfriend in a fit of jealous homosexual pique.'

Again Carole felt herself blushing under his sardonic gaze.

Theo chuckled. 'I'll tell you the truth, if you like.'

'Would you?' she asked pathetically. 'I mean, for a start, is Theo your real name?'

'Theo is my real name. I started off as an actor. And at one point I got involved in a production with one of those self-obsessed, power-crazed directors who builds up a show from months of improvisation.'

'Oh?' Carole didn't know a lot about the theatre. She hadn't heard of such a technique.

'Well, I was supposed to be playing a hairdresser in this show and so the director, true to his principles, sent me off to research my part by working in a real hairdresser's. I did three months. It could have been worse. I was lucky – one of the other actors had been cast as a cess-pool emptier's mate. Anyway, the usual thing – three months in the salon, three months of self-indulgent improvisation in the rehearsal room, and you end up with a show that would have been a lot better if the director had got a writer in in the first place.

'But after the run finished – and maybe because of what the show had been like – I go through a very bad patch work-wise. You couldn't give me away with soap. And after a long time sitting at home waiting for the phone to ring, I think: well, I'm going to have to get an income from somewhere . . . and I quite enjoyed that three months I spent in the hairdressing salon . . . so . . .'

221

'You became a hairdresser?'

'Exactly. I joined another salon, trained properly, and suddenly I was a stylist. Money's not great, but compared to being an out-of-work actor, anything's better.'

'And did you develop the, er . . . homosexual mask from the start?'

'Yes. As a joke at first. But then I saw the advantages. As I said, the customers like it, and it keeps them from prying into my private life. And there's a third big benefit – *they confide in me*. Things they'd certainly never tell their husbands or lovers, and a lot that they wouldn't even tell their girlfriends. You wouldn't believe the things a gay hairdresser hears about female behaviour.'

'Hmm.' Carole found she was beginning to relax, recognizing that Theo's sending her up was teasing rather than malicious. She gestured round the room. 'That still doesn't explain all this. I'm sure there are hairdressers who make a huge amount of money, but I'd have thought they're the ones with chains of salons and their own ranges of hair-care products. I can't think you make that much renting a chair at Connie's Clip Joint in Fethering.'

Theo grinned. 'Zara might have a lot of money.'

'Yes, I suppose she might.'

'But in fact she hasn't. Or she hadn't when I married her.' He stood up. 'Do you want to know the last part of my secret, Carole?'

'Please.'

'I'll tell you, but I really do want you to keep this to yourself. You're not to pass it on to anyone else.'

Not even Jude, was her first thought. Then she decided she'd wait to see what the last part of the secret was. If it involved illegality, then she might have to break the promise of confidentiality she gave to Theo.

He led her to a door on the left-hand side of the sitting room. With his family in the house, Carole now had no anxiety in following Theo anywhere. He ushered her into a beautifully designed office. On a desk in a window overlooking the sea stood a lone state-of-the-art laptop. Other purpose-built surfaces held the armoury of more electronic equipment without which no business can now flourish. On specially designed shelves on the back wall stood rows of new-looking books – hardbacks, paperbacks, many in foreign editions.

'Come on, has your brilliant sleuthing mind worked it out yet?'

The reluctant Miss Marple was forced to admit that it hadn't.

Theo took a hardback book from the shelf and held it across to her. On the jacket a determined-looking girl in a red dress stood on an outcrop of rock looking out at a departing steamship. The title was *The Sorrowful Sea*.

'Are you familiar with the *oeuvre* of Tamsin Elderfield?'

'No, I'm afraid I'm not.'

'Well, fortunately . . .' Theo gestured to the rows of shelves, '. . . lots of other people are.'

'You mean . . . you . . . ?'

'Yes.' He grinned. 'A third identity to confuse you, Carole. Theo the hairdresser in Fethering, Theo the family man in Brighton, and now – Tamsin Elderfield in virtually every bookshop in the world.'

'But . . . But . . . it's romantic fiction, isn't it?'

'It certainly is.'

'And you're a man.'

'Spot on. Can't pull the wool over your eyes, Miss Marple.'

'But, if you're such a successful writer, why on earth do you still bother with a day job as a hairdresser?'

'Because, Carole, that is *why* I am a successful writer. A lot of authors have difficulty answering the inevitable question: where do you get your ideas from? I don't,' he said smugly.

'You get them from Connie's Clip Joint.'

'Of course I do. I actually quite enjoy hairdressing, but that's not why I keep on doing it. No, Connie's Clip Joint is the rich seam of experience which furnishes me with my plots. I don't want to boast, but I think there are few men who have the depth of understanding of women's romantic aspirations and frustrations that I do . . . or indeed that any other gay hairdresser does.

'So, Carole, now you know everything – as do the police, incidentally. I've been quite open with them about my different identities and apparently I'm not breaking any laws. So I'm sorry – none of what I've done is even vaguely immoral. Well, except possibly for my lying to you about owning a little Westie called Priscilla.'

There was a long silence, as Carole tried to balance her feelings of surprise and embarrassment. Finally, rather feebly, she asked, 'So there's nothing you can tell me that'll help me find out who killed Kyra Bartos?'

'Sorry.' He too was silent for a moment, before saying, 'Well, there is just one thing . . . I don't know whether Nathan Locke killed the girl or not, but I would think finding the boy alive and talking to him might be the best way of getting to the truth.'

'Do you know where he is?'

'No. But I did overhear him once saying something to Kyra when he came to pick her up . . . something that might be relevant . . .'

'What was it?'

'I also told the police this, so it's no great secret. Whether they acted on what I said, I've no idea. It's just . . . I was in the back room at the salon one evening tidying up, and Nathan came in to fetch Kyra, and she was getting her stuff together and he was talking, rather romantically, of how he'd like to take her away some time, spend a few days with just the two of them. And he said he knew a lovely place, a secret place he'd been longing to show her ever since they met.'

'Where was it?' breathed Carole.

'In Cornwall.'

She still felt sheepish when she got back to the Renault. Theo had compounded the impression that he was patronizing her by giving her a copy of one of Tamsin Elderfield's paperbacks: *The Roundabout of Love*. With some force Carole threw it onto the back seat, before starting on the rush-hour crawl back to Fethering.

Chapter Twenty-three

Jude was round at the front door as soon as she saw the Renault slide neatly into the High Tor garage. Unaware of how Carole had spent the afternoon, she had her own news to impart.

So while her neighbour dropped her *Times* on the table and tried to regain favour with an aggrieved Gulliver by feeding him, Jude opened a bottle of wine and supplied edited highlights of her visit to the house in Summersdale. 'But,' she concluded, 'I still don't know why I was summoned there. Bridget Locke had nothing wrong with her, but she was very determined that I should go over. I wonder what she wanted . . . ?'

'I should think it was more a matter of what her husband wanted. Even though Bridget seems to be a strong woman, I get the impression Rowley dictates what happens in that household – and in the whole family, come to that. He's used to getting his own way and he'll use any means – even throwing tantrums – to ensure that that state of affairs continues.'

'All right, say she was only following orders . . . what was Bridget trying to find out? I imagine she must have got what she wanted before she fell asleep,

227

because she didn't ask me any supplementary questions afterwards.'

Carole was practical as ever. 'Just go through everything she said to you again. There must've been something that had a special meaning for her.'

Screwing up her face with the effort of recollection, Jude reassembled the conversation that had taken place in Bridget Locke's spare bedroom. At one point Carole interrupted her. 'Well, that's it!'

'What's it?'

'She effectively asked you whether you and I were investigating the case.'

'I suppose she did.'

'I think that's all she wanted – or all Rowley wanted. Confirmation that you and I were working together trying to find out who killed Kyra. And it would also tie in with the way Rowley's kept insisting that I should tell him any new developments I've found out about.'

'You reckon he's monitoring the progress of our investigation into the murder?'

'I would say that's exactly what he's doing, Jude. Which could mean quite a lot of things . . .'

'The most obvious being that he knows the truth of what happened and doesn't want us to get too close to it.'

They were both silent as the implications of this sank in.

'I also,' said Jude eventually, 'witnessed the two little Pre-Raphaelite models playing that ridiculous game.'

'Oh, God. The Wheel Quest.'

'Yes. What on earth is all that about? I couldn't make head nor tail of it.'

'I agree. Tolkien's got a lot to answer for,' said Carole darkly.

'You can say that again. But the girls were so caught up in the whole thing. I'm afraid I've never seen the attraction of all that Dungeons and Dragons nonsense or any of those fantasy computer games.'

'Be careful, Jude. Never compare the Wheel Quest to a computer game when Dorcas Locke is present. She'll bite your head off. She did mine.'

'Well, I thought it was all nonsense. Honestly, the way those two girls went on, all about Gadrath Pezzekan and Biddet Rock and the Vales of Aspinglad . . . just a load of meaningless words.'

'Like today's *Times* crossword.'

'Sorry?'

'I've got almost nowhere with it. Couldn't even do the anagrams, and I can normally spot those a mile off. Today the clues were like a jumble of nonsense words.'

'Well, maybe the answers are too, Carole. Try putting in some of that stuff from the Wheel Quest: "Ordeal of Furminal" . . . "Prince Fimbador" or—'

'Fimbador?'

'Yes, that was the name of one of the characters. The hero, so far as I could gather. Why?' Jude looked curiously at her friend's puzzled face.

'It's just something . . . Prince Fimbador . . . Fimbador . . . There's something at the back of my mind that . . .' She suddenly clapped her hands together. 'Fimby! The family nickname for Nathan is Fimby!'

'And you think that's short for Fimbador?'

'Yes.'

Jude was less than convinced. 'Well, it could be I suppose, but—'

'Come on, come on. Was there anything else the girls said that could have applied to Nathan?'

'Well, only . . . Let me think . . . Oh, they did say – that is, Chloë, in the character of Prince Fimbador, said: "I defy you and your false accusations!"'

'Did she?' Carole's pale eyes were sparkling with excitement. 'And just a minute – what did you say the name of the castle was? The castle where Prince Fimbador was going to escape by the Wheel Path?'

'Biddet Rock.'

'How many Ds? Quick, write it down, write it down!'

Jude found a pen and scribbled the letters down in a space next to the crossword. (It was a measure of her neighbour's excitement that she made no comment – normally she hated anyone touching her copy of *The Times*.) Carole narrowed her eyes and focused on the letters of Biddet Rock.

'Treboddick!' she shouted. 'Treboddick! "Biddet Rock" is an anagram of "Treboddick".'

'You know,' said Jude, 'I've a feeling we could be on our way to Cornwall.'

Jude had inherited a laptop from a former lover, Lawrence Hawker, who had died of cancer a few years back at Woodside Cottage. It was connected to the internet, though she had never mentioned this fact to Carole. Partly this was because the subject had not come up in conversation and also her neighbour was of the view that, having managed this far through her life without the new technology, there was no need to embrace it in her fifties. Another reason for Jude's reticence was the fact that she used email a lot to keep in touch with a wide variety of friends and lovers from her varied past. Knowing Carole's exclusive and jealous nature, Jude did not want to complicate matters by bringing to her friend's attention the life she had outside Fethering.

But for the task they faced that Tuesday evening the internet was the perfect tool, so they adjourned next door, where Jude immediately led her neighbour upstairs to the nest of a bedroom which spread across the whole frontage of Woodside Cottage. Carole had rarely been in this inner sanctum, and she could not help thinking of the lovers who had shared that broad bed – Lawrence Hawker for certain, but also many others (most of whom, it has to be said, existed only in Carole's fevered imagination).

'I don't know what you think this is going to achieve,' she said stuffily. 'It's not as if we even have an address for this place the Lockes have in Cornwall.'

'We have a name, though. That'll be enough.'

'How do you mean?'

'Ssh. Let Google work its magic.'

Carole watched in silence, as Jude summoned up a screen and typed into a dialogue box the single word

'Treboddick'. Within seconds a list of references appeared.

'Well, that wasn't so hard,' said Jude. 'Got the right one first time.'

'Just like that?' Carole looked curiously at the screen.

'Yes, well, I don't think "Treboddick" is that common a word. Quite possibly the one in Cornwall is the only one there is.' She scanned down the listings. 'Ah, here we are.'

Leaning over her friend's shoulder, Carole read: '"Treboddick Holiday Cottages – Perfect tranquillity in exquisitely renovated miners' homes in one of the most beautiful seaside settings in the British Isles."' There was a colour photograph of a terrace of stone buildings capped with slate roofs. Nearby were picturesque ruins of chimneys and outhouses, presumably vestiges of the mine workings. The position certainly was stunningly beautiful. Beneath the illustration were contact numbers. 'So what do we do – ring up the unfortunately named Mopsa and see if we can book in?'

'Let's make email contact first. Don't want to risk the phone being answered by Rowley Locke and him recognizing our voices.'

'But he's not down in Cornwall, is he?'

'Who knows? He wasn't at the house this afternoon when I went to see Bridget. I think it'll be safer if we remain anonymous at first.'

'Well, you can't remain anonymous on email, can you? Surely, if you want to get a reply, you're going to have to give your name?'

'You're going to have to give *a* name. I've got a "Jude" account, but I've also got others in the name of "Nichol" and "Metarius".'

Carole was excited by the direction the conversation was taking. Since she'd moved into Woodside Cottage, Jude had always been vague about the precise details of her past, particularly of her marital history. Now Carole was being given the perfect opportunity to get a little concrete information on the subject. She had heard the names from Jude before, but never had their provenance defined. 'Now one of those is your married name, isn't it?' she asked.

'They're both married names,' said Jude, muddying the waters even further.

'So you mean you have a third name too – the one you were born with?'

'That's right.' But before any supplementary questions could be asked, Jude had, as ever, moved on. Scribbling down the Treboddick email address, she announced, 'I think this is a job for Mrs Metarius.' As she made her way into the relevant account, she continued, 'Just a general enquiry first. Came across your details on the net . . . hear that the cottages are in a lovely part of the country . . . wonder if you have any availability . . .'

'When?'

'As soon as possible. We could leave tomorrow, couldn't we?'

'What?' This went against Carole's every instinct. Granted, they were going in the cause of investigation, but a trip to Cornwall sounded very much like a

233

holiday to her, and you couldn't just shoot off on holiday without preparation. She remembered organizing
family trips when Stephen was little. They had to be
planned months and months ahead, with all the attention to detail of a major military offensive. First, dates
had to be agreed with David, who always needed a
lot of warning and thinking time before he got close
to making a decision about anything. And then there
had to be long discussions about the venue and the
optimum form of transport to be used, and then . . .
and then . . . You couldn't just shoot off to Cornwall
overnight.

'Do you have a problem with that? Have you got
something booked?'

Trying not to sound pathetic, Carole was forced to
admit that no, she didn't have anything booked for the
next day. Or for a good many days after that. But she
kept that information to herself.

Jude was busy at the keyboard, typing in her
enquiry. Signing off with 'J. Metarius', she sent the
email off.

'How soon will you get a reply?'

'Depends how often Mopsa – or whoever happens
to be there – checks her email. From the impression
the Lockes have given of their financial situation, it
should be quite often.'

'So what do we do now?'

'We go downstairs, Carole, and we have another
glass of wine.'

*

Their other glass of wine led to further conversation about the case. Carole had missed the opportunity to get back on to Jude's marriage – or marriages – but she did somewhat shamefacedly describe her encounter with Theo. (She couldn't see any reason to abide by the confidentiality he had demanded.) When she heard what had happened, Jude was very good and just managed to stop herself from laughing. After the update, they went upstairs to find that there had already been a response from Treboddick Cottages. Mopsa was being appropriately vigilant.

Yes, there was current availability. Maybe J. Metarius would like to email back a more specific enquiry? Or telephone?

'Telephone,' said Jude firmly. 'I'll use the mobile. A Fethering dialling code might be a bit of a give-away.' She got through to the number on the screen. 'Good evening. My name's Metarius. I've just received your email.'

'Hello, so glad you've got in touch,' lisped the voice from the other end of the line. Had Jude met Dorcas, she would have recognized that Mopsa's voice was identical.

'Can I ask who I'm speaking to?'

'Yes, of course. My name's Mopsa Locke. I'm in charge of the lettings of Treboddick Cottages.'

'Oh, good. I'm glad I've got the right person. Now the fact is that a friend and I suddenly have some free time and we were wondering how soon we could book in to one of the cottages.'

'As soon as you like. They're all empty.' Mopsa

decided that this last comment made her business sound too needy, and went on, 'That is to say, they're all *currently* empty. You know, between bookings. But we could fit you and your friend in. When would you like to come?'

'Tomorrow would be ideal.'

'And how long would you be wanting to stay?'

'Well, till after the weekend at least.'

I can't suddenly go off and leave Fethering for nearly a week, was Carole's instinctive reaction. But when she thought about it, she realized that there was nothing at all to stop her. She couldn't even pretend to be restricted by Gulliver. The dog could come with them. There's nothing he'd like better. Gambolling on Cornish cliffs would be his idea of heaven. On the other hand, she wouldn't tell Jude that yet. She'd keep the potential problem of Gulliver up her sleeve in case she needed a get-out.

'Normally our minimum booking is for a week,' said Mopsa.

'Well, that's fine,' Jude responded airily. 'We'll book it for a week.'

What, thought Carole, and where's the money coming from? Although her Home Office pension and prudent savings habits meant she could easily have booked a round-the-world cruise at that very moment, a week in a cottage in Cornwall still sounded like an unwarranted extravagance.

'I'm not sure,' Jude went on, 'exactly what time we'll arrive tomorrow evening. Is there some arrangement we should make about picking up the key . . . ?'

'It's fine. I'm here all the time. I'll be able to let you in.'

'Good.'

'And there will be a Welcome Pack of basics in the fridge when you arrive. You know, bread, milk, butter.'

'That sounds fine. Oh, one thing . . . Is it all right if we have a dog with us?' The question showed that Jude was ahead of Carole. Gulliver wasn't going to be allowed as an excuse to get out of the trip.

'Yes, that's fine. Lots of our guests bring dogs. There are some lovely walks along the cliffs.'

'Great. Now which of the cottages is free, Mopsa? Which one would you recommend?'

'As I say, they're all free . . . just briefly. I live in Number One. Two and Four are really one big double room and one small single. Since there are two of you, Three would be best. That's got two large single bedrooms.' There was a slight hesitation at the other end. 'That is, if you don't want the double . . . ?'

Well, these days you had to ask. Jude suppressed a giggle and decided she wouldn't pass on that part of the conversation to Carole. Her neighbour was clearly already having difficulty accommodating the idea of the two of them swanning off to Cornwall for a week. The suggestion that they might be mistaken for a lesbian couple was probably more than she could cope with.

'No. Number Three sounds the right one for us. Now are you going to need my address?'

'If you can just give me a credit card number, that'll be fine. You can fill in the forms when you arrive. We

237

take a non-refundable hundred pound deposit, and that'll come straight off your card. I'm sorry, but we have had unfortunate experiences in the past.'

'I'm sure you have. Can't trust anyone these days, can you? Just a sec. I'll get the card.' Jude reached into a capacious handbag and took out a battered wallet, from which she extracted one from a choice of credit cards.

Carole saw the name: 'J. Metarius.' 'Do you have another in the name of "Nichol"?' she whispered.

'Yes.'

'And in your birth name?'

'Yes.' But Jude wasn't about to elaborate. 'Hello, Mopsa. It's a MasterCard, and I'll give you the number . . .'

When the call finished, Carole was about to go into a long diatribe about how rash and extravagant they were being, but she was prevented by Jude immediately keying in another number.

'Who?'

'The Lockes. In Chichester. Ssh.'

Carole watched in frustrated silence while her friend spoke. 'Hello, who is that? Mr Locke, my name's Jude. Yes, I came to see Bridget this afternoon about her back . . . That's right. Just ringing . . . a sort of after-service call, to see if she's still feeling better. Oh, good, that's excellent news. No, don't bother her. If it's still fine, I don't need to talk to her. And if she gets any more trouble . . . well, she's got my number. Thank you so much. Goodbye.' She switched off the phone.

'Do you give "after service" calls to all your patients?' asked Carole sourly.

Jude didn't bother to argue with the choice of word. Her neighbour knew she preferred to call them 'clients' and was only being annoying. 'Not all of them, no.'

'Then what was the purpose of that?'

'The purpose of that was to find out from Bridget whether her husband was around. But he saved me the trouble by actually answering the phone himself.'

'Ah.' Carole understood. 'Because if Rowley is currently in Chichester . . . then we know he's not at Treboddick.'

'Exactly,' said Jude. 'Now, one more glass of wine, and then I guess we should do some packing.'

Chapter Twenty-four

There was one call Carole had to make when she got back to High Tor. Her affront about the idea of suddenly swanning off to Cornwall (as she still thought of it) had now been replaced by a sensation that came quite close to excitement. Since the break-up of her marriage, she hadn't really done holidays. Partly this was due to the instinctive frugality of her nature, but she also had to admit to herself that she didn't like the idea of setting off somewhere to have a good time on her own. The prospect of booking into a cruise ship and being thrown in with all kinds of people she had never seen before was her worst nightmare. And there were no friends with whom she felt relaxed enough to risk exposing her personality to them over a sustained period. Jude was probably the person to whom she was closest, but the parameters of their relationship would not, to Carole's mind at least, encompass the suggestion of their holidaying together. So the forthcoming trip to the West Country, although in the cause of their murder investigation, had suddenly become rather an attractive proposition. As soon as she heard they wouldn't be sharing a room, Carole had become quite keen on the idea.

To her surprise, Stephen answered the phone. She hadn't expected him to be in his Fulham home, and had anticipated having to call his mobile number. Carole still felt a little old-fashioned about mobiles, as if they were new and experimental technology. She was never confident that a message left on a mobile didn't immediately vanish into the ether. Jude kept saying she ought to get one, but Carole didn't feel the need. She didn't get many calls on the landline at High Tor. What was the point of having two phones that didn't ring?

'I just rang to ask about Gaby.'

'She's still in hospital.' Stephen sounded weary. 'They say there's nothing to worry about, but they still want to keep her in, probably until the baby's born. Which is something I can't exactly understand, if there's "nothing to worry about".'

'I'm sure it's just precautionary. The blood pressure.'

'That's what they say.'

'She'll be fine.'

'I hope so.' Carole had never heard so much strain in her son's voice. The responsibility of approaching fatherhood, maybe even the masculine guilt about having put his wife into her current hazardous condition, was weighing him down.

'In a month you'll have a lovely little baby and you won't remember any of the anxieties you went through.' Stephen didn't reply to this. Perhaps he didn't think it was worthy of reply. 'Look, I'm ringing because I'm going to be away for a few days.'

'Oh? How long?'

'Well, it could be as much as a week.' Though somehow she didn't think it would be. That had been another reason for her shock at Jude's extravagance. Her neighbour seemed unthinkingly to write off a week's rent for an investigation that might only last a couple of days. And, come to think of it, what were they investigating? Because of some extremely iffy clues, they were hoping to find Nathan Locke at Treboddick. But, given the fact that the police had already searched the place, how small were their chances of success?

'Where are you going, Mother?'

Oh dear, he was back to formality. 'Cornwall,' she replied.

'Good.'

'Why do you say "good"?'

'Because you could do with a break.' A break from what, was Carole's instinctive reaction. Since the Home Office had decided to dispense with her services, she had never quite lost the sensation that she was totally unproductive. The work ethic remained strong within her, and she still felt people without work were, at some level, worthless.

'Are you going on your own?'

'With Jude.'

'Excellent.'

'As I say, it may not be a full week, but . . . Anyway,

if there are any problems with Gaby, you'll let me know, won't you?'

'Of course. Though I'm not sure how. You haven't got round to buying a mobile yet, have you?'

'No,' came the shamefaced reply.

'You really should. It's so convenient.'

'Yes,' she agreed humbly. 'But I'll call you when I get down there. There's probably a phone in the cottage.'

'Or you could just give me Jude's mobile number.'

But that somehow didn't seem right. Carole wasn't sure of the etiquette of mobile ownership, but she thought it must be bad form to give out someone else's mobile number as a personal contact – even though she knew that Jude would be the last person in the world to worry about something like that.

'I'll phone you when we get down there.'

'All right,' he said in the voice a cotton mill owner might have used to a potential Luddite. 'Oh, incidentally, Mum . . .' Thank God, he was relaxed enough to stop calling her 'Mother'. But Carole's joy was short-lived, as he went on, 'I was talking to Dad today.' He never seemed to have any problem using the word 'Dad'. 'He was saying he'd love to see you.'

'Why?' came the icy response.

'Well, look, you are both about to be grandparents.'

'That doesn't mean we cease to be divorced.'

'No, but I was thinking . . . you know, for the baby, it'd be nice if he or she was born into a family where everyone got on.'

'You and Gaby get on. That'll be the most important

thing for your child. And I'm sorry, Stephen, I wish that your father and I had "got on" like a perfect fairy tale couple, but we didn't, and at least we had the honesty to admit the fact.'

'I don't know. I think Dad would quite like you to get back together . . .'

This was more than Carole could cope with. Though aware of her son's fragile state of anxiety about Gaby, she couldn't stop herself from snapping, 'Well, I can assure you I do not share his opinion.'

After the phone call, she felt guilty about what she'd said. But by the time she went to bed – soon after ten, she and Jude were planning an early start – the reaction had receded. She'd have felt even more guilty if she'd lied about her feelings for David.

There was a feeling of holiday about their journey down to Cornwall. The Wednesday had opened to a cloudless sky, late September maintaining the illusion that winter wasn't just around the corner. And even as they drove along the M27 past Portsmouth and South-ampton, they got a feeling of life opening up. Jude had always been part of a wider world, but since her retire-ment Carole had felt her horizons narrowing down to Fethering and only Fethering. She felt exhilarated to be seeing somewhere new.

It was also interesting to have a different person in the navigator's seat. During her marriage Carole had done most of the driving, David beside her. Although he had a bad sense of direction and kept losing his place on the map, he was always convinced that he was right. As a result, the tension in the car quickly became palpable. So for Carole the mere fact of having someone else in the car was a stress trigger, even when the other person was Jude.

Though she had ferried her neighbour around on many short trips, they had never spent a whole day in the car together and, as ever in a new situation, Carole was anxious about giving away too much of herself. She had always eschewed intimacy. The idea that someone might know everything about her was appalling. The certainty that nobody did know quite everything was what kept her going.

But after about an hour of driving she relaxed. Jude was a very undemanding and unjudgemental companion. What was more, she had no interest at all in their route. She assumed that Carole knew the way she wanted to go and that was fine by her. Jude seemed more laid-back than ever. She didn't say much, but there were few uneasy silences. Indeed, Carole found herself talking quite a lot, even confessing the fears that she could never voice to Stephen about the health of his wife and their unborn child. Jude was predictably reassuring. She even volunteered the use of her mobile phone to check on the family, which made Carole feel very embarrassed. She knew she would only have had to ask.

They hadn't left quite as early as they'd intended. Eight-thirty had been the proposed departure time, and at eight-fifteen Carole had the Renault, packed with Gulliver and the luggage, parked outside Woodside

Cottage. But Jude hadn't been ready. She still had a couple of emails to do. Carole fumed quietly. It was all too reminiscent of travelling with David. Her husband had been the unusual and infuriating combination of a nit-picker and a bad time-keeper.

At about ten to nine Carole, unable to stand the wait any longer, had gone into Woodside Cottage to find out what was happening. Jude said she wouldn't be more than a quarter of an hour. Why didn't Carole have a cup of coffee? But Carole didn't want a cup of coffee. Apart from anything else, if she took on too much fluid, she might have to stop the car for an early toilet break, and that would be embarrassing. All she wanted to do was to leave at the time they had agreed to leave. So she just stumped around between the car and the two front doors.

Jude would normally have found the situation amusing, but she was preoccupied. She was sending an emotionally complicated email to a client who had just had breast cancer diagnosed. But she didn't tell Carole that. Eventually, they left at nine-thirty, 'exactly an hour after we intended to go, Jude'.

Only a couple of hours into their journey, however, there was already talk of stopping for lunch – from Jude, inevitably. This too went against everything Carole had grown up with. She was used to journeys during which you pressed grimly on until you reached your destination. If nourishment was required, you took sandwiches in Tupperware boxes. And yet Jude was proposing stopping at a pub for lunch, as if they were still in Fethering and wandering down to the

Crown and Anchor, rather than in the middle of a journey. The way Jude talked, it was as if travel could be an
enjoyable experience in its own right.

Still, Carole wasn't about to sound like a wet blan-
ket, so she didn't take issue with the pub idea . . . until
Jude suggested that they should look for the pub in
Lyme Regis.

'Lyme Regis? But that's not on the way.'

'It's not directly on the way, but it's not far off. Just
a minor detour.'

'But if we start taking minor detours, goodness
knows what time we'll get to Treboddick. Not till after
dark, at this rate.'

'So? Did we say a specific time that we'd arrive?'

'Well, no. But it's a strange place. If we arrive after
dark, we may not be able to find things.'

Jude couldn't suppress a grin. 'Carole, I think we'll
find that the Treboddick Cottages do have electric light.'

'Yes. Yes, but . . . Well . . .'

By the time she actually turned the Renault off the
A35 down the steep road that led to Lyme Regis, Carole
had almost become used to the novel idea of what they
were doing. 'But will there be somewhere I can take
Gulliver for a walk?'

'Perfect place. You can walk him round the Cobb.'

'Cobb?'

'*French Lieutenant's Woman*. Meryl Streep in black
with seawash all over her. Surely you remember that?'

'Well, I did see it, yes, but I wasn't really aware that
it was in Lyme Regis.'

'It very definitely was. Anyway, Gulliver will love

the Cobb. Lots of lovely smells of bits left by the fishing boats.'

Jude was right. Though at first annoyed at being kept on his lead, the Labrador soon responded to his environment. As they walked around the great stone harbour wall, his nostrils twitched with pleasure. This was better than being cooped up on the back seat of the Renault.

When they got back to where the Cobb began, Carole announced that she'd better put Gulliver back in the car. 'Nonsense,' said Jude. 'There'll be pubs we can sit outside. He'd much prefer that, wouldn't he?'

'Yes, he would,' conceded Carole, not convinced that dogs – or indeed anyone else – should be allowed to have what they preferred.

The pub they found was perfect, with lots of wooden tables at the front, commanding a view over the wide sweep of Lyme Bay. 'I'll get the first drinks,' said Jude and went into the bar.

First drinks, thought Carole. We're meant to be going on a journey, not a pub crawl.

Jude came out with a menu. Carole had, as ever, had in mind a small lunch, but was persuaded that not to take advantage of the local seafood would be sacrilege. So they both forced themselves – not that there was much force required for Jude – to order the Three Fish Feast.

'I won't eat this evening,' said Carole, but with diminishing conviction. She had a feeling that absti-nence was never going to be a major feature of travels with Jude.

Her friend looked out over the summery blue of the bay and sighed. 'Lyme Regis always does something for me.'

'Have you spent a lot of time here?'

'Nearby.'

'On your own?'

'No, with someone.' A deeper sigh. 'It didn't work out.'

'Ah.' Carole dared to ask a personal question. 'Was that with Mr Metarius or Mr Nichol?'

'No.' And once again the moment was lost. 'Incidentally, if you're worried about Gaby, do give Stephen a call.' Jude looked at her mobile. 'The signal here's quite good.'

Carole thought what she'd said about her daughter-in-law had been sufficiently casual, but Jude had read the depth of her underlying anxiety. Resisting her first instinct to say no, she gratefully accepted the offer. Stephen was at work, doing whatever it was he did, but unusually he didn't have his phone switched to voice-mail. No doubt leaving lines of communication from the hospital open. And the news about Gaby was better. Her blood pressure was down, but they still wanted to keep her in for observation. And Carole's grandchild was moving around in a very vigorous and healthy manner.

'Thanks for that.' She handed the mobile back.

'No problem. I'd be worried sick, if it was happening to one of my children.'

Was this a hint of yet another secret from Jude's

past? Carole seized the opportunity. 'Do you mean that you've actually had children?'

Her friend roared with laughter. 'I can assure you that I would've told you by now if I had.'

'Yes.' Carole was about to say it was difficult to be sure, because Jude was always so secretive, but that didn't seem entirely accurate. So she went on, 'Have you ever regretted it?'

Jude screwed up her face wryly. 'Not really. There have been a couple of times, with certain men, when I thought having a child would have put a seal on the relationship, but the timing was never right. And in each case I'm very glad it didn't happen. A child would have made the break-up even harder. No . . .' She grinned. 'I can't say I feel *unfulfilled as a woman*.' She dropped into a New Age Californian accent for the words.

Then she laughed and, before Carole could pursue the subject, said, 'Daft, aren't we?'

'What do you mean?'

'Two middle-aged women wasting our money on a wild-goose chase to Cornwall.'

'Actually, Jude, so far we haven't talked about the money. You did the booking on your credit card – well J. Metarius's credit card.'

'You don't have to worry. It is legitimate. It's not identity theft when the identity you're stealing is one of your own.'

'I wasn't suggesting that. I just thought we ought to work out how we're going to split the costs.'

'You're providing the transport. You've paid for the petrol.' Jude shrugged. 'Don't worry. It'll sort itself out.'

Carole was not of the opinion that money matters ever sorted themselves out, but she didn't say anything. 'Anyway, why do you say we're on a wild-goose chase?'

'Well, what are we hoping to get out of our little trip? Based on the flimsiest of clues, we're setting off to try and discover the Lockes' lost Narnia. We must be out of our skulls.'

'You say the flimsiest of clues, but we have got the anagram of Biddet Rock from Treboddick.'

'Yes, but that could be a coincidence.'

'Unlikely.'

'All right, Carole, it probably is an anagram, but there's no reason why it should have anything to do with the disappearance of Nathan Locke.'

'Do you think the girls knew it was an anagram? Chloë and Sylvia – or whatever their wretched nicknames are?'

'I wouldn't think so. They've grown up with that Wheel Quest game. I doubt if they ever think about where the names come from.'

'So you don't think they'd know where Nathan is?'

'I'd doubt it.'

'And do you reckon,' asked Carole, 'that the person who made up the anagram was Rowley Locke?'

'It'd make sense, wouldn't it, given what we know of his character?'

'Mmm.'

'So we've just got the one anagram,' said Jude,

uncharacteristically negative. 'I wish we had another clue to confirm that one. No, when I come to think about it, "wild-goose chase" is a pretty accurate description.'

Carole was worried. She'd just relaxed into their journey. Her anxiety about Gaby had been relieved by the call to Stephen. And now her fragile equanimity was being threatened by Jude apparently being an unwilling partner in the enterprise. 'Oh dear,' she said. 'Do you wish we hadn't come? You say it's daft. Do you think it's a bad idea?'

'No,' replied Jude, her brown eyes sparkling. 'I think it's a *brilliant* idea.'

Chapter Twenty-five

It was evening by the time they got to their destination. Treboddick was almost the furthest point of the British mainland, on the Atlantic Coast some miles north of Land's End. Carole was not a speedy driver, and their journey had got slower as they progressed through Cornwall. She hadn't been there since childhood holidays and the change that struck her most was the development of the tourist industry. Almost every house seemed to offer Bed and Breakfast, with such extra inducements as 'En Suite Rooms' and 'Sky Television'. Every side turning was festooned with signs to hotels, pubs and other attractions. So many facilities were advertised that there seemed an air of desperation about their pleading. And the drabness of some of the towns their route skirted reinforced the suggestion that all was not well with the local economy.

Mopsa Locke had emailed directions to Jude, and they had a very clear map for the last part of their journey. After Penzance they had to turn north towards Newbridge, then take the road to Pendeen. From there on the route was on very minor roads and they certainly wouldn't have found their way without the instructions. Carole drove cautiously along the high-banked lanes ('narrow, with passing places'), the Renault seeming to fit snugly between the sides as if on a green bobsleigh run. She sounded her horn frequently. What would have happened if she had met some demented local speeding in the other direction she did not dare to conjecture.

Finally they actually saw a sign to Treboddick, a mere three-quarters of a mile away. The road climbed upwards. They had glimpsed the sea many times on their journey and now, though it was invisible, they could sense its closeness. As the Renault breasted the hill, they suddenly saw the Atlantic in all its glory. The sun had just dropped behind the horizon, but its glow still flushed the sky. And outlined the jagged remnants of old mine workings on the clifftop, glowing through a twisted tower of rusty metal, the glass-free windows of a roofless pump house and the scattered rubble of other collapsed structures.

In strong contrast to this scene of dilapidation was the terrace of cottages a mere hundred yards away. Probably decayed too after the Cornish tin mining industry failed in the late nineteenth century, at some point they had been refurbished to a very high standard. The roofs were neatly slated and each of the four cottages had a white-fenced front garden with well-tended gravel path and beds of hardy shrubs and grasses. The cottage nearest the mine – presumably the one that the Locke family kept for their own use – had an extension built to the side that probably doubled its size.

The setting on that September evening was magically serene, but the landscape also carried hints of great harshness. The few trees leaned away from the sea, cowering as if in fear of its cruel potential. In a winter storm, when the rain and spray lashed against them, the little cluster of buildings would be a bleak – even frightening – place to be.

The situation was certainly dramatic, a ready inspiration for any over-imaginative child who wanted to create an alternative universe. Carole wondered whether the old pump house had been the building which the young Rowley Locke had creatively turned into the Castle of Biddet Rock.

Adjacent to the furthest cottage there was a clearly marked hard standing area for cars, its only occupant a beat-up green Nissan so old that when bought it was called a Datsun. As Carole brought the Renault to a neat halt, a tall red-haired girl emerged from the largest cottage. If she hadn't known who to expect, Carole would still have recognized her. Mopsa and Dorcas were absolutely identical twins. Though dressed in saggy jeans and a faded blue T-shirt, the girl still carried something of her sister's Pre-Raphaelite elegance. She came towards them, beaming a professional welcome and lisped, 'Mrs Metarius?'

'Yes,' replied Jude without hesitation. 'And this is my friend Cindy Shepherd.'

'Very pleased to meet you,' said Mopsa, fortunately not seeing the thunderstruck expression on the face of the thin grey-haired woman. Carole was looking away, busy putting a lead on Gulliver. His long period of incarceration in the back of the Renault, compounded by the amazing new cocktail of smells that greeted him when he got out, had brought the dog to a peak of panting Labrador excitement.

'If you come with me,' said Mopsa, 'I'll give you the keys to Number Three and you can fill out the paperwork for me.'

She led them back to the door of Number One and said it was fine to bring Gulliver in. But given his ebullient state and the possibility of there being breakables inside, Carole instead tied the protesting dog by his lead to a ring attached to the stone frontage.

The interior of the cottage did not maintain the promise of its exterior. The hallway was untidy with hanging waterproofs and abandoned gumboots. And the sitting room into which Mopsa led them was also a mess. The table was covered with newspapers, magazines and congealed coffee cups; the grey plastic of the outdated computer on the work surface was smeared with many fingerprints. About the cottage hung the same air of neglect and lack of investment as in the family's home in Chichester.

Mopsa herself also looked grubby. Her T-shirt wasn't that clean and there was a mark of what looked like soot across the back of one of her hands. Despite all this, she made no apology for the chaos in the cottage and she seemed to share the general Locke view that people should take them as they found them – and be grateful for the privilege. The girl riffled through papers in an overfilled drawer, saying that she'd got some forms somewhere. Carole disapproved. Mopsa had had twenty-four hours to prepare for the arrival of her guests and appeared to have done nothing about it. And if the same standards of cleanliness were going to be maintained in Cottage Number Three, Carole felt the beginning of a complaint coming on.

'I'm sorry,' said Jude suddenly, 'but could I use your loo? Been sitting in the car for ages, and dying to go since before Penzance.'

'Yes, of course.' Mopsa pointed down a passage. 'There's a little bathroom down there, through the kitchen.'

'Thanks. Maybe Cindy can sign the forms.' Unseen by Mopsa, Jude grinned at her friend and was rewarded by a furious glare.

'No, I'm afraid, Mrs Metarius—'

'Please call me Jenny.'

'Right, Jenny. I'm going to need your name on the forms, because the booking's been made on your card.'

'Oh, fine. Won't be a minute.'

And Jude disappeared. Carole was also feeling pressure on her bladder after the long drive, but her willpower would force her to wait until they got into their cottage. Anyway, it hadn't been that long since they'd stopped at the service station near Exeter. What was Jude up to?

Mopsa didn't seem about to initiate conversation, so Carole observed that it was very beautiful at Treboddick and asked whether the girl had lived there long.

'Not full-time, no. But the place has been in the family since before I was born, so I've been coming here all my life. You know, for holidays and weekends.'

'Very nice too.' Carole wondered what she could ask next. She must be careful. Carole Seddon might know quite a lot about the Locke family, but Cindy Shepherd certainly didn't. And why on earth had Jude chosen such a ridiculous name? Cindy was far too young for her, apart from anything else. And it was also common.

She decided that even a complete stranger might ask Mopsa if she lived there on her own, and did.

'Yes, at the moment. Some of my family'll probably be down soon.'

'So do you work round here?'

The girl looked affronted. 'This is my job. I run the lettings of the cottages.'

'Oh yes, of course, I'm so sorry. You told Ju – J – Jenny.' It didn't seem to be much of a job. Taking the odd phone call, checking the website. When business was as slack as it appeared to be, the duties could hardly be described as onerous. And when she had got something to do, like getting the forms ready for new visitors, Mopsa didn't appear to have done it.

Carole looked round the room for some other prompt to conversation. Fixed on two pegs over the fireplace was an old-fashioned single-barrelled shotgun. Gesturing to it, she asked, 'Is that a trophy or something? An antique?'

'Antique it may be,' Mopsa replied, 'but it still works. I use it when the rabbits get too close to the gardens.'

There was another silence, which the girl appeared quite happy to have maintained until Jude returned, but Carole thought she ought to say something more. 'I suppose you're very busy here during high summer?'

Mopsa jutted forward her lower lip. 'Not as busy as we should be. People don't seem to be coming in the numbers they used to. And there's lots of competition in self-catering accommodation.'

'Yes, I'm sure there is. We saw all those signs on the way down, offering "En Suite Bathrooms" and "Sky Television".'

'We don't have that kind of stuff here,' said the girl with an edge of contempt. 'Why, do you want an "En Suite Bathroom" and "Sky Television", Cindy?'

Carole winced. She didn't know whether she was more offended by the name or the suggestion. 'No, I certainly do not,' she replied icily.

Further awkwardness was prevented by Jude's return from the bathroom. As ever, her presence lightened the atmosphere. She signed the necessary form, listened to Mopsa outlining the small amount of housekeeping information new tenants required, and gratefully took the handful of crumpled flyers and brochures for local attractions.

'I'll show you Number Three now. Is there anything else you want to know?'

'Ooh yes. Is there by any chance a pub relatively nearby, where we could get something to eat?'

Carole's instinctive reaction was: again? But we had a pub meal at lunchtime in Lyme Regis. And we haven't even looked at the Welcome Pack in the fridge.

*

259

The pub Mopsa had recommended was the Tinner's Lamp in the village of Penvant, about three miles distant. Since she reckoned they stopped serving food at eight-thirty, Carole and Jude had only the briefest of visits to their cottage before hurrying off for supper. They did just have time to register, with some relief, that the standards of housekeeping in the rental properties were higher than in the Lockes' own cottage. (Probably there was a local woman who sorted them out, while Mopsa was responsible for her Number One.) Then Gulliver, tantalized by his brief taste of aromatic freedom, was once again consigned gloomily to the back of the car.

Very little was said on their way to the Tinner's Lamp, and Jude was pretty certain she knew the reason for her neighbour's frostiness. As soon as they had delivered their order at the bar, she was proved right. The pub was another stone-built building of considerable antiquity, but again skilfully and sympathetically modernized. There weren't many customers, but those present seemed definitely to be locals – not rustic fishermen with Cornish accents, but retired solicitors of the last generation to enjoy nice index-linked pensions.

At the solid wooden bar Carole had asked for white wine and been a little surprised to be offered a choice of five, including a Chilean Chardonnay, for which they inevitably plumped. Why did she imagine that, being so far from the metropolis, the Tinner's Lamp would not rise to the sophistication of a wine list? Pure Home Counties prejudice. Jude had then ordered a pasty –

'Well, after all, we are in Cornwall' – and Carole, feeling suddenly very hungry, had surprised herself by doing the same. Then, when they were ensconced at a small table between the bar and the open fire, Carole voiced the resentment she had been bottling up.

'Why on earth did you have to call me Cindy?'

'It was something I came up with on the spur of the moment,' replied Jude in a tone of well-feigned apology. 'I should have worked out names for us before, but I didn't think. It just came to me.'

'Well, I wish something else had "just come to you". Cindy! I mean: do I look like a Cindy?'

'We none of us have any control over the names our parents gave us.'

But Carole wasn't mollified by that. 'We might, however, hope to have some control over the names our neighbours give us.'

'I was thinking on my feet, and all I knew was that it was important to come up with a name that had the same initials as your real one.'

'Why's that?'

'Oh, really, Carole. Haven't you read any Golden Age whodunnits? The bounder who's masquerading under a false identity is always given away by the fact that the name he's chosen doesn't match the initials on his monogrammed luggage.'

'But I haven't got any monogrammed luggage.'

'Ah.' Jude suppressed a giggle. 'I knew there was a fault in my logic somewhere.'

'Cindy . . .' Carole muttered again despairingly.

'Putting that on one side,' said Jude, 'I do have a

261

result to report from my carefully engineered loo-break at Mopsa's cottage.'

'What? You didn't really want to go?'

'Not that much. But I thought . . . there we were actually in the place. Maybe it was a good opportunity for a little snoop.'

'And what did your little snoop reveal?' asked Carole, slightly miffed that she hadn't thought of the idea. 'Did you see Nathan Locke sitting in his hide-away, planning further murders?'

'No, not quite that. But I did see two steaks.'

'I beg your pardon?'

'You know I had to go through the kitchen to get to the loo . . .'

'Yes.'

'Well, on the work surface there was a meal being prepared. And there was a chopping board which had two slabs of steak on it.'

'Suggesting that Mopsa wasn't just cooking for her-self?'

'Suggesting exactly that, yes. Now, all right, maybe she's got a local boyfriend . . . some rough-hewn Cornish lad who is even now enjoying his hearty steak prior to enjoying the delights of Mopsa's wispy body . . . but if she hasn't . . . well, it might suggest that Nathan is on the premises somewhere.'

'If he is, he must be pretty well hidden. Don't forget that the police searched the place.'

'Yes, but if Mopsa was warned they were coming, there'd have been plenty of time to get Nathan out for the duration. There must be lots of places to hide along the coast round here.'

'Maybe . . .' Carole didn't sound convinced.

'Oh, come on, at lunchtime you were getting at me for talking about a wild-goose chase. Now you're the one who's going all wet blanket. I think those two steaks are going to be very significant. They're the closest we've got so far to confirmation that Nathan Locke is down here.'

'Hardly confirmation. There could be a lot of other explanations. Mopsa might just have an exceptionally healthy appetite.'

'She's very thin.'

'But very tall. Must need a lot of fuel for all that length.'

Jude's conviction was not to be shifted. 'No, I'm sure she was cooking for two.'

'We shouldn't really have come here then. Should be at Treboddick, watching out to see if a boyfriend has arrived.'

'Too late now. And, looking at what's just coming out of the kitchen, I think by being here we made the right choice.'

Carole also looked up to see the chubby landlord's wife bearing two plates, each swamped by a huge Cornish pasty. 'This right, is it? Some people want them with veg, but you didn't ask for that, did you?'

'No,' said Jude. 'A proper Cornish pasty's got lots of veg inside, hasn't it?'

'You're right, my lover.' The woman set the two plates down on the table. The smell that rose from them

263

was wonderful. The pastry was solid – not the nasty flaky kind that features in so many mass-produced pasties – and there was a neat finger-pinched seam along the top of the plump oval. 'And the pasties at the Tinner's Lamp are certainly proper ones. Now do you want any sauce?'

'Again, a proper Cornish pasty shouldn't need any sauce.'

'You're right again, my lover. But we get so many emmets down here who want to smother them with ketchup and brown sauce you wouldn't believe it.'

'Have you had a busy summer?' Carole yet again envied her neighbour's ability to slip effortlessly into conversation with total strangers.

The landlord's wife pulled a glum face. 'Not that good. Weather's been fine, but the tourists've stayed away. Nope, lot of people round here have felt the pinch. All the B&Bs and what-have-you been half-empty. So where are you two staying?'

'Treboddick.'

'Ah.' There was a wealth of nuance in the mono-syllable. The landlord's wife knew exactly where they meant, and exactly who ran the place. And she had some reservations about the owners. 'Don't think they've had a great summer either. Worse than most people round here, I reckon.'

'We've only just arrived, but it looks to be a beauti-ful spot,' Carole contributed.

'Oh yes, no question about that. But everywhere in Cornwall's beautiful. You've got to provide more than beauty if you're going to get the punters in.'

'"En Suite Bathrooms" and "Sky Television"?'

'All that certainly. But you got to do a bit more. Make your guests welcome, not treat them like you're doing them a favour by letting them stay in your place.'

The implicit criticism struck a chord. Mopsa's lack of interest in them and lack of preparation for their arrival was characteristic of the Lockes. Rowley welcoming guests to his precious Treboddick would no doubt be even more condescending.

'How long're you staying down here?'

'Oh, probably just till the weekend.'

'Well, it's a lovely area for walking. And if you want to go out for a day's fishing, just let me know. My brother can organize all that for you.'

They thanked her, but thought it unlikely that they would want to go out fishing.

'He does just pleasure trips too. There's some bits of the old mine workings and that you can only get a good view of from the sea.'

'Well, thank you. We'll bear it in mind,' said Carole politely.

'Looks like there was a mine at Treboddick,' Jude suggested.

'Oh, certainly, that's Loveday. There are mines all along the coast here. Hence the name of this pub. Tin mining was very big in the mid-nineteenth century. That and smuggling, of course. There've been attempts to revive it since – the tin mining I'm talking about now – but not very successful. If you want to see how it works, though, they've got this kind of working museum just down the coast at Geevor. That's worth a look. Most of the places, though, it's just ruins. Particularly of the pump house. A lot of the mine workings was under the sea, so they had to be constantly pumping the water out.'

'It looks like the remains of one of those at Treboddick.'

'You're right. About all there is left of Wheal Loveday.'

Carole and Jude exchanged looks. Of course! Now they really had got something. They'd both known that the Cornish word for a mine was 'wheal', but neither of them had made the connection. They'd never seen it written down, but now they both felt sure that what they'd observed the young Lockes playing was 'The Wheal Quest' with an 'a'; and that its inspiration definitely came from Treboddick.

Chapter Twenty-six

Whether because of the long drive or the Tinner's Lamp's excellent pasties and Chardonnay, both Carole and Jude slept exceptionally well that night. By her standards, Carole in fact overslept, waking at seven-thirty in a panic about getting Gulliver out before he soiled the cottage floor. Neither of the women were big breakfasters – except on those days when Jude suddenly felt like an All-Day Special – and they made do with the rather meagre Welcome Pack which Mopsa had left in their fridge.

It was warm enough for them to sit in the little back garden and look out over the sea as they finished their morning drinks – herbal tea for Jude, black instant coffee for Carole. Gulliver panted restlessly at their feet, the loop of his lead round the leg of a chair. His nose was giving him lots of impressions, the most dominant being that they were in excellent walking country. If the smells around the cottage were good, how much better might they be along the coastal path.

'So we're here,' said Carole. 'What do we do now?'

Jude looked out across the Atlantic, apparently not ready to commit herself.

SIMON BRETT

'I mean, Gulliver's definitely going to need a long walk.'

'Yes, and in these wonderful surroundings it would be madness for us not to go for a long walk.'

'On the other hand . . .' Carole lowered her voice histrionically, '. . . what are we going to do about . . . *the case*?'

'Well, anything we are going to do about *the case* . . .' Jude echoed the drama of Carole's diction, '. . . is going to involve getting inside Cottage Number One. And we can either do that when Mopsa is there, which is going to set every alarm bell in the world ringing, or . . . we wait till she's gone out and see if we can get in then.'

'So that means we have to watch her front door all day until she goes out.'

'It might not be all day.'

'How do you mean?'

'Well, she might go out early.'

'Really, Jude, I don't think you're taking this seriously.'

'No. Sorry. I am really. Promise.'

'Huh.'

'Of course, there is another way of discovering when Mopsa's going out.'

'Which is?'

'We could ask her.'

'What!'

Jude was only away a few minutes. Carole was washing up their breakfast things when she returned, humming. 'Mopsa's going out to the shops at about eleven.'

'How do you know?'

'Like I said I was going to, I asked her.'

'But didn't she think it was odd?'

'No, of course she didn't. She has no suspicion of us. She just thinks we're a pair of punters who are – thank God – paying some rental money at the end of what's been a very bad season.'

'So what did you say?'

'I said: "Are you by any chance going to the shops because if you are would you mind getting a few things for us?"'

'What things?'

'Oh, I thought of some stuff. Muesli, yoghurt.'

I might have known it wouldn't have been anything useful like bacon and eggs, thought Carole.

'And Mopsa said that was fine. And I gave her some cash, and she's going to give me some change. It wasn't very difficult.'

'And did she say where she was going shopping? Because that'll give us an idea of how long she's likely to be away.'

'Yes. Like the man with seven wives, she's actually going to St Ives.'

'Must be half an hour each way.'

'At least.'

'Give her half an hour for shopping . . . we've got at least an hour and a half to investigate the cottage . . . assuming, that is, that we can get in.' Carole looked at her watch. 'So what do we do in the meantime?'

'We do exactly what two mature ladies with a dog would do if they were staying in a rented cottage in

Cornwall. We go for a walk along the cliffs. But before we do that . . .' Jude held out her mobile, '. . . you ring Stephen. Then you can relax properly into a day's sleuthing.'

Carole did as she was told. Anxiety about what was happening in a London hospital was a constant background to all her other feelings. Her son sounded less tired and stressed than he had on their previous call. Gaby was getting very bored lying on her back all day. She just wanted the bloody baby to arrive, so that she could get on with her life. Stephen thought this bolshieness was a good sign.

Carole was deeply sceptical about Gaby's idea that the baby's arrival would allow her to get on with her life, but she didn't say anything. Every woman had to come to terms in her own way with the inevitable disruptions that motherhood would bring.

Still, she felt cheered by the call, and did give Stephen Jude's mobile number to use if there were any further developments.

The clifftop walk brought Gulliver to an eighth heaven, beyond all his previous doggy imaginings.

And they timed their return to perfection. Just as Treboddick came into view round a curve of the cliff path, they saw the ancient Datsun leave the parking space and set off inland. Soon it was out of sight over the brow of the hill. Mopsa had gone on her shopping errand.

'Oh dear,' said Carole. 'I should have asked her to get something for me too.'

'What?'

'A *Times*. Somehow I never feel complete if I haven't got a crossword to do.'

'Don't worry. Maybe there'll be other clues for you to solve right here. After all, you were the one who worked out that "Biddet Rock" was an anagram of "Treboddick".'

'That's true,' said Carole. And she felt a warm glow.

When they got back to their cottage, Gulliver was locked in. He let out one feeble bark of protest, and then settled down comfortably to dream of all the exotic sights he had seen and smells he had smelled. Fethering Beach may have been seaside, but it wasn't seaside on the scale that Cornwall was.

'How're we going to get in?' whispered Carole out of the side of her mouth as they walked across to Cottage Number One. Although there was no one in sight, she felt as though an entire battery of surveillance cameras was focused on her every move.

'Well, first we'll see whether Mopsa locked up or not.'

'Oh, come on. She must have done.'

'I don't know. Everything down here seems pretty laid back. There's nobody about, and Mopsa doesn't seem to be the most diligent of guardians. It's quite possible she's left the cottage open.'

'I'd doubt it. But, anyway, Jude, I'm not sure that we should be looking at the cottage.'

'Why not?'

'Well, you said when Chloë was playing the role of Prince Fimbador, she talked about the Wheel Path . . . and we thought that was something to do with wheels that go round, but now we know that it was a "wheal" as in Cornish tin mine. So shouldn't we look at what's left of Wheal Loveday first.'

'Good idea.'

Their search didn't take long. In the bottom of the ruined pump house and round about there were a few old shafts, but all of them had been blocked up to the surface with stones and rubble. Grass had grown over some, so that they were little more than indentations in the hillside. The fact that there were no protective railings around them meant that they must be safely sealed. They offered no possible access to the tunnels below.

'That was worth trying, but I've a feeling what we're looking for has to be in the cottage.'

Carole nodded, still feeling the scrutiny of a thousand unseen cameras as they moved towards the door. Jude's fantasy that Mopsa might have left it unlocked turned out to be exactly that, a fantasy. But the girl's burglar-deterrent system proved not to be very sophisticated. They didn't have to lift many of the potted plants around the front door before they found what they were looking for.

'I wonder,' mused Jude as she lifted it up, 'whether this is the Key of Clove's Halo . . . ?'

'Looks more like a Yale to me,' said Carole sniffily. She was feeling a prickling at the back of her neck at the illegality of what she was doing, and this intensified as they went inside the cottage.

'Quick tour, looking for obvious hiding places,' said Jude. 'You do downstairs, I'll do up.'

But they both looked crestfallen when they met again at the foot of the stairs. Every available door and cupboard had been opened. Not only had they not found anyone, they hadn't even found a space big enough for anyone to hide in.

Carole looked nervously at her watch. 'Nearly forty minutes gone, from the time Mopsa drove off. What do we do now?'

'Well, if there is a secret entrance . . . the Face-Peril Gate . . . we haven't found it. Come on, you're more logical than I am. Tell me what I should be thinking.'

Carole was touched by the compliment – though she thought it no more than an accurate assessment of her character – and concentrated hard to come up with something that would justify it. 'Presumably what we're looking for is a hiding place that has something to do with the mine workings. The Wheal Path . . . that's where Prince Fimbador was going to hide . . .'

'Right.'

'So logically we should be concentrating on the side of the cottage that is nearest to the ruins of the mine buildings.'

'I like it. This is good.'

'Maybe there's some secret entrance in the new extension . . . though I think that's unlikely . . . It looks

273

like it was built in the last twenty years, and I'm not sure how many modern builders are up for making secret passages.'

'Something in the older part would also make more sense, because it might have some connection with smuggling. Most of the secret passages and hidey-holes around here would have been built for hiding contraband goods.'

'Good point. So if it's not in the extension . . .' Carole moved through as she spoke, '. . . the place which is closest to the mine workings is the kitchen . . .' Jude followed her in, '. . . and this one must be the closest wall.'

They both looked at it. There was a door to a larder, but Carole had already checked that. Otherwise, it was just a stone wall that could have done with another coat of whitewash, about a third of whose width was taken up by a deeply recessed fireplace. The floor was stone-flagged, and the individual slabs looked too heavy to hide any cunning trapdoors.

'There's something here, there's something here . . . I can feel it.'

'Oh, Jude, you're not about to tell me the place has an *aura*, are you?'

'No, I know you too well to bother saying that. Mind you, it does have an aura.'

'Huh.' Carole sat defeatedly on a kitchen chair and fiddled with a pencil and piece of paper that lay on the table. 'If only . . . if only . . .' A thought came to her. 'Just a minute . . .'

'What?'

'Well, look, I got the "Biddet Rock" anagram because the words looked funny. That's how you usually spot anagrams in crosswords. The words don't look quite right – or their juxtaposition doesn't, so you start playing with them. Yes, I think whoever invented "The Wheal Game" likes anagrams. "Biddet Rock" sounds and looks funny . . . Good God, so does "Face-Peril Gate"!'

Carole scribbled out the letters in a circle, the first two opposite and the others next, going round clockwise in turn. It was the way her father had done anagrams for his crosswords and one of the very few things that he had passed on to his daughter. She looked at the ring of letters and narrowed her eyes, hoping that the solution would leap out at her.

'No, it won't come. I can get "place" out of it.'

'Well, that's good, isn't it? We're looking for a place, aren't we?'

'Yes, but then the rest of the letters . . . it doesn't leap out at me.'

'Well, maybe there are too many letters? Maybe you shouldn't be using all of them?'

'That's not how anagrams work, Jude. You've got to use all the letters, otherwise . . . Oh, my God . . .' Carole's jaw dropped as she moved forward to the paper. 'You're right. Forget the "Gate". Just concentrate on "Face-Peril" . . . which is an anagram of . . . "fireplace"!'

They both turned to look at the shadowed space, blackened by centuries of cooking and heating. Jude moved excitedly forward, saying, 'And Mopsa had a streak of soot on her hand! There must be something here!'

Close to, there were definitely vertical lines either side to the grate, lines that could be the outline of a door. And the soot had been worn thin along the lines, as though the edge had been moved quite recently.

'It's here! It's here! This is the Face-Peril Gate. But how on earth do we open it?'

'Is there a keyhole?'

Jude, oblivious to the soot that was smearing her hands and clothes, scrabbled away at the back of the fireplace. Her fingers found a narrow slot. 'Yes, yes, there is! But what do we use to open it?'

'Presumably,' said Carole, 'we use the Key of Clove's Halo.'

'And what the hell is that?'

This one came easily. 'Forget the "Key". And the "of". Is there a "Coal Shovel" anywhere, Jude?'

There was. An ancient implement, rather too narrow to be practical for lifting much coal. The scoop was curved and thin, more like a garden tool for cutting plant-holes than a coal shovel. It was black, except where, abraded by familiar grooves, the dull original metal shone through.

'I'll see if it fits,' said Jude. 'I'm so filthy already, a little more soot's not going to make any difference.'

The end of the coal shovel slipped into its predestined slot with the ease of long practice. Tentatively, anticipating resistance, Jude turned the handle to the right. But no resistance came. The smugglers of the nineteenth century had known their craft. The key turned.

Cunningly counterweighted so as to move as lightly as a cupboard door in a designer kitchen, the great plate of soot-covered steel gave way, moving almost soundlessly on rollers, to reveal a set of stone steps leading down into the void.

Chapter Twenty-seven

Both knew they should have made some kind of plan, but they hadn't. After all, if their surmise was correct, they were about to confront a young man who might well be a murderer. Having guarded his privacy so fiercely for three weeks, how was he likely to react to the discovery of his hideaway? If he had already killed Kyra Bartos, would he be worried about the killing of two inquisitive middle-aged women, so long as it kept him safe from the attentions of the police?

The opening of the door at the back of the fireplace, though quiet, had not been entirely silent. It was a sound their quarry would know well. Mopsa had quite possibly told him that she was going out, so he would know they were intruders. The welcome he was preparing for them could be ugly.

And yet still neither of them said anything. Instinctively, Jude drew back and let Carole lead the way. They didn't even look around for a torch. From whatever was at the bottom of the steps a thin light flowed.

They had not defined in their minds what they were expecting to see, but neither had anticipated the bright airy space they stepped into. The light was natural, sunlight streaming in individual, focused beams through narrow fissures in the natural rock of the walls. These openings, created by the erosion of the exterior cliff face, were too high up the walls to offer any hope of escape. But the chamber their light illuminated was not the primitive cave Carole and Jude's imaginations had suggested. It appeared to be a section of a circular vertical mineshaft, some twenty feet across, which would have reached the surface right next door to the Lockes' cottage. But, many years before, the space had been separated off by a wooden floor and ceiling to form the hidden room. The carpentry had not been professional, there was a rough-hewn quality to everything. But it looked sturdy and secure. The smugglers of Treboddick had known what they were doing when they constructed the Wheal Chamber.

These were the peripheral impressions of a nanosecond, because what arrested the attention of both women was the figure sitting at a table facing the sea. They had seen the family photographs and had no doubt that it was Nathan Locke.

The shock they both felt, though, arose from their assumption that he had hidden away of his own accord. They hadn't expected the chain from an iron ring on the wall which was attached to the boy's ankle.

Chapter Twenty-eight

Whoever Nathan Locke had expected to come down the stairs into his lair, it wasn't a pair of middle-aged women. He looked at them in frank amazement. But rather than reacting with violence, he remained seated and asked politely, 'I'm sorry, but who are you . . . ?'

No time for aliases now. 'My name's Carole Seddon. This is my friend Jude.'

The blankness on the boy's face told that he had never heard of either of them.

'And what are you doing here? Are you from the police?' His natural good manners couldn't completely exclude a note of disbelief from the question. He looked scruffy, a wispy three-week growth of beard around his chin, but not as though he had been mal-treated.

'No, we're nothing to do with the police. You don't need to be frightened. You're quite safe with us.'

He let out a bitter laugh. 'I think I might be safer with the police than I am here.' He gestured to the chain on his ankle. It gave them a moment to take in the space in which he was incarcerated. There were loaded bookshelves, a cassette player, even an ancient-looking television. Jutting out from one wall was a shed-like structure with two doors, possibly leading to a kitchen and bathroom. The area had more qualities of a furnished flat than a prison.

Jude moved forward alongside Carole. 'Listen, Nathan, we know who you are and we know why you're here.'

'Oh, do you? I sometimes wish I did.'

'It's in connection with the death of Kyra Bartos.'

The name hit him like a slap. His lip trembled and tears glinted in his eyes. At that moment he looked less than his sixteen years. 'Kyra? What do you know about Kyra?'

'That she's dead.'

'And that I killed her? Do you know that? Just like everyone else who seems to be so sure of it?'

'We don't know that. But we'd like to talk to you about it.'

'Would you? Well, there's a novelty.' The bitterness was back in his voice. He still wasn't being overtly rude to them, but there was in his voice a deep weary negativity, an acceptance that he had entered a world in which normal logic did not operate.

'A novelty, why? Because nobody else wants to talk to you?'

'Nobody else wants to talk except to give me orders. No one wants to listen to what I have to say.'

'We'd very much like to hear what you have to say.'

He was tempted by the sincerity in Jude's voice, but his scepticism remained. 'Oh yes?'

Carole decided it was her turn. Jude had been

trying the good cop approach, without marked success. Maybe something harder might be more effective.

'Listen, Nathan, you know you're in a lot of trouble. Circumstances dictate that you're the major suspect for Kyra Bartos's murder. And the fact that you've run away only exacerbates the problem.'

'Excuse me.' The boy looked affronted. 'What's all this "running away" business?' He indicated the chain round his ankle. 'Does it really look as though I'm stuck down here voluntarily?'

'Are you saying you were kidnapped?'

'Not exactly. No, I came down to Cornwall of my own accord. In all the confusion of what happened – and the kind of mental state I was in – yes, lying low for a few days did seem a good idea. In retrospect I'm not so sure it was, but I wasn't thinking very straight after I heard about . . . what happened at the salon.'

'Who did you hear about it from?' asked Carole.

'My uncle.'

'Rowley Locke.'

He looked at them curiously. 'Are you sure you're not police?'

Jude promised that they weren't.

'Because you do seem to know rather a lot about me.'

'Everyone in the West Sussex area knows a lot about you. There's been blanket coverage in the papers and on television.'

'Yes, I suppose there would be.' He sighed and gestured to the ancient set. 'That doesn't work. Not that I'd get Sussex local news down here anyway.'

'No.'

Carole picked up his narrative. 'So you were saying
. . . you came down here of your own free will . . . ?'

'Yes. More or less. Uncle Rowley can be very per-
suasive.' Both women shared the thought that they
were sure he could be. 'But when they got me here . . .
suddenly he says I've got to be chained up.'

'Does it hurt?' asked Jude.

'Not really. It's quite slack. Only hurts if I try to
get out of it, and I gave up on that idea after the first
couple of hours. And the chain's long enough so's I can
get to the bathroom.' He grinned wryly. 'No, as prisons
go, I suppose this is a very humane one.'

'But don't you get bored out of your skull?'

'Well . . .' He gestured to the bookshelves. 'I've got
plenty to read. And I keep comforting myself with the
thought that it's not for ever.'

'For how long, though?' asked Carole. 'Did your
uncle give any indication of that?'

Nathan shrugged. 'Not precisely. Presumably he's
just keeping me here until the police find out who
actually did kill . . .' Again emotion threatened. Something in his throat rendered him unable to speak his
late girlfriend's name.

'Hmm.' Neither Carole nor Jude was persuaded by
the explanation.

'Uncle Rowley did say I was being kept here for my
own good. He said if the cops got their hands on me, I'd
never escape. They'd stitch me up good and proper.'
That sounded in character from what Carole had heard
of Rowley Locke's estimation of the British police force.

'I have to listen to what Uncle Rowley says,' Nathan continued lamely. 'He does know what he's talking about.'

This was a tenet of Locke received wisdom to which neither Carole nor Jude subscribed. They both had strong suspicions about Rowley Locke's agenda.

'Well,' Carole announced practically, 'the first thing we should do is get you free from that chain.'

The suggestion brought a light of paranoia into the boy's eye. 'Oh, you'd better not do that. There's a girl – my cousin Mopsa who—'

'We know all about Mopsa. She's gone off shopping.' Carole consulted her watch. 'She won't be back for at least another twenty minutes.'

'So,' asked Jude, 'should we find some tools upstairs to cut through the chain?'

'You don't have to bother with that.' He gestured towards the foot of the stairs. 'There's a key to the padlock hanging over there. Just about six feet beyond my reach. Don't imagine I haven't tried to grab it.'

'Right,' said Carole. 'Then the first thing we do is get that key.'

'I don't think so.'

They all looked up at the sound of the lisping voice. Mopsa stood halfway down the stairs, back-lit from the kitchen above. In her hands was the shotgun that had been hanging on the sitting-room wall.

Chapter Twenty-nine

Carole was unfazed. 'Put that down.'

'No, you back off. Get away from that key, or I'll shoot.'

'Don't be ridiculous.'

'Move back,' hissed Nathan's anguished voice. 'She means it. She will shoot.'

Something in the girl's eye told Carole that her cousin was speaking the truth. She retraced her steps until she and Jude stood together, an inadequate defence in front of the chained boy. The chamber suddenly felt very small.

Mopsa moved on down the stairs. 'I should have been on my guard. A sudden booking out of the blue this time of year. I should have known you were up to something.'

'All we were up to,' said Jude reasonably, 'was trying to find Nathan. The police are looking for him. He can't be hidden away here for ever.'

'Oh no? Prince Fimbador spent seven years night and day in the Wheal Chamber.' There was a gleam of fanaticism in the girl's eye as she said the words.

'Yes, maybe. But that's not real. That's just a story.'

'A story?' Mopsa was deeply offended. 'The Chronicles of Biddet Rock tell how Prince Fimbador resisted the evil hordes of Gadrath Pezzekan. The tale of the ultimate battle of Good against Evil is not just a story.'

Carole and Jude caught each other's eye, as into each mind sank the sickening truth. Mopsa was not sane. This was why she had not followed the course of her sister Dorcas to university. Her unhinged mind had swallowed the nonsense of the Wheal Game whole. For her the incarceration of Nathan as Prince Fimbador was completely logical. She was just fulfilling her role in the legend. And if the fulfilment of that role involved bloodshed, she would not shirk her duty.

She waved the shotgun dangerously in their direction. 'You have broken through the Face-Peril Gate. Already you have invoked the Great Curse of the Leomon! The fate of all who sully the purity of Karmenka is death.'

'Mopsa,' said Carole firmly, 'you are talking absolute balderdash.'

'Contempt has always been the fate of the Prophetesses of Biddet Rock.' 'Prophetesses' was really quite a mouthful for someone with a lisp. The situation would have been laughable but for the fact that the girl so clearly believed all the nonsense she was spouting.

'We rise above it,' she persisted. 'We know the Right Course and we still pursue it till the last drop of the blood of the Leomon is shed.'

'Yes, well, fine. Let the blood of Leomon be shed, but don't let's shed anyone else's. How about that?'

But Jude's jokey approach was not the right one either. The girl pointed the shotgun very definitely in the women's direction and gestured them to move away from Nathan's table, till their backs were to the sea-facing wall. Not quite believing the situation they were in, but all too aware of its gravity, they did as they were instructed.

'When you sacrifice your pathetic lives, acolytes of Black Fangdar,' said Mopsa, 'there must be no risk of harm to Prince Fimbador.'

Under normal circumstances Carole and Jude would have giggled, but there was nothing funny about the way Mopsa was sighting them down the barrel of the shotgun. Through both their minds went the thought that she could only get one of them with her first shot. Then, since it was a single-barrelled gun, she would have to reload. But neither felt very cheered by the increased odds on survival. And neither was about to volunteer to go first.

Mopsa cocked the rifle. The way she did it suggested a discouraging familiarity with the weapon. Her talk of shooting rabbits had not been mere bravado.

She shifted her stance, so that the sight was trained on Carole's chest.

'Mopsa, this is daft,' said Jude, the calmness in her voice masking the desperation in her mind. 'You can't just shoot us in cold blood. You don't even know who we are.'

'I know all I need to know,' the girl responded

implacably. 'You are intruders who have broken through the Peril-Face Gate into the Wheal Chamber. You are probably Grail-seekers, sent from Black Fangdar. You are certainly a threat to Prince Fimbador, which means that you must be in the pay of Gadrath Pezzekan.'

'We are not a threat to Prince Fimbador,' said Jude.

'No, we certainly aren't,' Carole agreed.

'We're here to help Prince Fimbador . . .' God, how easy it was to slip into this nonsense talk. 'Nathan. We are here to help Nathan.'

'And how do you propose to help him, you who betrayed Prince Fimbador at the Battle of Edras Helford?'

'For a start we'll get him away from here.'

'And then?'

Neither woman answered. Neither could, on the spur of the moment, come up with a reply that they could be sure would not enrage the girl further.

'How do I know that you will not hand him over to the police?'

Still they couldn't reply. Handing him over to the police was the solution uppermost in both their minds. The shotgun was still pointed firmly at Carole's chest.

It was Nathan's voice that broke the impasse. 'It would be good if I could talk to the police, Flops.' Oh, God, another of the Locke family nicknames. 'Clear up a few details about what actually happened that night . . . You know, the night when . . . when . . .'

Again he was unable to speak his dead girlfriend's name.

'No!' Mopsa's voice rang against the stone walls of the Wheal Chamber. 'My orders are to guard you. My orders are to keep you safe from the police. And to kill anyone who challenges your safety.'

'Your father didn't really mean that, Flops. He was just going over the top, as usual. You weren't meant to take it literally.'

'The Prophetesses of Biddet Rock pride themselves on obeying all of their orders *to the letter*.'

'Well, not that one about killing people. Look, Uncle Rowley wrote me a note . . .'

His scrabbling in the table drawer distracted her for a moment, long enough for Carole to step forward with her hands locked and knock the rifle barrel upwards. As it jerked in her hands, Mopsa pulled the trigger. In the enclosed space the report was shockingly loud. It prompted an enraged cacophony of complaint from seabirds on the cliffs outside.

Nathan's chain was long enough for him to leap across and snatch the gun from his cousin's hands. Unarmed, Mopsa lost all resistance and sank to her knees, overtaken by hysterical weeping. Carole crossed to the bottom of the stairs and finished what she'd been about to do when the girl disturbed them. She removed the key from the hook where it had tantalized Nathan for nearly three weeks, crossed to him and undid the padlock on his ankle.

'Thank God for that,' he said, flexing the constricted muscles of his foot.

Carole, aware of the danger in which she had been, and slightly shocked by her action in hitting away the shotgun, felt suddenly rather feeble. 'What do we do now?' she asked.

'We get the hell out of this place as soon as possible,' said Jude.

'But . . .' Even in these circumstances Carole could not repress the instinctive words 'we booked for a week.'

Her neighbour didn't bother to reply. Instead, she looked at the boy and asked, 'Are you going to come with us, Nathan?'

He looked at Jude for a long moment, and then slowly nodded. 'Yes. I've got to find out the truth . . . you know, about what happened to . . . to . . .' He still couldn't do it. A tear glinted in his eye.

'Right, let's assemble our things, and get out of here as soon as possible.'

As Jude moved towards the steps, Carole looked down at Mopsa, still limp as a rag doll on the wooden floor and crying in long shuddering sighs. 'What do we do about her?'

'Lock her in,' suggested Nathan. 'Give her a taste of the medicine she's been dishing out to me.'

'I don't think we need do that,' said Jude. 'We don't want to sink to her father's level.'

'If we take away the gun, are there any other weapons in the cottage that she could use?' asked Carole.

He shook his head. 'I'm pretty sure there aren't.'

'I don't think violence from Mopsa is going to be a

problem.' Jude looked down at the weeping girl. 'She's not a threat to us any more.'

Responding to the compassion in Jude's voice, Nathan knelt down beside his cousin. 'It's all right, Flops . . . Fimby's not cross with you. Fimby forgives you. And everyone else will forgive you.'

'No, they won't,' the girl wailed. 'I have failed in my appointed task. I have not defended Prince Fimbador of the Blood of Merkerin.'

'You will be forgiven.' Nathan Locke stood to his full height and held a hand over the girl in a majestic gesture. 'You have the word of the Grail-Holder Prince Fimbador that you will be forgiven!'

Mopsa apparently drew comfort from this mumbo-jumbo. The weeping eased. Nathan looked across embarrassedly to Carole and Jude and shrugged a shrug which seemed to say, 'Don't knock it. It worked.'

'Right. Let's get ready,' said Carole, very much the teacher in charge of a school trip. 'It'll only take us a couple of minutes to get our bags. Have you got much stuff, Nathan?'

'Very little. I was rather whisked away from Fethering the morning after—'

Jude interceded before the memory of Kyra could upset him again. 'Don't worry. You can tell us everything in the car.'

They left Mopsa in the Wheal Chamber, but did not close the Face-Peril Gate. For safety they put the shotgun in the Renault's boot, along with their luggage and Nathan's rather pathetic plastic carrier bag.

As Carole drove off, with the boy and Gulliver

sharing the back seat, they all looked back. Mopsa was standing outside Cottage Number One, talking into a phone. Though none of them voiced it, they would all have put money on the fact that the person the other end of the line was Rowley Locke.

Chapter Thirty

Maybe it was delayed shock that kept them quiet for the first half-hour of their journey back. The only one making any noise was Gulliver, who started off by panting excitedly. For him getting in the car gave the signal that he was about to be taken for a walk. But as the journey continued with no signs of stopping, he got less excited. Honestly, humans were so unreliable. The memory of the excessively long journey of the day before came back to him and he subsided into an aggrieved lump on the back seat, not even responding to friendly stroking from Nathan.

They had passed Penzance before the silence was broken. And, surprisingly, it was the boy who broke it. 'I'm sorry about Flops – Mopsa. She's . . . well, she's always had problems.'

'Mental problems?'

'Yes. She's got a twin sister called Dorcas.'

'I've met her,' said Carole.

'Well, Mopsa's . . . Incidentally, I don't understand how you know everything about my family.'

'Don't worry about that for the moment,' said Jude. 'Tell us about Mopsa.'

'Well, as I say, she's a twin. Dorcas has always been the bright one . . . school, university, she's done well all the way. And Mopsa could never quite hack it. In another family I think doctors or psychologists would have been consulted, but the Lockes always think they can sort everything out for themselves, so they've kind of protected her from the outside world.'

'As they were trying to protect you from the outside world?'

He let out a mirthless laugh. 'I suppose you could say that. Anyway, there's been a long history of Mopsa sort of dropping out of things, having breakdowns I reckon, but she's always been at her calmest and most sane down at Treboddick.'

'That was her most sane?' Carole couldn't help asking.

'No, obviously she lost it when she found you'd broken into the Wheal Chamber. She's . . . she's potentially quite dangerous.'

'That was the impression I got.'

'But do she and Dorcas get on?' asked Jude.

'Yes, very well. Distressingly well. Dorcas is a strong character. I think in a way with Mopsa – and indeed with the two younger sisters – Dorcas has made them what Shakespeare would have called her "creatures". She kind of controls them.'

'So how long has Mopsa been down at Treboddick?'

'She's spent an increasing amount of time down there, you know, since she dropped out of school, or since she dropped out of the last of a series of schools.

And then when Uncle Rowley remarried . . . well, Mopsa and Bridget were never going to see eye to eye.'

Carole agreed. 'No, Bridget seems quite a sensible woman.'

'Yes, she is.' He spoke with warmth.

'I gather you and she get on well.'

'Very well.'

'You both approach the whole Locke family bonding process with a degree of scepticism.'

'You could say that. As soon as I got into my teens I got rather bored with all that Wheal Quest business . . . little realizing that I would end up playing it for real during the last three weeks.'

'There's something that struck me about Bridget,' said Carole. 'I've met your father and mother, and Rowley, and Dorcas, and the younger girls and, of all of them, Bridget is the only one who seemed worried about what had happened to you, where you'd gone to.'

'Well, she would be. All of the rest of them knew exactly where I was.'

'But Rowley didn't tell his wife?'

'Of course not. As you said, Bridget is a sensible woman. The minute she knew that I was locked up at Treboddick – particularly being guarded by Mopsa – she would have contacted the police.'

There was a silence. Then Carole said, 'I think we'll have to get in touch with the police, Nathan.'

He made no objection. Though he didn't welcome what lay ahead, he recognized its inevitability.

'If only to clear your name.'

'Yes.'

Jude joined in. 'Did Rowley – your uncle – did he say precisely why he was locking you up at Treboddick?'

'He said he'd got my best interests at heart. He was afraid of what might happen to me under police interrogation.'

'Yes, he doesn't have a very high opinion of what he insists on calling "our fine boys in blue",' Carole recalled. 'So he thought they'd force a confession out of you?'

'Something along those lines, yes. Uncle Rowley said the police always liked to get a conviction, and weren't too bothered whether or not it was the right one.'

'That sounds like one of his lines. And do you think he thought you were guilty?'

'What?' Nathan Locke's surprise was so unfeigned that clearly the idea had never occurred to him.

'Well, if your uncle did think you'd strangled Kyra, then there'd be an even stronger reason for him to lock you away at Treboddick. To stop you from being arrested . . . until the family had worked out a more permanent way of keeping you from justice.'

'What kind of way?'

'I don't know.' Carole shrugged. 'Sending you abroad? Changing your identity? Maybe even plastic surgery . . . ?'

'Oh, come on, they wouldn't do that.'

After what they'd witnessed at Treboddick, Carole and Jude's estimation of what the Lockes might do had expanded considerably.

'I think Uncle Rowley really was doing the best for me.' But Nathan's insistence was wavering. 'At least what he thought was the best for me.'

'Hmm.'

'Presumably . . .' Jude posed the question very gently '. . . you didn't kill Kyra?'

'No, of course I didn't! I loved her! You don't kill someone you love.'

Many authorities, including Oscar Wilde, would have questioned that assertion, but Jude didn't take issue as Nathan continued, 'I can't imagine what happened. I mean – who would do that to her? She was a sweet girl . . . wouldn't hurt anyone. I can't even think of anyone she didn't get on with . . . well, except her father . . .'

And possibly Martin Rutherford, thought Carole as Jude asked, 'Yes, we've heard about some difficulties between Kyra and her father. What was the problem there?'

'I think basically he's just old-fashioned.'

'Did you meet him?'

'Just the once. K – Kyra . . .' He did actually manage to get the word out that time, '. . . she took me home to meet him, thought it'd be all right.' He sighed wearily. 'It wasn't. He virtually showed me the door.'

'What was it about you that he disapproved of?'

'In a way, I don't think it was anything about me. Kyra said I shouldn't take it personally and I tried not to. It was just that I was interested in his daughter. He would have been equally down on any other person of the male gender who was interested in his daughter. He thought she was too young to have a boyfriend.'

'But, she was . . . what?'

'Seventeen.' He gulped down the emotion that the thought prompted. 'Yes, well old enough to . . . do anything she wanted. But that wasn't the way old man Bartos saw things. He got furious when she had her ears pierced and . . . It was . . . I don't know . . . something to do with the way he was brought up . . . in Czechoslovakia.'

I really would like to talk to 'old man Bartos', thought Jude. I've somehow got a feeling that he holds the key to this whole case. I wonder if Wally Grenston could set up a meeting . . . ?

'Nathan,' said Carole, her voice only just the right side of sternness, 'you did go to Connie's Clip Joint that evening with Kyra, didn't you?'

There was no attempt at evasion. 'Yes, I did. Perhaps it was a silly thing to do, but . . . well, it was very difficult for us to be alone together. Her father's attitude ruled out the possibility of meeting at her place and then my parents . . .'

'They wouldn't have objected to you taking a girl back to the house. They told me as much.'

'Yes, but it would have been hideously unrelaxing – particularly for Kyra. My parents can sometimes be so "right-on" that it hurts.'

'Constantly saying how broad-minded they are . . . how delighted that you feel sufficiently relaxed to bring your girlfriends into the house . . . ?'

He grinned without amusement. 'You've clearly met them, Carole.'

'Yes. Yes, I have.'

'So what happened that evening?' Jude prompted gently.

'Well, as I say, Kyra and I found it very difficult to be alone together . . . you know, unless we were in one of the shelters on the sea front at Fethering . . . or on the golf course . . . neither of which were particularly romantic . . . or relaxing . . . And then that day she rang me on the mobile and said that Connie had given her the keys to the salon because she wanted her to open up the next morning and . . . it would be our opportunity to . . . you know, to do what we hadn't had a chance to do before . . .'

'You mean make love to each other?'

He nodded agreement to Jude's question. His speech slowed as he clawed back the painful recollection. 'Yes, it was going to be our big night. I felt bad about sort of being in Connie's salon without her knowing, but I did want to . . . you know . . . And Kyra said if I joined her there at about ten, there'd be nobody about, and it'd all be fine. So I bought some beer and vodka and . . . you know, some cigarettes . . . because I wanted us to be relaxed about it all and . . . I was dead nervous. I think Kyra was too.'

'So what happened when you got there?'

'Well . . . I don't know whether I should tell you this . . .'

'You're going to have to tell the police,' said Carole, 'so you might as well have a dry run.'

SIMON BRETT

Nathan saw the logic of that. 'All right. Well, it's embarrassing, but . . .' He took a deep breath. 'Basically, it didn't work. Nothing worked.'

Jude's voice was mesmerizingly soft as she asked, 'You mean the sex?'

He nodded, now looking very young and confused. 'Maybe I was too nervous. There'd been such a long build-up and . . . I don't know . . . I wanted it to be a really romantic moment.'

Hence the dozen red roses, thought Carole.

'But when I actually got there . . . you know, in the back room of the salon . . . I just lost it. In a strange place, afraid we'd be interrupted at any moment . . . I mean, at one stage it seemed to be going all right, but then I thought I heard someone coming in . . .'

'You mean coming into the salon?'

'Well, I thought I heard the back gate bang, and then like footsteps . . .'

'Are you sure?'

'No, I'm not sure. As I say, I was terribly nervous . . . and also I'd got through most of the vodka . . . and I was worried about what Kyra would think of me. Anyway, it didn't work . . . you know, the sex,' he concluded lamely.

There was a silence before Jude asked if he and Kyra had quarrelled.

'No, not exactly. It was . . . just awkward. I felt kind of humiliated . . . She said it didn't matter, but . . . I just had to get away. I feel dreadful about it now . . . after what happened, but I left her on her own.'

'What time was that?'

'I don't know exactly. Half-past twelve . . . one o'clock . . . ?'

'You didn't see anyone outside?'

'What?'

'You said you'd heard the gate bang.'

'That was a lot earlier. And I could have imagined it. I don't know.' He let out a little gasp. 'I suppose, if there really was someone there, it could have been the murderer.'

Jude agreed that this was quite possible, then Carole asked, 'Why didn't Kyra go home?'

'Because she'd set up this big alibi with her dad. You know, she was supposed to be with some school friend for the night, so she couldn't suddenly say she wasn't. Also she'd been drinking, and if her old man had smelt that on her breath . . .' He didn't need to complete the sentence.

'And what about you?' asked Carole. 'Did you go straight home?'

Nathan shook his head, still traumatized by the images he had brought back to life. 'No. I don't know what I did really. I was pretty wasted, for a start. I'd drunk most of the bottle of vodka. And I felt terrible about, you know, what'd happened.' He let out a bark of pained laughter. 'Or rather what hadn't happened.'

'So where did you go?'

'I wandered along the beach. I don't know how long I did that. Just walking back and forth, back and forth, thinking terrible thoughts. You know, I loved Kyra . . .' there was a naked appeal in his voice, '. . . but I couldn't, you know . . . When it mattered, I couldn't . . .'

'So when did you go home?'

'Not till the morning. I don't remember exactly what happened, but at some point I fell asleep in the dunes . . . you know, about as far along Fethering Beach as you can go. I felt dreadful, but I'd slept through till after half-past ten. So I started back home.'

'I'm surprised no one saw you at that time of day,' Carole observed.

'I kept off the roads. I didn't want to be seen. So I was on the beach and then up by the side of the Fether. There's a way into our back garden from the tow-path. Anyway, by the time I got back to Marine Villas, Uncle Rowley was already there. Mummy had some-how heard about Kyra's body being found . . .' Another triumph for the Fethering bush telegraph, thought Carole. 'And Mummy had called Uncle Rowley and—'

'What did your father do?'

'He did what he always did – waited for Uncle Rowley to come and make the decisions.' He said the words with resignation rather than contempt.

'Anyway, as soon as I saw him, Uncle Rowley said I was bound to be the police's prime suspect because I'd been going out with Kyra and he soon got me to tell him that I had actually been to the salon to see her . . .'

'Did he ask you what had happened when you were there?'

'No, he'd already made his plans that I should lie low at Treboddick. As soon as I'd got my stuff together, we drove off.'

Carole and Jude exchanged looks. As alibis went, Nathan Locke's was not of the greatest. Poor boy, he wasn't going to have an easy time when they handed him over to the police. Neither of them believed that he had strangled Kyra Bartos, but the circumstantial evidence was against him. It had become even more imperative that they should find out who had really committed the murder.

Carole and Jude knew it would be late when they got back to West Sussex, but no one suggested breaking the journey, except for a brief stop and a taste-free Little Chef meal. Though none of the Lockes had any power to identify or stop the Renault on its way, the two women still wanted to get home as soon as possible. In both of their minds suspicions of Rowley were developing apace, though they knew they should not share such ideas with his nephew.

They outlined what they proposed to do, and Nathan was docile in his agreement to their plan. They would take him to the police station in Littlehampton, from which the investigation into Kyra Bartos's murder was being co-ordinated.

Jude said he could use her mobile if he wanted to call his parents to tell them he was all right, but he declined the offer. Arnold and Eithne Locke had presumably heard by now from Mopsa about their son's escape from the Wheal Chamber at Treboddick, and if he didn't want to talk to them, then that was his decision. The only person who'd seemed genuinely worried about the boy was Bridget Locke, and Jude decided she'd give the woman a call first thing in the morning. For the rest of his family, the longer they stewed in their own juice the better.

Before he got out of the car in Littlehampton, they wished Nathan luck. He looked very young as they deposited him outside the police station. They watched him go inside and then drove on the few miles to Fethering. No need for them to get involved at this point. There was plenty for the detectives to ask Nathan Locke about without Carole or Jude's names being mentioned. They thought he might need the luck they had wished him.

Chapter Thirty-one

When she got back to High Tor, Carole found a message on her answering machine. It was, predictably enough, from Rowley Locke.

Although by now the small hours of the morning, she immediately phoned Jude and they ended up opening a bottle of wine in the sitting room of Woodside Cottage.

'So what did Rowley say?' asked Jude as she poured Chardonnay into two glasses. 'Is he furious?'

'I'm pretty sure he is, but the message is a bit tentative. You see, he's only got Mopsa's description to go by, so he's not absolutely certain that we were Jenny and . . .' The name wouldn't come.

'Cindy.'

'Yes,' said Carole with distaste. 'So he's not accusing me of anything. All he's saying is that he's had some news on the whereabouts of Nathan, and he'd like to tell me about it.'

'Did he sound relieved?'

'Yes, he did quite a good impression of the concerned uncle. He said that Arnold and Eithne were ecstatic to have news of the boy.'

'So he wants you to ring him?'

'Yes, "ring and fix to meet up" was how he put it.'

Jude pursed her full lips. 'Could be risky. I mean, I'm sure Rowley Locke has worked out that we were the two women who went to Treboddick . . . and if he is actually the murderer . . .'

'But do you think he is?'

'I'm not sure. It would explain why he wanted Nathan kept out of the way. So that the boy remained the number one suspect.'

'A more charitable view would be that he was just trying to protect his nephew . . . if he wasn't the murderer himself, but he thought that Nathan was.'

Jude had the nerve to say, 'Unlike you to take the charitable view,' and Carole had the grace to smile. 'I've got to see Rowley,' she said. 'Got to find out what on earth he's up to.'

'Mmm.' Jude took a thoughtful sip from her wine. 'Incidentally, I did believe everything Nathan told us. Did you?'

'Oh yes. A boy of that age isn't going to make up that business about the sex . . .' Carole looked embarrassed, '. . . you know, not working.'

'No. Poor kid. Poor kid on many counts.'

'So . . . I'll ring Rowley in the morning.'

'I think if you do fix to meet him . . .'

'Yes?'

'. . . you should insist that I come too.'

'Safety in numbers?'

'That's it.' Jude suddenly raised her glass. 'To us. I think we've had a really good day today.'

'Found Nathan and freed him. Yes, not bad.'

'Now he's back in circulation, it's going to open the whole case up.'

'For the police certainly.'

'And for us too, Carole. We'll soon have a solution. I can feel the tumblers in the lock slotting into position.'

'Oh yes?'

'Yes. Definitely.'

This optimistic feeling was reinforced for Jude the next morning when she had a call from Wally Grenston. After greetings and a few lavish compliments (Mim was clearly not in the room), he said, 'Told you old Joe Bartos was thinking of going to the Czech Club on Wednesday . . . ?'

'Yes.'

'Well, I saw him there.'

'Did you tell him I wanted to talk to him?'

'I did, yes.'

'Did he agree?'

'No, he didn't.' Jude was suitably cast down, but Wally, playing his narration at his own pace, continued, 'I've just had a call from him this morning, though . . .'

'And?'

'And maybe he's changed his mind.'

'Oh?'

'Thing is, he's heard from the police that the boy – you know, Krystina's boyfriend, the one who'd disappeared – well, he's turned up.' Jude restricted herself to a non-committal response, waiting to hear what came next. 'The police won't tell Joe anything and he was thinking, you're interested in the case . . . maybe you know something. Maybe he should talk to you . . . ?'

That was her cue. 'Maybe he should. I actually spent most of yesterday with Nathan Locke.'

'Did you? How's that?'

'I'll tell you when you introduce me to Joe Bartos.'

The old man chuckled. 'Playing hard to get, are you?'

'No, not at all. Always available for you, Wally . . . assuming, that is, that Mim's not there.'

He chuckled more. She'd hit the right tone. They fixed that the meeting would take place at teatime. 'Four o'clock. On the dot. That's when Mim and I always have tea. Because I'm so English,' he added with a wheezy laugh. 'Oh, and one thing, Jude . . .'

'Yes?'

'Mim'll be there, so try not to make it too obvious that you fancy the socks off me.'

'I'll do my best.'

'But that's exactly the time I've arranged to meet Rowley Locke,' Carole complained.

'Well, I can't really change what Wally's set up. I get the impression Joe Bartos's goodwill towards me may be short-lived. I don't want to mess him around. Where have you fixed to meet Rowley? At Marine Villas?'

'No, I thought somewhere public was better. Safer.'

'Sure.'

'So it's the Seaview Café at four.'

'Oh, you should be all right there. There'll be lots of people around.'

'And I'm going to take Gulliver.'

'As a guard dog?'

'You must be joking. Gulliver hasn't got a suspicious bone in his body. He'd lick the hand of Jack the Ripper. But if I've got the dog with me, Rowley's not going to be able to abscond with me quite so easily.'

'Is absconding with you Rowley's style?'

'I don't think so. But who knows? It'll be very interesting to hear what he's got to say.'

'Certainly will. Is he coming on his own?'

'He didn't say. I'd doubt it, though. Those Lockes seem to go everywhere mob-handed.'

'Yes, Rowley can't function without his admiring audience. Tell you what, after you've talked to Rowley and I've talked to Joe Bartos, let's meet up in the Crown and Anchor to debrief.'

Carole bit back her instinctive reaction to say it'd be rather early to start drinking, and agreed that that was a very good idea.

Jude was just about to leave for her tea party on the Shorelands Estate, when she had a call on her mobile. She recognized the voice immediately, Martina Rutherford's distinctive accent. Strange how many Czechs seemed to be involved in the case. Could there be some undiscovered link between Martina and Joe Bartos? Or between her and Wally Grenston . . . ? Another idea to stir into the soup of conjectures that was swilling around in her mind.

'The reason I am ringing,' said Martina, 'is that I gather the boy Nathan Locke has been found.'

'Yes, he has.'

'And I hear a rumour that you were one of the people who found him?'

'There are always lots of rumours around down here.' Jude wasn't going to confirm that particular one until she had a clearer idea of what Martina was after.

'All I am asking,' said the Czech woman, 'is for you to confirm that the boy is in police custody.'

'I can do that. Though "custody" may be too strong a word. The police are certainly asking him some questions.'

'They will charge him soon,' Martina announced confidently. 'This will be a great relief to Martin.'

'Oh?'

'So long as the boy has been missing, Martin has been afraid he himself is a suspect.'

'You can see why the police would be interested in his movements.'

'I'm sorry?' Martina sounded puzzled.

'Well, Martin having been seen at Connie's Clip Joint?'

'You mean the night the girl died?'

'I don't know that there's any proof he was there then, but he was certainly seen coming out of the salon last Sunday.'

'Really?' The woman tried to maintain her professional cool, but was clearly shaken by the information.

'I had not heard this. I was away in Prague at the weekend.'

'So Martin didn't tell you? The police must have talked to him about it.'

'Oh yes, he said he had to see the police. I hadn't connected it with him being in Fethering on Sunday. Of course, now it makes sense.' The confidence was back in her voice, but Jude reckoned the cover-up was too slick to be true. Martina Rutherford hadn't known that her husband had been seen by Carole coming out of Connie's Clip Joint.

'Still, all I wanted, Jude, was for you to confirm that Nathan Locke is with the police. When I tell that to Martin, he will be very relieved. Thank you so much for talking to me.'

After the phone call Jude tried to define the emotions she had heard in the woman's voice. Shock certainly . . . but there had been something else as well. Suspicion. A new and sudden suspicion. For the first time Martina Rutherford had contemplated the possibility that her husband might have had something to do with the death of Kyra Bartos.

Chapter Thirty-two

During the summer season (which was coming to an end) tables and chairs spilled out of the Seaview Café onto Fethering Beach. Carole, arriving with Gulliver early as ever, took one of the seats furthest away from the self-service counter. She didn't go up there to order anything. She'd wait till Rowley Locke came and see how their meeting panned out. Her position, she reckoned, was well chosen. In sight of a lot of people, but good for a quick getaway. And also far enough away from the curious ears of Fethering for their conversation to be confidential.

Rowley Locke arrived on the dot of four. This time he wasn't heading a large family contingent. Only his brother Arnold, who was immediately despatched to fetch tea. Just tea. Carole had declined the offer of sandwiches and sticky cakes.

Rowley turned his innocent blue eyes on her. 'I assume it was you.'

'What was me?'

'Yesterday two women, matching descriptions of you and your friend Jude, abducted Nathan from our holiday cottage in Cornwall.'

'I'm afraid I take issue with the word "abducted". It might be used more accurately to describe the means by which he was taken to Treboddick in the first place.'

'Carole, you don't know the background to what you're talking about. This is a family thing.'

'I'll tell you what I do know – and that is that Nathan was being held down there against his will.'

Rowley Locke was unworried by the accusation. He shrugged and said, 'Sometimes young people don't know what's best for them. Then someone else has to take decisions on their behalf.'

'And if it's anything to do with the Locke family, then you're the person who takes those decisions.'

'Someone has to be a leader,' he said almost smugly.

'A leader like Prince Fimbador is a leader?'

She had managed to embarrass him. He looked away as he said, 'The Wheal Quest is a family game. You wouldn't understand it.'

At this moment Arnold arrived with the tea. After it had been poured, Carole turned her pale blue eyes on the weaker brother. 'You and Eithne must be very glad to hear that your son has been found.' He didn't respond. 'Or perhaps not, since you both connived at his imprisonment.'

'I think "imprisonment" is rather a strong word,' said Arnold feebly.

'Strong maybe, but it's accurate.' She turned back to Rowley. 'What on earth did you think hiding the boy away was going to achieve?'

'I hoped it would keep him safe until the police found out who really killed the girl.'

313

'Wouldn't it have helped the police more if they could have talked to Nathan? So that he could tell them what he saw that night, and help them to sort out a timetable of events?'

'I didn't want him to get into the hands of the police. Our fine boys in blue don't have a great track record when it comes to—'

And he was off again on his hobby horse. Carole couldn't stand any more of this tired old leftie agenda. 'Oh, for heaven's sake! You were deliberately perverting the course of justice. And I would imagine you'll be looking at a hefty prison sentence for what you've done.'

From his expression of dismay, this was clearly a possibility Rowley Locke had not considered. Like most control freaks, he was quickly vulnerable when threatened.

'I assume you've heard from the police in Littlehampton?' She addressed this question to the boy's father.

'Yes, they told me they were holding Nathan. He's "helping them with their enquiries". Eithne and I are going to visit him this evening.'

That would be an interesting encounter to witness. What do parents say to a son who knows that they've connived in having him imprisoned for three weeks? But that wasn't Carole's business. She moved on. 'Presumably you both know that Nathan didn't commit the murder?'

The look Arnold referred to his brother suggested

314

that at least one of them wasn't entirely convinced on the subject.

'Well, he didn't,' Carole continued. 'As I'm sure the police will find out in the course of their enquiries.'

'I wouldn't be so sure. The British police only want to get a conviction and they—'

'Oh, shut up, Rowley!' Carole was surprised by her own vehemence. So was its recipient. But she went on in similarly forceful vein. 'Listen, your ill-considered actions have wasted a lot of time. They've wasted police time, and they've certainly wasted time for me and my friend Jude.' In the magnificence of her flow neither man thought to question exactly what right she and Jude had to be involved in the investigation. 'What I suggest you do now, to make some kind of amends, is to tell me anything you know that might have a bearing on the case. Anything that you may have been holding back.'

Rowley Locke looked genuinely at a loss. 'I haven't been holding anything back. When I heard about Kyra Bartos's death, my only thought was that Nathan would immediately become a suspect. And that I had to get him to a place of safety.' Again he avoided Carole's eyes. 'I don't know anything else about the murder.'

'When I first came to see you, you told me that Eithne had met Kyra Bartos briefly in the street, but neither of you had. Is that still true?'

Rowley looked perplexed. 'Well, of course it's still true. The girl was already dead when we met you.'

'Yes. What I'm asking, though, is this. *At the time*

you said you hadn't met Kyra. Has your recollection maybe changed since then?'

'Are you accusing us of lying?'

'After what you said about Nathan's whereabouts over the past three weeks, don't you think I might have some justification?'

'Actually,' said Arnold quietly, 'I was lying.'

The announcement came as much of a shock to his brother as it did to Carole. They both looked at him in amazement as he went on, 'I did meet Kyra one evening a few weeks before she died. Eithne and I had gone out to a concert in Brighton. The Monteverdi *Vespers*, as it happened. Anyway, I had a bit of a stomach upset. My stomach has always been my Achilles heel . . .' He confided this mixed metaphor to Carole as though it would be of vital interest to her. 'So I went back to Marine Villas and found Kyra there with Nathan. Of course, I didn't mind his being there with the girl – Eithne and I have always made it clear that we have no old-fashioned moral scruples about that kind of thing – but I was a little upset that he'd done it without asking us. You know, choosing an evening when he thought we'd be out . . . it was all a bit underhand and hole-in-the-corner, if you know what I mean . . .'

Yes, I know exactly what you mean, and will you please get on with it, Carole thought.

'Anyway, when I found Nathan and the girl together that evening . . .' Arnold's pale features reddened, '. . . I must confess I was rather upset by what they were doing.'

'Do you mean they were having sex?'

'Oh, good heavens, no!' He dismissed the suggestion almost contemptuously. 'That would have been fine. Eithne and I wouldn't have had any problems about that. We've always brought up Diggo and Fimby to believe that sex is a perfectly natural and healthy act between two consenting—'

'Then what were they doing that you objected to?' demanded Carole, who had had quite enough of this spelling-out of right-on liberal credentials.

'Oh. Oh, well . . . they'd . . .' Arnold looked across at his elder brother, as though afraid of his reaction to the forthcoming revelation. 'They'd got out our box of the Wheal Quest.' He turned back to Carole. 'The Wheal Quest is a kind of family—'

'I know exactly what the Wheal Quest is, thank you.'

'What were they doing with it?' asked Rowley, suddenly alert.

'They'd got the game spread out on the floor, and I think Nathan must have been explaining to Kyra how it worked, and . . . and she was laughing at it.'

An expression of pale fury crossed his brother's face. 'Laughing at it?'

'Yes. And I think they must have been drinking, because the girl went on, saying how silly it was, and she even got Nathan to agree with her.'

Rowley snorted with anger at this betrayal.

'And I remember thinking . . .' Arnold went on quietly, 'this girl is not good for Nathan. She's a disruptive influence. She's trying to drive a wedge between him and his family. This relationship must be stopped.'

Carole had heard that cold intensity in a voice only the previous day. And when she looked at Arnold, she could see burning in his eyes the same demented logic that had driven Mopsa.

Chapter Thirty-three

Though in his eighties, Jiri Bartos was still an impressive man. Well over six foot and hardly stooping at all, he towered over Jude as he rose to shake her hand. There was still a full head of hair, white and cut to about an inch's length all over. His face was the shape of a shield, concave beneath high cheekbones, and his eyes were still piercingly blue. In the Grenstons' sitting room he seemed too large an exhibit, amidst the array of awards and the tables littered with tiny *objets d'art*.

While Wally made the introductions, Mim fluttered around over her tea tray, on which lay an unbelievable array of Victoria sponge, fairy cakes, tiny éclairs, coconut kisses and other fancies that Jude remembered from her childhood. There were even some slices of chequered Battenberg, which her father had always called 'stained-glass window cake'.

But Jiri Bartos did not appear interested in the spread of goodies. As soon as he sat down, he took a packet of cigarettes and a lighter out of his pocket.

'I'm sorry, Joe,' said Mim, 'but we don't smoke in the house.'

'I do,' he replied, lighting up. His voice was deep, like the creaking of old timber, and heavily accented.

'It isn't nice when we are eating food,' Mim protested.

'I will not eat food.'

'But I've prepared all this—'

'Walter . . .' He spoke it in the German way. 'We will have drink. Where is drink? Where is slivovitz? Where do you hide Becherovka?'

Mim tried again. 'Um, Wally doesn't drink in the afternoon.'

'Yes, he does. When with me he drink and smoke in afternoon.'

Mim turned to her husband, who studiously looked out of the window towards the sea. Then she turned back to Jiri Bartos. 'Listen, Joe, this is our house and—'

'Go. Leave us to talk. This is not wife's subject we talk of.'

She tried one more appeal to Wally, whose eyes still managed to evade hers, and then, with as much dignity as she could muster, left the room. As soon as her back was to him, her husband watched her go with a kind of wistfulness. Maybe he should have tried the Jiri Bartos approach a lot earlier in his marriage.

To Jude the exchange between Jiri and Mim had sounded unusual. Although his words were rude, he had not come across as ill-mannered. It had been a clash of wills rather than of words, and there had been no doubt whose will was the stronger.

Silently, Wally Grenston rose from his chair and went to a glass corner cupboard, from which he extracted a tall green bottle. He looked at Jude. 'You join us?'

'Please. I love Becherovka.'

Wally picked up three small glasses with a whirly design of red and gold on them. He put them on the table, unscrewed the Becherovka and after pouring about an inch into the bottom of each glass, handed them round.

He and his old friend looked into each other's eyes as they raised their glasses and in unison said, 'Na Zdravi!'

Jiri made no attempt to include Jude in the toast, but again for some strange reason this did not feel offensive. She took a sip of her drink, anyway, remembering and relishing the stickiness on her lips and the herbal, almost medicinal, glow that filled her mouth.

'I am very sorry about what happened to your daughter,' she said.

'Thank you.' Jiri Bartos left it at that. Jude did not imagine there were many circumstances in which he would let his emotions show. 'You find boy who police think killed her?'

'Yes. Yes, a friend and I went down to Cornwall and . . . we found him.'

Jude didn't particularly want to go into the details, but the old man insisted. Though hardened against showing any emotion about his daughter's death, he wanted to find out everything that might have some connection to it.

So Jude told him how Carole and she had tracked down the boy to Treboddick. She did not spell out the

321

fact that he had not been hiding there voluntarily. At the end of her narrative, there was a silence. Then Jiri Bartos asked, 'You think he kill her?'

'No.'

'Why not?'

'For a start, I don't think it's in his nature to kill anyone.'

The old man let out a guttural hawk of dissent. 'It's in all men's nature to kill when they have to. We know that – yes, Walter?'

Wally nodded uncomfortably. Jude wondered what secrets the two men shared, and reckoned it was pretty unlikely that they'd ever share them with her.

'So, if not boy, who you think kill Krystina?'

Jude was forced to admit she didn't have an answer. 'But there are quite a few suspects.'

Jiri Bartos shrugged at the inadequacy of her reply. 'Boy was there. Boy have motive.'

'What motive?'

'He want make love Krystina. She good girl, no want to. He lose control. He kill her.'

Jude would have liked to reveal the true nature of Nathan and Kyra's sexual encounter, if only to exonerate the boy, but she realized she would be betraying a confidence. So instead she said, 'You didn't approve of Kyra – Krystina seeing Nathan, did you?'

'Girl too young. One day she meet right boy. Now she too busy with job, look after house. Both too young.'

She decided to take a risk. 'You had another family once, didn't you? Another wife and children, in Czecho-slovakia?'

Wally didn't like the direction of the conversation. 'Jude, I don't think—'

'No. She ask me. I answer. Yes, I have other family. Not in Czechoslovakia. Well, first in Czechoslovakia. Then the name changed. Then it called "Protectorate of Bohemia/Moravia".'

'That was when the Nazis took over?'

'Of course.'

'What happened to your other family?'

The old man shook his head. 'They do not exist.' That was all she was going to get out of him on the subject. 'I come to England.'

'Do you think it was because of what happened to your other family that you were so protective of Krystina?'

The blue eyes looked at her bleakly. That question wasn't going to get any kind of answer. Someone like Jiri Bartos did not have time for psychology; his only imperative was survival. Jude tried another tack. 'Do you know Connie Rutherford . . . the one who runs the salon?'

'I meet. Pick up Krystina from work one day. Also she live near.'

'Near your house?'

'Yes. Two gardens meet at back, only fence between.'

Distantly this rang a bell with something she had heard from Carole. 'And did Krystina like Connie?'

'I think. Krystina happy in job.'

'But she wasn't happy in her previous job?'

Puzzlement etched new lines in his craggy brow. 'Not happy? This I not know.'

'She worked at Martin & Martina in Worthing. But not for long. Then she went to Connie's Clip Joint. Why?'

'Better job, she tell me.'

'No other reason?'

He shook his massive head.

'Did she say whether she got on with her boss at the Worthing salon? His name was Martin.'

'I know who you mean, yes. I've seen him around. Krystina say she like him very much.'

It made sense. If her father was so protective, Kyra wouldn't have told him about Martin Rutherford coming on to her. It could have made for rather an ugly confrontation.

Jude sighed and went back to the most basic of questions. 'Can you think of any reason why someone would want to kill your daughter?'

'If not boy, no.'

'I'm absolutely certain it wasn't Nathan.'

He shrugged. Tell me why, he seemed to be saying, you still haven't convinced me.

'Look, you disapproved of their relationship, Nathan and K— Krystina.'

'Yes, I disapprove. That not mean I kill my own daughter.'

'I wasn't suggesting that. But can you think of anyone else who might have disapproved of their relationship?'

'I don't know. I don't know boy at all. Maybe he have other girlfriend not happy.'

'From what I can find out, Krystina was his first girlfriend.'

'Then I not know. Unless his parents disapprove of my daughter.'

'Did you ever meet his parents?'

'Of course, no. I only meet boy once. But his parents . . . maybe rich. Maybe think they important family. Maybe not think daughter of Czech electrician good enough for boy.' He looked at her, challenging, almost amused through his pain. 'Maybe they kill her . . . ?'

It's a possibility, thought Jude, that I certainly haven't ruled out.

Chapter Thirty-four

Rowley Locke had been just as shocked as Carole by the sudden change in his brother's manner. 'Arnold, what are you saying?'

'I am saying that that girl Kyra was not worthy of Nathan. We can't allow anyone into the Locke family who thinks that the Wheal Quest is funny. That girl would only have been a disruptive influence.'

Rowley now looked positively worried. 'I agree, it's a family thing, and it should be kept within the family.' And then he said something so out of keeping with his usual attitude that it showed the extent of his anxiety. 'But we shouldn't take it too seriously. The Wheal Quest is only a game.'

'No, it's more than that! It's a philosophy, it's a life system!' The sudden vehemence with which Arnold spoke drew disturbed glances from people at adjacent tables. The serenity of Fethering Beach on a September afternoon was rarely broken by shouting.

But if the geriatric onlookers had been shocked by Arnold's outburst, they were about to get more free entertainment. Before he could say more, the group at

Carole's table was joined by a fast-striding Bridget Locke, with an embarrassed Eithne in her wake.

'Rowley! What the hell have you been doing?'

He quailed visibly under his wife's onslaught and asked feebly, 'What are you talking about?'

'You know bloody well what I'm talking about! What you did to Nathan.'

'I did it for his own good. I was trying to protect him.'

'Rowley, that is so much crap! I can't believe that you didn't tell me what you'd done. I've spent the past three weeks worried sick about the boy, when you could have put my mind at rest at any moment by telling me where Nathan was.'

'But I thought if you knew, you'd have told the police.'

'Too bloody right I would.'

'Bridget, if the police had got hold of him, God knows what would have happened. Our fine boys in blue are not—'

'Oh, shut up, Rowley! You sound like a record whose needle's stuck. I've had enough of your right-on *Guardian*-reading claptrap to last me a lifetime!' (Carole was rather enjoying this conversation. What a very sensible woman Bridget Locke was. She thought exactly like Carole did.) 'You weren't thinking about Nathan at all! I wonder if you've ever thought about anyone else apart from yourself, except to see if you can make an anagram out of their name. As ever, with Nathan in trouble, your first thought was about you. A Locke family crisis? Someone's got to take control here. And, because the rest of the family are so bloody pusillanimous, it had to be you, didn't it? He's only your nephew, not your son, but it's still got to be you who comes to the rescue. Don't worry, Rowley can sort everything out! Here comes the hero, galloping up on his white charger.

'And then what did you do? What was your solution to the crisis? You made it all part of a game. Yes, the bloody Wheal Quest. And you took advantage of your vulnerable daughter Mopsa and made her play along with your stupid, sub-Tolkien fantasy. And you never for one moment thought of what you might be doing to Nathan!'

Bridget Locke paused for breath. Her geriatric audience settled in their seats, and took another sip of tea in anticipation of Act Two.

'How do you know all this?' Rowley managed to ask.

'I know because the police rang the house to tell me that they were questioning Nathan. Because he's a juvenile, they wanted a family member there.' She turned the beam of her displeasure on the shrinking Eithne. 'And apparently I was the one who he wanted to be there with him.'

'But surely you should be at work?'

'Yes, Rowley, it's a Friday. I should be at work. But some things are more important than work. Listen, that call I had from the police was the first I knew that the poor boy was still alive. So, since I couldn't get hold of you anywhere, after I'd been to the police station to see

Nathan, I went straight round to Eithne's, and made her tell me what the hell had been going on.'

Arnold's wife appealed apologetically to the two brothers. 'I'm sorry. You know what she's like when she gets forceful.' She still looked to Carole like Mrs Bun the Baker's Wife, but the game was no longer Happy Families.

'Anyway,' Bridget steamed on, 'the police are extremely interested in talking to you, Rowley. I'm sure they won't have any problem finding you, but you might make things easier by turning yourself in.'

'What do you mean, "turning myself in"?' he asked petulantly. 'I haven't committed any crime.'

'No? I think the police could probably think of a few. "Perverting the Course of Justice" . . . ? I don't know the proper terms, but I'm sure there's one called "Abduction of a Juvenile". And there's certainly "Unlawful Imprisonment".'

'For heaven's sake, Bridget! These weren't crimes. They were all in the family.'

'God, Rowley, that sums you up, doesn't it? "All in the family." Everything's all right so long as it's kept within the magic circle of the Lockes. That's always been your escape. When you fail publicly, when you lose a job . . . never mind, because you're still a little god within the family. And everyone in the family does as you say. I've even done it myself. Pretended to have a bad back, so that you can find out if some woman's snooping on you. But that's always been your approach. Never mind your inadequacies in the real world – in the Wheal Quest you are still a hero. Rowley, if you only knew how bloody pathetic you are!'

He rose from his chair with an attempt at dignity. 'I'm not going to stay here to be insulted.'

'Fine. Go to the police. Let them start insulting you instead.'

'That kind of remark is not worth responding to. Come on, we're going.'

Arnold rose obediently to his feet and crossed to his wife, who had yet to sit down. Rowley joined them, then looked back at Bridget. 'Are you coming?'

'No. Certainly not now. And I'll have to think about whether I ever come back.'

He did not respond to that, but led his acolytes back across the sand towards the front. The animated language of his back-view showed that he was telling Eithne off for her betrayal of Locke confidentiality. And Arnold was joining in the castigation.

Exhausted, Bridget dropped into a seat next to Carole. 'Sorry about all that. I was just bloody furious. Letting off the steam of a good few years, I'm afraid.'

Realizing the climax of the play had passed, Fethering's elderly matinee-goers returned once more to their tea and cakes.

'Yes.' Now the others had gone, Carole felt awkward. The dissection of the Lockes' family life – and indeed marriage – had been rather public. She didn't quite know where the conversation should move next. Jude, she knew, would instinctively have found the right direction.

Still, there was always one safe English fallback. 'Would you like me to get you a cup of tea?'

The drained woman looked pathetically grateful for the offer and accepted.

By the time she returned with a fresh pot for both of them, Carole had decided which tack to take. 'How did Nathan seem when you saw him?'

'Oh, fine. No physical harm, anyway. Though what effect it's going to have on him emotionally, I hate to think.'

'What's he doing now?'

'Asleep. He didn't get much sleep last night. The detectives are being quite gentle with him.'

'Rowley would never believe that.'

'No.' She sighed. 'I just feel so sorry for Nathan. I mean he's still in deep shock about that poor girl's death. He did love her, you know, with that intense adolescent passion of a first love. He must be so cut up. And I can't think that being shut away for three weeks and ministered to by his loony cousin has made the grieving process any easier.'

'I'm surprised to hear you use the word "loony".'

'Yes, very remiss of me, isn't it? If I wasn't in such an emotional state, I wouldn't have been so politically incorrect. Mopsa is, after all, my stepdaughter. But it's true. I've never managed to get through to her. I mean, she loathed me, because I replaced her beloved mother, but . . . there was always a problem there with Mopsa. Poor concentration, no grasp of reality. I'm sure there's a name for it . . . Somebody-or-Other's Syndrome, no doubt. But, of course, the Lockes never

had her properly diagnosed. No, as ever, they reckoned they could sort everything out themselves.'

'Do you know why Rowley's first wife left?'

Bridget Locke smiled grimly. 'After the scene
you've just witnessed, do you need to ask?'

'Maybe not.' There was a silence, broken only by
the gulls and the soft swooshing of the sea, before
Carole asked what was, for her, a daringly personal
question. 'Do you think you will go back to him?'

'I don't know.' There was a weary shake of the head.
'At the moment I'm so seething with fury that . . . I
won't make a quick decision. There is still something
there, you know. There's a side of Rowley that very few
people ever see. He can be quite enchanting.'

I'll have to take your word for that, thought Carole.
And again she asked herself the perennial question:
why do bright, intelligent women stay with such unsatisfactory men? But then she thought of the alternative,
the divorce she and David had shared. And wondered
whether that was actually a much better solution.

'I was wondering . . .' Bridget went on, 'you spent
most of yesterday driving Nathan back from Treboddick . . .'

'Yes.'

'Did he say anything to you . . . you know, anything
that made you think differently about who might have
killed Kyra Bartos?'

'Not really. I mean, he told me and Jude what he'd
done that night . . . which sounded pretty convincing to
us . . . though whether it'll convince the police . . .'

'As I say, the police are being much more sensitive

than I'd ever have expected. They very definitely want to question Nathan, but I didn't get the impression that they regard him as a major suspect.'

'Good. Well, the one thing he did mention was that that night, while he was in the salon with Kyra . . . he thought he heard someone trying to get in through the back gate.'

'The murderer?'

'Possibly. Whoever it was couldn't have got in then . . . but maybe came back later.'

'Hmm . . .' Bridget Locke swept her hands slowly through her long blonde hair and looked thoughtful. 'There was one thing that Nathan said to me, just now, at the police station . . . which I thought was interesting . . .'

'What was that?'

'He said that there were a dozen red roses in the back room at the salon the night Kyra Bartos died.'

'Yes, I saw them. Part of Nathan's romantic set dressing, I imagine. Which, given the circumstances, is pretty sad.'

'No.'

'What?' Carole looked curiously at the woman.

'Nathan said the red roses had nothing to do with him. They were there when he arrived.'

'Didn't he ask Kyra if they were hers?'

'Apparently not. He assumed they were something to do with the salon's owner . . . Connie, is it?'

'Yes. Did he say whether he had told the police about seeing the red roses?'

'I asked him and he said he hadn't. I got the

impression they'd been asking more about where he'd been for the past three weeks, and in the next session they're going to get on to the night Kyra Bartos died. But I thought the red roses were interesting.'

'Certainly. And one assumes that the police took them away from the salon as evidence?'

'I would think so, Carole. What were they then – a love token for somebody?'

'Perhaps.'

'So,' said Bridget Locke, 'the two obvious questions are: who brought them to the salon? And who for?'

So far as Carole was concerned, the answers to those questions were very straightforward. As soon as she got back to High Tor, she fed Gulliver, hardly noticing what she was doing. Her mind was racing.

She could only think of one candidate as the bearer of red roses for Kyra. Apart from Nathan, there was another man who had fancied her. Or at least come on to her. Maybe the girl hadn't been so immune to his attractions as she pretended.

Carole found the card and dialled his mobile number. Martin Rutherford answered immediately. She identified herself, and reminded him that he'd asked her to get in touch if she found out anything more about the murder.

'Well, I have found out something.' She told him about the red roses, and the fact that they hadn't been brought to the salon by Nathan Locke.

'Ah. Maybe we should talk . . . ?'

'Just what I was going to suggest.'

She looked at her watch. Just before five. Jude would surely be back soon. Maybe they'd have to delay their debriefing meeting at the Crown and Anchor. If she made an appointment to meet Martin somewhere at seven, they could both confront him. But that wasn't going to be possible. Martin wanted to meet earlier. 'The salon closes at six, and I have, er, other commitments for the evening.'

'So you're there now?'

'Yes.'

'I'll be right over.'

'Very well.' He sounded resigned to whatever the interview might bring.

After she'd put the phone down, Carole contemplated ringing Jude's mobile. But no, she didn't want to interrupt her neighbour's meeting with the elusive Joe Bartos.

Besides, once again Carole felt that charge of doing something on her own. She'd find the truth and present it to Jude, neatly gift-wrapped. She'd show she was no slouch in this investigation business.

Chapter Thirty-five

'Did boy say anything?' asked Jiri Bartos. 'Yesterday you drive long time with him. Did he say anything about Krystina?'

'He said that he loved her.'

The old man snorted dismissively. 'What boys of that age know about love?'

'I think they probably know quite a lot. They find it all very confusing, but they do know the strength of their own feelings.'

'Love often dangerous. Many murders committed for love.'

Wally Grenston, who had been silently topping up Jiri Bartos's glass throughout their conversation, moved forward again with the Becherovka bottle poised. The old man waved it away. 'No. Slivovitz.'

Wally nodded, returned to the drinks cupboard and produced a bottle of the famous Jelinek Plum Brandy. He poured some into a new glass, and handed it across.

'Not cold?'

'I'm sorry. It very rarely gets drunk.'

'Huh. Wife not like?'

Wally didn't argue. He had long since reconciled

himself to his henpecked image. With a nervous look around the room, he was no doubt anticipating trouble ahead, from his wife. It was surprising how much of a fug one man's chain-smoking could produce. And Mim's obsessively produced tea lay untouched. Wally Grenston might be in for a difficult evening.

And yet there was something about him that was relaxed, as if sitting drinking in a haze of smoke felt natural to him. It probably echoed previous evenings that Wally had sat with Joseph and other compatriots. Jude had the feeling that, if she wasn't there, the two men would be speaking Czech.

Jiri Bartos once again focused his bright blue eyes on her. 'Tell me more about boy. What he say he do night Krystina died?'

Jude replied accurately, but not completely. She recounted the timing of Nathan's arrival at and departure from the salon, but she didn't detail his unsuccessful love-making with Kyra.

'Huh. And boy not see anyone else around salon?'

'No. He thought he heard someone coming through the back gate at one point, but he didn't see anyone.'

'Who could that be?'

'Well, putting on one side the explanation that it could just have been a burglar who was trying to break in . . . there might be an argument for thinking that the visitor was someone who could get into the salon by the back door . . . in other words someone who had keys.' Jiri Bartos did not challenge her logic. 'So that would mean Connie Rutherford herself or the other stylist Theo or—'

'Not Connie. She not go out that evening.'

'How do you know?'

'I tell you, my garden back on to hers. When hot in evening, I sit on balcony with drink, can see her house. Summer no curtains drawn. That evening I see her all evening.'

'What was she doing?'

He shrugged. 'She move round house from room to room. Like she nervous. I don't know. But she not go out.'

'Are you sure she didn't? Even later? Midnight? One o'clock? Hadn't you gone to bed by then?'

'No. I go to bed much later. Sometimes not at all. No point in going to bed if you do not sleep. I did not see Connie leave all night.'

'Well, that's good, thank you. I'm glad she's off the hook. I'd hate to think of her being in any way involved in what happened to your daughter. But the one other person who we now know did have keys to the back door of the salon is her ex-husband, Martin Rutherford. Do you know who I mean?'

'I know him, I tell you. I live in house long time. I saw him back when they two still married.'

'Well, Martin's got an alibi for the night Kyra died. He was at a conference in Brighton and—'

'He not at conference in Brighton.'

'What?' asked Jude, thunderstruck. 'How do you know?'

'I see him.'

'You saw him that night? At the salon?'

'No, not at salon. I in my house all night. Eleven o'clock maybe I see him in Connie's house.'

'Really?'

'He come through back garden. Way into house people not see. Only I see. He go to back door. Connie let him in.'

'And then what happened?'

'I not know. They close curtains.'

Jude took a triumphant sip of her sticky Becherovka, and felt the cough medicine taste burn in her throat. This was a result. The night Kyra Bartos died, Martin Rutherford had actually been in Fethering.

Chapter Thirty-six

The Worthing branch of Martin & Martina was still busy when Carole arrived. All the stylists seemed to be occupied, and it looked unlikely that they could all be finished by the six o'clock closing time. There was no sign of either of the proprietors, but the girl at the desk said she was expected and directed her to the staircase that led up to Martin's office.

The two-room suite had been designed by the same person who had done the salon downstairs. The Martin & Martina logo was very much in evidence, and all the furniture featured black glass and brushed aluminium.

Martin, who must have been alerted to Carole's arrival by the receptionist, was standing in the outer office, waiting for her. He shook her hand, the model of urbanity, but she could feel the tension in his body. 'Please come through.'

She did as she was told, leaving the door between the two offices open. Although the presence of all the stylists and customers downstairs gave her some security, she still wanted to have an escape route.

Martin Rutherford gestured her to a chair and sat down behind the black glass top of his desk. As ever, he looked what he was, the successful entrepreneur, hair subtly darkened, teeth expensively straightened.

'So, what can I do for you, Carole? I'm sorry I can't be long. As I say, I have somewhere to go this evening.'

'With your wife?'

'No, Martina is going to Prague to see her mother, who's very sick. She gets the 21:05 flight from Heathrow. I have to be away by six.'

'What I have to say won't take very long.'

'Good. Now, something about red roses, wasn't it . . . ? How romantic.' The laid-back flippancy of his tone was contradicted by the unease in his darting brown eyes.

'Yes. As I say, I was told this by the missing boy Nathan Locke. When he arrived in the back room of the salon that night, the red roses were already there.'

'Perhaps Kyra had another admirer . . . ?'

'That's rather what I was thinking, Martin.'

He looked genuinely puzzled for a moment before he caught on to what she was saying. 'Oh, me? Are you suggesting that I had the hots for Kyra?'

'She used to work for you, right here in this salon.'

'A lot of young women work for me, in this salon and in many others. That doesn't mean I fancy any of them.'

'No, but Kyra Bartos left the job here, because you were sexually harassing her.'

'Oh, we're back to that again, are we? Incidentally, where did you hear about it?'

'Your ex-wife Connie told my friend Jude.'

'Ah. Yes.' The explanation seemed in some way to

relax him. 'Of course, your friend Jude. The other half of Fethering's very own Marple Twins.'

Carole didn't react to the gibe. 'So there might be a logical connection between your "coming on" to Kyra when she worked for you and your giving her red roses when she no longer worked for you.'

'There might be, but I wouldn't say it was that logical. Nor would I say it's the kind of thing that would be possible to prove.'

'Did the police ask you about the red roses?'

'Sorry? No, not at all. Remember, I only talked to them right at the beginning of the case. Then all they wanted to establish was the set-up at Connie's Clip Joint . . . you know, the fact that Connie was my ex-wife, what our financial arrangements had been since the divorce. They didn't ask me anything connected with the actual murder case.'

'I wasn't referring to the first time, Martin.'

'What?' He looked puzzled.

'Not the first time the police talked to you, immediately after the murder. I'm talking about when they questioned you about having been in Connie's Clip Joint last Sunday morning.' Now it made sense to him. 'Because Connie told them about that break-in. And you're not going to tell me they didn't follow up on it with you.'

'No. No.' Martin Rutherford looked thoughtful. Then he said, 'You know, Carole, I think you and your friend Jude are very stupid to get involved in situations like this.'

'Oh? Why?'

'Because they're potentially dangerous.' There was no twinkle in the brown eyes he fixed on hers. 'It's very common that someone who is about to be exposed for committing one murder doesn't have much compunction about committing another.'

Jude was full of her news. When she got back, she went straight round to High Tor to share it with Carole. But there was no reply, just a disgruntled barking from Gulliver.

She returned to Woodside Cottage, the information about Martin Rutherford still bubbling inside her. Then she rang through to the Crown and Anchor, to see whether Carole had gone there, according to their earlier arrangement. But Ted Crisp said she hadn't been in. Jude moved round the house, unable to settle to anything, and kept looking out of her front window to see whether the Renault had reappeared.

Martin stood up from his chair and moved round to the front of his desk. He sat on the edge, in what should have been a casual posture. But his body was tense, in the grip of some strong emotion. He was only a few feet from Carole, and she could feel the energy sparking off him.

'There's a lot you don't understand,' he said at length. 'A lot of secrets that should stay secrets.'

'If keeping things secret leads to people being murdered, then I would have thought perhaps they ought to be made public.' The sentence was a lot more articulate and confident than Carole felt.

'Huh.' Martin Rutherford rubbed the back of his hand wearily across his brow. 'It's terrible how easily things go wrong, how easily they get out of hand.'

'Are you talking about what you did to Kyra?'

'I did nothing to Kyra.'

'No? Do you deny that you went round to Connie's Clip Joint the night the girl died?'

He slowly blew out a long breath, then said, 'No, I don't deny it.'

'When did you go there?'

'About seven, before the girl arrived.'

'But you didn't stay?'

'No, I had to get back to Brighton.'

'For your Hair and Nail Conference?'

'Yes.'

'To establish your alibi.'

'If you like.' He now sounded very weary. 'Yes, I sat through a dinner there and talked to a lot of people.'

'But then you went back to Fethering.' He nodded. 'What time did you get back?'

'Ten, half past.'

'And you went back to Connie's Clip Joint?'

'Yes, but I didn't go inside.'

'Really? You expect me to believe that, Martin?'

'I don't know whether I expect you to believe that or not, but it's the truth.'

'So why didn't you go in?'

'Because the boy was there, with Kyra. I saw them through the window.'

'So you went in through the back gate . . .' That would explain the noise Nathan Locke had heard, '. . . you saw the young couple were there, and then you left?'

'That's exactly what I did, yes.'

'But surely you must have been furious to see Kyra with another man?'

'For heaven's sake, I had no interest in Kyra! I never had!'

'Never even when you came on to her downstairs in this very salon?'

'No. No. No . . .' The monosyllable got weaker with repetition. Martin Rutherford let out a deep sigh, then seeming to reach some conclusion, went on, 'Look, I'm going to tell you what actually happened. Not because I particularly want to, but because you seem to have got some dangerous ideas fixed in your mind, and if you start passing them on to the police . . . well, it could be very inconvenient.'

'And what if I pass on to the police what you're about to tell me?'

'It's possible that when you've heard it, you won't want to. And if you do, that may not be such a bad thing. I'm sick to death of lying.' His head sank into his hands. 'Maybe telling the truth will *take some of this bloody pressure off me*!' The outburst was so sudden and uncharacteristic that it was a measure of the stress he was under.

Carole waited while he composed himself. Then he started. 'Most of my life I must have heard the expression "living a lie", but only when it happens to you do you understand what it means. I've been living a lie for the past few years, and it's been destroying me.' Again Carole let him take his own time. 'Obviously you know that I divorced Connie and married Martina.' He gestured round the room. 'That had a very good effect on all this. Martina is a wonderfully talented businesswoman. I could never have built up Martin & Martina to this level without her.

'On the emotional side, though . . .' he was having difficulty framing the words, '. . . things didn't work out so well. Some people have said Martina only married me because she had her eyes on the business. I don't know whether that's true or not, but certainly after the first few months . . . the emotional side of the marriage . . .' You mean the sexual side, thought Carole. 'Well, it virtually ended, and I realized I had made a horrible mistake . . .'

'And was that when you started coming on to the young girls in the salon . . . like Kyra?'

He shook his head in exasperation. 'No! I've never come on to any girl in my salon. For a start, younger women have never appealed to me that much and, then again . . . well, it's one of the first things you learn. If you're going to run a successful business, keep your hands off the staff.'

'Oh, come on, Martin, that won't wash. Connie told Jude there was a great history of you touching up the juniors, going right back to when you were married to her.'

'Oh, God,' he groaned. 'How complicated things become. You invent one little untruth to get you out of a hole, and suddenly you find you're having to fabricate more and more of them, and the hole is getting bigger and bigger.'

'I think you'd better tell me about those little untruths,' said Carole in her most magisterial Home Office committee-chairing voice.

'All right. I said I'd made a mistake in marrying Martina, but I did it because I was infatuated with her. When the infatuation faded, I looked around and realized what I'd done. And I also realized that there was only one woman I had ever loved and that was Connie.'

'Did she feel the same?'

'Yes. I had to summon up a lot of nerve to ask her, but yes, she did.'

'So all that business about what a bastard you'd been to her . . . ?'

'That bit was true.' A wry chuckle. 'I had been a bastard to her.'

'But you touching up the juniors in your salons . . . ?'

'Was a complete fabrication. A smokescreen. Connie and I would do anything to hide the fact that we still loved each other.'

'But why? Surely if you'd divorced once, you could do it again?'

His lips tightened as he said, 'Not from Martina. Martina is a Czech Catholic. She doesn't believe in divorce. Or at least she didn't object to marrying a divorcee, but there's no way she'd let me divorce her.'

'But these days a lot of people don't bother with divorce. They just move out.'

'I don't think I could just move out from Martina.'

The chill with which he spoke made it abundantly clear that Martin Rutherford was actually terrified of his second wife. 'She is a very powerful woman.'

'So, going back to where we started this evening, were the red roses for Connie?'

He nodded. 'It was very hard for us to meet. I had to fabricate alibis. Martina did not trust me being out of her sight. So the Hair and Nail Conference seemed perfect. I set up to meet Connie that evening.'

'In the salon?'

'Yes. I couldn't risk our being recognized in a hotel. Then where Connie lives – the house we used to share when we were married – well, there's a snoopy neighbour, old boy at the back who watches everyone's comings and goings, so that wasn't safe. But in the salon . . . I could park out of sight, go in the back way. It had worked well for us in the past.'

'But when you went back there that particular night, you found out that someone else had set up their own romantic encounter?'

'Kyra, yes. As I say, I went in early to set up the flowers, did the dinner in Brighton, and came back to find our little love nest occupied.'

'So you told Connie?'

'Our arrangement was that I'd get there and give her a call on my mobile, to say that the coast was clear, then she'd come and join me. But of course the coast wasn't clear.'

'What did you do?'

'I was stupid. I should have gone straight back to the conference hotel in Brighton. But I thought: I've actually managed to get a night off from Martina. I've got my alibi. Who knows when I'll next get a chance to be with Connie? So I went to her place.'

'And stayed all night?'

'Much longer than I should have done. We were just so happy to be together. The time was so precious. We talked and talked all night and well into the morning.'

'Was that why Connie was late into the salon? And why she hadn't done her hair or make-up?'

Martin Rutherford nodded ruefully. 'We talked about everything. About what we were going to do. About how I was finally going to face up to Martina and tell her it was all over. But then, when I heard about Kyra's death, everything had to be put on hold. Connie and I couldn't risk letting the police find out what we'd been up to. If they found out I'd been at the salon that night . . .' He shuddered, then concluded glumly, 'Everything still is on hold.'

'But you are planning to see Connie tonight, aren't you? Because Martina's going to Prague? Is that why you couldn't fix to see me later?'

His nod had something of bravado in it, the action of a cheeky schoolboy doing something he shouldn't. 'Sad, isn't it, a man having to set up elaborate deceptions so that he can go and see his ex-wife?' He looked at his watch. 'Connie's waiting for me in the back room of the salon even as we speak.'

They were interrupted by the sound of the outer office door closing. Carole looked up in alarm, but Martin said, 'Don't worry. Girls locking up. I must go down in a sec to check everything's all right.'

'Yes, well, I don't think I need to detain you much longer.' Carole looked at him sternly through her rimless glasses. 'You realize you are going to have to tell all this to the police?'

He sighed, then dropped his head. 'Yes, you're right. We probably are.'

'It could be material to their investigations. Now they're talking to Nathan Locke, they'll need all the information they can find on what actually happened that evening.'

'All right. I'll do it. But not tonight. Tonight's just for me and Connie. Tomorrow we'll face the consequences.'

'And stand up to Martina too?'

'Yes. I think facing the police is going to be easier than facing Martina.' He rose from his perch on the desk and picked up a briefcase. 'I'd better be off.'

'Just one thing before you go . . .'

'Yes?'

'We've established that you never came on to any of your juniors . . .'

'I hope we have, because I can assure you—'

'No, no, that's fine, but what I want to ask is: if Kyra Bartos didn't leave this salon because you'd been molesting her, why did she leave? She hadn't been here very long.'

'Ah.' Martin Rutherford looked embarrassed. 'Yes, there was a bit of a problem.'

'What was it? Come on, you've told me all the rest.'

'Well, all right,' he said wretchedly. 'The fact is, as I said, I've never touched any of the juniors. But the

pretty ones . . . well, occasionally I might say something. Nothing offensive, just a compliment. And Kyra
was very pretty, so . . . well, I never think it hurts to tell
a woman she's pretty. It was completely innocent.'

'Then why did it become a problem?' asked Carole
implacably.

'Because of Martina. Martina did not like me making these compliments to Kyra. She got the wrong end
of the stick. She thought that I fancied the girl.'

'So that's why Kyra had to go? Because Martina was
jealous of her?'

'Yes. Well, I suppose that's right.'

'How jealous is she?'

'What do you mean by that?'

'Well, if Martina had got it into her head that the relationship she imagined you to be having with Kyra was
still continuing, then she might have a motive to—'

'No, no, you're talking nonsense. Dangerous nonsense. Come on, I must go. Just check Kelly-Jane's got
everything tidied up.'

Down in the salon all was neat and swept clean.
The manic activity of half an hour before might never
have happened. A tall girl who must have been Kelly-
Jane stood with a bundle of keys, clearly waiting for the
all-clear to go home.

'Thanks, Kelly-Jane, looks great. Not sure whether
I'll be in in the morning or not.'

'Will Martina?'

'No, of course not. She's off to Prague.'

'Oh, I thought she might have changed her plans.'

'No, she'll be on her way to Heathrow now. Friday night traffic, she'll have left about five.'

'No, she was here.'

'Here? When?'

'Came in within the last half-hour. Went upstairs. I assumed she was talking to you in the office.'

'I didn't see her.'

Kelly-Jane shrugged. This wasn't her business. 'Well, I don't know what she was doing up there then.'

'Is she still here?'

'No, she rushed out about ten minutes ago.'

'Did she say where she was going?'

'She didn't say anything. She just swept out, looking absolutely furious.'

The realization came to Martin and Carole at the same moment. Martina must have been in the outer office. It had been she who had closed the door. She had heard all of their conversation.

'Oh, my God!' shrieked Martin. 'Connie!'

The speed with which he rushed out of the salon left Carole in no doubt as to who he thought was responsible for the murder of Kyra Bartos.

Chapter Thirty-seven

Jude had been expecting to hear from Carole, but not from such a panicked Carole as the one who rang from the Martin & Martina in Worthing. It took a moment for Jude to take in the information that her friend was on her way, but that Connie Rutherford was at her salon and in immediate danger. Carole was going to call the police, but could Jude get down there as soon as possible?

She rushed to Connie's Clip Joint as fast as her chubby legs could carry her. There was nobody around; the moment the shops shut, Fethering High Street became deserted.

A sleek green Jaguar was parked outside. No lights showed in the salon, but to her surprise when she tried the front door, it gave. Moving very slowly to avoid creaks, Jude advanced into the body of the shop.

The door to the back room was slightly ajar, and a pencil of light spread out across the salon floor. As Jude advanced towards it, she became aware of a passionate, heavily accented voice coming from the back room.

'. . . and I know he is coming here, because I follow him. I see him bring in red roses and I think it is for that girl who work here. Martin always fancied her, I could see from the way he looked at her. I didn't then know it was you he was visiting. I thought he had enough of you when you were married. I didn't expect Martin to be coming back . . . like, how do you say it . . . a dog to his own vomit?'

The lack of response to Martina's speech suggested that her victim had been gagged or otherwise incapacitated and, as Jude got close enough to peer through the slit of the door, this was confirmed. Connie was cowering in an old chair, a thin white towel tied tightly around her mouth. Her jaws moved as if she was trying to speak, but no sound came out. Ominously, the dome of a hair dryer loomed over her head.

'So there's a good cause of guilt for you, Connie. You start an affair with a married man and what effect does it have? An innocent girl gets killed. The blood of Kyra Bartos is on your hands, and for that reason I'll not feel so much guilt about having your blood on my hands.'

Even through the towel, the whimper that Connie let out at that could be clearly heard. Jude knew she had to move quickly. Martina was still invisible to her, probably with her back to the door. She certainly wasn't near the lead to the dryer, so if she was planning to replicate her previous murder method . . .

Jude decided quickly. She had to. If she burst in through the door, there was a good chance of knocking Martina off-balance, certainly of keeping her away from the electric flex. Jude put her shoulder down and barged forward.

She hadn't thought of a gun. Nor, when the automatic was pointed at her, did she think of arguing with it. Instead, she sat obediently on the seat next to Connie's.

'You, Jude. Of course, nosy Jude. Jude who so conveniently told me about my husband being seen here last Sunday. So now it will be three deaths you have caused, Connie. That's what you get for stealing someone's husband. And I'm afraid it will have to be your nosy fat friend who goes first.'

The gun was still pointing at Jude, but now Martina Rutherford brought up her other hand to steady it. Not one to mess about, thought Jude. Oh well, at least she'll save me from rheumatoid arthritis.

What happened next was so quick that only later could Jude piece together the sequence of events.

The back door crashed open and Martin Rutherford burst into the room.

For a moment his wife's aim wavered. Then she laughed and said, 'Don't worry, Martin. I'm not going to shoot you. You're mine.'

Just as she steadied the automatic to target Jude's chest, Martin leapt forward. In the small space the gunshot was hideously loud. He let out a gasp of pain and dropped to the floor. But in his hand he held the captured gun.

Martina let out some curse in her own language and rushed out of the front of the salon. As Connie and Jude crouched down with towels, trying to staunch the blood pumping from Martin's shoulder, they heard the Jaguar screeching off into the night.

Carole and the police arrived almost simultaneously.

Chapter Thirty-eight

'The trouble is these days,' said Mim, 'children don't even learn the rudiments of politeness. Not even the rudiments. I mean, there was someone in our road the other day . . . not just visiting, he actually lives in the Shorelands Estate, where you'd have thought at the very least you'd get someone who was well brought-up . . .'

'You'd hope you would,' Theo agreed.

'. . . and this man said to me . . . Ooh, not so much off the top there, Connie. We don't want you going round Fethering like a skinhead, do we, Wally?'

'No, Mim, we don't.'

'Anyway, this man, he had the nerve to say to me . . . to me, mind, and you would have thought he could see I was someone who had been brought up with standards . . . and he said to me . . .'

Jude grinned across at her neighbour, as if to say, 'See, I told you it was worth seeing.' Carole had not been keen on the idea of their having their hair cut at the same time, but the promised attraction of the Wally and Mim double act had won her round.

It was nearly three weeks after Martina

Rutherford's arrest, a Tuesday, five weeks to the day after the Grenstons' last joint appointment. Fethering had settled down after its recent excitements, and, though well into October, the weather had remained so tranquil that there were dark mutterings about the melting of the polar ice-cap.

Apart from the fact that Nathan had been allowed to return to his family after only twenty-four hours of questioning, Jude had heard nothing of the Lockes. She would like to know for sure whether Bridget had returned to Rowley, but felt gloomily certain she had. She would also like to have heard that Rowley Locke's recent experiences had made him less of a control freak, but didn't feel much optimism about that either. All she really hoped was that Nathan got good A-levels and went to a university as far away from Fethering as possible. Then he would be able to develop his own personality.

The Grenstons' haircuts were finally finished. At Mim's insistence Connie had snipped a little more off above her husband's ears – 'don't want him walking through Fethering looking like the Abdominal Snowman.' Theo waved a mirror around behind Mim's head for her to check her flame-red Louise Brooks look. 'There, you'll have all the men flocking round, Mim.'

'Just like you do, Theo,' she said rather daringly.

He giggled prettily at the idea, then caught Carole's eye and grinned.

Mim paid for the haircuts and carefully distributed the tips. While Theo was helping her into her coat,

Wally sidled up to Jude and winked at her. 'Our secret, eh?' he whispered.

'Our secret,' she confirmed. 'Oh, and I was sorry to hear about Joe Bartos.'

'Yes, well, probably best. Not one for showing his feelings, but losing Krystina . . . that destroyed him. You know, there had been his previous family . . . then his second wife . . . I saw Jiri the night before he died. He said he was tired, very tired. He suffered a lot through his life. He never talked about such things, but I knew. And the next morning he just did not wake up. Joe had had enough of suffering. No, very sad, but he went quickly. How we all want to go, eh?'

'What's he talking about then?' asked Mim, mentally scolding herself for letting her husband escape her surveillance even for a moment.

'I was talking about death,' he replied with some dignity.

'Oh, death,' she said dismissively. 'We won't have to worry about that for some time yet. Now, come on, Wally, are you coming or not? We can't be wasting these good people's time with all your idle chit-chat. Come along.'

'Usual appointments?' asked Connie. 'Five weeks today for the two of you?'

'Please. 'Bye, Theo. Lovely to see you, Connie.'

'And you, Mim. Goodbye, Wally.'

'Goodbye, Connie. And good luck with Marnie!'

'Who's Marnie?' asked Jude, as she was settled into her chair.

'Oh.' Connie blushed prettily. 'Just an idea Martin

and I had. Still some way off yet, but, well . . . the Martin & Martina branding has got to go . . . given the circumstances . . . so I thought of calling the chain "Marnie". It's Martin and Connie put together.'

'As you are.'

'Exactly.'

'How is he?'

'On the mend. But he will be permanently disabled. Won't be able to cut hair again.'

'I'm sorry.'

'Never mind. I'll cut the hair. He can run the business. Now . . .' She unpinned the shapeless topknot and ran her fingers through Jude's long blonde hair, '. . . how would you like to have it today, Madame?'

'Today,' replied Jude, with a huge beam, 'I would like to have it short.'

'Hooray! Did you hear that, Theo?'

'I did indeed. Well, well, well. Today's clearly a day for taking a plunge.' He looked in the mirror at his client. 'And what about yours, Madame? Are you going to take the plunge too? How would you like yours today?'

'Same shape, but shorter,' said Carole Seddon stolidly.

After Connie's Clip Joint, they went to the Crown and Anchor for lunch. Ted Crisp recommended the Chilli con Carne with Rice. It was surprisingly delicious.

While they ate, they watched the landlord holding up his fingers and gleefully demonstrating something to a customer. 'No, everyone gets that wrong, you know. The fingers that all hairdressers use are . . . yes, the thumb, like you said. But the other one isn't the middle finger. It's the one between the middle finger and the little finger. And do you know, that's the only one that moves. The thumb stays completely still.'

The customer was appropriately frustrated by getting it wrong. 'So, deal was if I beat you, you buy a pint for Les here. All right?'

Les Constantine grinned in anticipation. The old shipwright had recently given up his regular booth for a seat at the bar. Now Ted had made him the recipient of his winnings on the hairdresser bet, there was a plentiful supply of free pints.

'Hey,' the landlord went on to his customer as he pulled the pint, 'I must tell you . . . there's this joke I heard. Polar Bear walks into a bar . . .'

Jude looked across at her friend, and grinned.

When Carole got back to High Tor, she went through the automatic processes of emptying the contents of the tumble dryer, folding her clothes and putting them away. She was interrupted by the phone. Picking up the receiver at her bedside, she heard Stephen's voice.

'Hello, Granny,' he said.

BLOOD AT THE BOOKIES

To Jake,

hoping he gets lucky on the horses

Chapter One

'Come on, everyone likes a bet,' said Jude.

'Well, I don't,' sniffed Carole.

The response was so characteristic and instinctive that her friend couldn't help smiling. In a world where everyone was encouraged to be 'hands-on' and 'touchy-feely', Carole Seddon's approach to life was always going to be 'hands-off' and 'keep-your-distance'. But those idiosyncrasies didn't diminish Jude's affection for her. And that February morning the affection was increased by the diminished state her neighbour was in. The response to the idea of betting would always have been sniffy, but on this occasion it had been accompanied by a genuine sniff. Carole was drowned by a virulent winter flu bug, and Jude felt the last emotion her neighbour would ever wish to inspire in anyone – pity.

'Anyway, I've promised Harold I'll go to the betting shop and put his bets on, so I can't not do it.'

'Huh,' was Carole's predictable response. Her pinched face looked even thinner behind her rimless glasses. The pale blue eyes were bleary and the short grey hair hung lank.

'Come on, it's one of the few pleasures Harold Peskett has at his age. And he's got this wretched flu just like you. It's the least I can do for him. I can't see that there's anything wrong with it.'

'It's encouraging bad habits,' came the prissy reply.

'Carole, Harold is ninety-two, for God's sake! I don't think I'm going to make his habits any worse at this stage of his life. And it's no hardship – I've got to go to the shops anyway, to get my stuff . . . and yours.'

'What do you mean – mine?'

'You're in no state to go out shopping.'

'Oh, I'm sure I will be later. I've got a touch of flu, that's all.'

'You look ghastly. You should go straight back to bed. I don't know why you bothered to get dressed this morning.'

Carole looked shocked. 'What, are you suggesting I should be lolling round the house in my dressing-gown?'

'No. As I say, I'm suggesting you should go back to bed and give yourself a chance of getting rid of this bug. Have you got an electric blanket?'

'Of course not!' Carole was appalled by the idea of such self-indulgence.

'Hot water-bottle?'

With some shame, Carole admitted that she did possess one of those luxury items. Jude picked the kettle up off the Aga and moved to fill it at the sink. 'Tell me where the hot water-bottle is and I'll—'

'Jude!' The name was spoken with considerable

2

asperity. 'This is my house, and I'll thank you to let me manage it in my own way.'

'I'm not stopping you from doing that. But you're ill, and there are some things you can't do at the minute.'

'I am not ill!' Carole Seddon rose assertively from her chair. But she was taken aback by the wave of giddiness that assailed her. She tottered, reached for the support of the kitchen table and slowly subsided back down.

A grin spread across Jude's plump face. Her brown eyes sparkled and the stacked-up blonde hair swayed as she shook her head in the most benign of I-told-you-so gestures. 'See. You can't even stand up. There's no way you could make it down Fethering High Street even as far as Allinstore. I will do your shopping for you, and you will go to bed.'

'There's nothing I want,' Carole mumbled with bad grace. 'I'm well stocked up with everything.'

'Not the kind of things you need. You need nice warming soups and things like that. Lucozade, whisky . . . When you're ill, you need to feel pampered.'

'What nonsense you do talk, Jude.' But the resistance was already diminishing. Carole felt so rotten that even her opposition to the idea of pampering, built up over more than fifty years, was beginning to erode.

What defeated her residual contrariness was the issue of her dog. Gulliver, slumped by the Aga in his usual state of Labrador passivity, was going to need walking very soon or there might be a nasty accident on the kitchen floor. What was more, the house was

completely out of dog food. And Carole was just not
strong enough to complete either of these tasks. Much
as it went against her every instinct, she was going to
need help. And getting that help from Jude, who had
already witnessed her parlous state, was preferable to
involving anyone else, letting a stranger into her life.
Grudgingly, Carole Seddon bit the bullet and agreed
that her neighbour should add to her own errands the
task of walking Gulliver out to buy some of his
favourite Pedigree Chum.

She still showed token resistance to the idea of
pampering. She certainly wouldn't contemplate the
idea of Jude helping her undress and get back to bed.
But she did let slip where the hot water-bottle was to be
found.

Jude was discreet enough to tap on the bedroom
door before she entered with the filled bottle and a
steaming drink. She looked at the drained face peering
miserably over the edge of the duvet. 'There. At least
you look a bit more comfortable.'

'I'll be all right,' said Carole, who hated the notion of
being ill.

'Don't worry. We'll soon get you better.'

'What do you mean – "we"?' A spark of disgust came
into the pale blue eyes. 'You're not going to try and *heal*
me, are you?'

Again Jude had difficulty suppressing a grin.
Nothing would ever shift her neighbour's antipathy to
the idea of healing . . . or indeed any other alternative
therapy.

'I promise I am not going to try and heal you. It

4

wouldn't work, anyway. Bugs like this just sort themselves out in their own time.'

'Then who's this "we"?' Carole persisted suspiciously.

'For heaven's sake, it's just a figure of speech. "*We*'ll get you better" – it doesn't mean anything more than the fact that I'll keep an eye on you, see you've got everything you need.'

'Oh, but I don't want you to . . .' The words trickled away as Carole realized just how ghastly she did actually feel. She had no more resistance left.

'Anyway,' said Jude cheerily, 'we – or "I" if you prefer – have got to see you're all right by Sunday.'

'Why?'

'I thought you said that's when Stephen and Gaby are bringing Lily down to see you.'

But this reminder of her status as a grandmother didn't bring any warmth of Carole's manner. 'No,' she said, 'I've put them off.'

'What?'

'I don't want to breathe germs over the baby, do I?' replied Carole piously.

It was in a way the correct answer, but it stimulated an anxiety within Jude about how Carole was adjusting to her new role as a grandmother. Still, this was not the appropriate moment to follow up on that. She handed the hot drink across to her patient.

Carole sniffed. 'It's got whisky in it,' she said accusingly.

'Of course it has,' said Jude.

*

Jude was unused to walking a dog, but Gulliver's equable temper did not make the task difficult. His benevolence was more or less universal. When he barked it was from excitement, and his encounters with other dogs were playful rather than combative. Most important, he was never aware that Carole, not a natural dog person, had only bought one so that she wouldn't be thought to be lonely as she was seen walking with him around Fethering.

After her divorce and what she still thought of as her premature retirement from the Home Office, Carole Seddon had planned her life in Fethering so that she would be completely self-sufficient. She didn't want other people in her life, and Gulliver had been just one of the defence mechanisms she had carefully constructed to prevent such intrusions.

But then Jude had moved into Woodside Cottage next door, and even Carole found her resistance weakened by the charm of her new neighbour's personality. Jude rarely spoke about her past, but the details she did let slip led Carole to deduce that it had been a varied – not to say chequered – one. There was something of the former hippy about Jude. She was a healer and had introduced into the bourgeois fastness of Woodside Cottage such exotic items as crystals and wind-chimes. It would have been hard to imagine a more unlikely friend for Carole Seddon, but, though Carole would never have admitted it out loud, she valued the friendship more than almost anything else in her life.

Jude took Gulliver on to the beach and let him scamper around off the lead, playing elaborate war games with weed-fringed plastic bottles and lumps of polystyrene. She allowed him twenty minutes of this, while she scrunched to and fro on the shingle. Then she let out a hopeful whistle, and was gratified that Gulliver came obediently to heel and let her reattach the lead.

It was a typical early February day. Though the people of West Sussex bemoaned the lack of winter snow and spoke ominously of global warming, the weather proved itself able still to come up with good old-fashioned coldness. Jude's face, the only part of her not wrapped in a swathe of coats and scarves, was stung by the air, and underfoot the pebbles were joined by links of ice.

She did her shopping at Allinstore, the town's only supermarket (though many Fethering residents reckoned the prefix 'super' in that context was an offence under the Trades Descriptions Act). Jude bought organically when it came to meat and fresh vegetables, but she was not proscriptive about it. There were also baked beans on her shelves and hamburgers in her fridge. She knew her own body and, though she generally ate healthily, she would occasionally indulge in a massive fry-up or a fish supper in one of the local cafés. Jude believed that in all things well-being came from variety.

As well as the Pedigree Chum and a couple of other items her neighbour had asked for, Jude bought some of the things she thought Carole *needed*. As she had said, warming soups, Lucozade and whisky. Jude was very definite about the style in which one should be ill.

Illness made you feel miserable, so there was no point in making yourself feel even more miserable. Pampering was the answer. Oh yes, and of course, magazines. *Country Life* and *Marie-Claire*. She bought them, already relishing Carole's reaction to such frivolous extravagance.

As she emerged from Allinstore the heavens opened, vindictively spitting down a fusillade of hailstones. The parade was suddenly evacuated, as the denizens of Fethering rushed for shelter. So fierce was the blizzard that Jude, scuttling to her destination, could hardly see a foot in front of her face. Fortunately, the betting shop had a projecting canopy over its frontage, and she was able to tie Gulliver's lead to a metal ring which would keep him out of the weather.

Fethering High Street still had an old-fashioned parade of shops. Although this meant there weren't many of them, it did ensure that they were all close together. But the choice was limited. You could still get your hair styled at what used to be Connie's Cuts but had now been made-over and rebranded as 'Marnie'. You could still investigate house purchase at Urquhart & Pease or one of the other estate agents. But in the previous ten years the independent butcher and greengrocer had both closed and been replaced by charity shops.

And Sonny Frank's, the former independent bookmaker's, had been taken over by one of the major national chains. This Jude knew from no less an authority than Sonny Frank himself, who had been unable to cut his links with the business completely and was still a fixture on the premises. Sonny, who in his days as a bookie had been known as 'Perfectly' Frank, always sat on a tall stool near the betting shop's central pillar, from where he could command a good view of the wall of television screens, as well as the enclosed counter where bets were taken and winnings paid.

And, sure enough, there he was at one-thirty that Thursday afternoon, when Jude hurried in from the sleet to put on Harold Peskett's bets. Sonny Frank was a small man, whose arms and legs seemed almost irrelevant appendages to the round ball of his body. On top of this was another ball, his head, across which dyed black hair had been combed over so tight that it looked as though it had been painted on. He wore a frayed suit in subdued colours but large checks, and he greeted Jude cheerfully. Sonny Frank greeted everyone who went into the shop cheerfully, as though he were still its owner, but he held back an extra ration of cheerfulness for attractive women.

Though Jude had popped in sporadically since she'd been a Fethering resident, during the fortnight of Harold Peskett's flu she had become a regular, so Sonny knew her name. 'Hello, Jude darling. You look like you just come out of the fridge.'

Sure enough, in the short dash from Allinstore to the betting shop, her head and shoulders had taken on an encrustation of ice.

'Yes, look at it out there. It's quite revolting.'

'I would look at it, but I can't see a thing.' It was

9

true. The opposite side of the road was invisible through the icy downpour.

'So we're all much snugger in here, Jude. So . . . got a hot tip for me today, have you . . . as the actress said to the bishop?'

'You're much more likely to know something than I am, Sonny,' Jude replied, as she brushed the ice off her shoulders. 'You're the one with the inside knowledge.'

'Don't you believe it, darling. What you've got and I haven't is women's intuition.'

'A fat lot of good that's ever done me.'

'What, with the men or the horses?'

'Either. Both totally unreliable.'

'What's old Harold up for today then?'

'Heaven knows.' She reached into her pocket and flourished a sheaf of closely written betting slips. 'All his usual trebles and Yankees and goodness knows what. I don't understand what he does – I just put the bets on.'

It was true. Harold Peskett's betting system was arcane and deeply personal. Every morning he spent two hours religiously scouring the *Racing Post* and checking the tips given in the *Sun*, *Daily Express* and *Daily Mirror* before coming up with his recipe for 'the big win'. This involved a complex combination of horses at meetings across the country in formulations which, to the untrained eye, made Fermat's Last Theorem look straightforward. The total sum invested never exceeded two pounds, so it didn't make too many inroads into his pension. And at least his betting habit kept the ninety-two-year-old off the streets.

Jude handed over the betting slips to the vacuously beautiful blonde behind the counter, whose name badge proclaimed her to be 'Nikki'. She got an automatic 'Thank you', but not the automatic smile she would have received had she been a man. Behind the girl, the shop's manager, Ryan, fiddled on the keyboard of a computer. He was an edgy and uncommunicative man in his mid-thirties, thin with nervous dark eyes and with spiky black hair that could never quite be flattened by comb or brush. He always seemed to be sucking a peppermint. Both he and Nikki were dressed in the blue and black livery of their employers. Supported by other part-time staff, Ryan and Nikki provided the continuity of the betting shop. Though there was a lot of banter flying about the place, they never really joined in. They produced the manufactured smiles they had been taught during their training, but neither gave much impression of enjoying the job.

'So . . .' asked Sonny Frank, as Jude passed him on the way to the door, 'know anything?'

It was another of his regular lines. And anyone incautious enough to ask what he meant – as Jude had been when he first said it to her – would be treated to the full explanation. As a young man Sonny had actually met Edgar Wallace, who, as well as being a prolific writing phenomenon, was also an obsessive gambler. And Wallace's opening gambit to betting friends had always been the punter's eternal search for the life-changing tip: 'Know anything?'

'You've already asked me, Sonny, and I've already said you're the one with the inside knowledge.'

The ex-bookie looked elaborately furtive, then leaned forward on his stool till his cracked lips were very close to Jude's ear and his purple cheek brushed against the hanging tendrils of her hair. 'Well, as it happens . . . I do know a good thing.'

'Oh?'

'1.40 at Wincanton. Hasn't raced for over two hundred days. Gonna romp home.'

Jude looked out of the window. Still the sleet fell relentlessly. But Gulliver, under his sheltering roof, had lain down with his front paws forward and looked perfectly content. Maybe she could leave him out there a little longer. 'Which horse are you talking about?' she whispered, knowing that Sonny wouldn't broadcast his tip to the entire room.

He pointed up to the screen displaying the odds for the Wincanton race. 'Seven down,' he murmured. 'Number Four.'

The horse's name was Nature's Vacuum.

'If you're going to bet, do it quickly. That twenty to one won't last.'

Jude looked at the central screen, where the horses were ambling their way towards the start. Down in Wincanton the weather looked almost springlike. She wished she were there rather than Fethering.

'Go on, are you going to have a punt?'

She took one more dutiful look out of the window. In spite of the ice bouncing off the pavement only feet away from him, Gulliver's tail was actually wagging. He really did have a very nice nature.

'Why not?' replied Jude.

12

Chapter Two

As she sat down and looked around her at the punters
trying to read the runes of the racing pages spread over
the walls, Jude reflected on the unique egalitarianism
of betting shops. She had encountered a few that had
been silent and dour, but she'd never been in one
where she'd felt uncomfortable. True, a less secure soul
might have objected to the casual sexism that was
the norm in such places, but she had never found the
remarks flung at her less than good-natured. With an
inward giggle, she wondered whether Carole would feel
equally at ease in the environment.

Her bet was placed. Five pounds on Nature's
Vacuum. And she had managed to get the twenty to
one – Nikki had written the price on her slip. As Sonny
predicted, the odds on the horse had come down in the
minutes before the off. Somebody knew something.
The twenty to one gave way to sixteen to one. Fourteen
to one. The starting price might even be twelves.

With the instinctive reaction of all punters, Jude
was already beginning to feel that she was in profit.
At fourteen to one, a fiver on the win would only bring
in seventy pounds. Whereas the fiver she'd put on

at twenty to one would bring in a hundred. She was thirty quid up even before the race started. That there was a hot odds-on favourite called Girton Girl and that Nature's Vacuum remained a rank outsider were irrelevant details. In the mind of a punter the law of probability never carries as much weight as the law of possibility. And in the extraordinarily unlikely event of Nature's Vacuum not winning, Jude reckoned the rush of excitement she was feeling at that moment was well worth a fiver.

She looked around at the betting shop's other occupants and recognized plenty. There was a pair of decorators whose names she knew from overhearing their conversation to be Wes and Vic. The spatters of fresh paint on their overalls suggested that they were actually working, but the frequency with which they rushed in and out of the betting shop made Jude glad they weren't working for her. Over the years she'd seen them almost every time she had been in, which prompted the bizarre idea that they only took on decorating commissions within walking distance of the place. Wes and Vic were not men who kept their emotions to themselves. Every hope and disappointment was vocalized. Horses and greyhounds, subjects of veneration and hope before their races, were quickly and loudly vilified when they lost.

The other infallible attendees were the waiters from Fethering's only Chinese restaurant, the Golden Palace. There were never less than two and sometimes as many as five, all young, dressed in their uniform of

BLOOD AT THE BOOKIES

black shirts and trousers, constantly chattering to each
other in high chopped tones.

Another regular was a grey-haired man, dressed
unfailingly in a suit and sober tie and carrying a briefcase. He looked like an accountant, who in retirement
had chosen to continue working in a variation of his
former profession, turf accountancy. And, according to
Sonny Frank, that's what he was. He noted his bets,
successes and failures in an old-fashioned ledger, and
his face remained impassive, regardless of the outcome. Though he had never spoken directly to her,
Jude had overheard him placing bets at the counter.
His accent was extremely cultured.

There was also a female regular, whose presence
might have reassured a less confident woman than
Jude about entering such a predominantly male
enclave. A dumpy, white-haired woman, whom again
Jude had seen whenever she'd been in. Every day the
woman sat in the same chair and, without being particularly outgoing, seemed to be perfectly friendly with
everyone. Her name was Pauline, and she was habitu-
ally surrounded by scraps of racing pages torn out of
newspapers. In the early days Jude had always seen
her with a fag in her mouth and a full ashtray in front
of her, but now the woman was obedient to the smoking ban. The attraction of betting was apparently
stronger than that of tobacco.

Sonny Frank, who always spoke nostalgically of the
past history of bookmaking, and thought things had
gone downhill since the days when his father and he
took illegal bets in the back rooms of pubs, reckoned

15

the smoking ban was another nail in the coffin of the industry he loved. 'Punters just won't come in,' he'd say. 'And now they can do it all at home online, anyway. Soon won't be any high street betting shops left.'

While his prognostication might be true in the long term, Jude reckoned the Fethering business still looked fairly healthy. And, from her own point of view, she thought the smoking ban was an inestimable improvement. It was now possible to spend five minutes in a betting shop without emerging reeking of tobacco.

As the horses on the screen lined up for the 1.40, a change came over the room. Even with the number of races scheduled – at least three meetings for the horses, interspersed with the greyhounds, not to mention computer-generated virtual racing – there was still a moment of intense concentration before the 'off' of each one.

'Come on, Girton Girl, you can do it,' said the decorator Wes.

'No way,' said Sonny Frank. 'Iffy jumper if ever I saw one. Came down three out last time out at Uttoxeter.'

'But that was the jockey,' Vic, the other decorator, countered. 'Useless apprentice. She's got McCoy up today.'

'Which is why she's down to eleven to eight,' Wes contributed.

'Still an iffy jumper.'

'What you on then, Sonny?'

'The winner.'

'Oh yeah? So you're on Girton Girl too, are you?'

The globular old man chuckled. 'No, no, I recognize rubbish when I see it. Remember – bookies never lose.'

'*Ex*-bookies do,' said Wes.

'Ssh, they're away,' said Vic.

There was an animated exchange between the Chinese waiters and then a moment of relative silence – interrupted only by the endless jingles from the slot machines and the hiss of the sleet-storm outside – descended on the room as the punters listened to the race commentary. One horse had got left at the start and, by the time it got into its running, was some seven lengths away from its nearest rival. The horse was Nature's Vacuum. Oh dear, thought Jude.

The odds-on favourite, Girton Girl, meanwhile, seemed contemptuous of her opposition and swept over the first fence four lengths ahead of the rest of the field.

'Gone too soon,' shouted Sonny Frank.

'Cobblers,' came the riposte from Wes. 'That horse stays like the mother-in-law.'

'Others never going to catch her,' Vic agreed.

'Don't you believe it,' said Sonny.

Amongst the desultory cries of 'Yes, yes!' and 'Move it, you lump of cat's meat!' Jude was vaguely aware that a new customer had come into the betting shop. He was a man in his twenties, his face pale and pinched. The reddish hair was cut very short and he was muffled up in a dark blue overcoat that looked almost naval. His head and shoulders were frosted with ice. He stood by the doorway, as though looking for someone. He swayed slightly. Perhaps he'd had too good a lunch at

17

the Crown and Anchor. Jude was too preoccupied with the race to take much notice of him. And a shout from Sonny Frank of 'What did I tell you, Jude?' brought her attention firmly back to the screen.

And yes, after that pathetic start, Nature's Vacuum was slowly picking his way through the field. First past the exhausted stragglers, then the one-paced hopefuls, till he'd got himself up to fourth place.

Jude found herself instinctively joining in the shouts of encouragement. 'Come on, Nature's Vacuum!' she yelled.

Three fences to go. Nature's Vacuum looked full of running. But then so did the favourite. The distance between Girton Girl and the second horse was increasing rather than diminishing. She avoided the fate that had ended her hopes at Uttoxeter, and sailed over the third from last like a gazelle.

'Hang on in there, Nature's Vacuum!' shouted Jude. But for the first time she was assailed by doubt. Sonny's tip had been right in a sense. Nature's Vacuum was a good prospect, certainly much better than the odds suggested, and maybe he'd soon win a race. But it didn't look like being this one at Wincanton.

The contest wasn't over yet, though. With an effort of will she clamped down on her negative thoughts. Her horse remained upright, she was still in with the chance of a hundred quid. 'Come on, Nature's Vacuum! You can do it!'

At the penultimate fence the horse came up alongside the long-time second, and put in a flying leap which gave him a length advantage. But he still had five lengths to make up on the leading filly, who looked to be coasting home.

'That's the way, Gertie!' shouted Wes.

'Go on, my son!' roared Vic. (People in racing have never been too specific about the names and genders of horses.)

Sonny Frank and Jude just sat and watched.

Running up to the last, Nature's Vacuum maybe picked up half a length, but it looked like being too little, too late. Wes and Vic's beams threatened to split their faces. 'Come on, my son!' they roared together. There was no way Girton Girl could lose.

National Hunt racing, though, is an unpredictable sport. The favourite approached the last at a slight angle, cleared it fine, but then veered alarmingly off towards the rail. Nature's Vacuum took a dead straight line and put in a superb jump. That, together with Girton Girl's detour, meant that by the time the two horses were again together on the run-in, the second was less than a length behind. Both jockeys flashed away with their whips and used every ounce of their own energy to drive their horses forward. Nature's Vacuum drew alongside, then Girton Girl seemed to find a new reservoir of strength and regained the lead. But neither wanted to come second, and Nature's Vacuum surged again.

They crossed the line together and the photograph was called.

'Which one was it?' shrieked Jude.

'Gertie got there,' declared Wes with dispiriting certainty.

'I wouldn't be so sure,' said Sonny. 'The angle's deceptive at Wincanton. I think the other one's the winner.' Still he didn't declare an interest in either horse.

'And I think the result's coming . . .' the commentator announced.

'Number Four,' boomed over the racecourse's PA system. 'The winner was Number Four. Second, Number Seven. Third, Number Two. The distances were a short head and seven lengths.'

Jude turned with glee to look at Sonny Frank. The old bookie winked at her.

'Always knew it was a crap horse,' said Wes, crumpling up his betting slip.

'Iffy jumper,' Vic agreed, doing the same.

And the two of them went off to do a few minutes' decorating before the next race. Outside, the sleet had stopped as suddenly as it had started.

In a state of euphoria Jude rushed towards the counter. The young man in the naval overcoat was still swaying by the doorway. She grinned at him, feeling benevolent towards the entire world, and was rewarded by a weak but rather charming smile which revealed discoloured teeth.

Jude went to collect her hundred and five pounds (a hundred winnings, five pound stake) from an impassive Nikki and once again turned to thank Sonny.

'Going to have a flutter on the next?' he asked, as he folded a large pile of winnings into his back pocket.

Like all punters, she was tempted. Maybe this wasn't

just a one-off win . . .? Maybe it was the beginning of a winning streak . . .? Maybe her luck was in . . .?

But a glimpse of Gulliver outside reminded her of her priorities. The hailstorm might have ended, but the poor dog must be feeling pretty cold. No, she wouldn't bet again. She would do what all gamblers intend – and almost always fail – to do: stop after a big win. She thanked Sonny Frank profusely for the tip and, picking up her Allinstore carriers, made for the door.

The young man in the blue naval overcoat was no longer there. Off to lie down somewhere, sleep off the booze, Jude conjectured.

And then she saw it. A circle of dark fluid seeping into the carpet tiles by the door. Against the blue the red turned almost purple. She didn't have to touch it to recognize it was blood.

More drips had stained coin-sized marks, tracing the man's exit from the betting shop. Without a word to anyone, Jude followed them.

Outside, she freed Gulliver from the ring he'd been tied to and held his lead tightly. As she pulled him in the direction the red spots on the pavement indicated, the Labrador sniffed at one and then almost pulled her arm out of its socket as he followed the track. His first experience of being a bloodhound, and Gulliver liked it.

The trail of blood, though diluted by the melting sleet, was still easy to follow.

They didn't have far to go. Alongside the betting shop was a narrow alley which led round the back of

the building to a small area of scrub that gave access to
Fethering Beach.

He hadn't made it all the way down the alley. The
bloodspots grew bigger and bigger until they coalesced
into a widening stream.

At the end of which lay the man in the navy overcoat.

He hardly breathed and his eyes were glazing over.
As Jude knelt down beside him, he murmured some-
thing in a heavily accented voice. It sounded like
'Fifi . . .'

A moment later the man was dead.

Chapter Three

Jude had rung Carole on the mobile to say she would be delayed in bringing her shopping back, though she didn't specify the reason. And when she finally got back to Woodside Cottage after being questioned by the police, she rang again on the landline. They had long ago exchanged spare keys, but Jude knew that her neighbour never liked being surprised by an unannounced visit, even from her. Carole Seddon endeavoured to organize her life so that it involved the minimum of surprises. The slipping in and out of people's houses in which some people indulged was anathema to her. It was one of those habits for which Carole reserved one of her adjectives expressing major disapprobation: northern.

Inside High Tor, Jude, having served Gulliver a large helping of his long-wished-for Pedigree Chum, went upstairs to see the invalid.

It was a measure of the severity of Carole's flu that, having granted permission for the visit, she hadn't got out of bed to greet her guest. And in her reduced state even the news of a suspicious death in Fethering High Street didn't bring the animation it usually would have done. The questions she asked were listless, and Jude almost had to insist on telling her the known details of what had happened.

'As ever, the police didn't volunteer much information, but then I don't think they had much information to volunteer. Until they've established the identity of the dead man, they haven't really got anything to go on. I can tell you, though, that he wasn't a regular at the betting shop.'

Jude waited to be asked how she knew that, but with no question forthcoming, continued her monologue. 'The detectives took me back into the shop after I'd shown them the body, and they asked general questions to everyone who was there. Most of the punters hadn't even noticed the guy, but Ryan the Manager – who I guess makes it his business to clock everyone who comes in – said he'd never seen him before.'

She waited for a further prompt, but didn't get one. 'Obviously, having only seen him in the overcoat, I don't know which part of his body the blood was coming from, and it could be something natural . . . a haemorrhage of some kind . . . but I'm afraid my first thought was murder.'

This word did bring a small spark to Carole's pale blue eyes. Probably the activity she'd most enjoyed since her retirement to Fethering had been the investigation of murders with Jude.

'If it was murder,' her neighbour went on, 'then the most obvious thought would be that it was a stabbing. I suppose it could also be a gunshot wound . . . Either

24

way, the actual attack didn't happen in the betting shop.'

'Are you sure?' asked Carole, intrigued in spite of herself.

'Positive. He came in through the front door.'

'Is it just the one room?' asked Carole, who prided herself on never having been inside a betting shop.

'Well, there are offices behind the counter . . . and there are the toilets . . . and presumably there is a back entrance,' Jude added thoughtfully. 'But he definitely came in at the front. It was as if he was looking for something . . . Or maybe someone.' The skin around her brown eyes tightened as she tried to work it out. 'And I'm pretty sure he must have put the overcoat on after he was stabbed – or shot or whatever it was.'

'What makes you think that?'

'The lack of visible blood. It was a thick coat. If he'd put it on after he'd been wounded, then it would have taken a while for the blood to seep through.'

'There's one odd thing . . .' mused Carole, now firmly hooked in spite of her illness.

'What?'

'Why didn't he ask for help?'

'Sorry?'

'Here's this man, seriously wounded – mortally wounded, as it turned out – and he must know that he's hurt . . . and he staggers into a public place, the betting shop, surrounded by people . . . and he doesn't say a thing. You'd have thought, in those circumstances, almost anyone would have said something . . . would have asked for a doctor to be called, or an ambulance . . .

But he didn't say anything. Or did he, Jude? Did he say anything to you?'

'Not in the betting shop, no. He just smiled.' And the image of that weak smile brought home to her the horror of what she had witnessed. An involuntary shiver ran through her plump body.

'Well,' Carole continued, joining the links in her chain of logic, 'the fact that he didn't say anything . . . didn't draw attention to himself, even though he was dying . . . suggests, wouldn't you say, that the man had something to hide?'

'Yes,' said Jude, 'I suppose it could.'

'And if we find out what he was trying to hide, then we'll probably be a good way to finding out why he was killed.'

Jude wasn't really convinced by that line of enquiry. But it was the only one they had.

Both women realized that they had been letting their imaginations run away with them. They didn't even know that the death had been unnatural, and already they were building up pictures of a man with a guilty secret. Both were sheepish, feeling that the wildness of their conjectures was about to be shown up, as they waited for the early evening television news. Carole had roused her aching limbs and come down to the sitting room to watch. Jude had offered to bring the television upstairs, but her neighbour had been appalled by the idea. For Carole having a television in a bedroom was an unpardonable offence against decency, on the level with actually watching the thing during the daytime (though there was an afternoon chat show to which she was becoming almost addicted, but that was a secret vice).

The killing in Fethering was deemed sufficiently important to make the national news, and the bulletin did at least provide them with some solid information. The dead man had been identified as Tadeusz Jankowski, aged twenty-four. He was a Polish immigrant who had been in Britain less than six months. He had died of stab wounds and the police were launching a murder investigation.

Though it was an awful thing to think, both Carole and Jude would have been terribly disappointed if he'd turned out to have died a natural death.

That evening Jude, still more shaken than she liked to admit to herself, decided that she'd have supper at Fethering's only pub, the Crown and Anchor. Before she left High Tor she heated up some soup, but the invalid didn't seem interested in eating. Carole just sipped a little Lucozade and looked with affronted fascination at the magazines she had been given. Jude had a feeling that the minute she was alone in the house, Carole would pounce on them and start reading. The offer of a hot toddy was refused, but Jude said she'd come in later and maybe make one then. After her surge of excitement over the murder, Carole had now slumped back into total lethargy and voiced no objections to the idea of another visit from her neighbour.

In the Crown and Anchor it didn't take long for the subject to get round to Fethering's latest murder. After his usual pleasantries to Jude and the quick provision of her customary large Chilean Chardonnay, the landlord Ted Crisp was on to it straight away. 'Nasty business down by the betting shop this afternoon.'

'Tell me about it. I was the one who found the poor soul.'

'Were you? Blimey, you and your mate Carole certainly have a knack of being in the wrong place at the wrong time. Where is she, by the way?'

'Laid up with flu.'

'Poor thing. Give her my best.'

'Will do.' It was still at times incongruous to Jude that her fastidious neighbour had once had a brief fling with the scruffy bearded landlord of the Crown and Anchor. That evening he was in his habitual faded jeans, though in deference to the cold weather he was wearing a faded zip-up hoodie over his customary faded sweatshirt.

'Immigrant, I gather from the news,' he said darkly. In spite of his background as a stand-up comedian, Ted Crisp was capable of being, to Jude's mind, distressingly right-wing.

His point was quickly taken up by another customer, a man in his fifties, dressed in tweed jacket, salmon pink corduroy trousers and a tie that looked as if it should have been regimental but probably wasn't. He was thick-set, but in quite good condition. His receding hair was sandy, freckled with grey. He was accompanied by a younger, similarly dressed version of

28

himself, who had to be his son. The boy was probably mid-twenties, large and slightly ungainly, with a thick crest of auburn hair. What might once have been a well-muscled body was on the verge of giving way to fat.

Jude knew the older man by sight. He worked in one of Fethering's estate agencies on the parade (however small the town in West Sussex, there always seemed to be business for more than one estate agent). The agency was called Urquhart & Pease, though whether the man had one of those as his surname Jude didn't know.

'Been only a matter of time before something like this happened,' he announced in a voice that had been to all the right schools. 'Ever since the wretched EU opened up our boundaries to all and sundry, it's been an accident waiting to happen. I mean, I'm the last person to be racist . . .' Wasn't it strange, Jude reflected, how people who started sentences like that always ended up being exactly what they denied they were '. . . but I do think we ought to have a bit of a say in who we let into our country. We are islanders, after all, with everything that goes with that . . . and we have a long history of doing things our way. And I'm not saying all immigration is bad. I'm as tolerant as the next man . . .' Which in West Sussex, thought Jude, wasn't saying a lot '. . . and I've got friends and colleagues who . . . What are you allowed to say now? Have different ethnic backgrounds . . .? Pakistani chap works as our accountant, and he fits in, you'd never know . . . Doesn't he, Hamish?'

The younger man agreed that their Pakistani

accountant did fit in, and listened dutifully as the estate agent pontificated on. 'But I still do think you have to draw the line somewhere . . . or we'll see more things happening like we did today.'

Jude didn't want to get drawn into the conversation – she knew she'd be on a hiding to nothing – but she couldn't help asking, 'So you think this man was murdered because he was an immigrant?'

'Obviously.' He flashed her an urbane and slightly patronizing smile. 'I'm sorry, we don't know each other. Ewan Urquhart.' So he was one of the partners in the agency. 'And my son Hamish.'

'This is Jude,' said Ted Crisp, as though he'd been remiss in not making the introduction before.

'I've seen you walking along the High Street,' said the estate agent. 'Never fail to notice an attractive woman, you know.' It was a knee-jerk compliment, a little too smoothly delivered. Jude decided she would not buy a house from this man.

'But, Mr Urquhart, you were saying—'

'Ewan, please.'

'Ewan. You seemed to be making the assumption that this man's death must have happened because he was an immigrant . . .?'

'Well, my dear, in a situation like this the law of probability kicks in, doesn't it? Get the country full of foreigners and they bring their own ways with them. So you get welfare scroungers, gangs, people traffickers . . .' He seemed to be picking randomly at *Daily Mail* headlines. 'And then with the ones from the Indian subcontinent you get these so-called "honour killings". Bumping your sister off because you don't like her choice of boyfriend. I mean, what kind of behaviour is that?'

'Barbaric,' his son supplied.

'You're right, Hamish. It's barbaric. A culture of violence. We never used to have a culture of violence in this country.'

'No? What about our good old traditional soccer hooligans . . .?' Jude was tempted to add, 'or our good old traditional public schools . . .?', but didn't.

Ewan Urquhart smiled blandly. He was clearly a man who thought he had a way with women and knew how to deal with their little foibles. 'Ah, now I think you're just being perverse, Jude. Much as we'd all like to believe there's no connection between increased immigration and the crime statistics, I'm afraid the facts don't leave much room for doubt. If you leave your borders open, it's inevitable that you're going to get a lot of riff-raff coming in. For me, I'm afraid, it all goes back to joining the Common Market. Worst move this country ever made.'

He was clearly preaching to the converted as far as Ted Crisp was concerned. 'Couldn't agree with you more, Ewan. I don't want to be ordered about by bloody Brussels.'

'Nor me,' Hamish managed to slip in before his father continued. 'Being British used to be a cause for pride. Not showing-off pride like some other countries are so fond of. Not standing up and saying "Aren't I wonderful?" pride. But that quiet British pride that just does the right thing without crowing about it. And where's that gone, I ask you? God knows. Now our bloody politicians seem to be apologizing all the time . . . desperate not to offend anyone "of a different ethnic background". Margaret Thatcher never used to apologize for being British.'

Surely Ted was going to take issue with that? In his stand-up days Thatcher-bashing had been a major ingredient of his material. But he said nothing, as Ewan Urquhart steamrollered on. 'Things like this murder should be a wake-up call, you know. Get people to stop and think what we're actually doing to this country by allowing uncontrolled immigration. As I say, I'm not a racist, but I do think there comes a point when you have to recognize that enough is enough.'

'You're too right, Dad,' said Hamish.

Jude had intended to have supper in the Crown and Anchor. But as Ewan Urquhart continued his tub-thumping, and as Ted Crisp and Hamish continued to agree with him, the prospect became less attractive. When she'd finished the one Chilean Chardonnay, she went back to Woodside Cottage. She'd find something in the fridge.

Chapter Four

Carole Seddon's flu was slow to shift, but after the weekend the prospect of life continuing in some form did once again seem a possibility. She was pleased to feel better, but also guiltily relieved that it had lasted as long as it did. The weekend had been one she was dreading, and she was glad that the flu had prevented her from participating in it. Being Carole Seddon, she was also worried about the extent to which she had used the illness as an excuse.

The event she had avoided was a meeting with her son Stephen, his wife Gaby and their four-month-old daughter Lily. But it wasn't them Carole didn't want to see. Since the baby's birth she had actually bonded more with the young couple, happy on occasions to go and help her daughter-in-law out at their Fulham house. And she found Lily a miracle. That something so tiny and so perfect could suddenly exist was a source of constant amazement to her. Though she was the last person to go all gooey in public about babies, Carole did find she was suffering from considerable internal gooeyness. Of course she didn't vocalize such self-indulgent thoughts, but they did give her a warm glow.

It was all so different from when she'd had Stephen. Then she'd been in such turmoil, finding herself in the one state she had tried to avoid all her life – out of control. The strange things that had happened to her body, the demanding new presence in her life, the realignment of her relationship with her husband . . . everything conspired to make her feel threatened and useless. Had she gone to a doctor about her feelings, there might have been a diagnosis of mild post-natal depression, but Carole Seddon had always believed that doctors were there to deal with physical problems, not feelings. And depression was something that happened to other people.

So she hadn't been worried about seeing Lily and her parents at the weekend. In fact she longed to witness her granddaughter's every tiny development. But Stephen had included another person in the proposed visit to Fethering.

His father. Carole's ex-husband David. Stephen was still under the illusion that, because he'd seen his estranged parents together at social events – like his wedding – when they hadn't actually come to blows, a new rapprochement between them was possible. With a wistful innocence that made Carole feel even guiltier, her son was desperate to be part of a happy family. And, now Lily was on the scene, of a happy extended family.

It was an ambition that Carole couldn't share. Getting over the divorce had taken a good few years and at times it still felt like an open wound. But one of the important components of rehabilitation into her new single life had been not seeing David. Even the sound of his voice on the phone could upset her hard-won equilibrium for days on end.

As a result of this, she had bought a new telephone with a Caller Display facility. If David were to ring her, she could then identify his number and choose whether or not to take the call. So far he hadn't called – and in fact David's was the one set of digits where Carole's usual facility for remembering phone numbers failed (a psychological block no doubt, though she would never have recognized it as such). But the Caller Display did give her a sense of security.

The thought of seeing David in Fethering made Carole feel even more unsettled. High Tor had been bought as a weekend retreat for both of them in happier times, when the marriage was still more or less ticking over. Under the terms of the divorce settlement, Carole had taken sole possession, and had managed over the years to expunge all memories of their shared occupation. Seeing David back on the premises would stir up a hornets' nest of unwanted recollection.

As soon as she'd made the arrangement for the weekend, Carole had regretted it. Stephen had caught her in an unguarded moment, when she had been cuddling Lily, and at such times all the world seemed benign and she hadn't been able to refuse him. So the fated weekend had continued to loom ever larger on her horizon until the threat was removed by the mercy of her flu.

She felt deeply relieved that the encounter hadn't happened. But she was sorry not to have seen Lily.

Still, now she was feeling better, she could begin to focus her mind on the death of Tadeusz Jankowski. With the return of her health came a prurient wistfulness, almost a jealousy, prompted by the fact that Jude had witnessed the young man's dying moments. If there was to be an investigation, Carole wanted to be part of it. So she sought through the weekend papers and cut out all the coverage of the murder, anything that might have relevance to the case. She found quite a lot of material. Immigration, particularly from Poland, was a topical issue, and the murder had unleashed pages and pages of ill-informed speculation.

Jude was surprised it took till the Monday for the police to contact her again. They'd taken all her details when they'd questioned her on the Thursday, saying they'd be in touch. And on the old principle that the first suspect in a murder investigation tends to be the person who finds the body, she had expected them to show more interest in her.

But the two young detectives who came to Woodside Cottage seemed very relaxed. They certainly didn't give her the impression that she was a suspect and, given her previous experience of dealing with the police, were surprisingly generous with information.

'We're pretty sure,' said the one who was called Detective Sergeant Baines, 'that the victim had nothing to do with anyone in the betting shop that afternoon.'

'No one in there knew him?'

'No. We took statements from them all, you know,

after you'd gone. None of them knew him from Adam. The manager, who makes it his business to see who comes in and out, had never seen him before.'

'So why did he go into the betting shop?'

'No idea. Maybe he was walking past and, feeling weak after being stabbed, just went in there to sit down. Or to get some shelter from the hailstorm.'

'Don't you think it's odd he didn't ask for help?' asked Jude, reiterating Carole's point.

Baines shrugged. 'Perhaps he didn't know how badly injured he was. Perhaps he was already too weak to speak. Or he could have been in shock. I don't know.'

'And do you know where he actually was when he was stabbed?'

The other one, Detective Sergeant Yelland, exchanged a grin with Baines and said, 'If we knew that, we'd be well on the way to solving the case, wouldn't we?'

'But it can't have been far away, can it? Or there would have been more blood at the bookie's, wouldn't there?'

Unlike previous detectives Jude had met, these two didn't seem to object to her working out her own theories. 'Maybe,' said Baines. 'They won't really know till they get the detailed post-mortem report. It could have been an injury that didn't bleed much at first, but then got worse. In fact, that must have been the case, because there was no trail of blood leading towards the betting shop, only away from it.'

Jude found his use of the personal pronoun interesting. 'They' would get the post-mortem report, not 'we'. The main part of the investigation was going on elsewhere. Baines and Yelland were juniors, minor players in the game. Realizing this encouraged her to ask more questions.

'I just heard the man's name on the television. And they said he was Polish. Have you been able to find out much more about him?'

Baines showed no reticence in answering. 'He was from Warsaw. Finished at university there last year. Been doing casual bar work over here.'

'Do you know where he lived?'

'Rented room in Littlehampton.'

'Not far away . . .' Jude looked thoughtful. 'Have his family in Poland been contacted?'

Detective Sergeant Yelland seemed suddenly aware of the incongruity of the situation. 'Just a minute. Aren't we the ones who're meant to be asking you the questions?' But he sounded amused rather than resentful.

'I agree that's traditional,' said Jude with a winning smile. 'But you haven't asked many, and we don't want to sit here in silence, do we?'

Both men grinned. 'Yes, his family have been told,' Baines replied. 'And there's been contact with the Polish police authorities.'

'Oh?'

'Well, makes sense. Most likely the reason he was attacked is something to do with his own community. Probably goes back to some rivalry back home.'

'Can you be sure of that?'

'Can't be sure of much in our business,' said Yelland.

Jude now understood the explanation for their relaxed demeanour. Neither Baines nor Yelland was particularly interested in the case. They were underlings who did as they were told. They had been told to interview her and they were following their instructions. But they had no expectations that anything she might say would be useful to the investigation. They regarded the murder as a foreign case, which just happened to have taken place on their patch.

Jude decided to test the limits of their goodwill and persist in her questioning. 'I just wondered . . . whether it might be more local . . .?' Remembering Ewan Urquhart's pontificating in the Crown and Anchor the previous week, she went on, 'There does seem to be quite a lot of resentment of immigrants round here.'

'Not that much,' said Baines. 'In some of the inner city areas, yes, there are problems. But down here, it's not as if they're taking people's jobs or anything like that. Maybe a bit of trouble in the bigger cities . . . Brighton, Portsmouth, Southampton. Get a bit of racial conflict at chucking-out time, you know, the odd fight. But not somewhere as small as Fethering. We don't get called out much on disputes with immigrants, do we?'

Yelland agreed that they didn't.

'I would just have thought—'

'I can assure you that they are investigating every possibility.' Again Baines's tell-tale use of 'they'. 'And if there is someone local involved, I'm sure they'll find out about it. But the initial enquiries will be focusing on the Polish community.'

'Right.'

'So . . .' asked Yelland ironically, 'is there anything else you want to ask us?'

'Not at the moment. But if there are any further questions, I'll be in touch.'

Yelland grinned at his colleague. 'Stealing all our lines, isn't she?'

'Yes,' said Baines. 'And if you remember anything else you might think is relevant, you be in touch too.'

'Will do.'

'Or if there's anything you want to add to the statement you made on Thursday . . .?'

'I can't think of anything at the moment.'

'Fine. Well, if there's an arrest, you'll hear about it on the telly.'

But Detective Sergeant Baines didn't sound optimistic. Jude got the firm impression that neither he nor Yelland expected an early solution to the case. And that they weren't that bothered.

Chapter Five

After the murder the betting shop had been closed while the police made their forensic examination of the premises, but it was allowed to reopen on the Monday. Which, Jude extrapolated, meant that they had been expecting to receive little information there. It wasn't exactly a crime scene; the crime had happened elsewhere. Apparently detectives had made enquiries at other premises along the parade, but did not seem to have identified where the stabbing had taken place. Or if they had, they were keeping quiet about it.

No unsuspecting punter entering the betting shop on the Monday would have been aware that anything untoward had taken place there. But when she arrived that afternoon, Jude noticed that new, brighter blue carpet tiles had replaced the ones on to which the dying man's blood had dripped. The originals were presumably under scrutiny in a police laboratory.

She had come in again to place Harold Peskett's bets. The old man's flu seemed to be hanging on. He felt lousy, but he still wanted to keep up with what he insisted on calling his 'investments'. This had obviously been a problem over the weekend, with the betting shop closed, but Jude had found a solution. Using a laptop which she had inherited from a deceased lover, Laurence Hawker, she had opened up an online account.

The process had been so seductively easy that it gave her something of a shock. She had discovered that in a matter of moments anyone, armed only with an internet connection and a credit card, could have the capacity to lose money at will in the privacy of their own home. Jude was glad she didn't have an addictive personality. Bankruptcy had never been so readily available.

But she only used her new account to put on Harold Peskett's bets that weekend. Once the betting shop reopened, she thought it quite possible that she'd never log on again. She felt comforted to have the account, though. It was a convenience. If she fancied the name of a horse she saw in the paper or suddenly wanted to have a punt on the Grand National . . . well, the facility was there.

The regulars were in their allotted places when she arrived that Monday afternoon shortly before one. And they greeted her as one of their own. Nor was there any tasteful reticence about bringing up the subject uppermost in all their minds.

'So, who're you going to murder this afternoon, Jude?' asked Wes.

'Surprised they've allowed you out,' said Vic. 'On bail, are you?'

Sonny Frank came to her rescue. 'Leave the lady alone. She might still be in a state of shock.'

'I'm not, actually. But thanks for the thought, Sonny.'

'Well, from what I see on telly, with all those Poirots and Morses and what-have-you,' Wes went on, 'the one the police always go for is the one who found the body.'

'So I'm supposed to have stabbed the poor bloke outside, am I? Before I came in here?'

'You could have done,' said Vic wisely. 'You're the only one of us who's a suspect, Jude. You found the body.'

'All right.' Jude held up her arms in mock-surrender. 'I did it. What are you going to do – call the cops again?'

'No, we'll let you get away with this one,' Wes conceded generously. 'But you murder someone else and you're in trouble.'

All of this dialogue was lightly conducted, humour as ever diluting the awkwardness of an unpleasant situation. None of them was unaffected by the stranger's death; they were just finding ways of coping with it.

'Have any of you had follow-up calls from the police?'

None of them had. 'Thank goodness,' said Pauline. 'My old man always told me to keep clear of the police. If you don't talk to them, they can't twist your words in court, he always said.'

'But I heard you speaking to them on Thursday,' said Jude.

'Hadn't got much choice, had I? They come in here and asked us all to stay. If I'd legged it right then, they'd have thought I was well dodgy.'

'Suppose so. Well, I must do these bets for old Harold.' Jude moved across to the counter. Nikki was seated at a table checking through sheaves of betting slips. Ryan came to serve her. 'Presumably they asked you if you recognized the dead man?'

'Yes,' the manager replied.

Characteristically, he didn't volunteer any other information, so Jude prompted him. 'And you said you'd never seen him?'

'That's right.'

He turned away, wanting the conversation to end there, but Jude persisted. 'But you do normally check out everyone who comes through the door?'

'Yes. Part of the job. There are some villains about. Head Office sends us photos of the ones we got to watch out for. So I look at everyone.'

'And you didn't recognize him either, did you, Nikki?'

The girl looked up at Jude from her betting slips, her beautiful eyes blank. 'Wossat?'

'I was asking if you'd ever seen the dead man before?'

'Nah,' she replied. 'I never.'

'But do you normally check who comes in and out of the betting shop?'

Jude received one of those curious looks that the young reserve for the old and mad. 'Nah. Not my job, is it? Ryan does that. I just do what I have to do. Take the punters' bets. I don't have to notice who they are.'

Jude was inclined to believe her. She noticed the girl sported an engagement ring. And no doubt she made some young man very happy . . . so long as his demands didn't stretch to the intellectual.

'Know anything?' asked Sonny Frank, as Jude returned from the counter.

'About the murder or the horses?'

'Let's stick with the horses. A murder's a nine-day wonder, but horse racing is forever.'

'Well, I'd give you the same answer if you were talking about the murder or the horses. No, I don't know anything. How about you? And I am talking about horses. Know anything?'

He screwed up his round face into an expression of dubiety. 'Dunno.'

'Come on, Sonny, you won me a hundred quid on Thursday. You've got a reputation to keep up. Give me another tip.'

'All right. Here's a good 'un.' He beckoned her forward and whispered into her ear. '"A successful gambler doesn't bet more than he bets."'

'Meaning?'

'The successful ones know when to stop. When they have a big win, they leave it for a while, wait to see how things go, ignore all the nearly-good ones, wait for the really-good one. They don't bet on every race.'

Jude shook her head ruefully. 'Then I'm afraid I'll never make a successful gambler. In spite of what happened afterwards, I'm still flushed with the thought of that hundred quid I won last week. I'm sure my luck's on a roll.'

'That's another thing you'll never hear a successful gambler say. No such thing as luck. Graft, application, weighing up the variables – that's how you make money.'

'I'm never going to make much then.'

'No, darling, I'm afraid you're not. And I'm not going to make any today either.'

'What do you mean, Sonny?'

'I been through all the cards. There isn't a single nag I fancy.'

'So you won't have a bet?' He shook his head. 'Then why are you here?'

'Because I like racing, Jude. Can't get round to the courses like I used to do these days, but I can sit in here and see the lot. Coo, what my old man would have thought of a place like this, where you can sit in comfort and have all the racing come to you. He spent his entire life dragging from one racecourse to another, lugging his boards and boxes about. Setting up in the rain, standing there all afternoon, shouting the odds. He'd have thought he was in heaven in a place like this.'

Jude didn't think she could do what Sonny did, just watch the races. So far as she was concerned, take away the gambling and the whole exercise became a bit dull.

She looked up at the screen displaying the runners and prices for the next race, the 1.20 at Fontwell Park, the nearest racecourse to Fethering. She had been there once or twice, so that already gave her a sense of special interest. And then she saw there was a horse in the race called Carol's Duty. 'I'm going to do that,' she said to Sonny.

'Why?'

'I've got a friend called Carole – spelt differently but

near enough, and she's got an overdeveloped sense of duty, so it was clearly meant.'

'What was clearly meant?'

'That the horse is going to win the race.'

Sonny Frank shook his head in exasperated pity. 'That is no way to pick a horse. You could make up some kind of personal reference to any one of those names, if you put your mind to it.'

'I've just got a feeling it's going to win.'

'Oh dear.' The ex-bookmaker's expression clearly demonstrated his views on 'feelings'.

The odds on Carol's Duty were eight to one. Jude was going to put on a fiver but then, remembering that you have to speculate to accumulate, she wrote out a new slip and gave Nikki ten pounds. Horse was still at eight to one – she asked to take the price. The girl scribbled on the slip, ran it through the till and handed over the copy.

By the time Jude had sat down, the price of Carol's Duty had gone out to ten to one. Damn, thought Jude, that means I'll win less.

'Nothing's going to touch this favourite,' said Wes.

'Though eight to thirteen on is a stinking price,' said Vic.

'Not if you compare it to other investments. You don't get that kind of return from the building society.'

'No, but then you don't stand a chance of losing every ten minutes with the building society, do you?'

'Anyway,' said Wes with satisfaction, 'this favourite's going to romp home like there's no other horses in the race.'

Jude glowed inwardly. Let them crow, they'd done the same before the race on Thursday. A fat lot of good it had done them. And the same thing would happen again. Carol's Duty would romp home. She looked up at the screen. Annoyingly, her horse had gone out to twelve to one. Never mind, eighty quid profit was still worth having.

The race was run to the customary barracking from Wes, Vic and Sonny. The favourite won. Carol's Duty pulled up after three fences. Jude gave Sonny a rueful smile. He responded with an I-told-you-so pursing of his lips.

'Most of 'em lose,' said a voice beside her. Jude realized she had unwittingly sat herself right next to Pauline, who was at her usual post, surrounded by shreds of racing newspapers.

'You're right,' Jude agreed. 'Did you have anything on the last race?'

The dumpy elderly woman shook her head. 'No, I don't often bet. Just once or twice a week.'

'But you just like horse racing?'

'Not that bothered really.'

'Then why . . .?'

A knowing grin came across the woman's powdered features. 'Nice and warm in here, isn't it? If I was at home, what'd I be doing? Sitting in a chair in front of the telly, paying God knows what on my central heating. Here I can do just the same, but someone else is paying.'

'But you do like it in here?'

'Oh yes, there's people around. Better than just sitting on my tod.'

'Have you been coming here a long time?'

'Since after my old man died, yes. And that was back before the place got taken over. When Sonny used to run it.'

The ex-bookie grinned acknowledgement of his name. Jude lowered her voice. 'And nobody minds you just coming in every day?'

'Why should they? I have a bet every now and then. I buy myself the odd cup of tea. I don't cause trouble. And I keep my eyes open.'

'What do you mean by that?'

Pauline grinned sagely. 'Neither more nor less than what I said.'

'Would you like a cup of tea now?' asked Jude.

'Wouldn't say no. Four sugars, please.'

Tea was dispensed by Nikki from behind the counter. It came in plastic cups and wasn't very nice. Still, it might prove a useful bridge to Pauline.

When Jude sat down again, another race was in progress. A couple of Chinese waiters had come in – Monday lunchtime business was clearly slack at the Golden Palace – and they added their incomprehensible comments to the raucous exhortations of Wes, Vic and Sonny. It was a good time for an intimate conversation.

'So tell me . . .' Jude began, 'Thursday afternoon, when Tadeusz Jankowski came in to the shop, you saw him?'

'Oh yes,' said Pauline, emptying sachet after sachet of sugar into her cup.

'Did you notice anything odd about him?'

'I thought he looked pale. At least I think he did. But that's the kind of thing you can think after the event. You know, since I've known he died, now maybe I've made myself remember that he looked pale. Memories are pretty unreliable things.'

The shrewdness of the comment seemed at odds with the old woman's vague manner. 'And when he went out of here, did you notice anything about him then?'

'No, not really. No more than I'm sure you did. He did seem to sway a bit, and it crossed my mind he might have had a few too many at lunchtime, but that was all.'

'Yes, I thought that too.' Jude's full lips formed a moue of frustration. 'It would be nice to know more about him, wouldn't it? But since he'd never been in the betting shop before . . .'

'Oh, he'd been in.'

'What?'

'I'd seen him in here.'

'When?'

'Last autumn.'

'Did you tell the police that?'

Pauline let out a derisive laugh. ''Course I didn't.'

'Why not?'

'My old man taught me to be very wary so far as the police are concerned. If they once start nosing into your life, you never get rid of them. "Never tell the cops anything they don't already know, Pauline," my old man used to say to me. And I've stuck to his advice on that . . . as well as on a lot of other things.'

'Ah.' The latest race came to its climax. Wes and Vic's shouts of confidence subsided into moans of disappointment. 'What did your husband do?' asked Jude.

Pauline gave her a little, mischievous smile.

'A bit of this . . . a bit of that . . .'

Jude looked across to the counter. Behind the glass Ryan was impassively counting through piles of banknotes. The Ryan who had assured everyone he had never seen Tadeusz Jankowski before the day of his death.

Maybe there was more connection between the murder victim and the betting shop than everyone had so far assumed.

Chapter Six

Fethering boasted two cafés. On the beach was the Seaview, open around the year, welcoming in the summer but a rather dispiriting venue in February. Much more appealing was Polly's Cake Shop, which was on the main parade, just a few doors away from the bookie's. And Pauline was more than happy when Jude suggested they adjourn there for a proper pot of tea. So long as she wasn't increasing her own heating bills, Pauline didn't seem to mind where she went.

Polly's Cake Shop restored an image which at one stage had almost vanished from the British high street. It had oak beams hung with horse brasses and warming pans, red and white gingham tablecloths and little lamps with white shades over candle bulbs. The waitresses wore black dresses and white frilly aprons. And they served such delicacies as toasted teacakes, cinnamon toast, cucumber sandwiches, 'homemade' coconut kisses, sponge fancies, éclairs and fairy cakes.

It was of course all an exercise in retro marketing. The beams had been affixed to the bare nineteen-thirties walls in the late nineteen-nineties, and the 'homemade' delicacies were delivered daily from a specialist manufacturer in Brighton. Those who liked to use pretentious terms could have described Polly's Cake Shop as a post-modernist gloss on the traditional cake shop. But the residents of Fethering were not bothered about such niceties, and the older ones relaxed into the environment as if it had been unchanged since their childhoods. The only difference was in the prices. Nostalgia never did come cheap.

Pauline wasn't a regular customer at Polly's Cake Shop, but, offered the chance of a free meal, wasn't going to waste it. From the variety of teas proposed she asked for 'ordinary tea', then added a toasted teacake and the 'selection of cakes' to her order. Jude went for the same tea, together with a huge (and hugely sinful) éclair.

'Nice place,' said Pauline, looking around. 'I used to be called Polly, you know.'

'Oh yes?'

'That's what my old man used to call me. Kind of pet name, I suppose.'

'How long ago did he . . .?'

'Twelve years now. Women live longer, don't they?'

'But have you got used to—?'

'You never get used to it. You just learn to live with it.'

Anonymous in the betting shop, on her own Pauline seemed a much stronger personality. Her little-old-lady looks, white permed hair and heavily powdered pinkish face presented an image that was perhaps more benign than the reality. The grey coat she wore over a flowered print dress also fostered the ideal of a cosy little grandmother, but Jude was beginning to think that Pauline might have a bit of the wolf in her too.

'Yes,' she said sympathetically. 'But you manage OK?'

Pauline shrugged. 'OK. Moved into a smaller place after he passed on. Got the pension and he left me a bit. Not much, considering how much'd been through his hands over the years, but . . . yes, I manage.'

'And your husband . . . you didn't say exactly what he did . . .?'

'No, I didn't.' Pauline did another of her mischievous grins. 'Let's just say that what my old man earned . . . well, the taxman didn't know much about it.'

'Right. I think I get your message.'

Jude might have asked more about the dubious past of Pauline's late husband, but their teas were delivered then, and the moment passed.

When the pouring was done and they'd both taken a comforting sip, Jude got straight to the point. 'You said you'd seen Tadeusz Jankowski in the betting shop before.'

The old woman looked her straight in the eye. 'Before I answer your questions, there's something I want to get clear.'

'What?'

'Why you're asking them.'

'There's been a murder. It's natural to be curious, isn't it?'

'Is it? It's natural to be curious if you're a police officer, yes.'

'I can assure you I'm not a police officer.'

'No? Because they use the most unlikely people in plain clothes.'

A beam spread across Jude's chubby face. 'Not as unlikely as me, I promise.'

The moment of levity seemed to have allayed some of Pauline's suspicion. 'So what's your interest in all this then? You another of Fethering's self-appointed amateur detectives?'

Jude found herself blushing as she admitted that she was.

Pauline chuckled. 'I don't know, place like this, a bit of crime gets all the old biddies excited.'

Jude wasn't bothered about being categorized as an old biddy. So long as Pauline would talk to her. Which now the old woman seemed prepared to do. 'All right,' she said. 'So yes, I had seen the Polish boy in the betting shop before.'

'Often?'

'Just the once.'

'When was it?'

'Last year. Late September, maybe early October, I'd say. He come in the shop in the middle of the afternoon.'

'You have a very good memory.'

The little old lady smiled complacently. 'It's a matter of training, you know. Everyone could have a good memory if they trained it. These old biddies who go senile . . . what do they call it now – Alzheimer's? If they'd trained their memories when they was younger, they wouldn't have no problems. My old man, he used to get me to train my memory. "Focus on things," he used to say. "Concentrate. Every face you see, clock it. Use your mind like a camera, store the image." And since he taught me how, that's what I've always done.'

'Why was he so keen for you to do that?' asked Jude, knowing that the question was slightly mischievous.

Pauline instantly picked up the nuance, and winked as she replied, 'Let's just say my old man had a well-developed sense of self-preservation. He was always watching his back, so he liked me to keep my eyes peeled in case there was anyone dodgy about.'

'With faces then, for you it's "once seen, never forgotten".'

'That is exactly right, Jude. For faces I got this photographic memory.'

'So the minute that young man walked into the betting shop last Thursday, you knew who he was?'

'Well, you're overstating things a bit there. I never knew who he was . . . not till I heard on the telly like you did. But the minute he come in the betting shop on Thursday I knew I'd seen him before. Mind you, I didn't know it was going to be important. I didn't know he was just about to die, did I?'

'Of course you didn't.' Jude took a huge bite of her éclair and felt the cream squirting. She wiped her mouth before asking, 'You didn't speak to him then?'

'No. He was just another punter coming into the betting shop.'

'You say a punter. The first time he came in, did you actually see him put on a bet?'

'Oh, come on, Jude. We're talking last October. I

may havc a photographic memory for faces. I can't do an instant replay of my whole blooming life.'

'Sorry. Thought it was worth asking. So, so far as you remember, you didn't see him put on a bet?'

'I don't recall seeing him do that. But I'm not saying he didn't.'

'You didn't hear him speak? You didn't notice that he had an accent?'

'I don't recall hearing him speak either. I just remember that I seen him in the betting shop last October.'

'Right. Thank you.' Jude didn't think she was going to get a lot more information out of the canny old woman, but it might be worth trying a slight change of direction. 'It's confusing, isn't it, all the different ideas that are buzzing around the grapevine? So far as I can see, everyone in Fethering seems to have their own theory about the murder.'

'Everyone in Fethering has their own theory about everything,' said Pauline with some asperity. 'People here have too much time on their hands, so they spend it snooping into other people's business. Load of blabbermouths they are.'

'But have you heard any of the blabbermouths saying anything that might have any relevance to the case?'

'Some, maybe.'

'So, what theories have you heard?'

Pauline focused on another fairy cake and slowly bit the tiny slice of angelica off the top. 'Well, I've heard theories ranging from Russian hit men to Mafia gang wars. The only sensible theory I've heard is that no one has a clue why the poor bugger was stabbed.'

'And do you have any theories of your own?'

Pauline looked at Jude shrewdly and said, 'What my old man always used to say was, "If a crime of violence happens, the first question to ask is why the issue couldn't have been sorted out without violence." And the answer to that might be because the people you're dealing with are psychopaths or people of a highly nervous temperament, or there could be any number of other reasons. Moving on to the matter of murder, my old man used to say, "The only reason for murdering someone is to keep them quiet. If you just want to put the frighteners on them, you don't have to go as far as murder. So you only murder someone when the consequences of what they might tell another party constitute a bigger risk than the risk of actually committing a murder." That's what he always said, and my old man knew what he was talking about.'

Jude nodded. 'That makes very good sense.'

But then Pauline added, rather mischievously, 'Though, of course, the reason for this murder could be something else entirely.'

'Yes, but going along for a moment with your husband's theory . . . the question we should be asking is: what did Tadeusz Jankowski know that represented a threat to someone else?'

'That's the question. Mind you, finding the answer might be more difficult, since we don't know anything about the poor bugger except for his unpronounceable name.'

Jude nodded ruefully. It always came back to the same thing for amateur detectives; they suffered from a dearth of information.

'And there's nothing else,' she asked without much hope, 'that you can remember about when you saw him in October? Presumably he wasn't wearing the big overcoat?'

'No, T-shirt and jeans, as far as I remember.'

'And you've said you don't recall him going up to the counter to place a bet . . . You didn't see him speak to anyone, did you?'

To her surprise, Jude's last despairing question brought a response. 'Oh yes, he did talk to someone.'

'Really? Who?'

'A woman who's often in there.'

A spark of excitement had rekindled in Jude. 'One of the regulars?'

'She used to be in there a lot. Well-dressed woman, early forties maybe.'

'What's her name?'

'Ah, I never found that out. Kept herself to herself. Put on a lot of bets, but never joined in any of the backchat.'

'But you could point her out to me if she came into the betting shop?'

'Oh yes, of course I could.'

Jude's pulse quickened. At least she'd got the beginnings of a lead.

'Mind you,' Pauline went on, 'she hasn't been in for some months.'

'Oh? Since when?'

'I suppose I stopped seeing her . . .' The old lady screwed up her face with the effort of memory '. . . quite a few months back . . . October probably.'

'Just after you'd seen her talking to Tadeusz Jankowski?'

'Yes, that's right,' replied Pauline, before cramming a whole coconut kiss into her mouth.

'I went back to the betting shop and asked around,' Jude told Carole. 'Most of them remembered the woman all right, but none of them had ever seen her off the premises.'

'Did you get a name?'

'No.'

'Well, couldn't you have asked the manager?'

'I did ask the manager, Carole.'

'Without giving away why you were interested?'

'Of course without giving away why I was interested. I said something about a woman matching the description of a friend of mine having been seen in the betting shop and described her as Pauline had to me.'

'You do seem to find lying easy, Jude.'

'Yes, never been a problem for me. Except in certain relationship situations.'

'Ah.' Though intrigued, Carole didn't feel moved to pursue that subject.

'Anyway, what did the manager say to you?'

'Like everyone else, Ryan remembered the woman, but didn't have a name for her.'

'Surely they keep records?'

'Placing a bet is an anonymous exercise. Generally speaking, you pay in cash and, unless you have an account, no one has a clue who you are.'

'Hm.' Carole still looked a bit pale, but she was a lot better than she had been at the end of the previous week. Her hands were wrapped round a cup of coffee in the kitchen at High Tor. By the Aga Gulliver snuffled comfortably. His mistress was taking him out for walks again and all was even more serene in his comfortable doggy world.

'So this woman,' she went on, 'used to be a regular at the betting shop . . .?'

'Semi-regular, it seems. She didn't go absolutely every afternoon, and she never stayed for long.'

'All right. So she was a semi-regular till round October . . . and then suddenly she disappeared?'

'I think that's over-dramatic, Carole. She stopped going into the betting shop, that's all. We have no evidence that she disappeared from the rest of her life . . . chiefly because we know absolutely nothing about the rest of her life. Anything might have happened. Most likely she moved out of the area. Or maybe she lost interest in the horses . . . or she underwent a religious conversion and decided that gambling was sinful . . . There are so many possibilities that, quite honestly, any of them could be viable.'

Carole looked thoughtful. Though she was still physically weakened by the flu, her brain was once again firing on all cylinders. 'So this unknown woman was in the betting shop one day last October . . . and

Tadeusz Jankowski came into the place and spoke to her?'

'That's what Pauline told me.'

'And did he speak to her as though he knew her?'

'Apparently, yes.'

'So we have got something to go on.'

'Not much. A man about whom we know nothing except his name met a woman whose name we don't even know . . . I think it'd be a while before we could get that case to court.'

'But it's interesting. Did any of the other regulars see Tadeusz Jankowski last October?'

'I asked them. They all said no. But although they're regulars, they're not there every single day. Or it's quite possible he did go in when they were there and they didn't notice. Not everyone has Pauline's photographic memory for faces.'

'But the manager . . .'

'Yes, there's something funny there. He told me it's part of his job to clock everyone who goes in and out of the place. And he also told me he'd never seen the dead man before last Thursday.'

'So something doesn't quite ring true, does it?'

'Well, unless Pauline's lying and, although I'm sure she's quite capable of it in the right circumstances, I can't imagine why she'd do so in this instance.'

'So what can we do?'

'I think, given our current lack of information, the only thing we can do is to try and get a quiet word with Ryan.'

Chapter Seven

Jude went into the betting shop the following morning, the Tuesday, at around eleven, thinking it would be a good time to talk to the manager before the main racing fixtures started. But Ryan wasn't there. His place had been taken by an older man of uncongenial appearance. Jude's immediate thought was that the police had spotted the same inconsistency in Ryan's statements that she had, and he was 'helping them with their enquiries'. But a question to the vacuous Nikki provided a much less dramatic explanation. Ryan was laid up with the 'nasty flu' that had been going round.

At a loose end, Jude decided that she and Carole should have lunch at the Crown and Anchor. Her neighbour initially opposed the idea – she opposed anything that smacked of self-indulgence – but was persuaded. She was, after all, in a convalescent state after her own bout of flu. She wasn't yet up to cooking for herself. A meal out would be a necessary part of her recovery.

Carole was secretly pleased at the plan. All morning she'd been putting off ringing her daughter-in-law. After the postponement of the weekend, she needed to fix another date to meet up with Lily and her parents. But Carole didn't feel up to the challenge of such a call. She was always shy of Gaby, and she knew that any discussion of rescheduling their meeting would also involve mention of David. She wasn't sure she felt strong enough to state the truth: that she didn't want to see her granddaughter with her ex-husband present.

So going off to the Crown and Anchor gave her the perfect excuse to put off her difficult phone call till the afternoon.

'Heard you'd been out of sorts,' said Ted Crisp when they arrived at the pub. 'Still looking a bit peaky, aren't you?'

Carole had to think about her response. Every fibre of her being revolted against the idea of ever 'making a fuss', but then again she didn't want anyone to underestimate how ghastly she had felt for the previous few days. So she contented herself with a brave, 'Getting better, but it's been a really nasty bug.'

'Tell me about it. Everyone in the pub seems to have had it. Can't hear yourself speak in here for all the coughing and spluttering. And my latest barmaid's using it as an excuse for not turning up.'

'Poor kid,' said Jude.

'I'm not so sure about that. Quite capable of "taking a sickie". She's a right little skiver, that one. Most of them seem to be these days, certainly the youngsters. Whatever happened to the concept of "taking pride in your work"? This lot all seem to want to get paid for doing the absolute minimum. Bloody work ethic's gone out the window in this country, you know.'

Jude was once again struck by how right-wing Ted was becoming. Ironic how almost all of those who had derided the establishment in their youth came round later in life to endorsing its continued existence.

'The younger generation are all hopeless,' he went on. 'But round here older people are too well-heeled to bother with bar work. Hey, you wouldn't like to be a barmaid, would you, Jude? You'd bring lots of custom in, someone like you.'

She grinned. 'I have a sneaking feeling the word "buxom" is about to be mentioned.'

'I wasn't going to say it.'

'But you were thinking it, Ted.'

'Well, maybe.'

'I'll consider your offer. If I run out of clients for my healing services. It's not as if I haven't done it before.'

Carole, reminded of this detail from her neighbour's past, shuddered to the core of her middle-class heart.

Ted Crisp grinned at her discomfiture. 'Anyway, I'm the one in charge of the bar for the time being. So, what are you ladies drinking? Is it the old Chilean Chards again?'

'I should probably have something soft,' said Carole. 'You know, I'm not a hundred per cent yet.'

'All the more reason why you need a proper drink,' Jude assured her. 'You should probably be having a quadruple brandy.'

'Oh, I think that would be excessive. But all right, a small Chilean Chardonnay, if you insist.'

'I insist,' said Ted Crisp, 'that it should be a large one.'

'But—'

'You pay for a small one. I'll top it up to a large one. Landlord's privilege.' Carole didn't argue. 'And I assume a large one for you, Jude . . .?'

'Please. And what's good to eat? Healthy nutritious fare to help restore Carole to her old self?'

'You won't go wrong with the Local Game Pie. Served with Special Gravy.'

'Two of those then, please.'

'Though I don't actually think I've got much of an appetite,' said Carole. 'I probably won't be able to eat it all, given the size of your usual portions.'

'You'll manage,' said Ted, writing down the order.

'By the way,' Carole asked, 'what is the Local Game today?'

Deliberately misunderstanding, Ted replied, 'The Local Game in Fethering is still trying to work out who killed that poor Polish bloke. Tell you, I've heard more theories in this pub than you've had hot lunches here.'

'Any that sound convincing?'

The landlord shook his shaggy head. 'Not unless you're a big fan of Cold War spy fiction, no. I think the trouble is, nobody knows what the poor bloke was doing in this country, anyway.'

'Bar work, I gather.'

'Yes, Jude, that's what he was doing, but surely that wasn't why he was here. As I know all too well, it's a crap job, bar work. That's why I can't get any decent staff. The pay's not good enough.'

'No, but for him it was still probably more than he'd get paid in Poland,' said Carole.

'He was living in Littlehampton,' said Jude. 'You know most of the pubs and bars around, Ted. You haven't heard where he was working, have you?'

'No. I could ask around, though.'

'Be grateful if you did.'

'All right,' said the landlord. 'But we're rather starved of information, aren't we? Nobody really knows anything about the bloke, what he was like, what he wanted from life. Those are the kind of things you want to know if you're going to find out why someone was murdered.'

Carole and Jude were already far too aware of the truth in Ted's words. After a little more desultory banter, they adjourned to one of the pub's alcoves with their drinks.

'What about the girl?' Carole asked suddenly.

'What girl?'

'You said there's also a girl who works regularly in the betting shop.'

'Oh yes, Nikki.'

'Well, maybe she's seen the mysterious woman Tadeusz Jankowski spoke to. Maybe she knows who it is.'

'Possible. Nikki doesn't come across as the most observant of people – or indeed the most intelligent – but I suppose it's worth asking her. She can't be as dim as she appears.'

The Local Game Pie lived up to Ted Crisp's recommendation. And the Special Gravy was delicious. In spite of her prognostications, Carole finished every last morsel, but the food – and a second glass of wine –

left her feeling very sleepy. 'But I can't sleep during the daytime,' she told Jude. Sleeping in the daytime – like watching daytime television – was a slippery slope for retired people, so far as Carole was concerned. Go too far down that route and you'll stop bothering to get up or get dressed in the morning. Then you'll start to smell and 'become a burden'. Carole's mind was full of imagined slippery slopes to cause her anxiety.

'You go straight back to bed,' said Jude, 'and have a nice long sleep. You're still washed out. Sleep's nature's way of making you better.'

Carole didn't argue any more. Sleeping during the day for health reasons was quite acceptable. But such indulgence must stop the minute she was fully fit again.

Before she took to her bed, she felt sufficiently buoyed up by the Chilean Chardonnay to ring Gaby. And, to her delight, her daughter-in-law suggested coming down to Fethering that Friday. Just her and Lily. The perfect configuration, and no mention of David. Exactly what Carole would have wished for. Heartened by the conversation, she was quickly nestled under her duvet and asleep.

Jude felt restless when she returned from the pub. Although she had a presence that spread serenity, inside her mind all was not always serene. She had had a varied life in many different places. Sometimes the quietness of Fethering soothed her, but at others it rankled and she felt a surge of wanderlust. There was so much world out there, so much yet to be seen. Maybe it was time that her wings were once again spread.

Normally she would ease such moods by yoga. The familiarity of the movements, the relinquishing of her thoughts to a stronger imperative, could usually be relied on to settle her. But that afternoon she'd had two large glasses of wine and she knew her concentration would not be adequate to the demands of yoga.

So she lit a fire and then sat down to read the manuscript of a book written by one of her healer friends. It was about control, not controlling others, but taking control of one's own life, developing one's own potentialities. Jude, who had read and been disappointed by more than her fair share of self-help books, thought this one was rather good.

But her mind kept straying. The pale image of the dying Tadeusz Jankowski recurred like an old reproach. What had happened to him? Why did he have to die? She hoped she would soon have answers to those questions.

The phone rang. Jude answered it.

'Hello. Is this, Jude, please?' The voice was female, young, heavily accented.

'Yes, it is.'

'It was you who found the body of Tadeusz Jankowski?'

'Yes.'

'Please, I like to meet you.'

'I'm sorry, who am I talking to?'

'My name is Zofia Jankowska. I am the sister of Tadeusz.'

Chapter Eight

The girl was in her early twenties, with hazel eyes and blonded hair divided into two pigtails. She wore jeans and a blue waterproof jacket. There were silver rings on her fingers and in her pierced ears. She had a feeling of energy about her, as if all inactive time was wasted, as if she couldn't wait to be getting on with something.

Zofia had come straight from the police, having rung Jude from the Major Crime Centre at Hollingbury near Brighton. And Jude had invited her straight over.

'They were helpful to me, the police, but not very helpful, if you understand.'

'Yes, I think I do,' said Jude. 'Can I get you something to drink? Or have you eaten?'

'I have a sort of plastic breakfast on the plane.'

'And how long ago was that?'

'The flight left at 6.20 from Warsaw.'

'You must be starving. Come through to the kitchen and I'll get you something.'

Bacon and eggs were the most obvious emergency rations and while Jude rustled them up, the two women continued their conversation. 'When you say the police were helpful and unhelpful, what exactly did you mean?'

'They were helpful in the way how they were polite to me and answering my questions, but they did not give me a lot information.'

'They gave you my number, though.'

'They give me your name. I find your number in phonebook. I don't think the police were keeping information from me. I think they just don't have a lot information to give.'

'No, that was the impression I got.' Jude sat the girl down at her kitchen table and dished up the bacon and eggs. 'What would you like to drink? Tea – or something stronger?'

'You have coffee?'

Jude had coffee. While she made it, Zofia wolfed down the food as if she hadn't eaten for months. Whatever her reaction had been to the news of her brother's death, it hadn't affected her appetite.

Jude sat down and waited till the plate was empty. 'Can I get you anything else?'

'No, I . . . You are very kind. You give me much.'

'I bought a rather self-indulgent ginger cake yesterday. Let's have some of that by the fire, and you can tell me everything you know.'

'I prefer you tell me what you know. You are the one who find Tadek.'

'Tadek?'

'I'm sorry – Tadeusz. Tadek is short name for him. In family and friends, we all say Tadek.'

'Right.'

They sat down in a heavily draped sofa. Jude hadn't put any lights on yet, though the February evening was encroaching and soon they would be needed. The flickering of the fire illuminated the clutter of Woodside Cottage's sitting room, its shrouded furniture, its every surface crowded with memorabilia from the varied lives of its owner.

'Were you close to your brother?' asked Jude.

'When we live together as children with my mother, very close. Then he go to university, we do not see so much of each other. Still we stay close . . . from a distance, can you say?'

'Yes. You said your mother . . . are your parents not together?'

'My father he died when Tadek and I are small children. There is just my mother.'

'She must have been devastated when she heard the news about your brother.'

'Yes, I suppose. We do not get on, she and I. But, in her way, she is upset. She do not understand. I do not understand. That is why I know I must come here. I stop everything, get a flight, come here.'

'How much did you have to stop? Do you have a job?'

'I do not. Not yet. Not permanent job. I was student. At university in Warsaw.'

'Studying English? You speak it very well.'

'No, not English. Not major in English, though I try to get it better, because it is important. But I studied journalism. I wanted to be reporter.'

'"Studied"? "Wanted"? Why the past tense? What went wrong?'

'I did not like the course, not good. I drop out. Wait tables, work in bars till I decide what I really want to do.'

'Maybe you've got enough reporter's skills to get to the bottom of what happened to your brother.'

'This I hope. This is why I come.' She pulled a small notebook out of the back pocket of her jeans. 'In this I write down my notes, everything I find out. I have to know something, have to know why Tadek was killed.'

'It must be terrible for you.'

'I think it will be. Now I am too full of . . . unbelieving . . . and angriness. Now I just want to know what happened. When I have found this out, then I think there will be time for sadness.'

'I'm sure there will.'

'So I must know everything that is known. This is why I need see you. Please, tell me about how you saw Tadek . . . my brother.'

As simply and sympathetically as she could, Jude re-created the events of the previous Thursday afternoon. It didn't take long. She could only say what happened. She had no explanations, nothing that might assuage Zofia's thirst for detail. Meanwhile the girl scribbled down notes in her little blue book.

When Jude had finished her narration, there was a long silence. Then Zofia spoke slowly. 'It is terrible. That you should see Tadek like that. That I did not see him. That I will not see him again. That is the thing

73

that is hard to understand. That he is not there any more, not anywhere any more.'

'When did you last see him, Zofia?'

'Please do not call me "Zofia". That is very formal. My friends have a special name for me.'

A sudden thought came to Jude. 'It isn't "Fifi", is it?'

The girl looked at her in bewilderment. 'No. "Fifi" I think is a name for a dog.'

Jude didn't think the time was right to elaborate the reasoning behind her question. 'I just thought . . . "Zofia" . . . it might be shortened to—'

'No, "Zosia". That is the name everyone calls me. Please, you call me "Zosia".'

'Very well. Zosia,' said Jude.

'Why you think I am "Fifi"?'

Jude explained about her brother's dying word, hoping that now she might get some explanation for it. But Zofia was as puzzled as she was. So far as the girl knew, Tadek had not known a "Fifi". He'd certainly never mentioned one. And no Polish word that he might have been trying to get out seemed to have any relevance.

'You ask me when I last see Tadek . . . Of course I did not know it was the last time I would see him, but it was in Warsaw in September. Just before he come to England.'

'Why did he come to England?'

'I do not know. He would not tell me.'

'What was he doing in Warsaw?'

'He finish a year ago a degree in music. He want make a career in music. He write songs, play piano, guitar. He love playing his guitar. Now he will not do that any more.' These reminders of her brother's absence did not seem yet to cause sadness to Zofia. Her reaction was more one of bewilderment, an inability to take in the sheer scale of what had happened.

'So did Tadek have a job?'

'Small jobs. Temporary work. Like me. He wanted to buy time to write his songs.'

'Do you think he came to England because he thought there would be better opportunities in the English music scene?'

The girl shrugged. 'Maybe. But I don't think so. He was enjoying his music in Warsaw. He was in a band with some friends, it all seemed to be going well. Then suddenly he tell us all he is going to England.'

'And you've no idea why he might have done that?'

'No. Tadek was not very . . . I don't know the word . . . not good at details of life, doing things that needed to be done every day.'

'You mean he wasn't practical?'

'I think this is the word, yes. He lived in the clouds. He had wild ideas which were not easy to make happen.'

'He was a romantic?'

'Yes. And an optimist. He think everything will come good some time. But of course he was wrong.'

'When you say he was a romantic,' asked Jude, 'does that extend to his emotional life? Was he romantic about women?'

Zofia nodded vigorously. 'Yes, even after growing

up with me and our mother, Tadek still put women . . .
up high . . . I don't know . . .'

'On a pedestal?'

'That is good word. Often he want to be with
women who are not right for him. Too old for him
sometimes. But he still . . . yes, put them on a pedestal.'

'So do you think it might have been a woman who
brought him to England?'

'It is possible. But he did not say anything to me
about a woman. Usually he tell me who is the new one
he has fallen in love with. And tell me when it has broken up – as they all did.'

'Did your brother have any friends in England? Was
there someone he could have stayed with when he first
arrived?'

'I do not know of many. Tadek had not been to
England before. I do not know of any English friends of
him. But it is possible he meet people. He travelled a
lot in Europe. To music festivals and such events, with
his band. But again it is unusual for him not to tell me
about people he meet.'

'Did the police ask you about his friends?'

'Of course. I cannot help them much – like I cannot
help you much. But they do tell me where he was living.'

'Littlehampton, I gather.'

'Yes, they give me address. I will go there. After seeing you, this must be the next place I go. Maybe I find
out something.'

'Well, if you do, please let me know.'

The girl's hazel eyes sought out Jude's brown ones. 'You also are wanting to find out how Tadek died?'

'Yes,' Jude replied simply.

After Zofia had left, Jude was tidying up in the kitchen when she heard the rattle of something coming through her letterbox. Too late for the post (even though that did seem to be getting later and later). She managed to get to the front window just in time to see the person who'd made the delivery moving on next door to High Tor.

Through the encroaching dusk, she recognized him from the previous week in the Crown and Anchor. Dressed in a Drizabone coat and tweed cap, it was Hamish Urquhart. Running errands for his father. Jude looked down at the mat to see what he had delivered.

The envelope was addressed to 'The Occupier'. From, as she might have guessed, Urquhart & Pease, the estate agents. They were always looking for new properties in the 'much sought-after' location of Fethering. Anyone looking to sell could not do better than engage the services of the long-established, efficient and courteous firm of Urquhart & Pease, who would be happy to offer a free valuation.

Normally Jude would have shoved such a letter straight into the bin. But that day, given her earlier restlessness, it had a pertinence for her. Maybe it was a psychic nudge, telling her she should be moving out of Fethering. The timing was interesting. And Jude was a great believer in synchronicity.

77

Chapter Nine

Shortly after Carole had put her flyer from Urquhart & Pease straight in the recycling bin, she had a phone call from Ted Crisp. He wasn't good at remembering numbers, but hers had stayed stuck in his head from the time of their brief affair, so he rang her rather than Jude.

'Been doing my bit on the old Licensed Victuallers grapevine,' he announced. 'Found out where the dead man did his bar work.'

'Oh, really? Well done.'

'Pub on the Fedborough road out of Littlehampton. Just by the river bridge. Cat and Fiddle. Do you know it?'

'No,' said Carole unsurprisingly. The Crown and Anchor was about the only pub she did know. Carole Seddon still didn't think of herself as a 'pub person'.

'Run by a woman called Shona Nuttall. Known in the trade as "The Cat On The Fiddle". One of those self-appointed "characters", of whom there are so many in the pub business.'

'Your tone of voice suggests that she's not your favourite person.'

'Does it?' He neither confirmed nor denied the impression.

'And what about the pub? How does she run that?'

'Not the way I would,' Ted Crisp replied eloquently.

The Cat and Fiddle's perfect riverside position ensured continuous trade throughout the summer, but it wasn't so busy on a cold Tuesday evening in February. Even before Carole and Jude entered, they were aware of why it wasn't the sort of pub Ted Crisp would have liked. The inn sign was a Disneyfied version of a cute cat with bulbous eyes playing the fiddle to a group of goofy-toothed square-dancing rabbits. Notices in the vast car park bore the same motif, as did the signs on the children's play area. Whether the Cat and Fiddle was a one-off business or not, it gave the impression of being part of a franchise.

This was intensified by the interior, open-plan with lots of pine divisions which were reminiscent of some immaculate stable-yard, an image encouraged by the romantic country music that filled the air. Pointless rosettes were pinned to pillars; halters and unused riding tack hung from hooks. The narrow awning over the bar was thatched, and the bar staff, male and female, wore dungarees over red gingham shirts. On the wall-mounted menus another incarnation of the goggle-eyed cat pointed down to a sign reading 'Good Ol' Country Cookin''.

The few customers did not sit on their show-home pine stools with the ease that identifies the true pub regular. Suited businessmen at single tables worked silently through meals piled high with orange chips. An unspeaking couple in a stable-like booth looked as if they were mentally checking through the final details of their suicide pact.

Behind the bar stood a large woman whose lack of dungaree livery meant she must be the landlady. Tight cream trousers outlined the contours of her substantial bottom and thighs, while a spangly black and gold top gave a generous view of her vertiginously deep cleavage. She had a tan that looked as if it had just returned from the Canary Islands and wore a lot of chunky gold. Earrings, necklaces, bracelets and a jeweller's windowful of rings. When she flashed a greeting to the two women, a gold tooth was exposed at the corner of her smile.

'Good evening. Welcome to the Cat and Fiddle.' Her voice was brash and slightly nasal. 'What can I get you? We do have a Special Winter Warmer Mulled Wine for these winter evenings.'

Carole and Jude, who shared the view that nothing spoiled wine so much as heating it up and shoving in herbs and sugar, both opted for a Chilean Chardonnay. Carole had intended not to drink alcohol on this rare second visit to a pub in the same day, but the atmosphere of the place seemed to require some form of anaesthetic.

They had wondered in the car how they were going to get round to the subject of Tadeusz Jankowski, but they needn't have worried. The landlady, who must be the Shona Nuttall Ted had referred to, brought it up almost immediately.

'You local, are you?' she began.

'Fethering.'

'Oh, very close. I haven't seen you in here before, though.' She beamed so far that the gold tooth glinted again. 'Well, now you've found us, I hope you'll get the Cat and Fiddle habit.'

Both women, while mentally forswearing the place for ever, made some polite reaction.

'It's a real old-fashioned friendly pub. Got lots of atmosphere,' said Shona Nuttall, in the teeth of the evidence. The many photographs pinned behind the bar all featured the landlady grinning hugely and crushing some hapless customer in her flabby arms.

'Mind you, though,' she went on, saving them the effort of even the most basic probing, 'we have had our sadnesses here recently . . .'

'Oh?' asked Carole, providing a prompt which probably wasn't needed.

'I don't know if you heard on the telly about that poor young man who was stabbed . . .?'

'Yes, we did,' said Jude.

''Course you would have done, living right there in Fethering. Well, do you know . . .' She gathered up her bosom in her arms as she prepared to make the revelation '. . .that boy only worked in here.'

'Really?' Jude sounded suitably surprised. 'Tadeusz Jankowski?'

'Yes, him. Mind you, I could never pronounce his name, so I just called him Teddy.'

'What did he actually do for you . . .? Sorry, I don't know your name . . .?' Carole lied.

First names were exchanged, then the landlady went on with what was clearly becoming her party piece. 'I'd got an ad in the *Littlehampton Gazette* for staff. I always need extra bodies running up to Christmas and New Year, then it slackens off, but some of my real stalwarts tend to take their holidays this time of year, so I'm still a bit short. Well, Teddy saw the ad and came along.'

'When would this have been?'

'Middle of October. That's when I have to start thinking about Christmas. Anyway, Teddy seemed a nice enough lad . . . well, considering he was Polish . . . so I thought I'd give him a try.'

'Was he working behind the bar?' Jude tried with difficulty to visualize the young man she'd seen in dungarees and red gingham.

'No, no. His English wasn't good enough for that. And, you know, handling the money . . . you can't be too careful . . . particularly with foreigners.' As she had been with Ewan Urquhart, Jude was struck by the endemic mild racism of West Sussex. 'My staff do a kind of probation period before I let them behind the bar.'

'What work did he do then?' asked Carole.

'Washing up mostly. You know, clearing the rubbish from the kitchen, helping the chef. No cooking, mind. Kitchen porter kind of thing.'

'But not mixing with the customers?'

'No.'

'Was he friendly with the other staff?'

'Oh yes, yes, he was a nice boy. Such a tragedy, somebody so young,' Shona said automatically. 'Look, that's how friendly he was.' She pointed to one of the photographs behind the bar. Out of deference to the deceased, somebody had pinned a black ribbon bow over it. Tadeusz Jankowski looked very small and embarrassed in his employer's all-consuming embrace. The photograph may have shown how friendly Shona Nuttall was; it didn't look as though the boy had had much choice in the matter.

'Any particular friends amongst the other staff?' Carole persisted.

'No, not really. Not that I noticed. He only did two-hour shifts, and he was kept pretty busy, so he didn't have much time to socialize.'

'Did he ever mention having a girlfriend? Or did you see him with one?'

The landlady shook her head. 'I was asked all these questions by the police, you know.' This was not said to make them desist in their interrogation; it was spoken with pride. The death of Tadeusz Jankowski had given Shona Nuttall a starring role in her own drama and she was going to enjoy every moment of it.

'Did he say anything about other friends?' asked Jude. 'Or why he had come to England?'

'The police asked me that too, but I wasn't able to help them, you know. I mean, I'm very good to all the people who work for me, but I do have a business to run, so that has to be my first priority. Not too much time for idle chatter with the kitchen staff, particularly when they don't speak much English.'

'Did the police question you for long?'

'Oh, quite a while. Half an hour, probably. And . . .'

Shona Nuttall slowed down as she prepared to produce her biggest bombshell '. . . I was actually on the television.'

'Were you?'

'Yes. You may have seen me. Friday I was on the news.'

Carole looked puzzled. 'I'm fairly sure I did see the news on Friday evening. I had flu, but I got out of bed specially to watch it. I don't remember seeing you, though.'

'Ah, well, I was just on the local news.' The landlady seemed put out to have to make this admission. 'Six-thirty in the evening.'

'No, then I wouldn't have seen that.'

'I do have the video.' Not only did she have it, she had it set up in the VCR on the bar. She pressed the relevant controls and told them to look up at the big screen. The practised ease with which she went through these motions suggested that Carole and Jude weren't the first Cat and Fiddle customers who had been shown the recording.

Shona Nuttall's moment of television fame was very short. A brief shot of the exterior of the pub was shown, followed by a close-up of her behind the bar saying, 'He seemed a nice boy. I can't imagine why anyone would want to hurt him.' Then, with one of those bad edits so beloved of local television news, they cut back to the studio and the presenter talking about the increase of the rat population in Worthing.

'You came across very well,' said Jude, and Shona Nuttall glowed with the compliment. What a sycophantic remark, thought Carole, but she was still envious of the way her neighbour could always say the right thing to put people at their ease.

'And did Tad . . . Teddy ever talk to you about his music?'

'Sorry?'

'He was a very keen musician. He wrote songs and played guitar.'

'I didn't know that. He wasn't into country music, was he?'

'I don't think so. More sort of folk.'

'Oh. Because we do have regular Country Evenings here at the Cat and Fiddle. Line Dancing too. I don't know if that's your sort of thing . . .?'

'Not really,' said Carole, suppressing a shudder.

They continued their conversation with Shona a little longer. Relishing her moment in the spotlight, she was happy to talk for as long as they wanted. But it soon became obvious that she had almost nothing to tell them. 'Teddy' had been employed as cheap labour in the kitchen of the Cat and Fiddle. She had had no interest in him apart from that. Though happy after his death to project the image of the big-hearted employer struck by tragedy, Shona Nuttall actually knew nothing about the young man.

And when in the course of conversation Jude revealed that she was the one who had been present at his death, the landlady could not hide her annoyance. She didn't want anyone else muscling in on her fifteen minutes of fame.

Chapter Ten

'You want me to go into a betting shop?' said Carole, appalled.

'The betting shop is, if not the Scene of the Crime, at least the only place we know related to the crime. It's going to be rather hard to find out anything about the case if we don't go back there. Shona Nuttall proved to be something of a dead end – not to say a dead loss – so the betting shop must be our next port of call.'

'But, Jude, what on earth will people think I'm doing?'

'They'll think you're going into the betting shop, that's all. People wander in and out all the time. Nobody'll take any notice of you.'

'But supposing there was someone I knew in there? Or someone I knew saw me going in there?'

'So?'

'What would they think?'

'They would think that you were going into the betting shop. Full stop. It's only a betting shop, Carole. It's not an opium den in Limehouse.'

'No, but—'

'I'm going there right now. Picking up Harold Peskett's bets on the way. Are you coming?'

'Yes,' Carole replied meekly. But not without misgiving.

As it turned out, Carole and Jude went to the betting shop that Wednesday morning before seeing Harold Peskett. They didn't go inside, but to the small alley where Jude had witnessed the young man's death. She'd had the thought as they were walking along Fethering High Street that revisiting the scene might spark some recollection, might set her mind going in a different direction.

Though the day was dry, the alley looked drab and uninviting, littered with burger wrappers and plastic bottles. A smell of urine hung in the air. It had been used as a comfort station by many beerful customers taking a short cut back from the Crown and Anchor.

Tied to a drainpipe near where Tadeusz Jankowski had died was a bunch of flowers. Though not yet wilting, they looked infinitely pathetic. Attached to the stalks was a card with words in a language that neither woman understood.

'Zofia's tribute to her brother,' said Jude softly.

Carole was silent. Though not as sensitive to atmospheres as her neighbour, she could still feel the piercing melancholy of the location.

'So why did he come down here?' asked Jude, as if thinking out loud. 'Why did he go into the betting shop? What was he looking for?'

'Maybe he was going to meet someone on the beach? Or round the back of one of the shops?' The alley led to a little service road behind the parade.

'We could look.' Jude tried unsuccessfully to banish the sadness from her face. 'Maybe we'll see something obvious that he was making for?'

But no. There was nothing obvious. Nothing unusual at all. A lorry was delivering what was undoubtedly the wrong stock to the loading bay behind Allinstore. There was no other sign of human activity. Towards the sea was an area of scrubland, rough grass snaking its way over sandy soil, too flat to be called a dune.

'Nothing springs to mind,' said Carole dispiritedly.

'No.' Jude turned away from the beach to face the overgrown back yard of the betting shop. Through wire-netting gates, she found herself looking straight at Ryan the Manager. He looked as shocked to see her as she did him.

Jude raised her hand in a little half-wave of acknowledgement, but the young man did not respond. Instead, shoving the bulky contents of a brown paper bag into his pocket, he turned on his heel and disappeared through the back door of the shop.

Harold Peskett lived in sheltered accommodation, a tiny flat in a purpose-built block with views over Fethering Beach. Though still suffering from the flu, he was up and dressed by the time Jude and Carole arrived.

A small, birdlike man, ninety-two years had whittled away at him, so that now there seemed to be only one layer of skin on his prominent bones. There was no hair on the blotched cranium, and he peered at the world through thick-lensed tortoiseshell glasses. In spite of the considerable warmth of central heating turned up high, he wore two jumpers under a tweed jacket whose elbows and cuffs had been reinforced with leather. His shoes were polished to a high gloss and he wore a thin, greasy dark tie with some insignia on it.

His room was meticulously tidy, the bed neatly squared off and lots of box files regimented on shelves. Only on the table in the window facing the sea was there disarray, an untidy spread of the day's racing papers, from which he had been working out his latest foolproof fortune-bringing strategy.

He was very glad to see Carole. Any friend of Jude's was a friend of his. And he was sick of the wretched flu. 'I still wake up every morning as weak as a kitten. Mind you, even when I'm a hundred per cent, I'm not much stronger than a kitten these days.' He chuckled, and through the lenses there was a sparkle in his clouded eyes.

'Carole's just recovered from the flu too.'

'Oh, have you, love?' Carole didn't really like being called 'love', but the ninety-two-year-old's charm enabled him to get away with it. 'Then you have my sympathy. Rotten one, this is. Hangs on like the smell of damp in an empty house. Nasty.'

'Yes, it certainly took it out of me.'

'Well, I'm glad to see you're on the mend. Hope I

will be soon. Then you won't have to come collecting my bets every day, Jude.'

'It's no hardship. I really don't mind.'

'That's very kind of you to say so, but I hope it won't be for much longer. Anyway, I like putting the bets on myself. Then I can say my own special little prayer to Lady Luck. "Come on, love, today you're going to give me the big win, aren't you?"'

'And does she usually oblige?' asked Carole.

'Oh, no. Never. Well, I'll get the odd little double, but never the big one I'm really after. Still . . .' He chuckled again '. . . at ninety-two, what would I do with all the money if I did have a big win? No, no, it's not the money that's really the attraction for me. It's pitting myself against the system, against the whole random universe, trying to impose order on total chaos.'

'You're a bit of a philosopher in your quiet way, aren't you?' said Jude.

'Guilty as charged.' The little man placed his frail hands on his chest in a gesture of submission. 'Now, can I offer you ladies a cup of tea or something?'

'No, really, we've just had some coffee. Anyway, Harold, you're not fit enough to be doing that sort of thing. Can I get you a cup of tea?'

'Well, Jude, if you don't mind . . .' This exchange had become a part of their morning ritual. Harold would make the offer of tea, Jude would refuse and offer to make some for him, and he'd accept.

While she busied herself in the tiny kitchen, Carole said to the old man, 'So you're normally a regular at the betting shop?'

'Never miss a day. Been doing the horses all my life. Back when I started the bookie's were on the street corners with their clock bags.'

'I'm sorry?'

'Clock bags. They had to be closed at a certain time before the race started, so's no one could cheat by knowing the result. While now . . . well, very plush all the stuff they got in those betting shops these days. Comfy chairs, get a cup of tea, everything.'

'But over the years, Harold . . . you know, the years you've been betting, do you think you're up or down?'

'In financial terms?'

'Yes.'

'Oh, down. Definitely down.'

An expression of puzzlement settled on Carole's face. But rather than actually vocalizing the thought, 'Then why on earth do you do it?' she moved the subject on. 'So, if you're in the betting shop every day, Harold, maybe you saw the poor man who was killed?'

'No. Didn't Jude say? I was ill last week.'

'I know that. I just thought you might have seen him before.'

'No idea. I don't know what he looks like.'

'Haven't you seen the pictures on the news?'

He gestured around the room. 'Don't have a telly, do I? There's one downstairs in what they call one of the "communal rooms". But I'm not going to spend my time sitting with those old biddies. They never put the racing on, anyway. Just watch these endless soaps and chat shows with everyone spilling their guts about

SIMON BRETT

everything. No one's got any shame any more. I don't
need the television.'

'And you don't get a local paper?'

'No, nothing much happens in Fethering, and what
there does I usually hear along the grapevine.'

At that moment Jude reappeared with a steaming
cup of tea.

'I was just asking Harold whether he'd seen Tadeusz
Jankowski in the betting shop . . . you know, before last
Thursday. But Harold doesn't know what he looked
like. Fortunately, though . . .' Carole reached triumphantly into her handbag '. . . I've brought along all
the cuttings I've collected about the murder.'

Harold Peskett was shown a photograph of the dead
man and immediately responded, 'Oh yes, I seen him
all right.'

'In the betting shop?'

'Yes.'

'When?'

'While back. Late summer, I think.'

'End of September, early October?'

'Could have been.'

'Did you see him speak to a woman?'

The parchment-like skin wrinkled around the old
man's eyes. 'Hard to remember that far back. Maybe he
did . . .'

'The woman we're talking about,' Jude said gently,
'was a regular in the betting shop . . .'

'Do you mean old Pauline?'

'No. Another one. Apparently used to be a regular
and then suddenly stopped coming.'

92

Again the thin skin was stretched with the strain of recollection. 'Doesn't ring any bells.'

'Younger woman . . . smartly dressed . . .'

'Ooh, just a minute. Yes, there was this lady used to come in, now you come to mention it. Yeah, looked like she had a few bob. Nice clothes, like you say.'

'Did you ever talk to her?' asked Carole.

'Well, only to, like, pass the time of day. You know, say "bad luck" when she had a loser, that kind of thing.'

'Did she have a lot of losers?'

He shrugged 'All punters have a lot of losers.'

'Yes, but I mean – did she bet a lot?'

'Mm, think she did. Put something on every race, she would.'

'Big stakes?'

'Dunno. You never really know what other punters are putting on, unless they draw attention to themselves. And she was a quiet one, that woman. That's why I had trouble remembering her.'

'Do you know her name?'

He shook his head. 'Like I say, she was quiet. Almost, like, a bit secretive. And people who come in on their own, well, you never hear their names. Different with those decorators, Wes and Vic, a right double act they are. And Sonny "Perfectly" Frank, everyone knows him. But that woman . . . haven't a clue.'

'Did you see her talking to Tadek . . . to the man in the photograph?' asked Jude.

The wizened old man shook his head. 'Don't recall. She might have done, but, you know, there's a lot of comings and goings in a betting shop. You don't notice all of them.'

'Of course not.' Jude looked at Carole, as if to indicate that they weren't going to get much more information from this source, and said, 'Have you got all your bets done, Harold?'

'Been ready for an hour,' the old man replied, producing a pile of closely scribbled betting slips from the table. 'Ooh, and could you bring me some more of these, Jude love? I'm running out. I mean, hope I'll be better tomorrow and be able to go down there under my own steam, but just in case . . .'

'Yes, of course. I'll pick them up and drop them in tomorrow morning.'

'That's very good of you.' He looked at his watch. 'The first bet's on a twelve-thirty race.'

'Don't worry, we're on our way.'

'Well, good to see you. And nice to meet you, Carole love. You going down to sort out your day's investments, are you?'

'I beg your pardon?'

'You going down the betting shop to have a bit of a punt, are you?'

'Good heavens, no,' said Carole.

Jude smiled. 'Don't bother to get up, Harold.'

But he was on his feet before she had finished the words. 'No, no, I may be old and decrepit and full of flu, but I'm still capable of seeing ladies to the door of my own home.'

Harold Peskett moved stiffly across to the door and

opened it for them. 'And that poor geezer with the funny name got stabbed, did he?'

'So it seems, yes.'

'Rotten luck. He didn't seem the sort to get on the wrong side of anybody.'

Carole stopped in her tracks. 'You speak as if you know him.'

'Well, don't *know*, but I chatted to him a bit when he come into the betting shop in the autumn.'

'When he spoke to the mystery woman?' asked Jude.

'Maybe. Come to think of it, yes, I did only see him in bookie's just the once.'

'And when you spoke to him, what did you talk about?'

'Oh, nothing important. Just like passed the time of day.' He screwed up his face with the effort of squeezing out more detail. 'Ooh, and I remember . . . I did give him some directions.'

'Where to?'

'Well, as I recollect it, that's why he come in the betting shop, to ask the way. That's probably why he talked to the woman . . . you know, the one you were asking about.'

'Where did he want to go to?' Carole insisted.

'He was looking for Clincham College,' replied Harold Peskett.

Chapter Eleven

'I've heard of Clincham College, but I don't know much about it,' said Jude, as they walked briskly along the front towards Fethering High Street. 'Presumably it's in Clincham?'

Carole affirmed that it was. Clincham was a largish coastal town some ten miles west of Fethering. It had a well-heeled retired community, and a matching set of boutiques and knick-knack shops to cater for them. It also had a growing population of students, a lot of them foreigners studying at the town's many language schools.

'The place has been around for a long time. As a college, or it may even have been a poly. Not very academic, did courses in estate management, animal husbandry, catering, that sort of thing. Most of the students there were local, and I gather they still are. I always think that's the difference between a college and a university. A university is a place where young people go to get away from home, to spread their wings a little, start to find their own personalities, whereas a college . . . Anyway, in recent years, *following govern-ment policy . . .'* Distaste steeped Carole's words as she spoke them '. . . Clincham College has been accorded university status. So, rather than dishing out diplomas and certificates, Clincham College is now dishing out degrees. Which, I would imagine, are about as valuable from the academic point of view as the diplomas and certificates they replaced.'

'Does it take a lot of foreign students?'

'That I wouldn't know. I don't think more than the average so-called university.'

'Well, it'd be fairly easy to check if Tadek was enrolled there.'

'But how could he have been, Jude? If he was, surely the police would have described him as a "student", not a "bar worker"?'

'He could have been doing a part-time course. Or maybe he started something and dropped out. A lot of students do.' Her neighbour didn't seem particularly impressed by this new area of potential investigation. 'Look, Carole, we do now have at least one connection for Tadek and the Fethering area. Apart from Madame Ego at the Cat and Fiddle. He was looking for Clincham College. It's a lead.'

'About the only one we've got,' said Carole frostily.

Silence reigned between them until they reached the High Street. The cold wind off the sea stung their cheeks. Jude noticed with amusement how, the closer they got to the betting shop, the more the anxiety in Carole's face grew. At last, when they were only yards away, she burst out, 'Is there anything I ought to know? I don't want to look a fool. I don't want people staring at me. I don't want to do the wrong thing.'

'Carole, it's a betting shop we're going into, not the temple of some obscure religious sect. Nobody will take any notice of you. And if you do feel self-conscious, just study the sheets from the newspapers stuck up on the walls. They'll show all the runners and riders.'

'And nobody will think it odd if I don't bet?'

'Nobody will think anything about you.'

'Oh.' But she didn't sound reassured.

'Know anything?' asked Sonny Frank, the minute the two women entered the betting shop.

'Sorry. Nothing,' Jude replied.

'How's about your friend?'

'Sonny, this is Carole. Sonny Frank – Carole Seddon.'

'Good afternoon.'

'How do? And what about you – know anything?'

'Well,' Carole replied, primly mystified, 'I know quite a lot of things, I suppose. In which particular area were you interested?'

'Horses,' said Sonny. 'Wondered if you knew a good thing on today's cards?'

Carole looked to Jude for help, which was readily supplied. 'Sonny was wondering if you had a tip for any of today's races.'

'Oh, good heavens, no. I'm afraid I don't know any-thing about horses.'

'Join the club,' said Sonny Frank. 'The great inter-national conspiracy of mug punters.'

'Ah.' Carole still looked confused.

'You know anything, Sonny?' asked Jude.

'Might be something in the 3.20 at Exeter.'

'Oh?'

'From a yard in the north. Long way to travel if the trainer reckons it's a no-hoper.'

'So you're saying it's a cert?'

'No such thing, darling.'

'Are you going to tell me the name?'

The round head shook, its plastered-down hair unstirred by the movement. 'Maybe later. See what form the jockey's in first.'

Jude nodded acceptance of his reticence and crossed to the counter to hand in Harold Peskett's bets. Carole felt stranded. Sonny Frank had returned to his *Racing Post*, three Chinese waiters chattered incomprehensibly, the gambling machines recycled their interminable jingles. She didn't know whether to follow her neighbour or just sit down as if her presence in the betting shop had some purpose. Then she remembered Jude's advice and drifted across to look at the newspaper sheets pinned to the wall. The lists of runners and riders from Exeter and Lingfield meant nothing to her, but she stared at them with the concentration of an aficionado.

'The ground hasn't really thawed out after the frost,' said a cultured voice behind her. 'The going shouldn't be too heavy.'

'Oh. Really?' Carole turned to see a smartly suited mature man with an impeccably knotted tie. He was the former accountant whom Jude knew as a regular, but to whom she had never spoken.

'I don't believe I've seen you in here before.'

'No, I am not an habituée.' Why on earth had she

said that? Was it some form of inverted snobbery that put her gentility into overdrive in a common place like a betting shop?

'Well, I am, I'm afraid. Gerald Hume.' He stretched out a hand and formally took hers.

'Carole Seddon.'

At the counter, Jude had had Harold Peskett's bets scanned by the manager, but lingered. Ryan looked sweaty and ill at ease. Once again Jude was aware of the strong peppermint smell that was always around him. 'I was wondering if my friend and I could talk to you about something . . .?'

'What's that?'

'About Tadeusz Jankowski . . . you know, the person who died.'

The young man was instantly suspicious. His dark eyes darted from side to side as he said, 'I only saw him the once, that afternoon. I told you that. I've already told you everything I know.'

'Yes, but we'd like to talk to you a bit more about it. Amongst other things . . .'

'Why, what do you know?' There was a note of panic in his voice.

'Oh, this and that,' Jude replied, casually – and mendaciously. 'We thought it'd be nice to have a chat and bring you up to date on what we do know. And you're the person who knows everything that goes on in this betting shop. You, as it were, know where the bodies are buried.'

His pupils flickered like trapped tadpoles. 'I can't talk now,' he said.

'What time do you finish?'

'Five-thirty this time of year.'

'Meet in the Crown and Anchor?'

'OK,' he grunted reluctantly.

Someone's got a guilty secret, thought Jude. She wondered if Ryan's manner towards her had something to do with their encounter earlier that morning. Had he been doing something he shouldn't have been in the betting shop's back yard? And did he think she was a witness to his wrong-doing? Had her random talk of knowing 'where the bodies are buried' triggered some guilt in the manager?

These were her thoughts as she crossed back towards her neighbour, who she was surprised to see was in earnest conversation with the man whom Sonny Frank had once identified as a retired accountant. Animated by talking, he didn't look quite as old as he had before. Probably only early sixties, steel-grey hair and a lean face with unexpectedly blue eyes. When he smiled, he was almost good-looking.

'Oh, Gerald, this is my friend Jude,' said Carole in a manner which was, by her standards, fulsome.

The introductions were duly made. 'Yes, I've seen you in here before, but never known your name,' said Gerald.

'Same for me with you. And indeed with a lot of other Fethering residents.'

'You're certainly right there. Isn't that typical of England – everyone knows who everyone else is, but they never speak to each other?' He seemed slightly embarrassed by his own seriousness. 'Carole was just giving me her views on the first race at Lingfield.'

'Was she?' asked Jude, with some surprise.

'She fancies Deirdre's Cup, and I can see the way her mind's working, but I just wonder whether he can produce his turf form on the all-weather.'

'That's obviously the big question,' said Carole, trying to avoid her friend's eye. Out of Gerald Hume's sightline, Jude let her jaw drop in a parody of stunned surprise.

'Well, I might be swayed by your opinion,' said the retired accountant. 'I'll wait till just before the off, see how the market rates Deirdre's Cup.'

'Good idea,' said Carole.

'We can actually go now,' said Jude. 'Our meeting's going to be later in the day.'

'Oh,' said Carole. 'Well, may as well just stay and see this first race at Exeter.'

'Yes, wait and see if Deirdre's Cup floweth over,' said Gerald Hume, rather pleased with this verbal felicity.

'Very well,' said Jude, still bemused.

In the few minutes before the race, the odds on Deirdre's Cup grew shorter and shorter till he was see-sawing for favouritism with the horse which had started the day odds-on.

'Someone knows something,' observed Gerald Hume. 'Where do you get your information from, Carole?'

'Oh, here and there,' she replied airily. 'One keeps one's ear to the ground.' Again she looked studiously away from Jude, on whose face was a pop-eyed expression of disbelief.

'Right, I'm going to grab that eleven to four while stocks last,' said Gerald Hume and hurried up to the counter with open wallet.

'Are you not betting?'

'No.' Carole still avoided Jude's eye.

'Well, I'm going to do something. I can't watch a race without having a financial interest in it.'

Jude went each way on a wild outsider called Lumsreek, which she got at thirty-three to one. Already planning how she'd spend her winnings, she rejoined Carole and Gerald, who seemed as relaxed as if they'd known each other since schooldays.

Before the race started, Wes and Vic rushed in from some other abandoned decorating job and just managed to get their bets on in time, so the actual running was accompanied by their raucous shouts of encouragement.

Not that they did much good. In both cases, the horses whose praises they had been singing before the 'off' were condemned at the end as hopeless nags. Deirdre's Cup did better, though. Never out of the first four, he put in a big challenge in the last furlong, actually leading for a few strides before the favourite reasserted its class and got home by a short head.

'Worth watching, that horse,' said Gerald Hume. 'Going to win a race soon.'

'Yes,' Carole agreed sagely.

'So how much did you lose?' he asked.

'Oh, I didn't bet on it.'

'Canny. You fancied it, but you knew something . . .?'

'Well . . .'

'Thought he needed the race?'

Carole wasn't quite sure what the question meant, but it seemed to invite agreement, so, ignoring the flabbergasted look on Jude's face, she agreed.

'Yes, I should have thought it through,' said Gerald Hume. 'Are you going to do something on the next?'

'Oh no, I think Jude and I had better be off. Things to do, haven't we?'

Jude, still mystified by Carole's behaviour, agreed that they did indeed have things to do. 'Also,' she said, 'if the way my luck's going is characterized by the running of Lumsreek . . .' Her fancy had come a very distant last '. . . I think I should keep out of betting shops for the next few days.'

'Still, maybe I'll see you in here again?' asked Gerald Hume, directing the enquiry very firmly towards Carole rather than Jude.

'Oh, I don't think so. As I said, I'm not an habituée.' This time she didn't feel so stupid saying the word. In fact, she felt rather classy. Confident even.

'Well, I hope we will meet again somewhere,' said Gerald.

'I'm sure we will. Fethering's a very small place, and I only live in the High Street.'

'Good heavens, I'm in River Road.'

'Very close then.'

'I'm sure we'll meet up.'

The two women were nearly back at their respective homes before Jude asked, 'So what was all that about, Carole?'

Her friend looked all innocent. 'What?'

'Gerald Hume. Had you met him before?'

'Never.'

'Well, you behaved as if you knew each other very well.'

'Yes. Strange, that, isn't it . . .?' Carole mused.

'Any explanation . . .?'

'No, it's just . . . there are some people one meets, with whom one just . . . clicks. Do you know what I mean?'

'Oh, definitely,' said Jude, suppressing a smile. 'I've fixed to meet Ryan in the Crown and Anchor soon after five-thirty. Are you coming?'

'I certainly am,' Carole replied.

'Very well. See you then.' And Jude went into Woodside Cottage, her bewilderment by no means reduced.

Carole went into High Tor, feeling really rather good. She really had clicked with Gerald. For a moment she toyed with the unfamiliar sensation of being a bit of a femme fatale.

Chapter Twelve

'I speak to Tadek's landlord. Nothing,' said Zofia. Her voice down the phone was cold and disappointed.

'What do you mean – nothing?' asked Jude.

'It is like he do not know who he rents his rooms to. So long as they pay, he doesn't care who they are. Tadek was just another student for him. If the police had not questioned him, he would have forgotten my brother's name.'

'So you didn't get any idea of how Tadek spent his time?'

'The landlord does not live near the house with the rooms in. It is just for money. He might as well be taking profits from slot machines.'

'Did you go to the house?'

'Yes.'

'And did you manage to speak to any of the other residents?'

'Not many are in. Two I speak to. They also only remember Tadek because the police have been round asking questions. How can people live so close and not know each other?' the girl asked plaintively.

'They can do it because they're English,' Jude

replied. 'I'm afraid there's a strong tradition in this country of "keeping oneself to oneself". Have you heard the expression: "An Englishman's home is his castle"?'

'No. And certainly where Tadek was living was not a castle. It was very bare, not a nice place.'

'So what you're saying, Zosia, is that you've drawn a blank? You haven't met anyone who knew your brother?'

'I meet the woman at the pub he work. Cat and Fiddle. But she no use. She did not seem to know him at all.'

'Shona Nuttall. A friend and I met her too, and that was the impression we got. I think your brother was just cheap labour to her. She seemed to be a bit of a slave-driver.'

'She not even know Tadek was interested in music. That means she did not know him at all.'

'No.'

'It is strange, Jude. Tadek is a warm person, he always have friends. But no one in the house at Littlehampton know him. And that woman in the pub, she not interested in him.'

'I don't think Shona Nuttall's interested in anyone but herself.'

'No. But, Tadek . . . how can he come somewhere and make no friends?'

'He may not have made friends where he lived, but perhaps he had some somewhere else.'

'Where?'

'At college?'

'Tadek was at university in Warsaw. I tell you. He finish there last year.'

'Yes, I know. But we've got a lead that he might have had some connection with a college near here. Clincham College. Now called the University of Clincham.' Jude briefly outlined the information they had got from Harold Peskett. 'Tadek didn't say anything to you about going to college here?'

'No.'

'I mean, he was in touch with you, was he?'

'Tadek was never very good at keeping in touch. Oh, he always meant to, but other things would take his attention. He was a dreamer. So, since he leave for England, maybe he send one letter to our mother.'

'Was he close to her?'

'No. Like me, he did not get on with her.'

'But was he in touch with you?'

'More. But not a lot. A few texts on the mobile phone.'

'When was the last one you had from him?'

'I do not remember. Not since Christmas perhaps.'

'Well,' said Jude, 'I'm planning to make contact with Clincham College. Just see if anyone there knows anything about your brother.'

'Yes. You will tell me, please, if you find out something.'

'Of course.'

'You will keep in touch, Jude?' The appeal in Zofia's voice was naked. She sounded much younger than the nineteen or twenty that she must be. Jude felt a sudden rush of pity for the girl. Already shaken by bereavement, she had rushed to a country where she had no contacts, and had just experienced encounters with the English at their most aloof. She must have been feeling very alone.

'Zosia, have you got somewhere to stay while you're here?' Jude asked gently. 'Where did you spend last night?'

'Last night I was fine.' She clearly didn't want to give details. Jude wondered if the girl had slept rough. Not very pleasant when the weather was cold.

'And what about tonight?'

'I will find somewhere.' The girl dismissed the question as if it wasn't a problem. 'Somewhere cheap. A *pension*, a . . . what is it called in England? A Bed and Breakfast?'

'That's what it's called, yes. But if you'd like to, Zosia, you could stay here with me.'

'Oh, but I couldn't. No, I don't want to be trouble to anyone. I can do on my own.'

It took a bit of cajoling; not much, though. The girl's pride obliged her to put up some resistance, but Jude's arguments soon blew it away. There was a spare bedroom in Woodside Cottage; it made sense that it should be used. Jude didn't mention money, but she couldn't imagine that Zofia had much with her. The cost of living in Poland was a lot lower than in England, and even in the off-season B and Bs along the South Coast could be quite pricey. She was pleased when the girl gratefully accepted her offer, and suggested she should come straight from Littlehampton to Woodside Cottage.

109

By the time she arrived, the spare room would be made up for her.

As she put the phone down, Jude felt a double glow of satisfaction. Part came from the altruism of doing something that would be of help to someone in need. The other part was more selfish. Having the victim's sister on the premises might well prove very useful in the murder enquiry on which she and Carole had embarked.

Her recapitulation of what Harold Peskett had said about Clincham College prompted a new question. Had the old boy told the police what he had overheard Tadek say in the betting shop? Were they aware of the Clincham College connection?

She rang through to Harold. No, he hadn't been contacted by the police. Why should he have been, Jude reflected. He hadn't been in the betting shop on the relevant afternoon.

Jude was now faced with a moral dilemma. She had information which the police might not have. And her sense of duty told her that she should immediately share it with them. She felt certain that was the course Carole, with her Home Office background, would have recommended. An immediate call to the police was required, to alert them to Tadek's connection with Clincham College.

On the other hand . . . The police might have heard about the young man's enquiry from another of the betting shop regulars . . . There was a very strong temptation to leave them in ignorance . . .

No, she should do the right thing. Unfair though it

was – because she knew there was no chance of the
police reciprocating by sharing their findings with an
amateur detective – she should let them know what
she'd heard.

Reluctantly, Jude rang the number Detective
Sergeant Baines had given her. She got his voicemail.
She didn't give details of what she knew, merely said
that there was another regular of the betting shop
whom it might be worth their contacting for information in connection with the case of Tadeusz Jankowski.
And gave Harold Peskett's number.

She put the phone down with mixed feelings. Her
sense of virtue at having done the right thing was tran-
sient. Stronger was the hope that the police might clas-
sify her message as just the witterings of a middle-aged
woman, over-excited by her proximity to a criminal
investigation. That, in fact, they would ignore it.

Zofia Jankowska had very few belongings with her, and
the clothes she unpacked looked pitifully cheap. But
she was extremely grateful to her hostess. 'Please, I pay
you money . . .?'

'No need,' said Jude.

'But for food? Already you cook me one meal.'

'All right. If that happens more often, you can make
a contribution.'

'Please. You not ask how long I stay?'

'It's not a problem.'

'No, but I not be trouble you long. I go when I find

out all I can find out. I just want to know why my brother died.'

'Which is exactly what I want to know,' said Jude.

Ryan the betting shop manager looked more nervous than ever when he appeared in the Crown and Anchor very soon after five-thirty that evening. He wore a fur-hooded anorak over his uniform, but made no attempt to remove or even unzip it when he sat down in the booth opposite Carole and Jude. The latter introduced the former. He told Carole his name was Ryan Masterson and accepted Jude's offer of a drink, asking for 'A double Smirnoff, please, just with some ice.'

The two women had planned the way they wanted the conversation to go. From her snatched exchange with him in the morning, Jude had concluded that Ryan thought she knew something discreditable about him. She reckoned that was probably the fact that he had denied ever seeing Tadek in the betting shop before the afternoon of his death, but it might be something else, possibly something he thought she'd witnessed that morning. So she and Carole had decided to keep the one bit of information they did have on hold, and see if the manager had anything else to reveal.

'Busy day?' asked Carole uncontroversially.

'All right. Not too frantic this time of year.' The answer was automatic; there was tension in his voice.

'Do you know,' said Carole, uncharacteristically winsome, 'today was the first day I'd ever been into a betting shop.'

'Yes, I saw you come in.'

'You take note of everyone who enters the premises, do you?'

'Have to. There are a lot of villains around.'

'What, they're likely to cause fights, are they?'

'Not that. Some shops, maybe. Not in Fethering.'

'So what kind of villains are they?'

'Crooked punters. There are some who've got systems going. Multiple bets on fixed races, gangs of them going into a lot of different betting shops. We have to watch out for them.'

'Ah.' There was a silence. The question about his taking note of everyone who came into the shop had brought Carole the perfect cue to ask Ryan about Tadek's former appearance, but that was the one thing she didn't want to raise yet. And she couldn't think of anything else to ask him about.

Fortunately, Jude arrived at that moment with their interviewee's large vodka. As ever, her presence relaxed the atmosphere, though Ryan remained taut and watchful.

'Have the police been back to the shop since the weekend?' He shook his head and took a swig of vodka so urgent that it might have been some life-saving medicine. 'So you don't know what their current thinking on the murder is . . .?'

He shrugged. 'That the bloke was stabbed somewhere else and just came into the shop to sit down.'

'But he didn't sit down.'

'No. Thank goodness for that. If he'd actually died on the premises, I'd have had even more hassle.'

SIMON BRETT

'You didn't see which direction he came from, did you?' asked Carole.

'No. The way that hailstorm was coming down, you couldn't see anything outside. I was only aware of him when he was actually inside the door.'

'And did you think anything particular when you saw him? Was there anything odd about him?'

'Well, he was swaying about a bit. I thought he might be trouble because he'd been on the booze.'

'Do people on the booze often cause trouble in betting shops?'

Ryan looked up sharply at Jude's question, then mumbled, 'Can happen.'

'And watching out for that kind of thing is part of your job?'

'Yes, we're trained to stop trouble before it starts.'

'Hm.' Jude twisted a tendril of hair around one of her fingers. 'And do you think the same as the police do, Ryan – that the young man came into the betting shop by chance?'

'What else is there to think?'

'Well, if you listen to Fethering gossip . . .'

'If you listen to Fethering gossip, you waste a lot of time.'

'But you must hear a lot, being in the shop all day.'

'I manage to tune most of it out.'

'Do you like your job?' asked Jude suddenly.

'What's that to you?' he responded aggressively.

'Just a detail that might shed light on other details.'

Jude wasn't sure whether her answer actually meant anything, but it seemed to contain some threat to Ryan, because with commendable honesty he said, 'No, I don't like my job.'

'Why not?'

'Well, it's dull and repetitive, for a start. The hours are long, particularly in the summer. And you have to spend your day smiling at people you wouldn't normally give the time of day to. You don't exactly choose your own company. Some of the punters are pretty rude. Then you get the down-and-outs and the Care in the Community lot. Some of them smell, too.'

'Then why do you stick at it?'

'It's secure. I'm paid just about enough to make me think that the idea of giving it up and retraining for something else is a bad one.' For a moment he looked haunted by self-doubt. 'Don't know whether I've got it in me to train for anything else now – don't know if I could hack it. Anyway, I've got a wife and two kids – not the time to cut loose. I can't afford to take risks.'

'Risks that might mean you'd get fired?'

Ryan evaded a direct answer to Jude's question. He just shrugged and said, 'It's a job. Probably no better and no worse than any other job. How many people do you know who enjoy what they do?'

Jude did actually know quite a lot, but it wasn't the moment to say so. 'Why did you agree to meet me?'

Her question seemed to make him even more nervous. He swallowed and his voice was strained as he replied, 'You wanted to talk. I can't really do that while I'm in the shop.'

'I said I wanted to talk about Tadeusz Jankowski.'

'Yes.'

115

'Which is why you agreed so readily to meet me.'

'OK, yes. Him coming into the shop and then dying wasn't exactly good for business. Head Office are keen that the publicity is kept to the minimum. They would approve of my meeting you if it means there's less chat around the shop about what happened.'

It was a relatively convincing answer, but Jude reckoned he was still holding something back. And a straight question seemed as good a way as any other of finding out what that was. 'Is there anything you know about the case that you've been keeping to yourself?'

'No,' he replied. 'I've given the police my full co-operation.'

There was a silence. Ryan took another desperate swallow of his vodka. Jude exchanged a look with Carole which confirmed that neither of them expected to get much more out of the interview. Time to put the big question.

Carole did the honours. 'I believe you told the police that you'd only seen Tadeusz Jankowski on one occasion.'

'I did, yes. The afternoon he died.'

'Well, we've heard from other regulars in the betting shop that he actually went in on a previous occasion.'

'Last October,' Jude supplied.

'Yes,' said Ryan. 'I heard that as well.'

'Then why didn't you tell the police you'd seen him before?'

'Because I hadn't. I was on holiday last October.'

He answered so readily that they could not doubt the honesty of his reply. As simple as that. Ryan

Masterson had not seen Tadeusz Jankowski the previous October because he had been on holiday with his family. Annual leave. It could be checked, presumably, with his employers, but neither Jude nor Carole thought the effort would be worth it. He was telling the truth.

And dealing with the question seemed to relax him. If that was all they were interested in, his manner seemed to say, then no problem. He downed the remainder of his drink – just melting ice, he'd long since finished the vodka – and said he should be on his way.

'Couple of other things we'd like to ask you . . .' said Jude.

The panic returned instantly to his dark eyes. He thought he had been off the hook; now it seemed he wasn't.

'Nikki . . . ?'

'Yes.'

'She says she never notices anything that goes on in the shop.'

'Don't I bloody know it? Doesn't notice anything that goes on anywhere. Walks around in a dream, planning how she's going to decorate her sitting room when she gets married. Only thing she thinks about is her bloody wedding, and it's still over a year away.'

'That might be a front,' Carole suggested. 'And all the time she's really keeping her eye on everything that goes on?'

Ryan looked at her pityingly. 'Tell you, with Nikki, what you see is what you get. She is seriously thick.'

'Oh.' This didn't seem very gallant, but presumably he knew the woman he worked with.

'If that's it, I'd better . . .'

'One more thing . . .' Jude raised a hand to detain him. 'I asked you about this before. There's a woman who's a regular at the betting shop . . .'

'There are a few.'

'Well, I say she is a regular. I should have said *was* a regular. Stopped coming in around October last year.'

'People come and go, that's up to them.'

'This one was well dressed, sort of middle class.'

Ryan narrowed his eyes with the effort of recollection. 'I think I know the one you mean.'

'You wouldn't know her name, would you?'

He shook his head. 'Some people tell us their names, some don't. If they don't, we've no means of knowing.'

'No. And I suppose if you don't know her name, the chances of you knowing where she lives . . .'

'Are about as slender as those of one of Harold Peskett's bloody accumulators coming up.' This moment of levity showed how relaxed he now was. 'Why do you want to know about her?'

'Apparently Tadeusz Jankowski spoke to her when he went into the betting shop last October.'

'Ah, well, I wouldn't know about that,' said the manager with something approaching smugness. 'I was on holiday.'

Shortly after he reiterated that he must be on his way and left.

'There goes a relieved man,' said Jude.

'How do you mean?'

'He was very relieved when he found out what we were interested in – just whether he'd seen Tadeusz Jankowski before. He had no worries about answering that enquiry. Which means . . .' Jude grimaced '. . . that there was something else he was afraid we wanted to talk to him about.'

'Any idea what?'

'Well, only conjecture . . . but I'm pretty sure I'm right. Seeing the way he put away that vodka . . . and given the fact that he's always sucking peppermints, I would think it's a pretty fair bet that young Ryan has a drink problem.'

'And he thought we wanted to talk to him about that?'

'That's my theory. When I saw him in the back yard this morning, he was out there having a swig from his secret supply. He thought I'd actually seen him drinking. That's the only reason he agreed to meet us. He was afraid we might shop him to Head Office.'

'But why on earth would he think that?'

'Alcoholics are paranoid. Like all addicts. Including gamblers.'

'Well,' said Carole sniffily, 'you'd know about that.'

Chapter Thirteen

The decision to stay in the Crown and Anchor for another glass of the Chilean Chardonnay was quickly made. And they were soon joined by other after-work regulars. Shortly after six Ewan Urquhart and his younger clone Hamish appeared. Maybe they did this every evening after a hard day's estate agenting (though Jude sometimes wondered whether 'a hard day's estate agenting' wasn't the perfect definition of an oxymoron). Certainly the speed with which Ted Crisp set up a pair of unordered pints for them suggested a daily ritual.

Father and son took the first sip together and both smacked their lips in appreciation, another part of the ritual that needed to be observed. Then Ewan Urquhart took in the occupants of the pub and nodded recognition to Jude. She smiled back.

'Cold enough for you?' he asked, falling back, as most Englishmen do in casual conversation, on the weather.

'Pretty nippy,' Jude agreed, following the convention. She decided it wasn't the moment to engage in further talk. On their previous encounter Ewan

Urquhart had not endeared himself to her. But the introduction had been made and who could say when a tame estate agent might suddenly become a useful source of information? She continued to talk to Carole about Friday's impending visit of Gaby and Lily. But through their desultory conversation they managed to hear what the Urquharts were saying at the bar. Doing so was in fact unavoidable. Ewan Urquhart was one of those men who thought it was his God-given right to talk loudly.

'Do you know, Ted, what an absolute chump my son has been today . . .?'

'Tell me about it,' said the landlord.

'He only managed to turn up for a viewing of a property having left the keys in the office. Client wasn't best pleased about that, let me tell you.' While the litany of his incompetence was spelt out, Hamish's reaction was interesting. He looked apologetic, but at the same time almost grateful for the attention, as though undergoing such criticism was an essential part of the bond with his father. Hamish had apparently been cast early as the family buffoon, and it was a role that he played up to.

'Client was one of these city slickers,' Ewan Urquhart went on, 'investing his obscene bonus in a country cottage. Kind of guy for whom time is money. Wasn't best pleased to turn up to the property and find he couldn't get in. Gave you a bit of an ear-bashing, didn't he, Hamish?'

'Yes, Dad,' came the sheepish reply.

'So, needless to say, a call comes through to the

office and I have to leap into the Lexus, take the keys and smooth the city slicker's ruffled feathers. Turns out all right, actually, because when I get chatting to the chap, turns out he's an Old Carthusian just like me.'

'What's that when it's at home?' asked Ted Crisp.

'Old Carthusian? Means I went to a little educational establishment that goes by the name of Charterhouse. Rather decent public school, as it happens. So of course when the city slicker finds out we went to the same school we're all chums . . . and of course Hamish wouldn't have had the same connection, because you were too thick to pass the Common Entrance, weren't you?'

'Yes, Dad,' Hamish agreed, once again apparently proud of his inadequacy.

'Anyway, so once again I got the boy out of a mess. Which means that you're bloody well paying for the drinks tonight.'

'Of course, Dad.' The young man's wallet was out immediately; as yet no money had changed hands.

'And you can buy a drink for your sister when she arrives too.'

'Will do.' Hamish Urquhart looked at his watch. 'She said she'd be along about six-fifteen. Got some class or other up at Clincham College.' Carole and Jude pricked up their ears at that. 'Guarantee she'll be on the G and Ts. Ted, could you take for the pints and do me a large G and T too?' The young man's bluff bonhomie sounded like a parody of his father's. 'And won't you have one yourself?'

'No, thanks,' the landlord replied. 'I don't have anything till the end of the evening. Otherwise I'd drink myself into an early grave.'

'And we don't want that happening, do we?' said Ewan Urquhart heartily. 'I'm sure you're just like me, Ted, want to keep going as long as possible, becoming more and more curmudgeonly with every passing year, eh?'

'I reckon I'm pretty curmudgeonly already,' said the landlord as he poured tonic into a double gin with ice and lemon.

'Nonsense, nonsense. You're a fine upstanding English gentleman. Which is more than can be said for that fellow we had in the office this afternoon, eh, Hamish?'

'I'll say. He was very much an "oriental visitor".' The young man put on a very bad cod-Indian accent for the words.

'Not that we weren't punctiliously polite to him, of course. And, actually, nowadays it's all right. I mean, even ten years back I'd have had to be very discreet with someone like that . . . you know, suggesting that the Shorelands Estate in Fethering was maybe not quite where they should be looking . . . maybe they could find something more suitable in Brighton. But now half of the people on the Shorelands Estate are of dusky hue.' Ewan Urquhart let out a bark of laughter. 'Soon I would imagine the Residents' Committee there will be worrying about white people moving in next door to them!'

Ted Crisp guffawed too readily at this for Jude's liking. But she and Carole were distracted by the

SIMON BRETT

appearance through the door of a girl who was undoubtedly Hamish's anticipated sister. In her the ginger tendency of her father and brother was transformed into a mane of pale golden hair and their thickset bodies had been fined down into a slender voluptuousness. Her pale skin was flushed red, presumably by the February cold. She wore a Barbour over jeans and big fleece-topped boots. There was no doubt from the expression that took over Ewan Urquhart's face that she was the apple of her father's eye.

'So what's kept you, Soph?' he asked, as he enveloped her in a large hug. 'I didn't think you had classes as late as this.'

'No,' she said lightly. 'Had to do some work in the library.' Her voice had been trained at the female equivalent of Charterhouse.

'Well, I'm not sure I approve of all this book-learning for women. Women are only really good for three things. Cooking and cleaning are two of them . . . and . . .' Hamish and Ted Crisp joined him in a chortle of male complicity. He had spoken in an over-inflated tone of self-parody, but deep down he clearly believed in what he was saying.

'Anyway, your timing's good in one respect. Your brother's just bought you a drink.'

'Oh, thank you, Hamish.' She took a grateful swig of the gin and tonic.

'No prob, Soph.'

'And shall I tell you why the drinks are on him tonight?' Without waiting for a prompt, Ewan Urquhart once again recounted the tale of his son's ineptitude. At the end the girl gave her brother a little hug and said, 'You are an idiot.' Her tone was the affectionate one that might be used to an over-eager puppy.

'So what have they taught you today?' asked Ewan, sharing his next observation with Ted Crisp. 'Have to be doing a constant cost analysis on this higher education lark, you know. The amount they get charged for tuition fees these days, you want to know where the money's going.'

'Yes,' the landlord commiserated, 'I've heard about it. The debts these kids come away from university with, all those student loans, they're never going to get out of the red, are they?'

'Well, at least young Sophia doesn't have that problem.' He pronounced the second two syllables of her name like 'fire'. Then, with a tap to his back pocket in the vague proximity of his wallet, he explained, 'Muggins here's footing the bills for everything. So come on, what did they teach you today?'

'We had a class on Eisenstein, and then some work-shopping in the Drama Studio. It's for this show we're doing.'

'Huh, play-acting,' her father snorted. 'Not my idea of hard work. You know what my daughter's studying, Ted? Drama and Film Studies. They seem to be able to do degree courses in anything these days. Media Studies, Dance, Pop Music, Fashion, you name it. Probably be doing degrees in bloody Shopping before too long. Wasn't like that in my day . . .'

'Why, what did you study at university then, Ewan?'

For the first time the estate agent looked discomfited

by Ted's question. 'Oh,' he replied, quickly recovering, 'didn't go down the university route myself. Got out into the real world, got down to some real work. I'm sure you'd agree that's the best way to go about things, wouldn't you?'

'Dunno,' the landlord replied. 'It's not what I did. I went to university.'

'Really?' The surprise of the eavesdropping Carole and Jude was as great as that of Ewan Urquhart.

'Well, of course,' Ewan continued defensively, 'I studied later. You know, got my ARICS qualifications . . . eventually.' The recollection was clearly not a happy one, so he moved swiftly on. 'What did you study then?'

'Nuclear Physics.'

'Good Lord. So you have a degree in Nuclear Physics, do you, Ted?'

'Well, no, I don't actually. I left halfway through my second year. I was starting to spend more of my time doing stand-up than on my studies, so I thought I'd give it a go professionally.'

'And did it work out?'

'Ewan, do you have to ask?' Ted Crisp's large gesture, encompassing the whole of the Crown and Anchor, was sufficient reply.

'Anyway, Soph, I wonder if what you learnt today is ever going to prove of any use to you . . .'

The girl shrugged easily. 'Who knows, Daddy? Some people say that education shouldn't be about direct application of skills to commercial challenges, that it should be about training and broadening the mind.'

'What a load of poppycock. It's not a broad mind that's going to help you succeed in the marketplace, it's applied skills. Isn't that true, Hamish?'

'Certainly is, Dad.'

The set-up was perfect. With a guffaw, his father responded, 'And maybe, when you get some applied skills, you'll have a chance of succeeding in the market-place too!'

Shamefacedly, Hamish Urquhart rode the laughter. Carole and Jude exchanged looks and decided it was time to be getting back home.

Chapter Fourteen

The next morning, the Thursday, Carole drove Jude in her neat Renault up to Clincham College. They had tried ringing, but the woman who answered the phone said she wasn't allowed to give out any details about the students. Maybe an in-person approach would prove more productive.

The entrance to the campus was flanked by boards thanking local companies and other institutions for their sponsorship, giving the impression of a business park rather than a seat of learning. As the Renault nosed its way up the drive towards the visitors' car park, they passed a few students, looking impossibly young and clutching armfuls of books and folders. In warmer weather they might have been drifting more lethargically, but the brisk February air kept them on the move.

The main building of Clincham College had always been an educational institution, though it had undergone various metamorphoses before its recent attainment of university status. Originally built by a late Victorian philanthropist as 'an academy for the furtherance of Christian knowledge', the humourless tall grey edifice had at various times been a boys' prep school, a girls' public school and an outpost of a minor American university, peddling expensive degrees to students mostly from the Middle and Far East. Before its recent elevation it had for some years been a technical college. Now, as the biggest board at the entrance proudly proclaimed, it was 'The University of Clincham'.

The portico through which Carole and Jude made their way to the Reception area was elaborate and imposing, though it presented that quality of tired shabbiness which infects all educational establishments. The modern lettering of the various signs attached to the tall pillars was at odds with the period of their design.

Inside, more students were draped around the central hall, talking in groups or on their mobile phones. Their manner was loud and over-dramatic, trying to assert their personalities in their new supposed maturity.

Carole and Jude followed the signs to Reception, a glassed-off area with a counter, at which sat a daunting woman in a black business suit. Behind her in the office area stood a tall man reading through a stapled set of spreadsheets.

'Good morning,' said the woman, following some script that had been imposed on her. 'Welcome to Clincham College.'

'Hello, my name's Carole Seddon, and I wonder whether you could help me?'

'That's what I'm here to do,' said the woman, though her manner belied the welcome in her words.

'We're trying to make contact with someone who we believe may have been a student here.'

The woman's face shut down immediately. 'I'm afraid I'm not allowed to give out information about the students at the university.'

Jude thought she'd see whether charm might succeed where Carole's confrontational approach had failed. 'No, I'm sure that's the rule, but all we wanted to know—'

'I'm sorry,' the woman interrupted. 'I cannot let you have any information about the students.'

'Is there someone else we could speak to?' asked Carole frostily.

'You could write to the Principal with your enquiry, and it's possible that he might reply to you.' The woman didn't make that sound a very likely scenario.

'Look,' Jude persisted, 'all we want to know is the answer to one very simple question.' There was no point in pretence. Everyone in the locality knew the name of the recent murder victim. 'We want to know whether Tadeusz Jankowski, the man who was stabbed in Fethering last week, was ever actually enrolled in the college here.'

The woman went into automaton mode. 'I am not allowed to give out any information about any of the students in—'

'Ah, so you're admitting he was a student here?'

'I am not doing—'

She was interrupted by a voice from behind her.

Tadek's name had distracted the man from his spread-sheets. 'It's all right, Isobel, I'll deal with this.'

Leaving his papers, he emerged through the door from Reception and approached the two women. 'My name's Andy Constant. Lecturer in Drama Studies. Also Admissions Tutor.' Carole and Jude gave their names. 'Would you like to come and have a cup of coffee?'

They agreed that they would and, without further words, he led them to an adjacent snack bar. 'Don't worry, the coffee's all right.' He gestured to a well-known logo over the door. 'Outside franchise. Like everything else in this place. The academic life has ceased to be about learning. It's now all about raising funds and doing deals. I'll get the coffees. What would you like?'

As he went to the counter, Carole and Jude found a table and studied him. Long and gangly, Andy Constant moved with a laid-back swagger. His face receded from a beak of a nose and surprisingly full lips. His grey hair was worn long, rather in the style of Charles I. He had on black jeans, Timberland boots and a grey denim blouson over a white T-shirt. His voice was as languid as his manner.

He brought over the coffees, a cappuccino for Jude, the 'ordinary black' Carole had ordered, a tiny cup of espresso for himself, and sat down opposite them.

'Bit of excitement in a little place like Fethering, a murder, isn't it?' His tone was joshing, sending up the intensity of their interest. But he was at the same time alert, apparently trying to deduce the agenda that had brought them to the college.

'Bound to be,' said Jude easily.

For the first time he seemed to take her in, and he liked what he saw. 'Yes. And everyone's got their own theory about what happened.'

'The students too?'

'And how. Big excitement for them. Also rather frightening. A young man killed, possibly murdered, only a few miles away in Fethering. Comes a bit near home for them. Current crop of students have been brought up to be afraid of everything. The Health and Safety Generation, I call the poor saps. All afraid of being attacked, the girls afraid of being raped . . . Whatever happened to the innocence of youth?'

'Did it ever exist?' asked Carole.

'Maybe not, but I think when I was their age I did at least have the *illusion* of innocence. I kind of trusted the world, was prepared to give it a chance. I wasn't afraid of everything.'

'You say they're afraid of everything,' said Jude, 'but you're talking about a generation who think nothing of shooting off round the world on their gap years.'

'True. Except that's just become another form of package tourism these days. For me it takes the excitement out of far-flung places, knowing there'll be a nice familiar Macdonald's waiting when you get there.'

'Maybe.' He had taken over the conversation so effortlessly that Jude wanted to find out more about Andy Constant. 'You said you lecture in Drama. Does that mean you used to be an actor?' A theatricality about him made this quite a possibility.

'Very early in my career. Moved into directing for a while. Since then, teaching. Mind you, that involves a certain amount of directing too. And acting, come to think of it.'

He had considerable charm, and a strong sexual magnetism. The latter got through to Jude at an instinctive, visceral level, and she wondered whether Carole was aware of it too.

'Anyway,' Andy went on, 'I couldn't help overhearing what you said to Isobel at Reception. Sorry, I'm afraid she's not the most imaginative of women. Whatever the question, she always comes up with the party line. But I heard you mentioning the name of Tadeusz Jankowski. I wondered why you were interested. Are you just another pair of Fethering residents fascinated by their proximity to a murder?'

Carole and Jude exchanged a look. The true answer was probably a yes, but they needed to come up with something a bit better than that. Jude thought of a solution which certainly had elements of truth in it. 'The sister of the dead man came to see me. Naturally enough, she's trying to find out everything she can about her brother. I just thought Carole and I could possibly help her.'

He nodded, as if he accepted this justification for their presence. 'But why have you come here? What reason do you have for connecting the young man with Clincham College?'

Quickly Jude recounted what she had heard from

Harold Peskett, about the young Pole's earlier visit to the betting shop.

'Ah. That would explain something else.'

'What?'

'The police have been here too.'

'Asking about Tadeusz Jankowski?'

'Yes, Carole. Maybe they got the lead from the same source as you did.'

'When were they here?' asked Jude.

'Monday.'

'Then it wasn't the same source as mine. I only suggested they should contact Harold yesterday – and up to then he said they hadn't had any contact with him. So they must have heard about the Clincham College connection from someone else.'

'Not necessarily,' said Andy Constant. 'Apparently they didn't seem very focused when they came here, more like it was just a routine enquiry.' Yes, thought Jude, 'unfocused' is a pretty good description of the approach Baines and Yelland had used when they interviewed her.

'I mean, I suppose it makes sense,' Andy went on. 'Young people tend to congregate together. The dead man was young and had been living round here, so there's quite a reasonable chance that he would have hooked up with some of the students from the college.' Carole noticed he didn't use the word 'university' and wondered whether this was because he hadn't yet got used to the idea or whether he was as cynical about the place's status as she was.

The lecturer took a sip of his espresso and then continued in a different tone. 'Anyway, one thing the police did say was that we on the staff here should keep our eyes and ears open for anyone who came here expressing interest in the murder victim . . .'

'Oh.'

'I thought I should warn you.'

'Why warn us?'

'Well, I'm sure you don't want to be questioned by the police, do you? It's very time-consuming and can, I believe, be quite unpleasant. I mean, you're fine now. Isobel at Reception won't say anything – that would involve her using her initiative and she doesn't do that. And you can rely on me to keep quiet, but I can't guarantee that the rest of the staff here would be so accommodating.'

'So what are you actually saying?' asked Carole.

'I'm saying that we've been told to let the police know if anyone comes here enquiring about Tadeusz Jankowski, and so I think there might be an argument for you not taking your investigations at Clincham College much further.'

'You're warning us off,' said Jude.

He gave a relaxed laugh. 'That sounds a little over-dramatic. Let's just say I'm trying to avoid your being inconvenienced.'

'That's very thoughtful of you. But the police have already questioned me, and I didn't find it a particularly inconvenient experience.'

'Fine.' He shrugged. 'Only trying to save you hassle.' Jude felt his grey eyes seeking out her brown ones and saw the half-insolent smile on his face. Andy Constant knew he was attractive and he knew that she was responding to him. He couldn't know that part of the attraction came from his similarity to Laurence Hawker, another tall academic with whom she had spent time until his premature death a few years before. While she couldn't deny the pull that Andy Constant exerted, Jude resented feeling it. In spite of the superficial likeness to Laurence, there was something about him that struck warning chords within her, something dangerous. Which of course only served to add to his appeal.

Carole, who seemed unaware of the subtext between them, took up the conversation. 'You said you were Admissions Tutor.'

'I did, yes.'

'Then maybe you can at least answer the question we came here to ask.'

'Try me.'

'Was Tadeusz Jankowski ever enrolled here as a student?'

Andy Constant was silent for a moment, as if deliberating over his reply. He took another sip of his espresso, then put the tiny cup down on its tiny saucer. 'I can't actually see what harm my giving you that information can cause. Well, the answer's no. Tadeusz Jankowski was never enrolled in any course at this university.' It was the first time he had used the word.

'And had he ever made enquiries about the courses he might have enrolled in?' asked Carole, pushing her luck.

'Not so far as I know. I suppose he might have made

an approach by letter or email, but none of my colleagues has mentioned anything about his doing so.
And, needless to say, given the amount of media coverage, people have been talking a lot about him. I think if
anyone had had an approach from someone called
Tadeusz Jankowski, they'd have said so. It's not the
kind of name you'd forget, is it?'

Jude joined in. 'So you can't think of any connection he might have had with Clincham College?'

'No.'

'Do you know if he'd ever even been on the premises?'

'Not to my knowledge,' replied Andy Constant, and
then he gave Jude another of his lazy, but undeniably
sexy smiles. 'Still, if I hear from anyone that he has
been seen here, I'll let you know.' He smiled again.
'Maybe you'd like to give me your number, Jude . . .?'

As she was scribbling it out on a scrap of paper, a
girl came into the canteen. She was dark and pretty in
a Hispanic way, dressed in the typical student uniform
of jeans and layers of sweatshirts. Long black hair cur-
tained her face. 'Andy,' she said as she approached their
table. Her voice sounded slightly Spanish.

He looked up and seemed pleased with what he
saw. 'Yes?'

'Andy, I thought you said we'd meet up in the
Drama Studio at eleven.'

He looked at his watch. 'Oh, sorry. Hadn't noticed
the time.' He turned the full power of his smile on to
Carole and Jude. 'Ladies, you will excuse me?'

And, pausing only to snatch up the piece of paper

137

with Jude's number on it, he walked with long strides out of the café. The dark-haired girl followed, her eyes glowing with puppy love.

Jude was too old for puppy love, but she couldn't deny that Andy Constant was a very attractive man.

Chapter Fifteen

Jude heard the sound of crying as soon as she came through the door of Woodside Cottage. Zofia was hunched up on one of the sitting room's heavily draped sofas, her shoulders shaken by the sobs that ran through her body. On the floor beside her were a battered suitcase and a scruffy backpack. Immediately Jude's arms were round the girl and her lips were murmuring soothing words.

'I am sorry,' was the first thing that Zofia managed to say. 'I hear from the police this morning that I can come and collect Tadek's things, his possessions, and seeing them . . .' She indicated the bags '. . . it makes me realize that he is really gone from me.'

'Do you want me to put them away somewhere, until you are ready to deal with them?'

'No, Jude, thank you.' Zofia wiped the back of her hand against her face to dismiss the tears. 'No, I am ready to deal with them now. Maybe there is something in here that tells me what has happened to Tadek. I must not be emotional. I must try to piece together from his possessions what he was doing here in

England, and perhaps the reason why someone want to kill him.'

'All right,' said Jude. 'I'll help you. But first let's have a drink of something. What would you like, Zosia?'

'Coffee, please. Black, that would be good.'

'Don't start opening the bags until I'm there.' Jude didn't fool herself that her words were spoken from pure altruism. She was being offered a unique chance to further her investigation into Tadek's death.

'Did the police say anything,' she called through from the kitchen, 'about why they were letting you have his belongings so soon?'

'They just said they'd finished what they needed to do with them, and the landlord wants to rent out the room again as soon as possible so the stuff can't go back to Littlehampton. Would I like to take it, please?'

'Did you go back to the house?'

'No, I collect from police station.'

'I wonder if their letting you take the stuff suggests the police are winding up their investigation?'

'I do not know.'

'Well, if they've made an arrest, we'll hear pretty soon on the news.'

'Yes.'

When Jude came through with the coffee, Zofia had curbed her tears but she still looked lost and waiflike on the sofa. Her pigtails emphasized her vulnerability. 'Come on,' said Jude, once the drinks were poured, 'let's be very unemotional about this. Try to distance yourself from what you're looking at, Zosia.'

'I will try, but it is not easy.'

'I'm sure it isn't. But just try to forget it is your brother whose things we are looking at. Imagine it is an assignment you are doing as a journalist. You have to write a story based on the information you can glean from what you find here.'

'Yes, this is a good way. I will try this.' She produced her blue notebook and opened it at a clean page. 'I am writing a story about a murder investigation. And I will write my notes in English.'

'Right. Open the suitcase first.'

Zofia did as she was told. The contents of the case were pitifully few, mostly clothes, and fairly worn and threadbare clothes at that. Though they must all have been redolent of memories, the girl was commendably restrained as she neatly piled them up. She made a kind of inventory in her notebook.

'Nothing here that he didn't have at the time he left Warsaw,' she announced when the suitcase was nearly empty. She picked up the last item, a sponge bag, and unzipped it.

The contents once again were unsurprising. Shaving kit, deodorant, shampoo, toothpaste, toothbrush, paracetamol. And in one compartment a pack of condoms.

'So it looks like something was happening in his life . . .' suggested Jude.

'Or just that Tadek was, as he always was, optimistic.' Zofia was making a joke at the expense of her brother's romantic aspirations, but she could not say it without a tear glinting in her eye.

She moved on to the backpack. This had seen a lot

of service. Its fabric was slack and discoloured, covered with a rough patchwork of stickers, old and illegible ones covered over by newer designs whose colours showed up against them.

'Are these all from your brother's travels?'

'No. He was given the backpack by a friend, who I think himself had bought it second-hand. The only ones Tadek would have put on are those from music festivals he goes to.' She pointed to a bright printed circle. 'This one in Leipzig . . . I remember he goes there after he finish university last summer. A celebration . . . to play some of his own music, he said, and to listen to people who play music better than he does.'

She pulled the backpack towards her and tackled the buckles. 'Maybe here we will find more secrets about what he do in England.'

There was some evidence of Tadek's activities, but nothing very interesting. Zofia itemized everything in her blue notebook. Programmes and tickets suggested he'd been to a few music gigs, but none further afield than Brighton. Some torn-out newspaper advertisements indicated that his career ambitions might have extended beyond bar work. A well-thumbed dictionary and an old language course on cassette bore witness to a determination to improve his English.

And there was also an English rhyming dictionary. Zofia looked at this with some confusion, before opening it to check the contents. Then she nodded slowly.

'Does that tell you something?' asked Jude.

'I think, yes. It is something Tadek speak of occasionally. He say writing good songs in Polish is good for

Poland, but not for the world. To write songs that are very successful, you must write in English – or American.'

'So you think he was writing songs in English?'

'I think he tries, yes.'

'He wanted to be very successful?'

Zofia Jankowska grimaced. 'Not exactly that. Tadek did not want a lot of money. Well, we would not have minded, but for him money was a . . . was what he could do with it . . . I think there is an expression in English . . .?'

'"A means to an end".'

'Yes, this is good. This is how Tadek see money. It helps him to do things he want to do. For him money is "a means to an end".'

'So writing songs in English would have made him more money? That would be his reason for doing it?'

'Perhaps. More with Tadek, though . . .' The girl smiled wistfully '. . . he might want to write songs for English women.'

'What do you mean?'

'I tell you he is romantic. He fall for women who are not right for him . . .'

'Yes, you said. And often older women.'

'That is what Tadek does, very often. And because he is romantic, and because he does not have much money to buy presents for the women he loves . . .'

'He used to write songs for them?'

Zofia nodded. 'That is what he always does.' She picked up the rhyming dictionary again. 'So perhaps this means he had fallen in love with an Englishwoman.'

She pulled a small pile of songbooks out of the backpack. They were mostly much-used copies of folk and protest songs from the nineteen-sixties, songs made popular by artistes like Bob Dylan, Joan Baez, Donovan and the Byrds.

'Your brother had rather old-fashioned tastes.'

'Yes, this is the music he likes. He plays a lot of these. Not electric guitar. The songs he write are in this style too. Perhaps that is why he does not make money from his songs, in any language. As you say, they are old-fashioned.' Emotion threatened for a moment, as she realized that she had heard the last of her brother's songs, but she controlled it. 'Right, that is nearly everything. Just a few more bits.'

She took out the remaining contents of the backpack, again arranging them neatly in piles on the floor. She made more notes in the little blue book. A couple of novels in Polish, a crucifix, other small ornaments. There was nothing that seemed out of place to Jude, but Zofia sat there for a long time saying, 'It is strange, it is very strange.'

'What's strange? Is there something there that shouldn't be?'

'No,' the girl replied. 'It is the other way round. There is things not here that should be here.'

'What?'

The pained hazel eyes fixed on Jude's. 'Tadek lived for his music. There is nothing of that here, except for the sheet music. No notebooks with songs written out,

144

no lyrics, no cassettes, no CDs. Most of all, there is not his guitar.'

'What was the guitar like?'

'It was not electrical. It was . . . I don't know the word.'

'Acoustic.'

'Yes, it was acoustic. An acoustic guitar.' Zofia seemed to savour the adjective on her lips. 'Tadek would never give his guitar away. Where is it? It is such a special guitar.'

'Special meaning valuable?'

'No, no, probably after what Tadek has done to it, it is less valuable. He painted it red and he paint two eyes on the front, you know, like the hole behind the strings is the mouth, so the guitar has a face. In the band he play with with his friends, they all paint faces on their instruments. It is something they do, so that always people recognize them. And they call the band "Twarz". That means "face" in Polish.'

'Did you ask the police about the guitar when you picked up this lot?'

'I wasn't thinking. But they tell me here is everything they find in his room.'

'It might be worth checking. They could still be doing forensic tests on the guitar. Have you got a number for them?'

Zofia Jankowska had. She rang through and spoke to the officer from whom she had picked up the bags that morning. He told her everything was there except for the clothes her brother had been wearing at the time of his death. There had been no sign of a guitar amongst his belongings.

Being told this prompted another question from Jude. 'That overcoat he was wearing, was that his?'

Zofia nodded. 'I was with him when he bought it. In a street market in Warsaw for old clothes. It was from Russian navy. A lot of clothes like that are for sale in Poland.' Jude remembered thinking at the time that the coat had looked naval.

'You don't think he might have sold the guitar? If he needed the money?'

'Tadek would never do that. He might sell anything else, he might go without food, he would never sell his guitar. That was like part of him. Besides . . .' She picked up something that looked like a polished wooden cigar-box, turned it over and clicked a secret catch that revealed a false bottom. Inside was probably two hundred pounds in English notes. 'You see, Tadek had money.'

Zofia squatted back on her haunches in something like despair. 'So where do we find his guitar?'

'And where,' asked Jude thoughtfully, 'do we find the English woman to whom he was writing love songs?'

On her walk with Gulliver late that afternoon, Carole found herself passing Fethering's parade of shops and felt a very uncharacteristic urge to go into the bookie's. She managed to curb it and keep walking, but the strength of the impulse surprised her.

She knew it was partly to do with Gerald Hume. She didn't know whether she was attracted to him – she'd hardly been in the man's company long enough to form an opinion – but she was still warmed by the impression that she'd received of his being very definitely attracted to her. She wasn't convinced that the attraction was sexual, but they had definitely clicked at some level. The knowledge gave her a slightly heady feeling of power.

But Gerald Hume wasn't the only cause of her urge to go in. The betting shop remained the focus of the enquiry into Tadek's death. Perhaps it was no longer the focus for the official investigation – the police no doubt had new avenues to explore – but for Carole and Jude everything still came back to the betting shop.

Not for the first time Carole tried to guess at the young man's movements in the moments before he entered the place the previous week. That was the big question: where had he actually been when he was attacked? His thick coat could only have served as a temporary barrier to the flow of blood, so the scene of the stabbing could not have been very far away. Had the confrontation taken place on the beach or in one of the nearby houses or shops? Surely if it had happened in public there would have been some witnesses? And yet the powerful news-gathering agency of Fethering gossip had produced not a single clue even as to the direction from which the dying man had entered the betting shop.

Then Carole remembered the hailstorm. Under her duvet, drowned in flu, she had only been aware of the

rattling of the icy downpour against her windows, but
from Jude's description it had been really ferocious,
obliterating all of the town's familiar landmarks. That
was why no one had witnessed Tadek's approach to the
betting shop.

Carole looked again along the parade. Allinstore,
Marnie's Hairdressing, Polly's Cake Shop, the estate
agents, the charity shops. It seemed unlikely that the
young Pole had come out of one of them and yet what
other explanation was there for his sudden appearance?

At that moment a car drawing up alongside her
reminded Carole of another possibility. The young Pole
could have arrived at the parade by car. But if he did,
where had he come from? And who with?

Chapter Sixteen

Any social encounter that involved Lily had to be arranged around her schedule. Like most babies – particularly first babies – her arrival had immediately changed the pecking order in her parents' household. Gaby and Stephen were her slaves, and their lives now revolved around the vagaries of their daughter's feeding and sleeping patterns.

As a result the visit to Carole on the Friday was rigidly circumscribed by time. If Gaby left Fulham on the dot of ten, Lily would sleep all of the hour and three-quarters' drive to Fethering. Then they'd have to leave on the dot of two to ensure an equally peaceful return journey.

This suited Carole well. She liked arrangements to be fixed and defined. Nothing caused her greater anxiety than the concept of 'an open-ended visit'.

And she was hungry for the sight of Lily. Even in the few weeks since their last meeting, the baby had developed exponentially. Her smile was no longer something that could have been mistaken for wind. It was now a definite expression of pleasure, and one that could be bestowed on those around her like a rich gift.

Her mother still got most of the smiles. She and Lily had bonded instantly, and the baby's arrival had changed Gaby's personality. Though she hadn't lost her sparkle, she was calmer. And her conversation no longer revolved about show business. She seemed to have no wistful nostalgia for her work as a theatrical agent, she was totally absorbed in the new life which had come into hers. Carole thought it might be some time before her employers would see Gaby back in the office.

Serenely even-handed, that day Lily granted smiles to her grandmother as well as her mother. There had been some discussion with Stephen and Gaby as to what Carole should be called in her new role. All the possibles – Gran, Granny, Grandma, Nan – sounded dispiritingly old, but there was no avoiding making a choice. She had settled for 'Granny' as the least offensive, and indeed the name her own almost-forgotten grandmother had been known by.

With Lily there as a catalyst, Carole was surprised how much more relaxed she felt with her daughter-in-law. She had always liked Gaby, but felt an edge of unease when Stephen was not there and there were just the two of them. She had a bit of that feeling when she was alone with anyone. Her insecurities rose to the surface, she was always afraid that the other person was making judgements and finding her wanting.

But now with Gaby and the baby, Carole experienced something she had never relaxed into before, a kind of gender solidarity. Though she didn't rate her own maternal skills very highly, the shared experience of motherhood had brought the two women closer. Carole was amazed how unperturbed she could be by Gaby openly feeding Lily. She felt a kind of regret for her own time with Stephen as a small baby, when social convention and her own modesty had made breast-feeding a rather furtive exercise.

But perhaps what she appreciated most was the ease that her daughter-in-law showed in her presence. Gaby did not question Carole's right to be included in the care of her baby. She even asked for advice and reassurance over Lily's little quirks of development.

So at two o'clock sharp Carole was sorry to see them go, but warmed by the encounter. She felt bonded with the next two generations of women, and she looked forward to watching the development of the new person in her life.

She also knew that the visit would not have been nearly so satisfactory had her ex-husband been present.

So she was already in a good mood when the phone rang at about half-past two, and the ensuing conversation cheered her even more.

'Is that Carole Seddon?' The voice was cultivated, precise and vaguely familiar.

'Yes.'

'I found your number in the local directory.'

'Well, you would. It's in there,' said Carole rather fatuously. She still couldn't identify the voice, but was not left in ignorance for long.

'It's Gerald Hume speaking. Remember, we met in the betting shop yesterday.'

'Yes, I remember. I'm surprised you're not there now.'

'Oh, I am. As you may recall my saying, I am an habitué.' His use of the word echoed their conversation of the previous day. 'Well, to be strictly accurate, I am not inside the betting shop. I'm standing outside the premises. The mobile phone signal is better here, and also I don't like having my telephone conversations listened to by all and sundry.'

'Nor do I. That's one of the reasons I don't want a mobile phone.'

'I understand.' There was a brief silence. 'I thought you might have come in today.'

'Good heavens, no. As I believe I told you, yesterday was the first time I've crossed the threshold of a betting shop.'

'I thought you might have got the taste for it.'

'Certainly not,' came the instinctive, Calvinist response.

'Well, Carole,' said Gerald Hume with a sudden change of tone, 'I wondered if we could meet for a drink.'

'Meet for a drink?' she echoed stupidly. 'You and me?'

'Yes. I enjoyed meeting you yesterday. I thought it would be nice to talk at further length.'

'Well . . .'

'I'm sorry. I hope you don't think me forward.' Which was a comfortingly old-fashioned word for him to use. 'If you don't relish the idea, you have only to say no.'

Carole found herself saying 'Well . . .' again. The proposition was so unexpected that she couldn't immediately adjust to the idea.

'If you'd rather not, you needn't be embarrassed by refusing.'

'No, I'm not embarrassed.' To her surprise, Carole realized this was true. And suddenly she could see no reason to refuse his suggestion. 'Yes,' she said. 'Yes. Let's meet for a drink. When were you thinking of?'

'Would this evening be convenient?'

'This evening would be most convenient.'

Jude also had an invitation that afternoon. She had been half-expecting the call, with foreboding but an undercurrent of excitement. From the moment she'd met Andy Constant, she knew that something had connected between them.

On the phone he sounded even more languid and laid-back. The offer was made very casually, as if the manner of asking somehow took the curse off it. If she refused, his manner implied, it had never been any big deal anyway.

'Thought it'd be nice to meet again,' he said.

He was taking a risk. He knew nothing about her. She might be in a long-term relationship. But still he asked. Jude had already got the impression that Andy Constant was used to getting his own way with women.

'Well, yes, it might be,' she responded. She was taking a risk too. But she reassured herself that it wasn't only because she was attracted to him. He still might have some information that was of relevance to the murder of Tadek. To keep in touch with him would be in the cause of pursuing their investigation, she told herself with knowing casuistry.

'Thing is, I'm doing a show at the college with some of the Drama students. Wondered if you'd like to come and see it. Then we could have a drink afterwards.'

Again, he made it sound very casual. Quite clever too, Jude thought. Not a direct request for a date. He made it sound as if the main purpose of the invitation was for her to see the show. And hopefully be impressed by it, perhaps warm to him because of his skills as a director. Then have a few drinks and maybe fix to meet again. There was something disquietingly practised about his approach.

'What is the show?' she asked.

'It's called *Rumours of Wars*. Something the students have built up through improvisation and I've kind of tailored into a script. I promise you it's less dreary than it sounds. They're a bright lot of kids, some real talent in there.'

'When are you talking about?'

'Short notice, I'm afraid. Show only runs for three performances. Saturday I have to entertain a lot of college bigwigs. So I'm talking about this evening.' Jude hadn't complained about the short notice, but he still seemed to feel the need to apologize. 'Ideally, I'd have asked you further in advance, but I hadn't met you then, had I? And I do think the show's something you might enjoy.'

Which Jude considered was a rather bold claim, since he'd had no time to assess her theatrical interests.

'It's in the college's new theatre. Building's worth seeing, apart from anything else. So tell me, do you fancy it?'

Again, he fostered the illusion of distancing himself. It was the show she'd be coming to see, not him. Jude had to acknowledge that his technique, though obviously well practised, was rather good.

'All right,' she said. 'I'd like to come.'

Chapter Seventeen

On a day when she had been feeling less good about herself Carole Seddon might have balked at Gerald Hume's suggestion that their meeting that evening should take place in the Crown and Anchor. The proposed encounter did have elements of a 'date' about it, and the pub's landlord was one of the very few men in Fethering who had ever shown an emotional interest in her. In less certain moods she might have agonized about some awkward scene arising between the two men. But that Friday evening Carole had no qualms about the venue. For a start, her affair with Ted Crisp was long over and their relationship had settled down into an easy friendship. Besides, the Crown and Anchor did have certain advantages. Apart from anything else, she would be on home territory and not far from High Tor, should the meeting prove to be uncomfortable. After all, she knew nothing about Gerald Hume.

He was sitting in óne of the alcoves nursing a half-pint of lager when she arrived. Dressed, as ever, in pin-striped suit and tie, his briefcase on the banquette beside him. Carole greeted Ted Crisp immediately, to establish her familiarity with the pub. Now the moment had arisen, it gave her a slight *frisson* actually to be in a pub talking to an ex-lover when she was about to meet another man.

She sat down while Gerald Hume went to the bar to buy her requested Chilean Chardonnay, and wondered what kind of man he would prove to be. She wasn't worried about finding out, though, just intrigued.

'Perhaps,' he announced when he had supplied her drink, 'I should explain why I wanted to meet up with you.'

To her surprise, Carole found herself saying, 'I don't think you need to especially. As you said on the phone, it's nice for us to have a chance to talk.'

'Yes.'

He hesitated, still seeming to feel he should provide some explanation, so she moved on, 'Did you have a good day on the horses?'

'A profit of three pounds fifty pence.' He spoke in a considered manner, as if carefully selecting each word with a pair of tweezers.

'And is that a good day?'

'Would you regard three pounds fifty pence as adequate recompense for five hours' work?'

'No, I suppose not. So you do think of what you do in the betting shop as work, do you?'

'Well, it's the only work I have now.'

'I heard a rumour that you used to be an accountant.'

'That's a very unusual rumour to hear.'

'In what way unusual?'

'Because it's accurate. Very few rumours in

Fethering share that quality.' Carole smiled. He clearly knew the area well. 'Yes,' he went on, 'I was an account-ant with the same company for thirty-six years. They then deemed that I was no longer fit to be an account-ant.'

Carole didn't quite like to ask for amplification, but seeing her reaction he provided it. 'No, no skulduggery on my part, no embezzlement of funds. Merely a company policy of retirement at sixty. Drinks with colleagues, a hastily mugged-up speech from my new much younger boss, the presentation of an unwanted carriage clock and "Goodbye, Mr Hume." So, given the fact that I used to spend eight hours of every weekday in the office, that did leave rather a large gap in my life.'

'Surely there were other things you could have done?'

'I suppose so. I could have set up in private prac-tice. I could have offered my services as treasurer for various local societies. But such options did not appeal to me. My pension was adequate and I had made some prudent though not very adventurous investments over the years. So I didn't need to do anything else to make money.'

'Isn't retirement when people are supposed to devote themselves to their hobbies in a way that they previously never had time for?' asked Carole, reflecting that in her own case this hadn't worked out. The only hobby she had was being an amateur detective and that was one she had developed after she retired.

'Perhaps. And I am quite a keen photographer. But I can't do that every day. I get bored, so it remains just a hobby. Spending time in the betting shop, however, does impose some kind of structure on my life. It also enables me to study the vagaries of horse racing over a sustained period.'

'You mean you . . . "study the form"? Is that the right expression? And, incidentally, Gerald, I should tell you here and now that, whatever impression I may have given to the contrary yesterday, I know absolutely nothing about horses.'

'That, Carole, was abundantly clear.'

'Oh.' She couldn't help being disappointed. She thought the way she'd behaved the previous day had been pretty damned convincing.

'Anyway, you asked if I study the form, and yes, I do do a certain amount of that, but I am more interested in the mathematical probabilities involved in the business.'

'Do you mean you are trying to work out a foolproof system to win on the horses?'

Gerald Hume chuckled. 'If I were doing that, today's profit of three pounds fifty pence might suggest that my system is as yet far from foolproof. But you're right in a way. I am trying to draw some conclusions from the many races that I watch every day. I analyse the results and, yes, there is the hope that such analysis might lead to a more informed pattern of investment.'

'And do you ever have big wins?'

'A few hundred pounds now and then. But such days are rare.'

'I still can't quite understand why you do it.'

'No, it may seem inexplicable. There is a commonly held view that racing is a mug's game, that there are too many variables for any kind of logical pattern to be discernible. But the attempt to impose order on such chaos does sometimes bring me the same kind of satisfaction that I used to derive during my working life from balancing columns of figures. Perhaps because my life has followed a relatively predictable course, I am fascinated by the random. Maybe, in my own perhaps pernickety way, I am trying to impose logic on the random.'

'I see.' And now she almost did.

'And it keeps me off the streets.' He smiled rather wanly. 'I'm not sure how I would fill my time without my regular attendance at the betting shop.'

There was a moment of silence before Gerald Hume, realizing the danger of sounding pitiable, abruptly changed the direction of the conversation. 'Still, enough about me. I don't have nearly that amount of information about you yet, Carole.'

'No.'

Her retirement from the Home Office and divorce were established with the minimum of comment.

'I see,' said Gerald. 'I never married.'

'Is that a cause for regret?'

'Rarely. I think I am probably not designed for connubial bliss. I tend to be rather analytical in all my dealings, which may lead to a level of detachment in my behaviour. And I have been given to understand that marriage requires engagement with the partner rather than detachment from them.'

'I think that is usually thought desirable, yes.'

Carole was touched by his quaintness, and found her own speech beginning to echo the formality of his. She had also by now realized that Gerald Hume wasn't and never would be a 'date'. The attraction between them was not physical, it was purely intellectual. This revelation did not bring her even the mildest flicker of disappointment. In fact it reassured her, clarified her feelings.

'May I go off on a complete tangent, Gerald . . .?'

'By all means.'

'. . . and ask whether you do crosswords?'

As Carole knew he would, he confirmed that he did. 'I do the *Times* and the *Telegraph* every morning before I go to the betting shop. One might imagine, given my interest in numbers, it would be the Su Doku that monopolized my attention, but no, it's words. Maybe because words are more resonant than numbers, because they carry with them a greater burden of semiotic information. And do I gather you are also an aficionado of the crossword . . .?'

'I usually do the *Times*,' said Carole.

'I knew you would.' This confirmation of his conjecture seemed to make him particularly happy. 'I am very glad that we have met, Carole. I think there are a lot of similarities in our personalities.'

Deciding that this was not a completely undiluted compliment, she moved on to another possible area of mutual interest. 'Gerald, have you ever applied your analytical mind to the subject of crime?'

He smiled with relish. 'I most certainly have. I

enjoy the process of deduction, very similar in fact to that required in the solution of a crossword. But I'm afraid the crime writing I favour is of an older generation. The so-called Golden Age, when authors played fair with their readers in regard to plotting. Though contemporary crime fiction may have gained in psychological reality, that has always been at the expense of the puzzle element. And for me it is in the puzzle that the appeal of the genre lies.'

'But have you ever applied your deductive powers to a real crime?' asked Carole.

'Might you be thinking of the recent regrettable incident, which occurred at the place where I spend a large portion of my days?'

'I was thinking of that, yes, Gerald.'

'Hm. The first time I have been so close to a murder, outside of fiction. I'm afraid, in my professional life – though accountants may frequently be thought to get away with murder . . .' He let out a small dry laugh at this small dry joke '. . . they are – perhaps fortunately – rarely involved in the real thing.'

'So have you joined in the increasingly popular Fethering pastime of trying to work out whodunit?'

'I have.' He sighed. 'But without much progress. I regret in this instance the Almighty Author has provided us with an inadequacy of information. Dame Agatha would never have been so parsimonious with the clues. Though we habitués of the betting shop were witnesses to one part of the tragedy – and your friend Jude witness to a further part – we have very few facts that link the poor young man to his penultimate destination.'

'Were you particularly aware of him when he came in that afternoon?'

'I can't say that I was, Carole. Yes, I noticed a young man I had not seen before come into the shop. The noise of the hailstorm was very loud when the door was opened, so I looked in his direction. But I very quickly returned to my investments. I can't honestly say that the young man made any impression on me at all.'

'Gerald, you said then that you had not seen the victim before . . .'

'That is correct, yes.'

'But last week's visit was the second time he had been in the betting shop.'

'Was it?' The ex-accountant looked genuinely amazed by this news. 'I had certainly never seen him before.'

'And you are there most days during opening hours?'

'Well, not opening hours – betting shops tend to be open for an increasingly long time these days – but I'm there during afternoon racing hours. I tend to arrive about half an hour before the first race and stay there until after the last.'

'And would you say you tend to notice everyone who comes in and out?'

'I do. I make a point of that. My researches into the randomness of gambling are obviously related to the demographic profile of the people who participate.'

'So you're sure you'd never seen Tadek before last week?'

'Tadek?'

'I'm sorry. Tadeusz Jankowski was always called Tadek.'

'I understand. No, I had definitely never encountered him before last week. When was he seen?'

'Round the beginning of last October.'

Gerald Hume's brow clouded as he tried to explain the anomaly, but then it cleared. 'Last October, yes. I remember now. I was unwell. I had a serious throat infection which kept me to my bed for a few days. I think it must have been during that period. Did Ryan the Manager see him?'

'It was while Ryan was on holiday.'

'So how do you know the young man was in there?'

Carole explained about Jude's conversation with Pauline.

'Ah yes. That would make sense. Pauline never does much in the way of gambling, but she always keeps her eyes on everything that's going on. A habit that she learnt from her late husband.'

'Oh?'

'He was a fairly considerable crook. Or so Fethering gossip has it . . . and this is another instance when I would be inclined to believe Fethering gossip.'

'Jude said that Pauline was one of very few women who go into the betting shop.'

'That is true. It is more of a male enclave . . . though a lot of the ladies put in an appearance round the

Derby or Grand National. Or down here when Glorious Goodwood is on, of course.'

A new thought came suddenly to Carole. 'Ooh, that reminds me. Other women in the betting shop!'

'I'm sorry?'

'Apparently when Tadeusz Jankowski went into the betting shop last year, he spoke to a woman who was often in there. Another regular. Very well-dressed, middle-class woman . . . does that ring any bells, Gerald?'

'Well, there are one or two fitting that description who come in from time to time . . .'

'This one used to be very regular, but then stopped coming . . . round about last October. Any idea who it might be?'

Gerald Hume beamed as the recollection came to him. 'Oh yes. I know exactly who you mean. I'm sorry, with her not having been in for a few months, I'd completely forgotten about her. But yes, she fits your description exactly.'

'Did you ever talk to her?'

'No. She kept herself to herself.'

More or less exactly what Pauline and Ryan had said. Carole asked, without much hope, 'So you wouldn't know her name, would you?'

This question produced another beam. 'As a matter of fact I do. Melanie Newton.'

'But if you didn't speak to her, how do you know that?'

Gerald Hume's expression combined shame with pride as he replied, 'One day when she was in the betting shop, she had made a note of her fancies on an envelope. When she went, she screwed it up and left it on a shelf. I'm afraid, out of pure curiosity – and because she seemed rather different from the average run of betting shop habitué – I uncrumpled the envelope and looked at it.'

'So do you have an address for her too?' asked Carole excitedly.

Gerald shook his head apologetically. 'I'm afraid I don't have a photographic memory for such things. Though I do have a vague recollection that she lived in Fedborough.'

Carole still felt good about herself when she got back to High Tor at about eight o'clock. She had a new lead. Melanie Newton. She was going to share the good news with Jude, when she remembered that her friend was out seeing some theatre show at Clincham College.

But as well as a new lead, she thought she might have something else. Though Gerald Hume would never be a lover (which was, if she was honest with herself, quite a relief), it was not impossible that over time he could turn into a very good friend.

Chapter Eighteen

Jude picked up the ticket that Andy Constant had promised would be left at the box office and went through into the theatre. The building was named after the company which had stumped up the money for its construction, with a view to raising their local charitable profile. (They had made a very favourable deal with the university, which would allow them free use of the halls of residence for conferences during the vacations.) As Andy had said, the theatre was new, new even to the extent of still smelling of paint and freshly varnished wood. And it was a rather splendid structure.

The auditorium was buzzing with the sounds of young people, fellow students there to support their mates, but there were also quite a few parents, coming to see what all those tuition fees were being spent on.

Jude had been presented with a programme, just an A5 sheet printed in black with a list of actors and production credits. The title of the evening's entertainment was *Rumours of Wars: The Interface Between Society and Violence*. She noted that the show had been 'Conceived and Directed by Andy Constant'.

She saw him briefly before the show. He gave her a

wave of acknowledgement as he bustled busily up the aisle from the pass-door by the stage. He was dressed exactly as when she'd last seen him, but there was now a greater aura of importance about him. In his wake scuttled the pretty dark-haired girl who had summoned him from the university coffee shop on their last encounter. As he passed Jude, Andy Constant said, 'If I don't see you in all the confusion after the show, let's meet up in the Bull. Just opposite the gates of the campus – do you know it?'

'I'll find it.'

'Won't be such a scrum there as there will in the student bar.'

'Can I set one up for you?'

'Pint of Stella would be wonderful.'

And he whisked his important way to the back of the auditorium, where the dark-haired girl was now waiting for him.

Just as the lights were dimming, Jude caught sight of Ewan and Hamish Urquhart a few rows in front, presumably there to cheer on Sophia.

The show was not bad, but it did feel slightly over-inflated for its own good. The subject of war is a big one and *Rumours of Wars* tried to take on all of it. There were the obligatory scenes of carnage from 1914–18, juxtaposed with the clinical battles of new technologies. There were scenes of everyman squaddies punctiliously obeying orders given to them by idiots, of bereaved mothers weeping over the deaths of children in air raids, of blimpish generals planning mass slaughter over post-prandial port.

All of this was realized in a form that involved much shouting, a certain amount of dance, some a cappella singing and a lot of mime (which was about as interesting as mime usually is). The show was built about a lot of tableaux of human bodies, dramatic images precisely engineered. It was all impressive and just a tad worthy.

Also old-fashioned. Andy Constant must have been very young during the sixties, but that was definitely the period when his ideas of theatre had been formed. Jude got the feeling that he'd definitely seen *Oh! What A Lovely War* at an impressionable age. There was a simplicity in his anti-war message which accorded better with the protest years of Vietnam, when there were still perhaps some illusions remaining to be shattered, than the cynical wartime of Iraq. The show seemed to be taking a battering ram to a door that was already wide open.

And the acting wasn't terribly good. The kind of slick ensemble playing required by that kind of theatre was beyond the capacity of the University of Clincham's Drama students. Though individual talents shone through in various areas, none had the all-round versatility that the piece demanded. And of all the cast Sophia Urquhart was probably the weakest. She looked pretty enough and went through the motions of what she had rehearsed, but didn't convince. However much she threw herself around the stage, she remained quintessentially a young lady of the Home Counties who had been to all the right schools. Wherever the girl's future lay, it wasn't in acting.

Her singing voice, though, was something else. In the one solo number she had, she was transformed. This, again harking back to the sixties, was Pete Seeger's 'Where Have All the Flowers Gone?' As the girl's pure unaccompanied soprano spelt out the message of pacifism, she seemed not only to evoke an earlier era, but also to swell with confidence and to take effortless control of the whole auditorium. As a singer, Sophia Urquhart might make it.

The best thing about *Rumours of Wars*, in Jude's view, was its length. An hour and twenty minutes with no interval. Quite long enough to preach to the converted that *war is a bad thing*.

Jude's overall impression of the evening was the dominance of Andy Constant. The show was supposedly built up from improvisation, but had all the hallmarks of contrivance. Yes, the students may have come up with individual ideas, but they had been welded into a preconceived form by the director. The iron will of Andy Constant lay behind every line and every gesture. In a way, the weakness of the material served only to highlight the skill with which it had been pressed into theatrical shape.

In her brief experience as an actress Jude had come across directors like that. For them the written text was an irrelevance, an obstacle to be overcome by their stagecraft. And working from improvisation gave them the perfect opportunity to impose their wills on actors. The aim of the production was only to show how clever they, the directors, were. The whole exercise was an ego-trip.

Jude knew that that was exactly how Andy Constant would have treated his students during the rehearsal period. What he was after was control, pure and simple.

And even as she identified the kind of man he was, she was aware of the way she was drawn towards him. She could regret, but she couldn't deny it.

Andy had said that the Bull pub would be less of a scrum than the student bar, but it was still pretty crowded, the regular clientele augmented by parents who had just experienced *Rumours of Wars*. From the conversations Jude overheard as she struggled towards the bar, they had thought rather more of the show than she had. Or maybe it was just because their offspring had been participating.

There were also quite a few of the students who'd been in the show, and a lot of their friends who hadn't. Jude saw the girl with long dark hair at the centre of a giggling bunch of youngsters.

Given the crowd, she was glad she'd suggested setting up a drink for Andy Constant. One trip to the bar took long enough. As she eased her way through the crowd with a Chardonnay and a pint of Stella, she found herself face to face with Ewan and Hamish Urquhart, both dressed in Drizabone coats over their corduroy.

'Ah, Jude, isn't it? I thought I saw you in there. So, what did you think of my little Sophia, eh?'

'I thought there was a lot of talent there,' she said tactfully.

'Yes. Bloody stupid thing for a girl to do, though,

isn't it? No security in acting. Hope she'll see the light soon and start doing something sensible. Mind you,' he couldn't help saying, with a father's pride, 'she is rather gifted, and she's pretty enough to make a go of it.'

'Let's hope so. Her singing is really excellent.' No need to say anything about the acting.

'Yes. Hamish, you get them in, will you?' Ewan Urquhart's son obediently scuttled into the melee around the bar. 'No, she's a good little singer, my Soph. You can catch her singing in here most Friday nights.'

'Really?'

He pointed to a poster pinned on to a board nearby. It had been printed up on a home computer by someone who had only just discovered how many fonts and colours it was possible to use, and advertised 'MAGIC DRAGON, Clincham Uni's Number One Folk/Rock Band'. A rather smudged photograph showed a long-haired figure who was recognizably Sophia Urquhart fronting two guitarists and a fiddler.

'Obviously they're not doing it tonight because of the show. But most other Fridays during term-time you'll find her in here singing her little heart out.'

'I must try and catch them one day. As I say, she has got an exceptional voice.'

'Yes.' Ewan Urquhart agreed in a voice that mixed pride with scepticism. 'Trouble is, if she goes into that kind of business – singing, acting – God knows what kind of riff-raff she's going to mix with. Funny lot, actors, aren't they?'

'Some of them. So there isn't any showbiz in your family?'

'Good God, no. I went to Charterhouse, spent all my time doing sport. No time for bloody acting.' Ewan Urquhart seemed to need to shoehorn his status as an Old Carthusian into every conversation.

'I thought maybe Sophia's mother . . .'

'Sophia's mother and I parted company some years ago,' he responded with some asperity. 'And if you're wondering whether Sophia got her acting or singing talent from that source, let me tell you my ex-wife had no talent of any description.'

Jude deduced from the vehemence of this response that it was Mrs Urquhart who had left her husband, rather than vice versa. And she didn't blame her.

She noticed that Andy Constant had just entered the pub and so, with an 'Excuse me', edged her way towards a table for two she'd just seen vacated.

He flopped down in front of his pint, long limbs drooping in a parody of exhaustion. 'God, I'm wiped out. I find directing takes more out of me than acting ever did. Particularly with these kids . . . you never quite know what they're going to do from minute to minute.'

'They seemed very disciplined to me, from what I saw on stage.'

'Yes, but it takes a while to get into their heads what acting's about. Very few of them understand the concept of an ensemble. They don't know that acting's not about the individual, it's about everyone working together.' Which Jude understood as 'everyone doing what I tell them'.

'Still, the show played pretty well tonight,' Andy

Constant went on complacently. 'I like it when the audience gasps.' The audience had indeed gasped, but only at the crowbarring-in of a few four-letter words, which Jude hadn't reckoned added anything.

'I'm intrigued that the show was worked out through improvisation,' said Jude. 'It all felt very structured.'

He grinned, as if she had given him a compliment. 'Yes, well, the ideas the kids come up with are not always very practical. You have to have someone there who's shaping the thing.'

'And in this case that person was you?'

He acknowledged the fact with a nod, took a long sip of his lager and then looked at Jude through narrowed eyes. She guessed that at some stage he had been told he looked sexy doing that, and was annoyed with herself for actually finding it sexy.

'So . . . Jude . . . I don't know much about you.'

'No.' That was, generally speaking, the way she liked things to stay. 'Well, I live in Fethering. Is that enough information?'

'I'd like to know whether you're married?'

'No.'

'In a long-term relationship?'

'No.'

'I'm surprised. You're an attractive woman.'

'Thank you.' Jude had never been coy about accepting compliments. 'And what about you . . . in the marital stakes?'

He ran his fingers through his long grey hair, flattening it either side of the central parting. 'I am technically married, in that my wife and I haven't bothered to divorce, but we haven't really been married for sixteen years . . . no, I tell a lie, it's seventeen now.'

'Children?'

'A couple.'

'How old?'

'Oh, finished with education. Off our hands.' The answer was airy and, to Jude's mind, calculatedly vague. He didn't want her to know exactly how old he was, which probably meant he was older than he looked.

This impression was confirmed by the way he immediately moved the conversation on. 'You haven't got any further in your search for the killer of Tadeusz Jankowski?'

'No further progress. Nor in finding a connection between him and Clincham College.'

That caught him on the hop. A momentary expression of anxiety was quickly quelled as he said, 'Well, I think you're very unlikely to find one.'

'Carole and I can keep looking.'

'Of course you can. It's a free country. Though, with the current government, I'm beginning to wonder . . .' It was a line he had to say, to maintain his pose as the free-thinking outsider.

Their exchange of information was still incomplete, so Jude asked, 'And are you in a relationship at the moment?'

He did the narrowed eyes routine again. 'Nothing I couldn't get out of if something better came along,' he murmured. God, the arrogance of the man.

'I think we should meet again,' he announced suddenly. 'When we have more time to . . . appreciate each other.'

'It's a thought,' said Jude, against her better judgement.

'A good thought.' He smiled lazily. 'I'd suggest extending this evening's encounter, but . . .' He shrugged '. . . I'm afraid there's some stuff I've still got to sort out back at the college.'

Jude didn't say anything. The bar was quieter now. The first rush of students had gone back to the campus. Her hand was lying on the table. Andy Constant moved his forward as if to touch it, then abruptly changed his mind as he caught sight of the approaching Sophia Urquhart.

'Andy, bit of a problem.'

He looked shaken and turned to face the girl. 'Something to do with the show?'

'No. A message from Joan.' She looked piercingly at Jude, not recognizing her but perhaps with a degree of suspicion. 'If I could just have a quick word, Andy . . .'

'Excuse me.' He shrugged, as if to apologize for the bad timing of all young people, and uncoiled his lanky body from the chair.

There was a short exchange between him and Sophia, then he ambled back to the table with a magnanimous smile. 'Sorry, she was just picking up on a note I gave her about tonight's performance.'

Which was a perfectly reasonable explanation for what had happened. But for the fact that Jude had exceptionally good hearing and had caught the words the two of them had whispered to each other.

Sophia had said, 'Joan thought her father would have gone straight after the show, but he's just offered her a lift home. So she can't come back with you tonight. She says she probably could tomorrow.'

'Tell her she'd better be able to,' Andy Constant had hissed. 'I want her.'

'I'll pass on the message.'

'Make sure you do,' he said intensely. 'Make sure she knows what I feel.'

Jude found the exchange, to say the least, intriguing.

Chapter Nineteen

Andy Constant looked at his watch, before turning his narrowed eyes back on to Jude. 'Actually, I could show you the college's Drama facilities now if you like . . .'

'I've seen the theatre.'

'But not the Drama Studio. I keep a secret supply of hooch in the Drama Studio. We could have our second drink there.'

'No, thank you,' said Jude firmly.

Andy Constant's reaction was like that of a spoiled child. He swallowed down the rest of his lager and, with a brusque 'Thank you for the drink – I'd better go and sort things out back at the college', left the pub.

Jude was appalled by his behaviour. If she read what had happened right, Andy Constant had had some kind of assignation set up with the Joan that Sophia Urquhart had mentioned . . . quite possibly back in the Drama Studio. Within seconds of hearing that Joan couldn't make it, he had, presumably on the 'bird in the hand' principle, asked Jude to share the delights of the Drama Studio with him. And when she, who hardly knew him, had refused, he had immediately thrown his toys out of the pram.

But Jude had a feeling that wouldn't be the last she heard from Andy Constant. She recognized the kind of man who wouldn't acknowledge failure when it came to women. He'd be on the phone again before too long, suggesting another meeting. And Jude hated herself for knowing that she'd probably respond to his invitation.

Oh dear, how weak she could sometimes be. Time to get back to Woodside Cottage. She reached into her handbag for her mobile to call a cab, and then realized she'd left it on charge in her bedroom. Never mind, there was bound to be a public phone in the pub. In fact there was a sign to it over the far side of the room.

As she approached the bar, she found herself passing the three Urquharts. 'Jude,' said Ewan bonhomously, 'are you after another drink? Please, allow me to do the honours.'

'That's very kind, but actually I was just on my way. Going to phone for a cab.'

'Oh, you don't need to do that. You're in Fethering, aren't you? So are we. I'll give you a lift.'

'Well, thank you.'

'And since the massed Urquhart clan are not leaving till we've had another dram, what can I get for you?'

Ewan Urquhart, as he never missed telling everyone, drove a large sleek black Lexus. It must have been recently cleaned. In the damp February weather cars in West Sussex were very quickly spattered with mud from the roads, and his shone as though it had just come out of the showroom.

The interior was also immaculate. Hamish had offered her the passenger seat, but Jude had said she was sure he needed the leg-room, so sat in the back with Sophia. She was aware of the girl's distinctive and very expensive perfume. She was also aware that Sophia seemed subdued and out of sorts. Perhaps it was just the come-down after giving of herself in *Rumours of Wars*.

The relative silence of his children didn't appear to worry Ewan Urquhart, as he continued the monologue which, from what Jude had seen, filled his every waking hour. 'I thought the show was pretty well done, but I'm not sure what the point of it was. I mean, good as a showcase for student talent perhaps, but not what you'd call entertainment. I can't imagine anyone who hadn't a vested interest . . . you know, some connection with the cast . . . voluntarily going to a show like that.'

'You don't know anything about theatre, Daddy,' said his daughter truculently.

'I may not know about theatre, but I know what I like,' he riposted with a self-satisfied guffaw. 'And what I like is something with a structure. A "well-made play" I think it's called.'

'An "old-fashioned play" is what I think you mean.'

'Nonsense, Soph. Certain standards are always viable. In my young day plays were crafted, not thrown together from the ideas of a bunch of self-dramatizing students. And craft is what plays should be about.'

'I didn't know you were a lover of the theatre, Ewan,' said Jude.

'Oh yes, there's some stuff I enjoy.'

'Really?' asked his daughter. 'But you never go to the theatre, Daddy.'

'I do.'

'Come on, before tonight, when was the last time you went to the theatre?'

'Well . . . Well, I . . .'

'See, you can't remember. Honestly, Daddy, sometimes you're so full of shit.'

He wouldn't have taken a line like that from anyone else, but when his beloved daughter said it, Ewan Urquhart just chuckled. 'You may be right, but I know what I like.'

'Do you get to see a lot of theatre, Sophia?' asked Jude.

'Oh yes, I go whenever I can. It's important, you know, because of the course I'm on. Andy sometimes organizes trips to the West End for us, and we get to see most of what's on in Brighton and Chichester.'

'Now Chichester used to do some good plays,' said her father.

'Yes, but you never went to see any of those either.'

'I remember you and Mum taking us to see some pantomimes there when we were little,' said Hamish, rather pathetically.

But his contribution to the dialogue was, as ever, ignored, as his father chuntered on. 'It's a very insecure business, though, the theatre. I'm just waiting, Jude, till young Sophia sees the error of her ways and starts doing something sensible.'

'It's my life,' said his daughter passionately, 'and I'll do what I want with it!'

Her father was instantly contrite. Clearly he didn't like to upset his precious Sophia. 'Yes, of course you will,' he said soothingly. 'I was only joking.'

'Dad's always joking,' said Hamish, contributing his bit to the reassurance. 'He's really not getting at you.'

'Huh,' was all the response they got from the girl.

There was then a moment of silence, which Jude broke by asking, 'Have you had singing lessons, Sophia? You've got a really good voice.'

'Not much. We cover it a bit in general voice work on the course. But I have sung a bit with bands round here, and I did some singing with people when I was on my gap year.'

'Gap year,' her father snorted. 'Weren't any gap years when I was growing up. You finished your education and you got down to work. Mind you, we didn't have a government then that wanted to keep as many kids as possible as students to massage the unemployment figures.'

Carole would agree with you on that, thought Jude.

'I think,' he went on, 'that university is just an excuse for not facing up to real life. I didn't go to university and it hasn't done me any harm.'

'Nor me,' Hamish agreed.

But of course he was just setting himself up for another parental put-down. 'Yes, but the cases were slightly different. I didn't go to university as a career decision. I reckoned the education I'd had at Charterhouse would be quite sufficient to see me through life. Which indeed has proved to be the case.

Whereas you, Hamish, didn't go to university because you were too thick to get in!'

As before, all the Urquharts, including Hamish, enjoyed this joke at his expense.

'So, Sophia, where did you go on your gap year?' asked Jude.

'Oh, just round Europe. InterRailing, you know. France, Germany, Denmark.'

'Did you get into any of the old Eastern Bloc countries?'

'No.'

'Thought you said you went to East Germany,' her father pointed out, nitpicking as ever.

'Oh yes, I did. Sorry, I wasn't counting that, because it's part of Germany now.'

'Geography never was your strong point, was it, Soph?' Another guffaw. 'Though I think that's actually just a women's thing. No good at navigating, women – have to keep stopping to ask for directions.'

'Whereas men get lost,' said Jude, 'because they never will stop to ask for directions.'

'Oh, touché,' came the response, but nothing was actually going to change Ewan Urquhart's view of the opposite sex. 'Now tell me, Jude, where is it you live?'

'On the High Street. Just drop me anywhere now, it's no distance.'

'Nonsense. I will escort you to your front door. One hears of such terrible things happening to unaccompanied women these days.'

'Well, thank you, I'm sure I'll be fine.'

But the Lexus had already turned into the High Street. 'So tell me, which house is it?'

'Just along there on the right. Beyond the lamp-post.'

'Oh, I've sold a good few properties along here, let me tell you. Prices skyrocketing. If you're ever thinking of selling, Jude . . .'

'Well, I had thought of having the place valued. You know, to sort of see where I stand.'

'We'd be happy to do it. All part of the service at Urquhart & Pease. Isn't that right, Hamish?'

'Yes, Dad.'

'By the way, I'm intrigued to know . . .' Jude asked. 'Who's Pease?'

'My partner?'

'Yes, the other part of Urquhart & Pease.'

'Ah.' Ewan Urquhart chuckled, before producing another well-rehearsed line. 'He doesn't exist. When I set up the business, I reckoned two names sounded more authoritative than one. So that's how Mr Pease got invented.'

'Thank you for explaining that. It'd been intriguing me. Anyway, I might take you up on your offer of a valuation.'

'Do, by all means.'

Then, as the big car slowed down, Jude asked Sophia, 'Tell me, while you were in East Germany, did you go to Leipzig?'

The girl looked at her with some surprise. Then the line of her mouth hardened as she replied, 'No. I've never been there.'

Chapter Twenty

Both Carole and Jude had shopping to do on the Saturday morning, but they joined up for coffee in the kitchen of High Tor at about eleven. Jude had not suggested meeting at Woodside Cottage because Zofia Jankowska had come in very late the night before and the poor girl needed her sleep. She was exhausted by the emotional rollercoaster she had been riding since she heard of her brother's death.

Carole was very pleased with herself about the information she had received from Gerald Hume and presented it to Jude with considerable aplomb. 'So at last we have a name. Someone who did actually know Tadek – or at least spoke to him in the betting shop.'

'Pauline implied that he knew the woman. Melanie Newton, eh?'

'And Gerald seemed to think she lived in Fedborough.'

'Sounds like a job for the local phone book.'

Flicking through the directory, they were beginning to wish their quarry had a less common name. There were forty Newtons listed. But when they narrowed the search down to Fedborough addresses, it looked easier.

Only four. None of them had the initial 'M', but, as Carole and Jude agreed, the listing might well be under the name of Melanie Newton's husband or another relation.

'Well, let's see if we get any joy. Are you going to call them or shall I?'

'You do it, Jude.' Carole was suddenly embarrassed by the idea of phoning up complete strangers. 'You're better at lying than I am.'

'Why do I need to lie?'

'You can't just ring up someone out of the blue, can you?'

'A lot of people do. The number of calls I get about replacement windows and making wills and investing in land . . .'

'Yes, or trying to sell you a mobile phone . . .'

'Perhaps I should do that. Make up some story. Pretend I'm from a call centre.' Jude made up her mind. 'No, I think it'd be simpler – as usual – just to tell the truth.'

'"Hello, I want to talk to you about someone you spoke to five months ago"?' suggested Carole with disbelief.

'Something along those lines, yes.' Jude phoned the first of the numbers. An answering machine message. She pressed the red button to end the call. 'Bob and Marie Newton are not available at the moment. No Melanie.'

She keyed in the next number. 'Oh, hello, could I speak to Melanie?'

She was informed, with some huffiness, that there was no one of that name living at the address.

'Two more to go,' she said as she tried the third. Again someone answered. A woman's voice.

'Oh, hello, could I speak to Melanie Newton, please?'

'I'm sorry. She no longer lives here.'

'You don't by any chance know where she lives now, do you?'

'I'm not sure. I got the impression the marriage was breaking up and I think she and her husband went their separate ways.'

'So don't you have any means of contacting her?'

'I've got a mobile number for her husband, Giles. I've never used it, so I don't know if it's still current.'

'Could you give it to me?'

For the first time the voice at the other end of the line sounded suspicious. 'Who am I talking to here?'

'My name's Jude.' Which was true. 'I'm an old friend of Melanie's.' Which was a lie. Carole raised her eyes to heaven.

'All right.' And the voice gave the mobile number.

'Thank you so much. And can you tell me how long ago the Newtons moved?'

'We moved in here on the third of November.'

As soon as she had finished the call, Jude keyed in the mobile number she'd been given.

'Hello?' said a wary answering voice.

'Is that Giles Newton?'

'Yes.' He still sounded guarded.

'You don't know me, but I'm trying to contact Melanie Newton and—'

Giles Newton ended the call.

When Jude returned to Woodside Cottage, Zofia Jankowska was up and dressed, making coffee in the kitchen. 'Aren't you going to have something to eat too?' asked Jude.

'No, I have too much food of yours already. You do not let me pay.'

'You don't need to pay.'

'It makes me feel not good. I do not like to be . . . what is the word I heard? A "sponger"? I read in newspaper that many Poles in England are spongers.'

'Then you should read different newspapers. You're not sponging off me. You're here as my guest.'

'I should be paying something. I do not know how long I will be here. If I could get a few hours' work, I could pay you.'

'Well, I'm sure you could get something if you really wanted to.' A thought came to Jude. 'Tell you what . . . the landlord of the Crown and Anchor was complaining how he couldn't get any decent bar staff.'

'That is the pub here in Fethering?'

'Yes.'

'Well, if I could work some hours for him, I could pay you some rent.'

'I've told you, you don't need to.'

'It would make me feel better. And I have worked in a bar a lot. I know what to do. In Warsaw I work in bars.

There of course I take money in zlotys, but I am quick learner. I soon catch on to money in pounds.'

'Well, I'll give him a call. His name's Ted Crisp.' Jude hesitated. 'I just wonder, though . . .'

'What?'

'Ted's . . . um, how shall I put this? Very English.'

'English in the way that he does not like foreigners?'

'Yes,' Jude admitted.

'This is perhaps because he has not met many foreigners?'

'Quite possibly, yes.'

'Then I think he should meet one. Me. Zofia Jankowska. I will show him how a good worker works.'

Jude chuckled and looked at her watch. 'I'll give him a call later. After the Saturday lunchtime rush. Ooh, by the way, there is something more we've found out about that woman your brother spoke to in October.' And she told Zofia the information she'd had from Carole. 'As I say, the husband hung up on me, but at least we've got a name, which is more than we had this time yesterday.'

'Maybe you will be able to find her.'

'I hope so.'

'I also thought of two people I could try to talk to.'

'Oh?'

'One is back in Warsaw. A friend of Tadek, called Pavel. He was in the band. I try to call him this morning, but his mother say he off playing music in Krakow. She will pass on message when he call her. But I think that will not be soon.'

'Why not?'

Zofia shrugged ruefully. 'Pavel like Tadek. Not good keeping in touch.'

'But your message will get through eventually?'

'Eventually, yes. But his mother say he not even picking up emails in Krakow.' She looked glum for a moment, but then a spark returned to her eyes. 'A second person I think of, though. I had forgotten about him until this morning, but there was another friend of Tadek who used to play in the band with him. In Twarz. Not for a long time. He was the drummer, but not a very good drummer. He left the band a year before Tadek finished at the university. He was called Marek Wisniewski and he used to get on well with my brother. But why I think of him is I remember he came to England. I think he get work as a waiter.'

'How long has he been here?'

'More than a year. A year and a half perhaps. But perhaps Tadek get in touch with Marek when he come to England.'

'Have you got a contact for him?'

'Not here in England, no. But I know his brother in Warsaw. I will ring him, see if he knows where Marek is working now.' The girl shrugged. 'It may be nothing, but everything is worth trying, isn't it?'

'Certainly,' said Jude.

They both made their phone calls that afternoon. Zofia got through to Warsaw and was given the address of a Brighton restaurant where Marek had been working when his brother had last heard from him. A bored man at the restaurant said he still worked there, but he was off on a few days' leave. He thought he would be back on the Tuesday. She asked the man to give Marek her mobile number, but she didn't feel very optimistic that the message would get through.

'Nothing else we can do at the moment,' Zofia said gloomily when she'd ended the call.

'No, but if you don't hear, we can go and see him. Brighton's not far away. Anyway, now I'll phone Ted.'

The timing couldn't have been better. The landlord of the Crown and Anchor had just been let down by one of the barmaids who was meant to be doing a shift that evening. If the girl Jude was talking about could come down straight away . . . 'That is, if she has had experience of bar work. I haven't got time to train anyone up.'

'Oh, she's had experience of bar work,' said Jude. She and Zofia had agreed that they would not mention her relationship to Tadek. That might make for an uncomfortable atmosphere in the bar of the Crown and Anchor. Nor on the phone did Jude mention the fact that Zofia was Polish.

Of course, it was something that Ted couldn't fail to notice when they were introduced. Behind the ragged beard his face took on a look of suspicion. 'From Poland, you say?'

Zofia Jankowska smiled brightly. 'Yes.'

'Well, you can help out tonight, because I've been let down,' he said grudgingly. 'But I don't know if I'll be able to offer you anything more.'

'Let's see how tonight goes, yes?' said Zofia, unfazed by his less than enthusiastic welcome.

'All right,' he conceded.

'Please, you show me where everything is, and where is written down the costs of the drinks.'

As Ted Crisp turned to get a price-list, he cast a reproachful eye on Jude. She'd put him in a situation where he couldn't really make a scene, and he felt she'd rather pulled a fast one on him. There were already far too many foreigners around the country; he didn't want any of them actually working for him.

Jude, however, went home happy. She felt confident that Zofia would do everything that was required of her. And also from behind the bar of the Crown and Anchor, the girl would be perfectly placed to hear any gossip relating to the death of her brother.

Chapter Twenty-one

Though Carole was not good at lying, that did not mean that she was incapable of deviousness. She woke in the small hours of the Sunday morning, frustrated by their inability to contact Melanie Newton. The only way to the woman was through her husband's mobile phone, and when Jude rang him Giles Newton clearly had not wanted to play ball. There had to be another approach. And by the time, an hour later, Carole drifted back into sleep, she felt confident she had found it.

She reckoned half-past ten was a reasonable hour to call someone on a Sunday, so after a brisk walk on the beach with Gulliver and a skimpy perusal of the *Sunday Telegraph*, she called the number they had been given by the new owner of the Newtons' house.

When Giles answered, she said, 'Good morning. My name is Carole Seddon, formerly of the Home Office.' Which was entirely true, but she hoped the words 'Home Office' would have such a strong effect on the man that he would hardly be aware of the 'formerly'.

'Oh yes?' He sounded puzzled, but not as if he was about to put the phone down. Which was already better than the response Jude had got.

'I'm calling in connection with the death of Tadeusz Jankowski.' Again, not untrue, but hopefully misleading about the level of officialness in her enquiry.

'Who?' He sounded genuinely mystified by the name.

'Tadeusz Jankowski. A young man who died in Fethering some ten days ago.'

'I've never heard of him.'

'There's been a lot of media coverage, on national television and in the papers.'

'I wouldn't have seen it. I've been in Dubai the last three months.'

'Oh?'

'I work in oil exploration. I tend to be away for long periods.'

'Ah. Well, in fact, it was your wife I wanted to contact. Melanie . . . is that right?'

'Yes.'

'She wasn't in Dubai with you?'

'No. So far as I know, she was here in England.'

'So far as you know?'

'Yes, as far as I know,' Giles Newton said testily. 'She may have gone travelling. She went abroad last summer, to Holland and Germany, I believe.'

'You *believe*?' Carole echoed again.

'Yes. Look, Mrs . . . I'm sorry, I didn't get your name.'

'Carole Seddon.'

'Well, Mrs Seddon, as you may well have deduced, the fact is that my wife and I are no longer together.'

'I'm so sorry,' said Carole automatically.

'I'm not sure that I am. At least I'm no longer involved in the messes Melanie gets herself into.'

'Messes?'

But echoing his words was not so fruitful this time. 'Look, Mrs Seddon, what do you want? If it's something to do with my wife, you're talking to the wrong person. What she does is her own business. I no longer have any contact with her.'

'But do you know where she's living?'

'No, I don't. We used to live together in a house in Fedborough, but since we sold that, we've gone our separate ways. And may I emphasize that I have no responsibility for her financial affairs. In fact, after some of the things she got me involved in, I hope I never see her again.'

'What kind of things did she get you involved in?'

The question was over-optimistic. 'Mrs Seddon, if my wife has once again got herself into trouble, I suggest you talk to her rather than to me.'

'Well, that's what I want to do, Mr Newton, but I don't have any means of contacting her.'

'I can give you a mobile number.'

'Is it still current?'

'I've no idea. I've made no attempt to contact Melanie since last November.'

And so it was that Carole got hold of Melanie Newton's phone number. The words 'Home Office' did still command a measure of authority.

She knew she should really share her discovery with Jude, but the temptation to present her neighbour with some kind of dramatic coup was too strong. Carole

195

rang the number. It went straight on to voicemail. No identification of the phone's owner, just a terse, 'Leave a message after the tone.'

A pity, but Carole's gratification outweighed her disappointment. She now had a name and a phone number for Melanie Newton. And she had heard the woman's voice.

Zofia Jankowska stayed in her bedroom late on the Sunday morning, but Jude knew the girl was awake because she could hear music. At about half-past eleven she tapped on the door. 'Just wondered what you'd like to do about lunch?'

The girl was dressed and sitting on her bed. She looked as though she might have been crying, her pigtails once again emphasizing her youth and frailty. After a quick look at her watch, she said, 'No, I don't think I have time for lunch. Ted wants me to do a shift at the pub starting at twelve.'

'So you must have done all right last night.' Jude had been in bed before Zofia returned from the Crown and Anchor.

'I think so. Not that you'd have known it from Ted. He watch me all evening like he thought I was about to steal from the cash register.'

'He'll get used to you. He's naturally distrustful.'

'Distrustful of "foreigners", yes.'

'If he's asked you to come back, he can't be too worried.'

'He does not make it sound like he is happy. He

offer me shift today only because he is very busy at Sunday lunchtime, and his other staff let him down. Still he don't say whether there will be more work for me.'

'You'll win him round.'

Zofia grinned. 'Yes, I think I will.'

'Well, look, would you like me to rustle up something quickly for you before you go?'

'No, I'm OK. I'll just have a cup of coffee.'

'How long's the shift?'

'Ted wants me to work till three.'

'I'll have something nice and hot waiting for you when you come back.'

'Please, Jude, you don't have to do this.'

'I want to.'

'You are very kind to me.'

Jude grinned and there was a silence between them. She became aware of the music. Soft acoustic guitar and a gentle voice in a yearning song, some kind of folk tune in a language Jude could not understand. The sound quality was not professional, as though a primitive microphone had just been placed in front of the singer in an ordinary room.

'This is your brother, Zosia?' The girl nodded and once again tears welled in her eyes. 'He's very good. Is it one of his own songs?'

The girl gave another nod, not daring to speak lest it start her weeping. Jude sat down on the bed and put her ample arms around the thin shoulders. 'We will find out what happened to him. Don't worry. I promise we will.'

'Yes.' Zofia's hazel eyes sought Jude's. 'That will not bring Tadek back, will it?'

'No, I'm afraid it won't. Nothing will do that.'

'But finding out who killed him, is that supposed to bring me . . . closure?'

'I hate the word. American psychological claptrap. But I think knowing how and why Tadek was killed may make it easier for you to live with what has happened. I'm not stupid or simplistic enough to tell you that the grief will ever go away.' Another silence. Jude could feel in the tension of the girl's shoulders how hard she was trying not to cry. 'I'm sorry, not knowing any Polish, I've no idea what this song is about.'

'What does it sound as if it's about?'

Jude listened to the music for a moment. 'Love. Yearning. A love that is doomed.'

'Then Tadek has written a good song, if you can understand the feeling without understanding the words. Yes, it is about a love that is doomed. He wrote songs for all of the women he loved.' She let out a wry little laugh. 'And with every woman he loved, I'm afraid the relationship was doomed.'

'You said most of them were older women?'

'Yes, this song was for one of his music teachers at the university. She was married with two small children.'

'So did they have an affair?'

'No, no. A lot of his relationships were not . . . what do you say? Hands on?'

'He worshipped from afar?'

'That is a good way of saying it, yes. The love was

mostly in his head. He put the women on . . . what was that word you told me . . .?'

'A pedestal.'

'That is correct.'

'What do the words of the song say?'

'I can't translate exactly, but Tadek is saying that, though he and the woman can never be together, this does not stop his love from being beautiful.'

Jude nodded. 'That explains it. Because, although the song is yearning, it doesn't actually sound sad. It isn't a miserable song.'

'No, sometimes I think Tadek likes it that his love affairs never work out. Perhaps he finds it is easier to write about an imagined woman than a real woman.'

'Typical romantic. It's much easier to remain romantic about an imagined woman than a real one.' There was a moment of stillness as Jude listened to the song. 'He was very talented.'

'I don't know. I like his music, but he is my brother. And he writes old-fashioned songs. If he could be successful in the commercial world, that I do not know.'

'Did he write songs about all the women who he . . . put on a pedestal?'

'Yes, I think so. I think it is these hopeless loves that make him able to write songs. Perhaps if he had had a real love affair that really worked, he would not have felt he needed to write songs.'

'So if, and I suppose it's possible, he came to England because of a woman . . . then you might have expected him to have written songs about her?'

'I am sure he would have done. I am sure Tadek

could not have been in England as long as he had without writing songs.'

'And yet there was no evidence of any in the belongings you collected from the police?'

'No, not only his guitar is missing. Also there are no notebooks, no CDs, no tapes.'

'So, if we could find those . . .?'

'If we could find those, where we found them might be a good clue to what happened to him.'

'Yes, and if the songs were written to another older woman here in England, finding that older woman would be another very good clue.'

At that moment Carole rang, to tell Jude the good news that she'd now got a mobile number for Melanie Newton.

Chapter Twenty-two

'The police could do it,' said Carole gloomily.

'Do what?'

"Track down where a person is by their mobile phone. The technology's there. It's just not yet available to amateurs.'

'Just as well for some.'

'Hm?'

'If you could always tell where someone was phoning from on their mobile, it would considerably slow down the activities of certain philanderers. "Oh, darling, I'm in the office," when in fact the speaker is in a Travelodge bedroom – and not unaccompanied. Would spell the death of adultery as we know it.'

Carole couldn't stop her face from looking disapproving at that. Though she was fully aware that adultery existed – indeed, even thrived – something in her background prompted a knee-jerk reaction of censure.

'So we're really no further on,' she continued in gloomy vein.

'How can you say that? We've not only got a name for the woman Tadek spoke to in the betting shop, we've now also got her mobile number. That's a huge advance.'

'Yes, but she's not answering the phone.'

'True.'

'So how on earth are we going to track her down?'

'I could try the internet. If she's in a phonebook, wherever she happens to be . . .'

'But if she only moved out of the Fedborough house in November, she isn't likely to be in a phonebook yet.'

'Maybe not, but there are other things I could try on the laptop. Just googling her name, see if that brings anything up.'

Carole was silent. She was still a bit of a dinosaur when it came to computers. Which she knew was silly, because she had the kind of brain that would respond well to that sort of technology. And indeed, had computers played much of a part in her work at the Home Office, she would have embraced them and developed her skills. But they hadn't, and as always when faced by something new, Carole Seddon didn't want to expose her ignorance.

'Well, you can try,' she said, her voice full of resentful scepticism.

'I will,' Jude responded, her optimism, as ever in such circumstances, even stronger than usual.

Carole looked at her watch. 'Is Zofia at the Crown and Anchor?'

'No, she's having a lie-down. We had some lunch together. She's exhausted. I think the reality of what's happened to her is beginning to hit home.'

'Yes. I'm surprised to hear that Ted would take on a

foreigner. He seems to be getting more right-wing with every passing day.'

'I kind of put him in a position where it was difficult for him to refuse. Give him a few days with Zosia and I bet he'll come round.'

'Zosia? I thought her name was Zofia.'

'Her friends call her Zosia. Apparently most people in Poland have kind of pet names. Like Tadek.'

'Ah.' A sudden thought came to Carole. 'I say, you don't think that what you heard the boy say, that "Fifi" . . . could be a reference to his sister? Zofia?'

'I asked her. No. He'd only ever called her Zosia.'

'Well, maybe "Fifi" means something in Polish?'

'I asked her that too. She said it could be the beginning of certain Polish words, you know, that he was trying to get out, but she couldn't think of any that had any potential relevance.'

'Ah,' said Carole, disappointed.

Her disappointment, however, was short-lived, as Zofia came rushing down the stairs, holding her mobile phone.

'Jude! Oh, hello, Carole. Listen, I have just had a call from Marek!'

'Is he back in Brighton?'

'No, not yet, but they did give him the message to call me when he rang the restaurant.'

'And had he seen Tadek since he'd been in England?'

'Oh yes. They were in contact, but Marek did not know about what happened to my brother.'

'How could he avoid knowing?' asked Carole. 'It's

been all over the national newspapers and on television.'

'Marek has been off travelling with a girlfriend the last week. He does not see any television.'

'When did he last see Tadek?' asked Jude.

'Round Christmas they meet and drink, but – and this is the interesting part – he fix to see Tadek on the day he die.'

'But he didn't see him?'

'No.'

'Where were they going to meet?'

'At Tadek's room in Littlehampton. The door is left open, in case Tadek is not there when Marek arrive. They are both not good with being on time. Marek gets to the room, he waits an hour, two hours, Tadek does not come. Marek goes back to Brighton. He has a shift to be at work.'

'So he was probably in your brother's room,' asked Carole, 'at the time the murder took place?'

'Yes, I think so.'

'Did he say what he did while he was waiting?'

'He sat around, being bored, he tell me. Then he find Tadek has a bottle of vodka, so he drinks some. He wants to play music, but there is nothing there.'

'No CDs, no nothing?'

Zofia shook her head so vigorously that the pigtails slapped against her face. 'No. And that is not like Tadek. Wherever Tadek is, he always has his music.'

'And his guitar.'

'Yes, and his guitar. So someone must have been

into the room to steal those things. And I do not know why anyone would do that.'

Jude pieced her thoughts together slowly. 'You said your brother always wrote songs about the women he was in love with . . .?'

'Yes.'

'So his songs, if he'd recorded them, would probably have identified the woman he was in love with?' Zofia nodded. 'And if that person had something to do with his murder, then she would try to remove anything in his room that might make the connection between them?'

'Certainly.'

'Then I think that must be the explanation. It becomes even more imperative that we find the woman your brother was in love with.'

'We may be closer to that than we were before,' Carole interposed with renewed pride. And she told Zofia of the advances they had made in tracking down Melanie Newton.

'This is good. There must be a way we can contact the woman.'

'I've tried the number a few more times. Still just get the voicemail.'

'But you will keep trying?'

'Yes, of course,' replied Carole, slightly affronted by Zofia's question.

'Mind you,' said Jude, uncharacteristically sceptical, 'we don't know for sure that a woman was the reason why your brother came over here.'

Zofia beamed. 'Yes, this we do know. This is another

thing Marek tell me. When Tadek first contact him, he say that he has come to England because he has met a woman with whom he has fallen in love and she lives in England.'

'He didn't volunteer her name?'

'No. He say no more than that he is madly in love, and that this is different from every other time he has been in love. Mind you,' Zofia concluded sadly, 'that is what he say every time he meet a new woman.'

'And your brother hadn't been to England before last summer? He couldn't have met the woman over here?' asked Carole.

The girl shook her head firmly. 'Tadek has travelled a lot in Europe. But this is the first time he come to England.'

'So we're looking for a woman who has been to Europe relatively recently.'

'Giles Newton told me his wife had been travelling in Europe,' said Carole with some satisfaction.

'Yes, we must talk to her.' Jude had another thought. 'Have the police spoken to Marek? Have they been in touch with him?'

'I ask him this and he tell me no. But the police might not know the connection between my brother and Marek. It is a long time ago they play in Twarz together.'

Carole looked bemused, but then had the name of the band explained to her. 'Well,' she announced, full of Home Office sternness, 'what you must do immediately is ring Marek back and tell him to phone the police in charge of the investigation.'

'But I cannot do that. As Marek was talking to me, the power on his phone run out. The battery needs recharging. And Marek tell me he will not be able to do this recharging until he is back in Brighton.'

'Oh, good,' said Jude.

Later that Sunday the phone rang in Woodside Cottage. Jude answered it, and was not wholly surprised to hear Andy Constant's voice.

'Listen, I'm sorry, I was a bit churlish on Friday.' Though this was undoubtedly true, she made no comment. 'Sorry, I was preoccupied with the show. You know, I get like that when I'm in production. A kind of creative tunnel vision, if you know what I mean.' Oh yes, I know what you mean, thought Jude. You're full of pretentious self-importance. 'Anyway, now the show's finished . . .'

'Did last night go well?'

'Bloody brilliant. Though I say it myself. Wish you'd seen last night, in fact, rather than Friday. It really gelled. The kids made me bloody proud of them, they kind of realized my vision.'

'I thought it was *their* vision that was meant to be realized.'

'Well, yeah, but, you know, *Rumours of Wars* was meant to be, kind of, an ensemble piece. A mutual vision, if you like.'

'OK.'

'But the reason I was ringing was . . . I wonder if my churlishness put you off too much . . .' He paused, but she wasn't about to put him out of his suspense '. . . or if maybe we could meet up again?'

'What are you suggesting?'

'Just a drink. I mean, not some heavy date or anything like that. I just thought, we got on all right, be nice to, you know, chat further about this and that.' His voice was by now so laid-back as almost to be comatose.

'When had you in mind?'

'After work tomorrow? Sixish?'

'I might not be able to do tomorrow.' Caution dictated that she shouldn't sound too available.

'Tuesday then, same sort of time . . .?'

'Might be possible. Where were you thinking of? As you know, I live in Fethering.'

'Yeah. Bit difficult for me to get down there . . . you know, what with my commitments at the college. But we could meet up in the Bull again. At least you know where that is . . .'

'Yes.' The lazy, arrogant, mean bastard, not prepared to make the effort to stray off his own patch, not even inviting her out to dinner.

'So, what do you say? Shall we meet up at the Bull at six on Tuesday?'

Against her better judgement, Jude said, 'Yes.' And once again she tried, without much success, to convince herself she'd only agreed to the meeting to further her murder investigation.

Chapter Twenty-three

'Is that Carole Seddon?'

'Yes.'

'Are you feeling lucky?'

'I'm sorry, who is this speaking?'

'It's Gerald. Gerald Hume.'

'Oh, I'm so sorry. I didn't recognize your voice.' She should have done. Those precise, clipped tones were very distinctive. 'How nice to hear from you.'

'Have you finished the *Times* crossword?'

'I did most of it over breakfast. About three clues left. But please don't—'

'Carole.' He sounded aggrieved by the imputation. 'There is honour among crossword-solvers. I would never give away an answer to a fellow cruciverbalist, unless specifically asked to do so. And if someone did ask me for an answer, I have to confess that I wouldn't regard that person as a proper cruciverbalist.'

'Good. We understand each other.'

'So I revert to my original question. Are you feeling lucky?'

'I don't think I ever feel lucky,' Carole responded with rather dispiriting honesty.

'I was referring to the likelihood of your being successful on the horses today.'

'I don't think I'm ever likely to be successful on the horses.'

'Why not? You have a keen analytical mind.'

'That's as may be. The fact remains that the only way of being successful on the horses is by putting bets on them, and since I never put bets on them, my chances of success in that arena are correspondingly diminished.' Strange, she thought, how whenever she spoke to Gerald, her locutions became as mandarin as his own.

'But if you were to come down to the betting shop and make some investments, your chances would be correspondingly increased.'

'But why should I come down to the betting shop?'

'Because you might enjoy it.'

'I don't think that's a good enough reason.' For anything, her puritan upbringing might have added.

'Then a better reason might be that I have some information regarding the woman about whom you questioned me during our last encounter.'

'Melanie Newton?'

'The very same.'

'I'll be down there straight away.'

He was sitting in his usual seat, in pin-striped suit and tie, his briefcase at his side and ledger open on the table in front of him. 'Ah, Carole,' he said, rising politely to greet her. 'I am so glad you could make it.'

The environment still felt alien to her. The walls covered with newspaper spreads, the banks of television screens, the eternal pinging of the games machines, Chinese waiters chattering in one corner. The only other women in the place were the girl behind the counter and the woman Jude had identified as Pauline.

'Well, what is it you have to tell me?' she asked, rather brusquely.

'Before we do that, I would appreciate your input into the knotty problem of the two-ten at Towcester.'

'Toaster?' Carole echoed in bewilderment, thinking of a kitchen appliance.

'Towcester as in the Northamptonshire town, whose racecourse is set in the Easton Neston Estate. Towcester being one of those English place names which so charmingly befuddle foreign visitors. In the same way that Leominster and Bicester can confuse the unwary. And indeed with British surnames there are many whose pronunciation is similarly at odds with their spelling. One need only mention "Chumley" spelt "Cholmondley", "Dee-ell" spelt "Dalziel" and "Fanshaw" spelt "Fetherstonehaugh" . . . though there is further confusion with the last, because some owners of that surname do insist on pronouncing it "Feather-stone-haugh".'

Carole couldn't help smiling. 'Yes, Gerald, I think I've got your point.'

'I am delighted to hear it. So, the two-ten at Towcester . . . a treat for lovers of alliteration everywhere.'

'I'd really rather you'd just told me—'

He raised a hand that was at once deferential and commanding. 'After the two-ten at Towcester.' He held out a copy of *The Times*, folded back to show the relevant runners and riders. 'Because of the recent frost, the going will be quite hard, which factor I am sure will affect your assessment of the race, Carole.'

'Gerald, I know nothing about horse racing.'

'Perhaps you don't have a great deal of education in the matter of horse racing, but you do have an instinct for the sport.'

'I don't. It doesn't interest me.'

'Carole, would you do me the kindness of approaching this race as if it were a crossword puzzle?'

'I would, if a horse race had any features in common with a crossword puzzle.'

'It has many. In a horse race there are many variables, but only one answer.'

'Yes, but—'

'And one reaches that answer by a process of deduction and elimination.'

She couldn't help being intrigued as well as amused. 'Could you spell that out to me a little?'

'Very well.' He pointed down to the list of runners. 'Here we have twelve horses, only one of whom is going to win the race.'

'Yes.'

'So, before we commence on the process of deduction, let us deploy our skills of elimination.'

'Remove from consideration the ones that have no chance?'

'Exactly. And to do this we look at the recent form.'

'Where is that?'

'In front of the horse's name. The position in which they finished in their previous races. You see, that list of numbers.'

'So that one with "4–6–5–6–0" . . .?'

'In its last race it was unplaced – that's the nought. In the previous one it came sixth, the one before that fifth, the one before that sixth again, the one before that fourth.'

'Not much of a prospect then?'

'No.'

'And what about this one? This has got letters too. Look . . .' She spelt them out. '"0-F-F-P-0-P".'

'That, Carole, is an even worse prospect. The zeros, as you know, mean that the horse was unplaced. And "F" stands for "fell".'

'The horse fell?'

'Yes. And "P" means "pulled up".'

'Sorry, I don't know what that means.'

'The horse was doing so badly that the jockey pulled it up. In other words, it didn't complete the course.'

'Ah. So in the form, letters are bad news?'

'Yes. "0FFP0P" . . .' He spoke the word as an acronym '. . . is not the horse to back. And there's another letter to watch out for, which is "U".'

'What does that mean?'

'"Unseated rider".'

'Again bad news?'

'Very.'

'So this one, Conjuror's Rabbit, whose form is "33211", is a much better bet.'

'Which is why it's the odds-on favourite. Look, it's down to thirteen to eight on.'

'All right, well, looking at the form, I would say there are seven of these horses that can be ruled out completely.'

'Excellent. You're catching on to the idea.'

'In fact, I'd say that Conjuror's Rabbit is definitely going to win.'

'Maybe.'

'Why maybe? It's obvious, Gerald. Look at the form.'

'Ah, but because of that form, because of those two recent wins in particular, the handicapper is making the horse carry more weight.'

'What, a heavier jockey?'

'More likely weights put into the saddle.'

'That seems rather a dirty trick. It's punishing success, isn't it? A horse wins and immediately something's done to make it less likely to win next time.'

'That's how it works, yes. But if one didn't have some compensatory system of that kind, the same horses would win all the time.'

'Well, that'd be fairer.'

'It might be fairer, but it would remove the excitement from the racing. The thrill of the unpredictable.'

'Generally speaking, I don't find unpredictability thrilling.'

'Oh, Carole, I'm sure you do.'

'I don't. So, anyway, this poor Conjuror's Rabbit is

now carrying too much weight to have a chance of winning?'

'No, no, it has a very good chance of winning. That's why it's favourite. And the ground's in its favour.'

'I'm sorry?'

'Back to what I was saying about the going. The overnight frost has made the ground hard, so it's easier for a heavy horse to move over it. If it were muddy, the weight would make a bigger difference.'

'Oh. I see what you mean about variables. Having to think not just about the horse's recent form, but also the weight it's carrying, not to mention the weather.'

Gerald Hume chuckled. 'And that's just the start of it. There's also to be considered the horse's breeding, the length of the race, which jockey's up on him, the horse's state of health, how well the trainer's yard is currently doing . . . I could go on.'

'I think I get the point. But I'm not sure that your crossword analogy is quite valid. There the only real variables are the number of words in the English language.'

'Yes, but you narrow those down in the same way. No, it can't be this word because the second letter's got to be an "m". No, it can't be that one, because the seventh letter isn't a "j". And so you go on till you reach the one, inevitable solution.'

Carole smiled at her new friend. 'I can see why it appeals to you, Gerald. And I can see why photography appeals too.'

'Ah, do you want me to start on the variables that

have to be considered when taking the perfect photo-graph? There's the shutter speed, the light, the—'

She held her hand up to stem the anticipated del-uge. 'No need. I'll take your word for it.'

'So, after all that exegesis of the form book, it is now two eight and fifty-three seconds. Are you going to make an investment on the two-ten at Towcester?'

'Well, I'm sure Conjuror's Rabbit is going to win.'

'And are you going to put your money where your mouth is?'

'Why not?' She opened her handbag, took out her purse and held up a two-pound piece.

'Last of the big spenders,' said Gerald Hume.

'Would you mind putting it on for me when you put your bet on?'

'Very well.' He went to the counter. Carole tried not to look self-conscious. She needn't have worried. Nobody was interested in what she looked like.

'So,' she asked, as Gerald returned, 'have you done the favourite too?'

'No.'

'So what have you done?'

'Ssh. They're under orders. I'll tell you when the race is over.'

They watched, along with the rest of the crowd, including Pauline, the Chinese waiters and Wes and Vic. The decorators were noisy with 'Go on, my son!'s. Conjuror's Rabbit showed his class from the start, eas-ing himself into third early on and holding that position until they turned into the straight with two fences to jump. Finding another gear, he moved smoothly forward to overtake the two ahead of him and sailed over the penultimate obstacle. Then, six lengths ahead, with the race at his mercy, he approached the last. Carole began to get a distant inkling of what the attraction of gambling might be about.

But the calculation of her modest winnings was interrupted. Suddenly Conjuror's Rabbit seemed to break his stride. He crashed into the top of the last fence, stumbled on landing and neatly deposited his jockey on to the ground. The second horse, a twenty-to-one outsider called Draggle Tail, clumsily crossed the last fence and had enough momentum to reach the winning post first.

'Well, that's stupid,' said Carole. 'You can't apply any logic to something like that. What a very unsatisfactory exercise – two pounds straight down the drain.'

'Not unsatisfactory for everyone,' said Gerald slyly.

'What do you mean?'

'I had a fiver on Draggle Tail.'

'What? But why? What possible logic could there be in that? No, I'm afraid your analogy with crosswords is completely destroyed by what's just happened.'

'No, it isn't.'

'How so?'

'I backed Draggle Tail because "Draggle" is, all but for one letter, an anagram of "Gerald".'

'And you call that logic? So much for all your talk of "mathematical probabilities".'

Carole was still fuming when Gerald Hume returned from the counter with his winnings. 'Having dragged me down here,' she said sniffily, 'to squander my hard-earned pension, you will now perhaps have the goodness to give me the information that you have about the betting shop's mystery woman.'

'Oh yes,' he said, with a twinkle. 'That would only be fair, wouldn't it?' He sat down on a blue plastic seat beside her. 'The woman you refer to is Melanie Newton, who has an address in Fedborough.'

'Yes, except that she has moved from that address, and has apparently split up with her husband and could be anywhere.'

'So you've no other means of contacting her?'

'I got a mobile number for her, but she doesn't answer it.'

'Have you left a message?'

'No. I don't want to put her off. If she thinks we're on the trail, that might be a prompt for her to make herself scarce.'

'Yes. Assuming she has something to hide. Which is rather a big assumption. You have no real reason to think Melanie Newton is involved with wrong-doing of any kind.'

'No,' Carole agreed. Though in her mind the scale of Melanie Newton's wrong-doing had been increasing disproportionately. 'The trouble is, with only a mobile number as a means of contact, she could be anywhere in the world.'

'Well, Carole, I am glad to be able to say that I can narrow the focus down a bit from the whole world.'

'I'm glad to hear that.'

'Melanie Newton is in Fethering – or at least was in Fethering yesterday.'

'How do you know?'

'Because I saw her.'

'Not in here? Is the betting shop open on Sundays?'

'It is, but it wasn't in here that I saw her. As I believe I mentioned at our first meeting, I live in River Road. And I am fortunate in that I live in one of the houses with a sea view. For this reason, to maximize that view, my sitting room is upstairs, and I was sitting there yesterday afternoon setting up some shots with my camera. I never tire of taking pictures of the view from my window at different times of year.

'While I was engaged in this activity, I noticed hurrying towards me from the direction of the river a woman whom I thought I recognized as Melanie Newton. She looked somewhat unkempt, and I could not be sure that it was her until she was virtually opposite my house. But when I saw her that close, there was no doubt. Thinking of your eagerness to identify her, I regretted that I had not had the presence of mind to take a picture of her. But still, the chance was gone, so I returned to my own photography.'

He paused, relishing the hold he had over her attention. Carole had to use great control not to ask what happened next.

'Well,' Gerald Hume continued in his own time, 'luck was on my side . . . as I must say it appears to have been this afternoon with the triumph of Draggle Tail . . .' Carole could have done without such excursions in his narrative, but again kept her calm and her silence. 'Because a mere quarter of an hour later, I saw Melanie Newton returning the way she had come, this time bearing two loaded carrier bags from Allinstore, which I'm sure you know to be the—'

This time Carole cracked. 'I know what Allinstore is!'

She spoke with such vehemence that Gerald Hume picked up speed. 'Anyway, I saw her coming towards me, I had time, and the outcome is: that I took a photograph of her.'

'Do you . . .?' she asked tentatively.

'Of course I do.' Gerald Hume reached down for his briefcase, lifted it up on to the table and opened it. He took out an envelope containing a colour print.

Carole had not seen the woman before. But at least she now knew what Melanie Newton looked like.

Chapter Twenty-four

'But surely, Jude, it suggests that she lives down by the river.'

'It could do.'

Carole found herself infuriated by her neighbour's reaction. 'It must do. Look, she walks up River Road to the High Street, does her shopping in Allinstore, then walks back down towards the river. She must live down there.'

'I agree, she might do, but we don't know that for certain. She could have just parked her car down by the river.'

'Why would she do that? She could have parked a lot nearer to Allinstore. And Gerald said she was weighed down by two quite heavy bags. She wouldn't have done that, unless she lived down by the river. If you've got heavy bags, you take the shortest route between where you've been shopping and where you want to get to.'

'Yes, usually.'

'Jude, why are you being like this? Normally I'm the one who's the wet blanket on everything.'

'I just thought I'd see what it felt like.'

'Oh, now you're being tiresome.'

'No, I'm not. I'm playing devil's advocate.'

'Well, it isn't a role that suits you,' said Carole grumpily and flopped back on one of Jude's draped sofas. She felt something hard through the bedspread that covered it, and pulled out a plastic potato masher.

'Oh, I wondered where that had got to,' said Jude.

Which didn't improve Carole's mood. As she looked round the soft curves of the Woodside Cottage sitting room, she longed for the antiseptic right angles of High Tor. But even as she had the thought, she knew that Jude's home had a warmth and welcome hers would never achieve.

'I think you're feeling grumpy because you're still not over that flu.'

'I am quite over that flu, thank you very much. And I am not feeling grumpy,' said Carole grumpily.

'Look, I agree with you that it is most likely that Melanie Newton lives somewhere down by the river.'

'She must do, because if she lived further along, you know, near Marine Villas, that area, then her quickest route to Allinstore wouldn't be along River Road.'

'Carole, I've said I agree with you. The question is how we find out exactly where she lives.'

Carole looked shame-faced, 'I did sort of . . . lurk about a bit down there this afternoon, just to see if there was any sign of her.'

'"Lurk about"?' Jude was intrigued and amused by the image. 'Were you in disguise?'

'Don't be silly, of course I wasn't. I just . . . well,

I took Gulliver down by the river for his walk. And I . . . made the walk rather longer and slower than I normally would. You know, I let Gulliver sniff at anything along the towpath that he wanted to. And then later . . .'

'What did you do later, Carole?' asked Jude, trying to keep the smile off her face.

'I drove down in the Renault and . . . parked there for a while.'

'You mean you did a "stake-out"?'

'I don't think there's any need to call it that, but I did kind of . . . well, look out to see who was coming and going.'

'How long did you stay there?'

'Till it got dark. Then I came back home.'

'Good. Because I wouldn't like to think of you being arrested for kerb-crawling.'

'Jude, I don't know why you're being so childish this evening.'

'No, nor do I. Sorry.'

'You may have lost interest in this murder investigation, but I haven't.'

'Nor have I. I promise, I promise.'

'Good.' Carole sighed. 'Oh, it's so frustrating! We've got this woman's name, we've got her mobile number, we know what she looks like, we have strong reason to believe she lives in Fethering, but we can't find her.'

'I'm sure, if we worked out the right thing to say, we could leave a message on her mobile that would make her ring us back.'

'What? "Hello, we're from the *Reader's Digest* and

we're ringing to tell you you've won a quarter of a million pounds in our prize draw."'

'No, it's got to be something she'll believe. Nobody believes it when the *Reader's Digest* says they're going to win a quarter of a million pounds – they know they're just being sold some rubbish CD. Maybe, if we just leave a message saying it's in connection with the death of Tadeusz Jankowski . . .?'

'If Melanie Newton's got anything to do with that, then there's nothing that would frighten her off quicker.'

'No, I take your point. Well, we can ask around in Fethering, about new people who've just moved in.'

'Let's be logical about it, Jude. If Melanie Newton only moved out of the Fedborough house in November and she moved into a new house of her own, surely her husband would have known about that. He'd have to, unless she's got a lot of money of her own, which he implied she hadn't. So that probably means she's currently renting. We don't have an in with any of the local estate agents, do we?'

'Well, perhaps we do. I was given a lift back here on Friday by Ewan Urquhart. Yes, I could give them a call.'

'I don't think estate agents are meant to give out details of their clients, but I suppose he might respond to your "feminine wiles".' Carole knew that Jude had these. She suspected that she herself didn't.

'I'll see how I go. And I think that's probably all we can do at the moment. Are you going to continue your stake-out of the towpath of the River Fether tomorrow, Carole?'

'No, of course I'm not.'

'Well, Zosia should be able to contact Tadek's friend Marek tomorrow. I'm pretty sure it was Tuesday he was due back. Let's hope he knows something.'

The Polish girl did indeed speak to her brother's friend the following morning. He was working in a café/bar/restaurant in Hove. His shift started at twelve, but if they could be there by eleven, he could spare time for them. He wanted to talk to Zofia; he still hadn't taken in the news of his friend's death.

'If we leave Brighton by twelve, can we be back in Fethering by one o'clock?' she had asked Jude.

'Certainly if we go by car. I'm sure Carole would be happy to drive us. But why do you need to be back by one?'

The girl had grinned. 'Ted wants me to do another shift.'

'Ah, coming round to the idea of employing *foreigners*, is he?'

'You would not think so, the way he speak. It is only short term, he tell me, just till he gets his proper staff back. He has not said anything yet that he is pleased with me, with how I work for him.'

'The fact that he keeps asking you back means he must be.'

'But he do not say so.'

'God, Ted can sometimes be so curmudgeonly.'

'I'm sorry? I do not know this word.'

'I'm not surprised. Well, it means . . .' Jude had been

225

perplexed as to how to explain it. 'It means the way it sounds, really. Think of Ted, think of any other grumpy old man and yes, you know what curmudgeonly means.'

'Oh, thank you.'

That morning Jude put into practice a plan that she had been nursing for a while. Remembering the circular letter she'd had from Urquhart & Pease, she rang the office and asked to have her home valued. She spoke to Hamish Urquhart, who sounded surprisingly efficient, and they made an appointment for him to come to the house on the Thursday morning at ten. Jude thought, with the young man actually on her premises, she could easily question him about rentals in the area. And maybe get a lead to Melanie Newton.

Carole readily agreed to take on the role of driving to Hove, because that meant she would be part of the next stage of the investigation. And so at a quarter to ten on the Tuesday morning (Carole always left more time than was needed and she knew that parking in the Brighton conurbation was notoriously hard to find) the three women set off in her immaculate Renault. As it turned out, they found an empty meter easily and so reached their destination nearer half-past ten than eleven.

The place where Marek Wisniewski worked was in Church Road, Hove, which ran parallel to and up the hill from the sea front. Virtually every business there seemed to be a restaurant of one ethnicity or another. Hove had always had the image of being more staid and geriatric than its louche neighbour Brighton, but that was changing and its plethora of restaurants and clubs suggested that young people could thrive there too.

The ethnicity of Marek's place of work had nothing to do with Poland. A glance at the menu suggested a more Mediterranean flavour, a mix of Italian, Greek and Turkish cuisine. But it was very much open for business at that hour in the morning – and indeed had been since seven-thirty – serving a variety of breakfasts and coffees to a predominantly youthful clientele, none of whom seemed in a great hurry to leave their conversation and newspapers to engage in the world of work. It felt a bit *young* to Carole, the kind of place she might have thought twice about entering on her own; she was glad to have Jude and Zofia with her.

The girl ordered for them, because she recognized the waitress also to be Polish and had a quick incomprehensible exchange with her. She would have a latte, Jude a cappuccino and Carole a 'just ordinary coffee, black, thank you'. Zofia also established from the waitress that Marek was not in yet. Another exchange in Polish followed, which left both the girls laughing.

'She says,' Zofia explained, 'it is good we fix to meet Marek at eleven. That means he will be in time for his twelve o'clock shift. He is not a good . . . what do you call it?'

'Time-keeper?' suggested Jude.

'Yes, that is it. So I know Marek has not changed. Always when Twarz are going to play some place, the other ones in the band are waiting for Marek.'

He finally put in an appearance round twenty past eleven. When he took off his anorak, he was wearing black trousers and a black shirt with the logo of the café embroidered on its short sleeves. Tall with a shaven head and mischievous blue eyes, Marek Wisniewski was greeted by Zofia with a kiss, immediately followed by what was clearly a dressing-down. Neither Carole nor Jude could understand a word of it, but the tone of voice and the body language made the nature of what the girl said absolutely clear.

When she had finished, Marek looked sheepish but not really cowed. 'I tell him,' said Zofia, 'it is bad to not be good time-keeper. It is bad for the image of Polish people here in England. Already people worry about us taking jobs. They call us "spongers". We must show we are efficient and hard workers, so people cannot criticize us for that.'

Then Marek, completely unsubdued by his carpeting, was introduced to Carole and Jude. He smiled, shook hands and greeted them in English which was adequate, though his accent was much thicker than Zofia's. He said how desolated he had been to hear of Tadek's death. 'He was good friend of me. I not really good musician, but he support me when I in band with him.'

Zofia had got out her blue notebook and was poised to record any information they got from Marek. Carole, too, was eager to get on with the business of investigation. 'Did you see a lot of Tadek since he came to England?' she asked.

'A few times I see him. We are both busy with work. It is not always easy to meet. But we stay in touch . . . messages, texts on phone.'

'That's a thought,' said Jude. 'What happened to

Tadek's mobile phone? It wasn't among the possessions that the police gave you, was it, Zosia?'

The girl shook her head. 'Perhaps the police keep it still? To check the phone calls my brother make?'

'I should think that's quite likely,' said Carole.

'Or perhaps,' suggested Marek, 'the phone is taken from his room by the person who take his other things.'

'You're certain that other things were taken from his room?'

'Yes. I go there to meet with Tadek at end of December. His room is like his room always is in Warsaw. Cassettes, CDs all over the place. And of course his guitar. When I go there two weeks ago none of these things is there.'

'So it does sound like someone cleaned them out,' said Jude.

'To avoid incriminating themselves,' added Carole. Then she fixed the focus of her pale blue eyes on the young Pole. 'Zofia told us that you had said her brother definitely came over here because of a woman.'

'This is what he tell me, yes. With Tadek it is always a woman.' He and the girl exchanged wistful grins. 'Always it is the big romance.'

'Which is not how you treat women, Marek,' said Zofia knowingly.

He grinned with shamefaced cockiness. 'No, with me it is always the big sex.'

'So this girl you have just been away with for a week . . .?'

'It is very good, Zosia. Good sex.' He grinned again. 'Now I think over. Time to move on.'

'You do not change, Marek.'

'I hope not. I like women very much, but not one woman,' he explained for the benefit of Carole and Jude.

Carole didn't think tales of his philandering were really germane to the current discussion. 'This woman,' she said, firmly redirecting the conversation, 'did you know her name?'

'Tadek do not tell me. But he say she is very beautiful, he has never felt like this before, she is the one.' Again he and Zofia exchanged rueful smiles.

'Did he say where he'd met her?'

'Yes. It was at a music festival last summer. In Leipzig.'

'Ah,' said Jude, pleased to have at least one of her conjectures confirmed. Zofia wrote down the new fact in her notebook.

'Did he say whether the woman was older or younger than him?' asked Carole.

'No, he do not say.' Marek looked at Zofia for endorsement as he went on. 'But with Tadek it is always older woman, no?'

The girl nodded. 'Well,' said Carole, 'there seems a strong likelihood that it was this woman . . . this older woman who cleared out his room of all his music stuff.'

The boy shrugged. 'Perhaps. Do you know who this woman is?'

'We may do.' But Jude didn't give any more information about Melanie Newton.

'I think,' said Zofia, 'that Tadek would have written songs for this woman.'

'Oh yes,' Marek agreed. 'Always if he is in love, he write songs.'

'But he didn't play you any?' asked Jude.

'No. Tadek knows I not very good with music. Only a drummer. When he was asked about the line-up for his band, he always say old joke: "Three musicians and a drummer." I join Twarz because I like other people, not because I have musical talent. Which is why,' he added philosophically, 'the others ask me to leave. So no, Tadek does not play me any songs. If he want to discuss songs, it is always with Pavel.'

'I told you about him, Jude,' said Zofia. Then she explained for Carole's benefit, 'Pavel is the other song-writer in the band. Very close friend of my brother. They write songs together sometimes. If Tadek write a song, he probably show it to Pavel.'

'What, he'd post a copy to him?' asked Carole.

She had turned on her the young person's stare that is reserved for Luddites and other dinosaurs. 'No, he'd email the MP3.'

'Oh. Right,' Carole responded, as though she had a clue what was being said.

'Why didn't I think of that before?' exclaimed Zofia.

'You speak to Pavel since Tadek die?' asked Marek.

'No, he is playing music in Krakow. But I will email him, ask if he has received anything from Tadek. If my brother had written new songs, I am sure he would have sent them to Pavel.'

'Aren't the police likely to have been in touch with him?' asked Jude. 'They would know the connection between the two of them.'

'Perhaps. The police in Poland maybe are following this up.'

'Speaking of the police,' said Carole severely. 'I think you, Marek, should be in touch with them.'

'Oh?' Immediately he looked defensive, guilty even.

'The fact that you had been in Tadek's room on the afternoon he was killed is something of which they should be informed,' she went on in her best Home Office manner.

'You think so?' the young man pleaded.

'Certainly. It's your duty to do it. You will, won't you?'

'Yes,' said Marek wretchedly.

As she drove the Renault demurely along the coast road towards Fethering, Carole announced, 'I'm very glad that Marek's going to tell the police what he knows. It may be relevant to their enquiries.'

'Yes,' said Zofia. 'I do not think he will do it, though.'

'What?'

'Marek does not want dealings with the police.'

'Why? Is there something wrong with his immigration status?'

'No. He just does not want dealings with the police.'

'You mean you don't think he will get in touch with them?'

'No. I am sure he won't.'

Carole snorted with exasperation. Jude didn't say anything, but she was delighted.

Chapter Twenty-five

Before she started her shift at the Crown and Anchor, Zofia just had time to send an email to Pavel from the Woodside Cottage laptop. She didn't know when she was likely to get a response. It would depend on how long he stayed in Krakow.

Jude's afternoon was committed to a client whose whiplash injuries after a car accident needed massage and healing. Carole said she was going to spend a quiet few hours reading. But in fact she had other plans.

Jude knew she had other plans. Why else would Carole have asked to borrow her mobile? But, as she handed it across, she didn't ask for any explanation.

The *Times* crossword was there as an ostensible reason for sitting in the Renault by the towpath at the end of River Road, but Carole had to admit she felt cold. Whenever she'd seen cops doing a stake-out on television, they seemed to have supplied themselves with bottomless hipflasks and a copious supply of cigarettes, and now she could understand why. Surveillance was very boring and unrewarding work.

Nor did her distracted concentration allow her to make much headway on the crossword. She knew

Tuesday's could sometimes be tricky, but her mind that afternoon was not dissecting and analysing words as it should have been. A few clues made sense, and she got them so quickly that she suspected the others were equally easy. But her brain couldn't see through the verbal obfuscation to the patent truth. She knew if she failed to complete the puzzle, the answers in the next morning's paper would make her kick herself for her ineptitude.

There was a phone number that could be rung to get answers to the day's crossword, but Carole Seddon would never resort to that. For a start, calls were priced at the exorbitant rate of seventy-five pence per minute, and then again . . . well, it just wasn't the sort of thing she'd do. She felt sure that Gerald Hume would be as much of a purist in such matters as she was.

The road by the River Fether was not busy on a chilly February afternoon. The few people out walking their dogs were what Carole thought of dismissively as 'pensioners' (until she realized that she and Gulliver would also fit the description). Between half-past three and four a few schoolchildren, defiantly coatless in the cold weather, returned to their homes. But as the shadows of the encroaching evening closed together and lights came on in the houses before their curtains were closed, the area was deserted.

It was nearly five o'clock and Carole could hardly even see the crossword, though she knew that two corners of clues remained intractable. There was a fifteen-letter word straight down the middle of the grid. She knew if she could get that, all the other answers would fall into place. She also knew that the solution was quite easy, but she could not for the life of her see what it was.

Stuff this for a game of soldiers, thought Carole. It was not an expression that she would ever have spoken out loud, but it was one she had learnt from her father and cherished. Time to get back to High Tor.

Before she turned the key in the ignition, however, movement from one of the houses along the road drew her attention. A woman was coming out of the front door. She moved, in a manner which to Carole's imagination looked furtive, towards the turning into River Road. In the deepening gloom, Carole couldn't make out the woman's face well, nor could she see Gerald Hume's photograph clearly enough to make comparisons. But the stranger was about the right age.

When the woman was close to her, Carole put the next part of her plan into action. On Jude's phone she keyed in the number given her by Giles Newton, and pressed the 'call' button.

The woman reacted. She didn't answer the phone, but she definitely reacted to its ringing.

She was Melanie Newton.

Chapter Twenty-six

Jude felt empowered after her session with the whiplash sufferer. There were times when her healing really worked and, though she might be drained by the transfer of energy entailed, she felt the peace of knowing she had actually done someone some good.

But her contentment was not total. There was something else that was making her feel bad. Her agreement to meet Andy Constant at the Bull that evening. She tried to convince herself that she'd only made the arrangement because he might be able to give her some useful information about the murder case, but she knew that was casuistry. She was going to see Andy Constant because she wanted to see him. And she knew he was seriously bad news.

Jude rather despised herself for the aromatic bath she took before her excursion. Also for the care she took with what she wore.

Andy Constant was an arrogant, selfish boor. He hadn't even had the decency to invite her on a proper date, just a drink in a location which involved her in either a train journey and a long walk or an expensive cab ride. He didn't deserve her attention.

But she still wanted to see him. Some instincts were stronger than logic.

Carole really did feel like something out of a television cop show. She waited till Melanie Newton was halfway up River Road before driving the Renault slowly along and parking again a little behind her. Then, when her quarry turned right into the High Street, she edged the car further up till she could just see round the corner. Melanie Newton's errand appeared to be the same as when Gerald Hume had seen her. She disappeared into Allinstore.

While the woman was in the shop, Carole turned the Renault round and parked at the top of River Road, facing towards the Fether. Sure enough, Melanie Newton soon passed by, carrying two loaded carrier bags, and retraced her steps. Carole waited till the woman was about to turn at the end of River Road and then drove the Renault back to where she had originally been parked. She was just in time to see Melanie Newton use a key to let herself into the house whence she had emerged some ten minutes earlier.

Carole hadn't really planned her next step. Having found where the woman lived was perhaps achievement enough for that afternoon, but not for the first time she wanted to present Jude with a more tangible advance in their investigation. Also she recalled that Jude had a client that afternoon and was then going out somewhere for the evening. Either Carole would have to wait till the following morning to tell her neighbour of their quarry's whereabouts, or she should try to consolidate her achievement straight away. She got out of the car.

It had felt cold inside, but that was as nothing compared to the freezing blast that hit her when she emerged. That cold evening in Fethering worries about global warming seemed seriously exaggerated.

She crossed resolutely to the house into which her suspect had disappeared. It was a semi, probably with three bedrooms. Before she had time for second thoughts, Carole rang the doorbell. A moment passed before it opened, and she found herself face to face with a young teenage girl in school uniform.

'Good afternoon, I'm looking for Melanie Newton.'

'She's in her room at the top of the house.'

'Could I see her?'

The response was one of those 'no skin off my nose' shrugs which only teenage girls can really do properly. After it, the shrugger seemed to lose interest in the proceedings and disappeared into the kitchen from which she'd presumably come.

Carole closed the front door behind her, and set off up the stairs. She found herself on a landing with four doors leading off, presumably to three bedrooms and a bathroom. But the girl had said 'the top of the house'. That must mean up the uncarpeted wooden staircase which led up to what must be a loft conversion.

Carole went on up. The final step at the top of the flight was not much wider than the others. She stood there for a moment, gathering her thoughts, and then knocked on the door.

There was a gasp from inside, then silence. She knocked again. This time she heard movement from the room, footsteps approaching, and the door was opened a fraction. In the narrow gap Carole could see the frightened face of the woman Gerald Hume had photographed.

'Melanie Newton?' Carole asked, although she knew the answer.

'How did you find me?' The voice was cultured but taut almost to breaking point. 'Who let you in?'

'A girl in school uniform.'

'She's not supposed to. The fact that I'm renting this room is supposed to be a secret. Her mother swore they wouldn't let anyone in.'

'Well, she let me in.'

'Who are you?'

'My name's Carole Seddon.'

'And which one of them do you come from? Who do you represent?'

Carole couldn't really supply an answer to that rather strange question, so she just said, 'I want to talk to you about Tadeusz Jankowski.'

The woman's reaction was mixed. Her face still showed fear and suspicion, but there was also something in it that looked like relief.

Andy Constant wasn't there when Jude arrived in the Bull. It was loud with University of Clincham students, taking advantage of the 'Happy Hour' offers and, in the time-honoured student fashion, converting their grants into alcohol. They looked very young, and completely harmless.

She was annoyed with herself for ordering a pint of Stella for Andy along with her glass of Chardonnay, but given the scrum at the bar it was once again the sensible thing to do. Sitting down at a table for two, she wondered again why the hell she was there. She had no illusions about the kind of man Andy Constant was, and she ought to be too old to go deliberately looking for trouble. And yet there she was.

Jude didn't recognize any of the students, but she saw again the poster for Magic Dragon with the blurred photograph of Sophia Urquhart. It reminded her that she wanted to ask the girl about Joan, the other Drama Studies student, and Joan's relationship with Andy Constant.

When he came in, though, sweeping back his long grey hair, she couldn't curb a little kick of excitement. It wasn't just his similarity to Laurence Hawker that got to her; Andy Constant affected her viscerally in a way that few men had. And the men who did trigger that response had always been bad news. Jude made a pact with herself to be extremely sensible that evening. No joining him in a guided tour of the Drama Studio.

He brushed his lips against her cheek, and slumped down into the chair opposite. He reached for the pint of Stella and took a long swig. 'God, that's good,' he said as he put the glass down. No thanks for the drink, just 'God, that's good.'

'Ooh, am I knackered?' he continued. He was one of those men, Jude felt sure, who were always more tired than anyone else, the implication being that they put so much more energy into their creative lives than mere mortals could even contemplate.

'What have you been doing – lecturing?'

'Why should I be doing that?'

'I thought that was your job description. When you first introduced yourself, you said you were a lecturer.'

'Yes, but in my discipline that doesn't mean giving many lectures. In Drama it's more role-playing, work-shopping, you know the kind of thing.'

'Which is what you've been doing today?'

'Kind of.' He said it in a way that implied she wasn't bright enough to understand a fuller explanation. 'The trouble is,' he went on, 'these kids are full of ideas, but their ideas are all so derivative. Based on the latest movies, based on what they've seen on television. It's a real effort trying to get them to think outside the box.'

'And that's what you've been doing with them today?'

'Sure.' He took another long draught of lager. 'Tough, tough, tough.'

'Was Joan one of your group?'

'Who?' he asked. But she felt sure he knew who she meant.

Jude spelt it out for him. 'The Joan whom Sophia Urquhart mentioned on Friday.'

'Ah, that Joan.' The idea seemed to amuse him. 'Yes, Joan was in the group.'

'But had to go home?'

'What do you mean?'

'When we were in here last Friday, Sophia Urquhart

241

SIMON BRETT

apologized that Joan couldn't go back with you, she had to get a lift back with her father.'

Andy Constant's brow wrinkled with aggrieved innocence. 'I'm sorry, I don't know what you're talking about.'

'I am suggesting that there is some kind of relationship between you and this Joan.'

'Hey, whoa, whoa,' he said sardonically. 'Aren't we getting a bit ahead of ourselves here? We're meeting for a drink for only the second time, and already you're telling me who I should and shouldn't see.'

'I'm not doing that, Andy. I'm just trying to clarify your personal situation. You told me about your defunct marriage . . . I assume that still is defunct?'

'Dead as a dodo. Has been for years.'

'Right, so that's the marriage dealt with. I was wondering if you were going to tell me about Joan too.'

'Nothing to tell.' He shrugged ingenuously. 'You have just got the wrong end of the stick in a very major way, Jude. Apart from anything else, it would be totally inappropriate for someone in my position to be messing about with one of my students. Maybe it's a long time since you've been in an educational establishment, but let me tell you, these days they're very hot on what's appropriate and what's inappropriate behaviour. And me having anything to do with a student would be a very big no-no.'

'I know what I heard on Friday,' Jude insisted.

'No. You know what you *think* you heard on Friday. Different matter altogether.'

He sounded so convincing that for a moment Jude

242

almost believed him. Perhaps she had misheard, or misinterpreted what she heard. She was aware of his hooded eyes lazily watching her, appraising, wondering what she'd do next. And she was aware of the power those eyes could exert over her.

But she resisted them. 'I think you're lying,' she said.

He spread his hands wide in a gesture of harmless self-depreciation. 'Do I look like a liar?'

'Oh yes. And if you're prepared to lie to me about this Joan, then it's quite possible you lied to me about Tadeusz Jankowski.'

'About who? Ah, the Pole. The one you came enquiring about. The one without whose existence we wouldn't have met.'

'Yes. Can I ask you again whether you know of any connection between him and Clincham College?'

'You can, my sweet Jude,' he said, 'but I'm afraid you'll get the same answer you got before.' A new idea seemed to come to him. 'Though just a minute . . . I have thought of some other admission files we can check . . . then we'll know if he ever did make any application to the college.'

'Where are the files?'

'Over there.' He jerked his head towards the university campus. 'Do you want to come with me and look through them, Jude?'

She should at least have thought about her answer, but immediately, instinctively, she said 'Yes.'

243

Chapter Twenty-seven

The room into which Carole was ushered was indeed a loft conversion. One wall was a large gable window, which must have provided a wonderful view over the River Fether to the English Channel beyond. But the glass was covered by thick curtains and the stuffiness in the room suggested they had been closed for most of the day.

There was very little light, only what spilled from an Anglepoise whose shade had been pushed down low to a table on which stood an open laptop, its screen idle. But Carole could see enough to recognize that the room was in a mess. As was the woman who faced her. If the descriptions the betting shop regulars had given on how well dressed Melanie Newton was were anything like true, then she'd certainly let herself go.

She was wearing jogging bottoms and a shapeless grey cardigan. There was no make-up on her haggard face and white showed at the centre of her roughly parted hair where the roots were growing out.

'What do you want from me?' she asked, half defiant, half frightened.

Carole reminded herself that she must be cautious.

She had succeeded in her primary objective, of finding Melanie Newton. Now she mustn't scare the woman off by clumsy interrogation.

But fortunately, before she could make a gaffe, the woman asked her another question. 'Are you from one of the agencies?'

'Agencies?'

'Debt collectors. Because I can pay it all back and—'

'No, no. Good heavens, no. I'm not a debt collector.' Carole Seddon's middle-class soul was shaken by the very suggestion.

'Really?' There was anguished pleading in Melanie Newton's voice.

'Really. I'm a retired civil servant from the Home Office.'

'Home Office?' The idea of contact with any authority seemed to upset the woman.

'Retired, I said. Retired. I don't mean you any harm at all, Mrs Newton. As I said, all I'm interested in is what you can tell me about Tadeusz Jankowski.'

'You mean the young Polish boy who was killed?'

'Yes.'

She looked puzzled. 'Well, I don't think I can tell you anything about him. Please sit down.' Now her anxieties about debt collection had been allayed, Melanie Newton remembered her manners. But she didn't make any move to put more lights on in the gloom. Carole noticed one of the Allinstore carrier bags on the table. A sandwich had been torn from its packet and half-eaten, as though its consumer needed fuel rather than food.

She sat on an armchair whose covers felt thread-bare under her hands. 'But you're not denying that you met him?' she asked.

'No, I'm not denying that. He came to see me.'

'Here in England?'

'Yes.'

'When you were living in your house in Fed-borough?'

Melanie Newton looked suspicious again. 'You seem to know rather a lot about me. Are you sure it's nothing to do with the debts?'

'I can absolutely assure you of that. I didn't know that you had any debts. The only thing I do know about you is that you used to be a regular in the betting shop here in Fethering and that early last October you were seen to speak to Tadeusz Jankowski in there.'

'Then how did you find me here?'

This was a potentially difficult question to answer. For Carole to describe her surveillance techniques might raise the woman's paranoia once again. So all she said was, 'Somebody told me you lived in Fedborough. I consulted the telephone directory and spoke to the new owner of your house.'

'She didn't know where I lived, did she?' asked Melanie Newton, once again alarmed. Maybe some of her creditors might go in person to her old address.

'No, she didn't. But she gave me your husband's mobile number.'

'I didn't know Giles knew I was here.' But it didn't seem to worry her that much. 'Not that he's likely to come looking for me.'

'No, I gathered there had been some . . . estrange-
ment between you.' Which was an odd word to use, but
the one that rose to Carole's lips at that particular
moment.

Melanie Newton let out a bark of contemptuous
laughter. 'You could say that. I've come to the conclusion that for a marriage to have any hope of success a
degree of proximity between the participants is
required. That's what Giles and I never had. His work
takes him off on contracts for considerable lengths of
time. Three months, four months, sometimes six
months at a time. Not the best recipe for connubial
bliss. Months of loneliness when they're away, interrupted by weeks of disappointment when they're
home.'

She seemed to be in confessional mode, so Carole
made no attempt to interrupt the flow. 'I think there
were probably things wrong with the marriage from
the start, if we could but have recognized them. But the
separations certainly didn't make it any easier. God
knows what Giles got up to while he was away. I think
there may have been other women. In fact, I found
proof that there was at least one other woman when he
was out in Mexico. And when I did find out, do you
know . . . it hardly worried me at all. I think that was
when I realized that the marriage was dead in the
water.'

Melanie Newton, who had been standing up until
that point, slumped into a chair, drained by her
revelations. Her movement must have jolted the laptop, because the screen came to life, displaying a highly

coloured roulette wheel and board. The woman's eyes could not help but look at it, and her hand moved involuntarily towards the keyboard.

'Your husband implied,' said Carole tentatively, 'when I spoke to him on the phone, that you had got into financial problems.'

'That was an understatement,' came the listless reply.

'And is it the gambling?'

Melanie Newton sighed a huge sigh, which seemed to encompass a whole world of troubles. 'Yes. I started . . . I don't know, a couple of years ago. It was at a time when Giles was away on one of his really extended trips, and I was feeling low. I think I'd just found out about the woman in Mexico, and that hadn't done a lot for my self-esteem. Then I went for a day's racing at Ascot. It was a corporate freebie. I work for a PR agency, get offered lots of stuff like that. Well,' she corrected herself, 'I say I work for them. What I mean is, I *did* work for them. Anyway, up until that point I'd never thought much about horse racing. Might put a small bet on the Derby or Grand National, join in the office sweepstake, you know . . . like most people, I could take it or leave it.

'But that day at Ascot I really enjoyed myself. I had a good day, I was with nice people. There was even a man there who made me think I might not be a totally unattractive has-been as a woman. And also, when it came to backing horses that day, I couldn't do anything wrong. First horse that won I remember was called Mel's Melon. And I backed it for purely sentimental reasons, because my friends call me "Mel" . . . well, used to call me "Mel". That romped home at twelve to one. And for the rest of that day it didn't matter what method I used, the form book, a horse's name that appealed to me, just sticking a pin in the paper . . . I was invincible. Came home more than five hundred pounds to the good.

'I didn't think any more about it for a few weeks, but then I had a rather upsetting phone conversation with Giles, who told me his contract had been extended by two months and he basically couldn't be bothered to come home for a break which he could easily have arranged. A bit of a slap in the face for me, as you can imagine . . . and I was feeling bad again. So at lunchtime that day I went out to the betting shop near where I used to work and . . . well, I had some good days and some bad days and . . .' She seemed to run out of words.

'It became a habit?' suggested Carole.

'Yes. Very good way of putting it. It became a habit. Though I think "habit" is too mild a word. "Obsession" might be nearer the mark. "Obsession" as in "love". I came to love the thrill of gambling. It replaced ordinary love for me. Giles was out of my life, so far as I was concerned. Whether he was abroad or at home, he wasn't part of me or anything to do with me. He had stopped loving me. Perhaps he never loved me. But I could close my mind to that. Gambling gave me hope, offered me the chance of making a new life for myself.'

'How?' asked Carole, incredulous.

'Because I'd win!' replied Melanie Newton, as if

speaking to an idiot. 'I'd win a lot of money and then have the freedom to do what I wanted.'

'But did you win a lot of money?'

'Sometimes,' came the defiant reply.

'Did you need a lot of money, though? If you had a good job in PR, and your husband must have been earning quite a bit in oil exploration . . .'

'I didn't need money then. And soon I won't need it again.'

'Why not?'

'Because,' she explained patiently, 'I'll soon have a big win. Soon I'll pay off all the debts, on all the credit cards. And then I'll get my life back on track.'

Carole indicated the computer screen. 'Through roulette?'

'I'm playing roulette at the moment. I'm on a winning streak on the roulette. You have to be sensible, you know. When you're on a losing streak, you must change games. Then your luck will change.'

'And does your luck often change?'

All that got was another recalcitrant 'Sometimes.'

'Melanie, have you ever asked for help?'

'Help? I don't need help. I can gamble perfectly adequately on my own, thank you.'

'I meant help with stopping gambling.'

This sparked another paranoia of suspicion. 'Has someone sent you? Is Giles behind this?'

'No, I have come completely of my own accord. I'm nothing to do with your debts or your gambling problem. I'm—'

'I don't have a gambling problem,' Melanie Newton

250

insisted. 'When I get the big win, everything'll be sorted out.'

'All right.' Carole held her hands out in a pacifying gesture. 'Then I'll just ask you what I came to ask you.'

'What was that?' The woman sounded distracted now. Her eyes kept darting to the laptop screen and her hand was itching for the keyboard.

'About Tadeusz Jankowski . . .'

'The boy. Oh yes.'

'How did you come to meet him?'

'He came to the house in Fedborough last autumn.'

'Just out of the blue?'

'No.'

'By arrangement then?'

'Yes.'

'So, after your first meeting in Leipzig you kept—?'

'What?' Melanie Newton asked curiously.

'Your husband told me that you went travelling in Holland and Germany last summer.'

'I wanted to get away. I wanted a clean break. Giles was abroad, as ever. I thought going off on my own might be the answer. It wasn't. I'd booked a fortnight and I came back after five days.'

'But during those five days you met Tadeusz Jankowski?'

'I don't know what you're talking about. He came to see me in Fedborough in answer to an advertisement.'

'An advertisement for what?'

'I put a card in the newsagent's window. Advertising a room in the house. I . . . Well, the fact is . . . I was rather hard up. Giles was going to be away for four months. He would never know if I got in a lodger – not that I'd have cared much if he did find out. We'd already decided to split up and sell the place. I thought a bit of income would help the interest payments on the credit cards, so I advertised. Tadeusz Jankowski was about the only response I got.'

'But he didn't take the room?'

'No. He didn't think he could afford what I was asking. He said he'd look around and get back to me. But he never did.'

'Though you did see him again in the betting shop?'

'Yes. That was while I still used to go in there.'

'Why did you stop going?'

The woman gestured to her laptop as if it were something of exotic and unparalleled value. 'Why bother making the effort to go into a betting shop when I can get all this at home?'

Carole found it sad to see how narrow the focus of the woman's life had become. 'So what did you say to Tadeusz Jankowski in the betting shop?'

'I can't remember. We're talking about last October. I don't know. I suppose I said hello, how are you, asked him about how his girlfriend was.'

'His girlfriend?' Carole, who had been about to question Melanie Newton about her affair with the boy, was completely wrong-footed.

'Yes. He mentioned a girlfriend when he came to see the room. He said she was why he had come to England. But that he just wanted the room for himself, they wouldn't be cohabiting.'

'Did he tell you her name?'

'No.'

'Anything about her?'

'Just that she went to the University of Clincham. He asked me how to get there. I didn't know where it was, so he asked somebody else. '

'Ah,' said Carole. 'Thank you.'

Chapter Twenty-eight

Andy Constant strode through the University of Clincham campus as though he owned the place. And the proprietorial manner was increased when he pulled out a large bunch of keys to open the block marked 'DRAMA STUDIO AND REHEARSAL ROOMS'.

'Is this where the admissions records are kept?' asked Jude, with some scepticism.

'I keep everything to do with me here.'

'A little empire?'

'Yes, one that has declared UDI from the rest of the university and its policies.' He pushed open the glass door and ushered her into the unlit lobby. As Jude knew he would, he put his arm around her ample waist as he propelled her into the darkness.

He opened another heavy door and she found herself in a space which felt larger, but was totally black. Andy released his hold on her and said, 'Just get some light on the situation.'

He seemed to know the way around his empire blindfold. There was a click of another door, then after a few seconds, the space was filled with light. Not bright light, but subtle warming light which seemed to focus on the edges and corners of the room. Jude looked up and saw the source, stage lights hanging from a gantry in the ceiling, their harshness muted by gels of pink and orange.

The space they revealed was painted matt black, a functional studio for drama workshops or even small-scale productions. Folding audience chairs were stacked against the walls. On the floor were large blocks, a free-standing door in a frame, other chairs, all painted matt black. Against the wall were a couple of crestfallen sofas and – surprise, surprise – a double bed mattress covered with black sheets.

Andy Constant appeared from the lighting box, a bottle of whisky and two not very clean glasses in one hand. 'Drink?' he asked.

Jude nodded. 'You seem to have got yourself very nicely set up here.'

He shrugged as he poured the drinks and gestured to one of the sofas. 'Need a versatile space for the kind of stuff I do.'

Jude wondered if the ambiguity was deliberate, and decided it probably was. She sat down on the sofa and he slumped beside her, passing across a glass of Scotch.

'Cheers.'

She echoed the toast and took a long swallow. The whisky burned its comfort down her throat. 'So . . . are you going to have a look through the admissions files . . . to see if Tadeusz Jankowski ever applied for a place here?'

'I'll do that in a little while,' he replied. 'Let's just enjoy a drink first. I've had a hard day. I need a break.'

They both took a long swallow.

'Workshopping, were you?'

'Yes. Right here. We were doing some role-playing about broken relationships.'

'Which no doubt involved a lot of rolling about on the bed over there?'

'A certain amount, yes.' He read the potential censure in her eye. 'Nothing inappropriate, I can assure you. This generation of kids are very hot on what's appropriate and inappropriate. What they get up to in their own time is not my problem; here on the campus they're quite sophisticated in their approach to gender politics.'

'And you have a position of trust with them?'

'Very definitely. A duty of responsibility. Which I take very seriously. I wouldn't last long here if I didn't.'

'Which could bring us back to the mysterious Joan.'

'It could, but it needn't.' His hand was now resting gently on Jude's shoulder. She could have told him to remove it, but she didn't want a scene. Not yet, not before she'd got some more information out of him. Besides, she was a grown woman. She could look after herself. And having his hand on her shoulder was not a wholly unpleasant sensation.

'So you deny that you're having a relationship with her?'

'I've told you. It'd be more than my job's worth. And it'd be far too public for me to do such a thing. A campus like this is a breeding ground for gossip. Everyone would immediately know all the details. How could I possibly manage it?'

'This place seems quite private. We didn't see anyone when we came in here this evening, did we?'

'The CCTV cameras would have clocked us.'

'Yes, and the security people might be interested in me. Because I have nothing to do with the university. But you . . . it's part of your job to come and go as you please. And presumably Joan's enrolled as a student here, so there's nothing odd about her wandering around. If she's studying Drama, why shouldn't she come into the Drama Studio?'

'Jude, might I say that you do have rather a one-track mind?'

'Maybe.'

His hand was now holding her shoulder rather than just resting on it. And he was moving his face closer, as if to kiss her.

Jude, tempted but strong, held up a hand. 'I came here because you said you kept the admission files here.'

'Yes, they're on my laptop.' Recognizing that he wasn't going to get anywhere with her at that moment, he raised himself out of the sofa's depths. 'I'll get it.' He went back to the lighting box.

Jude swallowed the rest of her whisky. She topped up her grubby glass from the bottle on the floor. She looked around the room. Andy Constant's convenient little seduction venue. Against the walls were racks of costumes, rifles, banners, swords, kitchen equipment, stepladders. All the impedimenta of the fantasies worked out by the students in the space. The fantasies which were engendered and controlled by Andy Constant during workshop sessions. And others that he realized out of academic hours.

He returned, holding his laptop open and already keying instructions into it. 'What period were you talking about?'

'He came over to England round the end of last September. Any time since then, I imagine.'

'University term starts at the end of September. He'd have had to apply much earlier than that if he wanted to enrol as a full-time student . . .'

'Are there part-time courses?'

'Some.'

'Could you check those too, please?'

'Jude, I would be within my rights to ask you why the hell you want to know all this stuff?'

'If you did, I'd reply that I want to know why Tadeusz Jankowski was murdered.'

'Whatever the reason for his death, I can assure you it had nothing to do with Clincham College.'

'The information I'm asking you to check could maybe prove that. You do have it there, don't you?'

'Yes,' he replied tartly. 'The main records are over in the Admin block, but I keep copies of everything here. It is my job, you know.' He seemed to resent Jude's insinuation that he might be less than diligent in his duties. Looking at the laptop screen, he said, 'No, the name's not here.'

'May I have a look?'

He sighed at her suspicion, but obediently sat down

and placed the laptop on her plump knees. 'OK, we're in the file "ALLAPP", short for "All Applications". As you see, the dates are on different tabs. Check along the period you are interested in. The applicants' names, you'll see, are in alphabetical order.'

Jude went through the files for the previous nine months. The name "Tadeusz Jankowski" did not appear. She handed the laptop back.

'So now do you believe me?'

'About that,' said Jude, 'yes.'

He deliberately closed the laptop and placed it down on the floor. Then he put his hand on her shoulder and moved it quickly round to her neck. He drew her face towards his.

He had cleaned his teeth. He had at least made that effort to meet her. She could smell the fresh mint from his mouth. She could feel the strength of his eyes as they locked with hers. And he did have very kissable lips.

Jude had no puritan instincts in sexual matters. She tended to let her actions be dictated by the promptings of instinct. Such an attitude had frequently led to disaster, but the way to that disaster had sometimes been a pretty one.

Their mouths engaged. It was pleasant. He seemed in no hurry. His lips teased and nibbled at hers, his tongue flicking against her teeth.

Their eyes had disengaged, and over Andy's shoulder Jude could see the contours of the room, the black walls washed by honey-coloured light, the jumble of stage equipment against the wall. She felt his hand slip over the curves of her shoulder towards the more rewarding curves of her breast. She liked the feeling. She didn't like the man, but she liked what he was doing to her.

Suddenly her eye was caught by a flash of colour amongst the black of the props. She saw the outline of a face, red, with two black and white eyes over a circular mouth.

Propped up against the wall of the Drama Studio was a red-painted guitar.

Chapter Twenty-nine

'He said he had no idea where it came from,' Jude announced. 'He'd asked the students to bring in musical instruments for some workshop they were doing. One of them brought in that guitar.'

'Which one?'

'He claimed he couldn't remember, Carole. He didn't notice. A lot of them brought stuff in.'

'Do you think he was telling the truth?'

'From what I know of Andy Constant, I'd think it was unlikely.'

'Hm.' Carole looked at her neighbour curiously. 'And how did you actually come to be in the Drama Studio with him?'

For the first time in their acquaintance, she saw Jude look embarrassed. 'Oh, I was just checking out with him whether Tadek had ever applied to the university.'

'And Andy Constant kept those records in the Drama Studio?'

'Yes, he did.' Although she was speaking absolute truth, Jude found herself blushing like the biggest liar on earth.

'I see,' said Carole witheringly. 'Anyway, that ties in with what I found out from Melanie Newton. About the connection with the University of Clincham.'

'Yes, I haven't congratulated you properly yet on tracking her down. That was a brilliant bit of detective work.'

Carole glowed in the beam of the compliment, which also, as Jude had intended, took the focus off her own discomfiture. 'Oh, it was Gerald Hume who gave me the lead. Once I'd got the photo from him, the rest was straightforward.'

'I'm still impressed.'

'Well, thank you.' Now it was Carole's turn to blush.

'So I don't think it would be too great a leap of logic to conclude that the girl from the University of Clincham with whom Tadek fell in love was the one who had taken the guitar from his room. And who then handed it over when Andy Constant asked them to bring instruments.'

'So who would that be? One of his Drama set, obviously. And the only one we know about of those is Sophia Urquhart.'

'There's also the mysterious Joan. The one I said he was having an affair with.'

'I thought you said he denied having an affair with her.'

'Yes, but Andy Constant is not the kind of man whose truthfulness I'd trust very far in matters of relationships. He's a born liar.'

'So you haven't even met this Joan?'

'Well, I wonder . . . You remember that day when

262

we went to see Andy up at the college, and he took us for coffee?'

'Yes.'

'The girl who came to fetch him . . . do you remember her?'

'Dark-haired? Looked a bit Spanish?'

Jude nodded. 'I saw her with him again just before that show I went to see. And she was in the pub afterwards, but then I didn't notice her there when Sophia gave Andy the message about Joan not being able to make it. I reckon there's a strong chance she's the one.'

'So how do we contact her?'

'Through the college – or university or whatever it wants to call itself.'

'We didn't have much luck there when we were trying to find out about Tadek.'

'No, but he'd never been enrolled. We've got more to go on with this girl. We know what she looks like, we know she's studying Drama with Andy Constant and we know her first name's Joan.'

'Any idea of her second name?'

'No . . .' Jude suddenly remembered. 'But I've got the programme for *Rumours of Wars* upstairs. I know she wasn't performing in the show, but I'll bet her name's there in the backstage crew!'

She rose excitedly from her sofa, but in the hall met an equally excited Zofia running downstairs, clutching Jude's laptop. 'I've heard from Pavel!' the girl shouted.

'What, about the songs?'

'Yes. He's back from Krakow, he reply to my email.

And we were correct. Tadek did write a song to his English girl. He sent a copy to Pavel.'

'Do you have the lyrics for it?'

'Better. I have a recording.' Zofia bustled into the sitting room and, after a quick greeting to Carole, placed the laptop on a pile of books on one of Jude's cluttered coffee tables. 'You are ready to hear it?'

'Yes, please,' said both women eagerly.

Zofia pressed a key and from the laptop's tiny speakers came the strumming of an acoustic guitar. Then followed a voice, an innocent light tenor, singing in heavily accented English.

> *You're my love and I love you like hell,*
> *Though I don't speak your language so well.*
> *You're the best in all the whole world,*
> *You are all that I want in a girl.*
> *I love you in good or bad weather,*
> *I love things that we do together –*
> *Sing, make love, talk on the phone.*
> *All the time you're just like Joan.*

Carole and Jude exchanged satisfied looks as their suspicions were confirmed. Tadek's song went into its chorus.

> *Just like Joan,*
> *I'm overthrown*
> *By the power of your love.*
> *Just like Joan,*
> *You're in my zone,*
> *Like an angel from above.*

Oh, how big my love has grown.
It's because you're . . . just like Joan.

There was a silence as the song ended. Tears glinted in Zofia's eyes. Hearing her brother's voice sounding so close and real brought home to her once again the hard fact of her loss. To fight off sentiment, she said in matter-of-fact tones, 'I think that is Tadek's first attempt to write a song in English.'

'Then it's pretty good,' Jude assured her.

'And,' said Carole, 'it also confirms the suspicion we've had about who his mystery woman is.' They quickly brought the girl up to speed with their thinking, and told her about the pretty dark-haired girl they had seen at the University of Clincham.

'Then I must see her,' said Zofia immediately. 'I must go to the university and talk to her.'

'Exactly what we were thinking.'

'But we must be careful,' Carole cautioned. 'If she has something to hide, she's going to be on the lookout.'

'Yes, she doesn't want anyone to make the connection between her and your brother,' said Jude. 'I think she has already gone some way to cover her tracks.'

The girl looked puzzled. 'I'm sorry. I do not understand.'

'Look, you say your brother was devoted to his guitar?'

'Yes.'

'So, however much he loved a girl, he'd never give it to her, would he?'

'No.'

'Which means that if – as seems likely – this Joan was the one who gave the guitar to Andy Constant, she must have got it without your brother's knowledge. Marek said, when he waited in Tadek's room on the day he died there were no signs of his music, no guitar, no CDs, no tapes. I think Joan must have gone into the room and cleared it all out.'

'Because it would link him to her?' Carole nodded. 'Yes, that makes sense. And if she did do that, it means she must have known that he was dead . . . or about to die. So she either killed him herself or at least knows who did.'

'I think, Zosia,' said Jude, 'that you should get back to your brother's friend Pavel again. He might know more about this Joan. After all, if, as we think, they got together at the music festival in Leipzig, then Pavel might well have met her.'

'Yes, that is good idea. But we must see her as soon as possible,' said Zofia urgently. 'We know she is called Joan. Do we have her other name?'

'Actually I was just on my way to check that when you came downstairs. I think her full name is likely to be in the programme for the show I saw at Clincham College.'

Jude hurried back up to her bedroom to fetch the printed sheet she had been given at the university theatre, but she came down more slowly, studying the text.

Back in the sitting room, the two women looked up at her expectantly.

'Well, that's very odd,' said Jude. 'There's no one on this programme whose first name's Joan.'

Chapter Thirty

'You're the expert in surveillance work.'

'Don't be ridiculous, Jude.'

'Come on, who was it who did that very successful stake-out to find Melanie Newton?'

'Well . . .' Carole couldn't help being flattered.

'And what we're trying to do here is much easier.'

'Is it?'

'Of course it is. We know the girl is a student at the University of Clincham, we know she's doing Drama, and we know her name's Joan. Much more information than you had when you tracked down Melanie.'

'Yes, but we didn't get much cooperation when we went to the university reception asking about Tadek, did we?'

'No. That's why I'm talking about surveillance. Look, there's only one entrance to the university. Which means all the students have to go through it every day.'

'Don't they have halls of residence? For the minority of students who don't live at home? If they do, a student could stay inside on the campus as long as he or she wanted to.'

'They do have halls of residence, but they're not right on the campus. Andy Constant told me. So all the students do have to go in and out through the main gates.'

'So, Jude, are you suggesting I spend the next few days sitting in the Renault outside the university's main gates until I get a sighting of this Joan?'

'No. I'm suggesting we go and have a drink in the Bull. It's right opposite those gates.'

'You mean now?'

'Yes.'

'But Zofia wanted to come too. And she's gone down to do another shift at the Crown and Anchor.'

'Carole, I don't think she'll mind, so long as we actually track the girl down.'

'No, I suppose not.'

'So off to the Bull, in we go. And you never know, we might get lucky.'

They did get lucky. Luckier than they had any right to expect. It was about five when they reached Clincham and the Bull was empty enough for them to get a table in the bay window, which commanded a perfect view of the university's main entrance. Darkness had fallen during their drive from Fethering, but the area was well lit and they could see the comings and goings of the students.

Mostly goings. Clearly many lectures or classes or seminars finished at five and a lot of the students were on their way home. They gathered in little knots, draped round each other, looking even younger in their muffled anoraks and hoodies. As always, they gestured flamboyantly, as though they were taking part in some adult performance of a play to which they did not quite yet know the words. Some were busy texting on mobile phones, some waving elaborately dramatic farewells to friends they would undoubtedly see the next day.

Carole and Jude had only been in their surveillance point for about twenty minutes when their luck kicked in. A bunch of students emerged from the campus, behaving even more flamboyantly than the others, and Jude was quick to recognize some of them from the cast of *Rumours of Wars*. She couldn't see Sophia Urquhart amongst them, but it was definitely the Drama set. Even better, it included the girl whose pretty dark face was framed by long black hair. Better still, she was one of the group who decided to have a drink to start off whatever entertainment the evening might hold.

The Bull's 'Happy Hour' seemed more or less permanent. The management recognized the value of their location and used low prices to encourage the students' alcoholic consumption (not that many of them needed much encouragement). The Drama lot equipped themselves with pints of lager for both genders and commandeered a large table over the other side of the bar. Their presence doubled the decibel level in the pub.

'Well, there she is,' said Carole. 'How do you propose that we start talking to her?'

'Not a problem,' said Jude, rising to her feet. 'If you

want to start a conversation with anyone involved in the theatre, all you have to do is to tell them how good their last show was. And fortunately I had the dubious pleasure of witnessing this lot's last show.'

Carole, as someone who hadn't seen *Rumours of Wars*, thought she should stay put, while her friend sashayed across the bar towards the loud assemblage of students.

Two of the boys were just coming to the end of some routine in cod French accents and Jude timed her entrance so that she rode in on a wave of laughter. 'Sorry to interrupt,' she said, 'but you lot were in *Rumours of Wars*, weren't you?'

Their attention was duly grabbed. Someone actually wanted to talk to them about their work. They confirmed that they had been in the show. One or two of them put on the faces they had practised in their mirrors for the moment when they would be interviewed on television about their professional lives.

Time for the tactical half-truth. 'I thought the show was terrific. Saw it on Friday. Really packed a punch.'

A couple of the girls agreed that it was powerful stuff. 'We felt, like, absolutely *drained* at the end of it,' said one.

'Yeah, like, the director really made us get into our parts. Even if it's only a couple of lines, he said, I want to *feel*, like, the energy you're transmitting to that person.'

Yes, I bet he said that, thought Jude. And a lot more garbage along the same lines.

Their eyes were gleaming, pathetically hungry for

praise. 'Well, I thought you were all terrific. I mean, I used to act and I do know what I'm talking about.' They lapped it up. 'And the staging, too. It was a real ensemble piece.'

'Yeah, that's what Andy – he's, like, the director – he said he wanted us to be an ensemble.'

'Yeah, he said we should be like the . . . Berlin Ensemble . . .?' the girl hazarded.

'Berliner Ensemble.'

'Right, whatever.'

'A lot of backstage effort went into that show too.' She looked at the dark-haired girl. 'I didn't see you in it. Were you part of the stage management?'

'No,' the girl said, in an accent that sounded very slightly Spanish. 'I was the assistant director.'

'Ooh yes. Like, working *very closely* with the director,' insinuated one of the boys.

'Shut up!'

But he'd got the others going. 'You sound guilty to me,' said one.

'Teacher's pet,' crowed another. 'Or teacher's heavy petting, maybe?'

'Just shut up!' the girl said again. But there was no vindictiveness in their banter.

'I wonder, actually,' said Jude to the girl, 'if I could just have a quick word with you . . .' Time for another tactical lie '. . . I'd love to ask you about how the improvisation element worked out.'

'Sure.' The girl seemed quite ready to detach herself from the teasing boys around her. Picking up her pint, she sidled out of her seat.

'Let's go and join my friend.'

'Is she interested in the theatre too?'

'Oh yes. Very,' Jude lied. Then, as they approached Carole, she continued, 'I was just saying how interested you are in the theatre.'

'Really?' Carole's pale blue eyes looked daggers at her neighbour.

'What was it you wanted to ask about?' said the girl as she sat down easily between them.

'Well, I know Andy Constant, and I just wondered how closely you worked with him on the production? You know, as his assistant?'

She grimaced. 'Not very closely at all, really. I mean, like, I had this title of assistant director, but really Andy did everything himself. I don't think he's very good at delegating.' No, I can believe that, thought Jude. 'Andy had all the ideas, he wasn't really interested in what I had to say.'

'But did you work with him on the improvisations?'

'Well, yes, but they were pretty useless. I mean, we all did improvisations, but Andy didn't use much of our stuff. It was like he had the whole thing planned from the start, almost like he was working from a script that was already written.'

'Something he'd done before?'

'It felt like that at times.' Which didn't surprise Jude one bit. She could imagine Andy Constant bringing out some long-written script, dusting it down, slotting in a few contemporary references and making his students think that they had worked it out through their own improvisation. That would be typical of his control-freak approach to his work. And would also explain why *Rumours of Wars* had felt so old-fashioned.

'You imply that being assistant director to Andy Constant wasn't the most rewarding creative experience of your life.'

'No way. He just used me as cheap labour. Photocopying, typing up rehearsal schedules – that was the extent of my creative input.'

'So was that why you didn't let them put your name on the programme?'

The girl's forehead wrinkled with bewilderment. 'My name was on the programme.'

'But I thought your first name was Joan.'

The bewilderment increased. 'I'm not called Joan.'

Her name, it turned out, was Ines Ribeiro. Her parents were part of the Portuguese community in Littlehampton. She had never been nicknamed 'Joan' by anyone. She didn't know anyone in the Drama set who was called or nicknamed 'Joan'. She had never met Tadeusz Jankowski. And, in spite of the insinuations of her friends, the suggestion that she might have been having an affair with Andy Constant shocked her to the core of her Portuguese Catholic being.

It was not Carole and Jude's finest hour. After a very offended Ines Ribeiro had left them, they hastily finished their drinks and beat an ignominious retreat back to Fethering.

Chapter Thirty-one

That evening Jude was getting ready for bed when Zofia returned from her shift at the Crown and Anchor. 'Please, I am sorry for intrusion,' said the girl. 'May I just check the email on the laptop?'

'Of course you can. But actually it's not here. I took it downstairs, so that you'd be able to get at it. It's on the kitchen table.'

'Oh, I am sorry. I did not look down there.'

'No reason why you should have done.' Jude belted her dressing-gown around her substantial waist. 'I'll come down and see if anything's come through.'

'I just wish to see if there is anything more from Pavel,' said Zofia, as they made their way down to the kitchen. 'I asked him if he knew about Tadek's Joan.'

'Well, let's hope he knows more than I thought I did.' And, while Zofia got to work on the keyboard, Jude spelt out the failure of her trip with Carole to the Bull.

'Ah yes, there is a reply from Pavel,' said the girl excitedly. 'Quite a long one. And look – he has attached another song as well.'

Jude looked at the lines of incomprehensible words on the screen. 'So what does it mean? What does he say?'

BLOOD AT THE BOOKIES

'I'll tell you. First I get out my notebook, make
some notes.' She opened the blue book on the kitchen
table. Then, as her eyes scanned down the text, the girl
translated from the Polish. 'He say yes, Tadek did meet
the English woman at the festival in Leipzig last summer. He say Tadek did call her "Joan", but he think perhaps it is a nickname. The girl come up on stage and
sing with the band one evening when they are in a
club. That is how my brother meet her. And Tadek is in
love . . . yes, yes, like he has never been in love before.
Always the same with my brother. And Pavel says the
woman is very beautiful.'

'What does she look like?'

'He does not say. Maybe later. It is a long email, and
Pavel writes like he talks, all out of order, just thoughts
as they come to him. Ah, and then he says the songs he
is attaching are ones Tadek recorded in Leipzig with the
girl, her singing to his accompaniment . . . Now he says
why Tadek call her "Joan". He think her voice like one
of his favourite singers, Joan Baez.'

'Of course. His other song was called "Just Like
Joan". We got it wrong. The girl's name wasn't Joan, she
was *like* Joan.' Jude was pretty sure now that she knew
the mystery woman's identity. 'Can we hear the song?'

Zofia's nimble fingers set up the playback. Again it
was an amateur recording. 'The Night They Drove Old
Dixie Down'. Another Joan Baez standard. With Tadek's
acoustic guitar accompanying the pure soprano that
Jude had last heard in the theatre at Clincham College
singing 'Where Have All the Flowers Gone?'

Chapter Thirty-two

Jude grinned with satisfaction. 'I think we're looking at an old-fashioned love triangle,' she told Zofia. 'Sophia Urquhart is loved by two men. Your brother Tadek who we now know met her in Leipzig during her gap year, and Andy Constant who came on to her once she became enrolled in his Drama course.'

'OK, let me write this down,' the girl responded excitedly. She took a biro, opened a clean page of her notebook and drew three separate crosses. 'Here are the corners of our triangle. We have Sophia Urquhart . . .' She wrote the names as she spoke them. 'Tadek . . . and Andy Constant . . . We draw a line here . . . Tadek to Sophia . . .' She scribbled down, 'He loves her.' 'And the same thing from Andy Constant to Sophia . . .' She wrote that down too, and nodded with satisfaction. 'It's beginning to make sense.'

'Yes. Of course, the one side of the triangle you haven't filled in is the relationship between Andy Constant and your brother.'

'You think . . . it is hatred perhaps? Hatred enough to kill someone?'

'It's possible, Zosia. At last we're getting somewhere.' Jude beamed. 'I think this deserves a celebration. How about a glass of wine before we go to bed?'

'I would like that very much.'

The buoyant certainty Jude had felt the night before received a predictable inundation of cold water the next morning. 'I don't see how you can be sure she'd even been to Leipzig,' said Carole, reverting to her customary wet blanket role.

'Carole, of course she was there. She was the woman Tadek talked to his friend Pavel about, the one he followed to England.'

'I don't understand how you can make that assumption.'

'I can make it because I heard Sophia sing in *Rumours of Wars*, and now I've heard the song she recorded with Tadek in Leipzig. I'd put money on the fact that it's the same voice.'

'You'd put money on anything.'

Jude grinned. She reckoned her neighbour was behaving like this because it was not she who had made this latest leap of logic. Carole could be very competitive at times and that quality, coupled with her recurrent paranoia, could make her a difficult companion.

'I'm not so sure,' Carole went on sniffily. 'Anyway, if what you say is true, who's our murderer?'

'Well, having seen the kind of anger Andy's capable of when he's thwarted, I think he has to be way up the top of the list.'

'You think he killed the boy?'

'Two rivals for the love of the same woman. Wouldn't be the first middle-aged man who's felt his virility challenged by a young upstart.'

'But . . . But, Jude, there's so much we don't know. Tadek came to England to follow Sophia Urquhart . . . all right, it sounds from what his friend Pavel said that that's true. So he was in love with her. But was she in love with him? And what did she think about her Drama teacher? Or him about her? It all seems terribly vague. You don't know Sophia was having an affair with her teacher.'

'I've told you, Carole. I overheard Sophia apologizing to Andy that "Joan" could not go back with him, because she was getting a lift home with her father. And that made him angry because he "wanted" her. We now know "Joan" didn't exist, but was a nickname for Sophia. And I actually travelled in the car from the university with Sophia, so it was her father who was giving "Joan" a lift home. It can't be plainer than that.'

'I don't know,' said Carole, infuriatingly unconvinced.

'Anyway,' Jude looked at her watch, 'I'll soon be able to find out about whether Sophia went to Leipzig or not.'

'How?'

'Because her brother Hamish is due here in ten minutes.'

'Why's he coming?'

'To value the house.'

'Oh.' Carole also looked at her watch. She had

already exercised her dog on Fethering Beach that morning, but she said curtly, 'I must go. Gulliver needs a walk.'

There was something of the play-actor about Hamish Urquhart. His manner was studied rather than spontaneous. Maybe, Jude reflected, being an estate agent was similar to the professions of lawyer, doctor and teacher, where young recruits took on the manners of people much older than themselves. In Hamish's case, of course, he took on the manners of his father, becoming a hearty facsimile of Ewan Urquhart.

He was dressed in a gold-buttoned blazer and mustard-yellow cords. Under his arm was a brown leather briefcase, from which he produced a clipboard, some forms and a pocket-sized laser distance measure. He also handed Jude his business card and some stapled sheets of details from houses Urquhart & Pease had recently sold.

'The property market's still very buoyant at the moment, I'm pleased to say. Particularly down here in the south-east. We could sell every house that comes on to the market three times over. Just not enough product, that's the problem. No, we'd have no problem in getting you a very good price for this.' He looked without total conviction around the clutter of the Woodside Cottage sitting room. Jude reckoned he was thinking, 'even in this condition'. But he was too courteous to vocalize the thought.

'Now, if you don't mind, I'd just like to go around

the property, take some details, make some notes. You may accompany me if you like, or . . .'

'No, you just wander round at your own pace. The place is empty apart from me. I do have a friend staying, but she's out this morning. Anyway, I've got some stuff to put in the washing machine.'

'Fine. Well, I'll have a look at the kitchen first, and then be out of your way doing the rest of the house.'

'Yes. Would you like a cup of coffee or something?'

'No, thanks. Just had some at the office.'

He quickly checked out the dimensions of the back garden and the kitchen, then said, 'It's not pivotal at this juncture, but when you do sell, you'll have to decide whether you'd want to take or leave your kitchen equipment. Oven, washing machine, what-have-you . . .'

'Oh, I'm not definitely thinking of selling. Just sort of . . . testing the water, trying to find out where I stand financially.'

'Yes, of course, Mrs . . . er, Miss . . .'

'Just call me Jude.'

'Right. Jude.'

She had decided that she'd question him about his sister after he'd finished the valuation, so she set her load of washing going while he surveyed the house. It didn't take long. Soon he was downstairs again, tapping at the kitchen door. They sat down either side of the kitchen table for him to give his verdict. Jude told him to push aside some of the clutter so that he would have room for his clipboard. She noticed that Zofia had left her notebook open on the table from the night before.

'Well, to be quite honest, Jude,' said Hamish cheer-ily, 'Urquhart & Pease could get you a buyer for this property tomorrow. No problems at all. Fethering is quite a property hot-spot, a much sought-after area, because it's still one of those villages which has kept its . . . Englishness.'

'I'm sorry? What do you mean?'

'Well, I mean, most of the people . . . Not to put to finc a point on it, you don't see too many coloured faces in Fethering . . . and you don't hear too many Eastern European accents when you're shopping in Allinstore.' The guffaw which followed this, not to mention the sentiments expressed, made him sound exactly like his father.

Jude didn't approve of what Hamish had said, but made no comment and let him continue. 'So, as I say, very much sought-after. And you'd be surprised how many wealthy city folk are looking for that ideal of a country retreat. Woodside Cottage would tick all the boxes for them. So far as I can tell, the structure's very sound, though . . .' A blush spread across his face and down to his thick neck '. . . not everyone might share your taste in decor. Some of the windows are getting a bit shabby, and the exterior paintwork needs to be done. So I think any potential purchaser would be look-ing to spend a bit of money on the place. Or you could have some of the work done yourself before you put the place on the market. Mind you, having a house redecorated with a view to selling doesn't always work, either. In a lot of cases, the new owners are going to want to redo everything, anyway.'

'Yes, it's supposed to be a natural human instinct. Marking one's territory. Like dogs peeing at lamp-posts.'

'Really?' The young man looked puzzled. 'I hadn't heard that.'

'So what sort of price would we be looking at?' Although she'd had an ulterior motive in asking for the valuation, Jude was still intrigued to know how much her property was worth.

After a bit of professional hedging and prevarication, Hamish Urquhart named a figure. It was considerably in excess of what Jude had been expecting. Of course she'd read the constant newspaper reports about the inexorable rise in house prices, but was still shocked to hear the sum spelt out for Woodside Cottage. She was sitting on a little gold-mine.

'That's very gratifying,' she said.

'Yes. As you say, you're not looking to sell at right this moment, but, you know, when you do make the decision, I hope you'll remember Urquhart & Pease. There are, of course, other estate agents around, the area's bristling with them, but many are branches of big chains, and I think you're guaranteed a more sympathetic experience dealing with a family firm like Urquhart & Pease.' He reached once again into his briefcase. 'I do have a sheet here, spelling out the terms of our business transactions, fee structure and so on, and I think you'll find Urquhart & Pease are competitive with . . .' He looked, puzzled, into the recesses of his case. 'Damn, I don't seem to have brought it with me.'

'Never mind, Hamish. I'm sure we can take those details as read. I've just put the kettle on. Are you sure I can't tempt you to a coffee?'

'Oh, well . . .' He looked at his watch. 'I've got a bit of time before my next appointment. Why not?'

Making the coffee gave Jude a good excuse to change the subject. 'Very interesting seeing that play your sister was in last week . . .'

'Yes. Pretty damned odd, I found it. I mean, I don't pretend to know much about the theatre. Like a good musical . . . you know, Lloyd Webber, that kind of thing. Something where you don't have to think too much. But that thing of Soph's . . . can't say I got all of it. I mean, she was very good, but . . . Also, the message it seemed to be putting across . . . I'm not sure I went along with it.'

'In what way, Hamish?' asked Jude as she put the coffee cup in front of him.

'Thanks. Well, the show seemed to be saying that war is always a bad thing.'

'And you don't agree with that?'

'Good God, no. I mean, I'm not recommending that countries should go around invading and bombing other countries whenever the fancy strikes them, but sometimes action has to be taken. Every country needs to have an army, and I reckon we've got one of the best in the world. So I don't like when I hear our brave boys being mocked. They do a damned fine job in extraordinarily difficult conditions. And they're bloody necessary. Always have been. I mean, if Mr Hitler had been allowed to go his merry way in 1939 without anyone trying to stop him . . . well, we'd probably now be conducting this conversation in bloody German!' Again he sounded as if he was quoting his father verbatim.

'Talking of Germany . . .' said Jude, snatching at the most tenuous of links, 'your sister was saying she'd been there in her gap year.'

'Yes. Lucky old Soph, actually getting a gap year. I didn't have one. Straight out of school into the family business. None of that university nonsense for me.' Hamish made it sound as if he had made a choice in the matter, but Jude remembered Ewan Urquhart saying it was lack of academic ability that had kept his son out of university.

'And she's such a good singer,' Jude went on, worming her way round to what she really wanted to ask. 'Do you know if Sophia did any singing while she was in Europe?'

'I think she did, actually. I know she went to some music festivals and things. She kept sending Dad postcards.'

'Where from?' Hamish seemed so innocent and unsuspicious in his answers that Jude didn't worry about pressing him.

'Berlin, certainly. I remember she was there. And Frankfurt, I think . . . and Leipzig. I remember that, because Dad made some comment about my sister being in the land of the Commie Krauts!' He guffawed once again at his father's wit.

Still, Jude had got what she wanted. Proof positive that Sophia Urquhart, in spite of her denial when asked about it, had actually been to Leipzig. So now Jude had a solid fact to underpin her conjectures.

'Are you musical too, Hamish?' she asked.

'God, no. Can maybe join in the chorus of some filthy song down the rugby club, but that's the extent of it. No, Soph's the one in the family with talent.' He spoke this as an accepted fact, one that he had been told about so many times that it caused him no resentment.

'And she's very pretty too,' said Jude, still angling the conversation in the direction she wanted it to go. 'She must be surrounded by boyfriends.'

'She hasn't had that many, actually.'

'Seems strange. I'd have thought the boys'd be after her like bees round a honey-pot.'

'Maybe some'd like to be, but they don't get far.' He let out another hearty laugh. 'You see, none of them can pass Dad's quality control.'

'You don't know whether she met anyone on her gap year?'

'No,' Hamish replied shortly. Then he clammed up. For the first time, he looked suspicious of Jude.

'Or what about at college? Drama students traditionally are supposed to have colourful love lives.'

'No, I don't think . . . I don't know . . .' He looked confused. 'I don't think she'd got anyone special, but . . . Why, have you heard anything?'

Jude shrugged, in part at the incongruity of the question. So far as Hamish knew, she had nothing to do with Clincham College, and yet here he was asking her for information about his sister's relationships there.

'Just rumours,' she replied airily. 'As you know, the main product of this entire area is gossip.'

'Yes,' said Hamish thoughtfully.

At that moment the doorbell rang. Jude went through to the hall to let in Ewan Urquhart, who with unctuous smoothness held her hand for slightly longer than was necessary and asked, 'Sorry? Is my idiot boy still with you?'

'Hamish is here. Through in the kitchen.'

Ewan Urquhart marched through, brandishing a couple of stapled printed sheets. 'Only forgot to bring the terms and conditions, didn't you, Hamish?'

His son admitted his error, looking like a guilty schoolboy. But once again he didn't seem genuinely shamed. His incompetence was an essential part of his personality. Perhaps within the family it was what made him lovable.

Ewan handed the sheet to Jude. 'Sorry. The old adage that if you want something done, you'd better do it yourself has never been more true than when it comes to dealing with Hamish. As I have learnt, to my cost, over the years. Anyway, I hope he's done a proper valuation for you.'

'Yes, he's been excellent,' said Jude, who was getting sick of hearing the young man constantly diminished.

'What price did he give you?'

Jude told him. The older man rubbed his chin sceptically. 'I think he may have overstated it. Exuberance of youth, eh? To be on the safe side, I'd say five thousand less.'

'Well, it's still a huge amount more than I paid for it.'

'I bet. Oh, you can't go wrong with property. Just sit at home and watch the money grow around you.' He let out a guffaw, exactly like the one Hamish had copied from him. Then he turned to his son. 'Come on. We've got a business to run. Can't sit around drinking coffee all day.'

The young man was on his feet before his father had finished speaking. Ewan Urquhart focused on Jude again. 'Just whenever you decide you want to sell, remember Urquhart & Pease. There are, of course, other estate agents around . . . the area's bristling with them, but many are branches of big chains, and I think you're guaranteed a more sympathetic experience dealing with a family firm like Urquhart & Pease.'

So Hamish had actually learnt the spiel word for word from his father.

Before he left the kitchen, Ewan Urquhart paused for a moment, looking at the clutter on the table. Jude couldn't be certain, but it looked as though he had seen the open notebook on whose page Zofia had spelt out his daughter's love triangle. Something certainly seemed to have changed his manner. As he said goodbye, there was a new beadiness in the older estate agent's eyes.

Next door at High Tor, Carole Seddon sat in a state of bleak desolation. Her lifelong instinct had been never to trust anyone, and once again it had been proved right.

Drop your defences, allow another person inside your comfort zone, and you're just inviting them to betray you. Only a matter of time before it happens.

Jude was selling Woodside Cottage. She hadn't thought it necessary to impart that decision to her neighbour. And Carole, who didn't have many, had thought they were friends.

Chapter Thirty-three

Jude would have gone straight round and told Carole about the confirmation of Sophia Urquhart's presence in Leipzig, but her friend had said she was going to take Gulliver out for a walk. So Jude rang Andy Constant's mobile.

'I wondered if we could get together.'

'I don't see why not.' His voice was full of lazy self-congratulation. The parting from their last encounter had not been harmonious. When she'd seen Tadek's guitar in the Drama Studio, Jude had broken from their kiss to question Andy about it. The interruption had destroyed the mood between them and certainly thwarted the plans he had been nursing for the rest of the evening. In his frustration he had become very childish and refused to answer her questions.

But there was still information Jude needed that she could only get from him, so another meeting was imperative.

Of course, Andy Constant, being the kind of man he was, interpreted her getting in touch with him as the action of a woman who had seen the error of her ways. Yes, she must have known she had behaved badly when they last met, but she obviously couldn't stop thinking about him. He reckoned the old Andy Constant animal magnetism was once again exerting its irresistible pull.

Jude didn't mind what he thought her motives were, so long as he agreed to see her again. Which he readily did. 'Don't let's bother with meeting in the pub,' he said, his voice low in a way that he knew to be sexy. 'Come straight to the Drama Studio.'

'Will I be able to get in?'

'I'll leave the building unlocked.'

'I meant – will I be able to get past security on the main gate?'

'There's another way in. There's a small door into the campus in Maiden Avenue. It's meant to be locked, but some of the staff have keys and it very rarely is. A lot of the students come and go through it.' There was something unappealing about the practised ease with which he went through these details. Jude wondered how many other women had been given these instructions before an assignation with Andy Constant.

'All right. I'll come in that way.'

'Good, Jude.' He sounded patronizing, as if speaking to a recalcitrant child. 'Let's say six o'clock. I'll really enjoy seeing you.'

I wouldn't be so sure about that, thought Jude as she finished the call.

She rang to see if Carole was back, but there was no reply. In the afternoon she had a couple of clients for her healing services, a man with a stomach complaint for which the doctors could find no explanation, and a woman who suffered from panic attacks. In both cases Jude felt she made some progress.

Just before she left for Clincham, she tried ringing her neighbour again. Still no reply. Must be out.

Inside High Tor, Carole looked at the Caller Display and did not pick up the phone.

The door in Maiden Avenue was, as Andy Constant had promised, unlocked. The road fringed Clincham's main park and there was no street lighting. The February night was dark. Jude slipped into the campus, reflecting on the laxness of the security. No doubt an alternative means of access was convenient for the staff, but it would only take one incident of violence by an outsider against a student for them to realize their foolishness in leaving the door unlocked.

Jude hadn't yet worked out the best approach to use with Andy Constant. Her suspicion was growing that the lecturer had killed Tadeusz Jankowski. Replaying the scene she had overheard between him and Sophia Urquhart in the Bull made her more certain than ever that they were lovers. He was having an affair with 'Joan' and 'Joan' was Sophia's nickname, at least for Tadek. Maybe she had told her Drama tutor that and he had relished the idea of using it as well.

Andy Constant was a spoilt and petulant man, used to getting his own way. He wouldn't have taken kindly to having a rival for his beautiful student's affections. Quite how he'd come to be in Fethering to meet and kill the young Pole, Jude didn't know, but she felt sure she could find out.

As she pushed open the door into the unlit Drama Studio block, she felt a little stab of fear. If Andy was the murderer and she threatened to reveal that fact to the world, he might not think twice about killing again. Pauline's late husband's view that the prime motive for murder was to keep people quiet came into her mind. She needed to be very circumspect in her approach.

There were no lights on in the lobby, but memory guided her towards the door of the studio itself. She pushed open its heavy mass. The only light inside came from an illuminated 'Exit' sign.

It wasn't a lot, but sufficient for her to see the body of a man lying on the double mattress. And sufficient to be reflected in the glistening of wet redness on his chest.

Jude heard a sound behind her in the lobby. She reached for her mobile and pressed the buttons to dial Carole's number.

In High Tor, as soon as the caller was identified, the phone remained untouched.

Chapter Thirty-four

There was a call that Carole did take later that evening, and selfishly she almost wished she hadn't. It was from Gaby, at her wit's end because Lily had developed a high temperature and would not be comforted. The doctor had been called and was going to come again in the morning. If the little mite wasn't better then, she'd be taken into hospital for observation.

For Carole, already desolated by Jude's betrayal, that was all she needed. She knew she wouldn't sleep a wink that night, expecting every minute a phone call with terrible news from Stephen or Gaby.

She had forgotten that awful panic that can be instantly summoned up by the sickness of a child. Lily was so perfect, but so tiny. The lightest puff of illness could blow her away, it seemed to Carole as she faced the long agony of the night. Everything in her life felt suddenly threatened and fragile.

Jude heard only the clattering of the external door of the Drama block. She shivered as she realized she must have passed within inches of whoever it was in the lobby. She must have been within touching distance of someone who was probably the murderer of Tadeusz Jankowski.

But her first priority was the man lying on the bed. She felt along the walls for light switches, but in vain. She remembered that Andy Constant had achieved his lighting effects from the box, but she didn't know how to get in there.

Still, if she concentrated . . . Her eyes slowly adjusted to the gloom. The light from the 'Exit' sign seemed to grow stronger.

Soon she could see clearly enough to recognize that the man on the bed was Andy Constant himself. Blood was pouring from his chest, but he was still breathing.

Jude rang the police.

They were much tougher with her this time than they had been after Tadek's death. To discover one stabbing victim might be considered bad luck; discover two and the authorities are bound to get suspicious. It took Jude most of the evening to convince the detectives that she had no responsibility for either crime. Their questioning remained polite, but they were very persistent.

Andy Constant, she was told, had been taken to hospital and was in intensive care. They promised to let her know when they heard anything about his condition. And meanwhile they kept going over the same ground, asking about her relationship with the lecturer, on and wearily on. She was suitably cagey on the subject, admitting that they had met for a drink a couple of times, but denying things had gone any further than that. Which was pretty much the truth.

In fact, Jude answered all the detectives' questions as honestly as she could, but she didn't volunteer any information they didn't ask her about. Above all, she didn't mention that she and Carole had been trying to solve the murder mystery themselves. She knew the derision with which professional policemen would greet that news.

To her surprise, in what the detectives said to her they did not seem to be linking the two attacks. Or maybe they were, but did not want her speculations going down that route. As an amateur, she had the usual difficulty in knowing how far the official investigation had proceeded. And she wasn't about to be enlightened on the subject. Jude was a witness and a possible suspect. The police weren't about to tell her their secrets.

Finally, around ten-thirty, the detectives seemed to decide that there really was nothing more she could tell them. They said that they were trying to keep what had happened secret for as long as possible and firmly forbade Jude to have any contact with the media about the stabbing. It was their hope to make some headway with their investigation before they had to deal with the intrusions of press and television. Then they thanked her politely for her cooperation and asked if she wanted a lift home, an offer of which she took grateful advantage.

It was an unmarked police car that dropped her outside Woodside Cottage. She looked up at High Tor, but the curtains of Carole's bedroom were closed. Oh well, she could bring her neighbour up to date in the morning.

Inside, she found that Zofia Jankowska was not yet back from the Crown and Anchor (where, though Ted Crisp would never admit it, she seemed to be becoming an essential member of staff). Jude didn't wait up for her. She was totally exhausted by the events of the day, so got to bed as quickly as she could and passed out.

Chapter Thirty-five

Gaby rang back at eight-thirty. Lily had slept well and, though a bit grizzly, no longer had such a high temperature. The doctor's return visit had been put off. Stephen had gone off to work. They were all right.

She hadn't rung her mother-in-law earlier because she hadn't wanted to wake her. To Carole, who'd been sleeplessly entertaining the most ghastly speculations all night, this was an unhelpful thing to say. But she didn't mention the fact, just said how relieved she was about Lily's improvement and asked for regular updates on the tiny girl's progress.

At least one cause of her perturbation was diminished. The other, she thought, might never be resolved.

Waiting for the call from Gaby had kept her at home when she would normally have been taking Gulliver down to Fethering Beach, so her next priority was giving the dog his walk.

As she opened the front door, dressed in her smart Burberry, thick scarf and hat, Carole found herself face to face with Jude, who had been on the verge of lifting the knocker.

'Good morning,' said Carole coldly. 'I'm just taking Gulliver for his walk.'

'Well, I'll come with you. Just give me a moment to get a coat.'

'I don't think it'll be necessary for you to come. I'll be fine on my own.'

And with that, Carole Seddon, with Gulliver in tow, stalked off down Fethering High Street in the direction of the beach.

Open-mouthed, her neighbour watched her go. But it wasn't in Jude's nature to let wounds fester. If something had come up between her and Carole, then she had to find out immediately what it was. She got her coat and set off after the figures of woman and dog dwindling into the distance.

Though not overtly looking back, Carole was aware of the pursuit. When she reached the edge of the beach, rather than going left towards the estuary of the River Fether, she turned right and strode firmly away, Gulliver off his lead and performing eccentric circles around her. That way the beach stretched on for miles. Carole's long stride took her ever further away from her pursuer, who not only had shorter legs but also had a lot more weight to carry.

After walking about a quarter of a mile and not making any inroad into her neighbour's lead, Jude stopped and sat on the end of a wooden breakwater where it nuzzled into the high shingle of the beach. There was no alternative route; Carole would have to come back the way she had gone. It was just a matter of waiting.

Jude sat there for over an hour. Carole must have known that she was making a fool of herself, but when she finally did come to where her neighbour sat, she looked all set to walk by without acknowledging her.

Jude wasn't having any of that. She stood up and blocked Carole's way. 'Look, will you please tell me what's going on.'

'Nothing's going on,' replied Carole icily.

Gulliver very much let the side down by going up to Jude and enthusiastically licking her hand.

'Carole, I have done something to offend you. I don't know what it is, but I can assure you it wasn't deliberate.'

'Don't worry about it. It's not a problem.'

Carole once again tried to manoeuvre herself past, but found her arm grabbed. 'Look, we're friends. And it's stupid for friends to split up over something trivial.'

'People have different definitions of trivial,' came the snitty reply.

'Listen, Carole, I have actually got a lot of new information on the murder case. You won't believe what has happened.'

Though clearly tempted, Carole wasn't going to succumb to curiosity. 'I'm sorry. I must be on my way.'

'No.' Jude kept her neighbour's arm firmly in her grasp. 'I am not going to let you go until you tell me what's bugging you.'

'All right,' said Carole with exasperation. 'You've just said we're friends. Well, I would have thought it was a rather strange person who moves house without telling her friend about it.'

'Moves house?' Jude looked at Carole with incomprehension. Then slowly the penny dropped. 'Oh, no . . . the valuation? You didn't think . . .? That was not because I was really selling the house. I set it up just to get some information out of Hamish Urquhart. And it worked. He confirmed that Sophia had been in Leipzig last summer, which is where she must have met Tadek.'

'Oh,' said Carole, suddenly feeling rather small.

'You idiot!' said Jude affectionately. 'You absolute idiot! Now will you please let me tell you what has happened in the last twenty-four hours?'

As the two women walked back up the beach, Carole heard everything, about the second stabbing and Jude's uncomfortable evening with the police. By the time they got back to Woodside Cottage, her bad mood had dissipated and she was once again totally caught up in the murder investigation.

'You haven't had any news as to how Andy Constant is?'

Jude shook her head. 'There was a lot of blood. I don't have the medical knowledge to assess how serious it was. The police said they'd keep me informed, but I doubt if they'll bother.'

'I'll put on the radio when I get in – and check the television . . . see if there's anything about the attack.'

'Yes, well, if I hear anything, obviously I'll let you know as soon as possible. And, Carole,' Jude went on as her friend moved towards High Tor, 'don't ever imagine that I would sell my house without telling you.'

'But are you thinking of selling it?'

'Not today,' said Jude enigmatically. And Carole had to be content with that.

The phone in Woodside Cottage rang at about five that afternoon. 'Is that Jude?' asked a well-spoken woman's voice she did not recognize.

'Yes.'

'You don't know me. I'm Esther Constant. Andy's wife.'

'Ah,' said Jude, fearing the worst. 'How is he?'

'Surprisingly good, actually. He's out of intensive care.'

'Wow, that was quick.'

'Yes, although there was a lot of bleeding, the wound itself wasn't very deep. He's still quite weak because he lost so much blood, but no, he's basically on the mend.'

'I'm delighted to hear it.'

'Yes.' Esther Constant was silent for a moment, as though uncertain how to phrase the next bit. 'Andy . . . he . . . he said he'd like to see you . . .'

'Oh. Really?' Jude was thrown. Was Andy's wife aware of his interest in her? 'Why is that?' she asked.

'He said so that he could say thank you.'

'Thank me for what?'

'Andy reckons it was your arrival which frightened his attacker off. He thinks you may have saved his life.'

*

The wounded lecturer was in a private hospital not far from the University of Clincham campus. Whether he had been put in there for reasons of security or because he had a good private health insurance, Jude didn't know. She'd gone by train along the coastal line to Clincham and got to the hospital's reception round seven-thirty. They were expecting her and when she asked for Andy Constant, a smartly suited woman directed her to a suite of rooms on the fourth floor. The decor of the hospital was all soothing pastel blues and greens. There were tasteful photographic prints on the walls and gratuitous reproduction coffee tables on the landings.

A nurse sitting behind a reception desk on the fourth-floor landing led her to a door which had a card marked 'Mr A. Constant' fitted into a plastic slot. She tapped on the door and Esther Constant's voice said, 'Come in.'

The scene that greeted Jude was one of long-standing connubial bliss. Andy was propped up on a lot of pillows, with an edge of bandages visible at the neck of his pyjamas. Esther, a pretty woman with short dark hair, was seated at his bedside, holding his hand. She rose and said, 'You must be Jude.'

'Yes.'

'I'm so grateful to you for coming. Andy really wanted to see you.'

The patient smiled weakly and gave a feeble wave. Jude felt the knee-jerk suspicion that she had in all dealings with Andy Constant. He wasn't as badly hurt

302

BLOOD AT THE BOOKIES

as he was pretending. Once again he was milking a situation for all it was worth.

'As I said on the phone,' Esther Constant went on, 'he really thinks you may have saved his life. His attacker would have gone on stabbing him if you hadn't arrived. Andy reckons the attacker must have heard you coming in through the main door of the Drama block, and that's what made him do a runner.'

'Maybe. I didn't see anything, but I think I must have passed him – or her – in the lobby.'

'Anyway, Andy says thank God you arrived.'

Jude's conjecture that the whole conversation might be conducted with Esther verbalizing her husband's thoughts ended, as Andy himself said, 'Yes, I can't thank you enough.'

Jude shrugged. 'I'm glad if that is what happened, but it was pure luck. A serendipitous accident of timing.' But in spite of his injured state, she couldn't help moving instantly into investigative mode. 'Did you see who it was who attacked you?'

'No. He – or she – was waiting for me in the lighting box. Must have known I switch on the studio lights from there. Leapt on me as soon as I got through the door.' His voice sounded pretty robust, considering he had just emerged from intensive care.

'Have you been questioned by the police yet?'

'Just basic stuff.'

'They're coming again tomorrow morning,' Esther Constant interposed. 'Assuming he's stronger by then.'

Andy Constant showed a brave smile. 'Which I'll hope to be.' Then he reached out and took his wife's hand. 'Esther love . . . I just want to ask Jude a few details about what she saw . . . and I don't want to make you go through the whole thing again. Maybe you'd like to ask the nurse to get you a cup of coffee?'

His wife, obedient to his every whim, took the hint and made for the door. 'I'll give you five minutes.' Then, explaining to Jude, she said, 'Important that he doesn't get too tired. He's very weak.'

Weak he may have been, but the minute Esther was out of the door, he sat up in bed and said urgently, 'Have the police talked to you yet, Jude?'

'Yes. At some length.'

'And did you tell them anything?'

'About what?'

'About you and me.'

'There isn't much to say about you and me, is there?'

'Come on. We've met a few times. But for . . . external events, we'd be lovers by now.'

Jude wondered how accurate that was. Any attraction she might have felt for Andy Constant had melted away in the last couple of days. But, looking back and being honest with herself, she had a nasty feeling his words might be true.

'Well, I certainly didn't tell the police that.'

'What did you tell them?'

'Just that we'd met for drinks a couple of times, that you'd asked me to go and see *Rumours of Wars* . . .'

'And what about last night?'

'I said that you'd asked me to join you for a drink in the Drama Studio.'

'Just that?'

'Pretty much, yes.'

'Hm.' He looked troubled. 'The thing is, it's very important that Esther doesn't find out anything about us.'

Jude saw him then for what he was. Just another cheap philandering husband. All his talk of the moribund nature of his marriage was so much guff. At home he was the dutiful husband, but he used those elastic moments between work and home to conduct his affairs. His favourite time for an assignation was not a dinner, not a whole evening. No, six o'clock in his own convenient little knocking-shop, the Drama Studio. Time for a furtive glass of Scotch and a quick sexual encounter. Then, no doubt, back home to Esther with an airy, 'Oh, met up with some people for a drink after work.'

Jude shuddered inwardly to think how nearly she had become involved with a man like that.

'Andy, I've said what I told the police. What they make of the information, how much further they want to go with it, that's not up to me.'

'I just don't want Esther to get hurt. She's quite fragile emotionally. I don't want her getting hold of the wrong end of the stick.'

Getting hold of the right end of the stick, thought Jude. Being made to realize what a bastard her husband really was. Yes, it was quite possible that Esther was completely unaware of Andy's finely practised seduction technique. As the saying went, the wife was always the last to know.

'I won't do anything to make the situation worse,' said Jude. Then, suddenly she asked, 'And what about you and Sophia?'

She wouldn't have thought it possible for his face to have gone paler, but it did. 'Me and Sophia? The police didn't ask about that, did they?'

It was the nearest she was likely to get to an admission that he had been having an affair with the girl, so Jude pressed home her advantage. 'No, they haven't asked me about that, but what do you want me to say if they do?'

'Do you think that's likely?'

She shrugged. 'I don't know which way the police investigation is going, do I?'

'Oh, God.' He looked really bad.

'So you're not denying that you were having an affair with her?'

'Look, these things happen.' He was trying to sound disingenuous, but it wasn't cutting any ice with Jude. 'Two attractive people who're attracted to each other, sometimes the emotion can just get too strong to cope with. Even with the difference in ages. I think in fact the difference in ages made it even more powerful. We could learn so much from each other. Come on, haven't you ever been in a situation like that, Jude?'

She had, but she wasn't about to tell him so. 'How long had it been going on?'

'I suppose the attraction was there since the beginning of the academic year, when we first met . . .'

That made sense. Sophia had met Tadek in Leipzig in the summer, he had followed her to England in late

September. Maybe they had begun or continued an affair. But round the same time Sophia had started her university career, and found the archetypal lecherous lecturer coming on to her. As Jude had deduced before, it was a classic love triangle.

'And when did you become lovers?' she asked implacably.

'I suppose it must have been in the run-up to Christmas. You know, there were lots of parties and things on the campus. And I was working closely with Sophia on some one-to-one role-playing exercises.' Yes, I bet you were, thought Jude. He shrugged helplessly, as he went on, 'And, you know, one thing led to another. We both admitted how much we fancied each other and . . .'

Jude suppressed her fury. Andy Constant had shamelessly abused his position of responsibility and was now trying to get sympathy for himself as a plaything of the gods, a man incapable of resisting the surging power of a *grand amour*. All she said, though, was, 'And are you and Joan still love's young dream?'

'Joan? How do you know about—?'

'I know it was Sophia's nickname. One given to her by her other boyfriend.'

'Other boyfriend?'

'Didn't she mention that she had another boyfriend?'

'Oh, yes,' he recalled. 'There had been someone, apparently. But she implied that that had been over for a long time.'

Taking a leaf out of your book then, thought Jude. 'No more details?'

'No, she said she'd got rid of him.'

'Hm.' Jude took in the implications of this for a moment, then said, 'I actually asked whether your affair with Sophia was still going on.'

'Well, no.' He screwed up his face wryly. 'We had had a bit of a falling-out, during the last week, really. I mean, often the really powerful loves have only a limited duration. "So quick bright things come to confusion", and all that. I had to tell her that it wasn't working. And, you know, I was beginning to feel guilty about Esther.'

Oh yes, very handy – the married man's time-honoured way of getting out of an extramarital entanglement: he's worried about his wife.

'How did Sophia take the news?'

He grimaced. 'Not very well, I'm afraid. She was terribly upset, talk of suicide, all kinds of things.' He smiled a put-upon smile. 'Clearly, the whole thing meant much more to her than it did to me.'

Once again Jude was struck by Andy's arrogance. He saw himself doomed to go through life as a babe-magnet, powerless against the devastating strength of his own attractiveness.

'So thoughts of Esther were the only reason you said your affair with Sophia must end?'

'Well . . .' He smiled winningly. 'There was another reason.'

'What was that?'

'I thought maybe things were going to work out with you.'

This time Jude had great difficulty containing her anger. Even from his hospital bed the sleaze-bag was coming on to her. One moment he was talking of breaking off one relationship out of consideration for his wife, the next he was proposing to start a new one. She calmed herself, and said, 'Going back to what happened to you last night, you didn't get any sight of your attacker, did you?'

He shook his head. 'It was pitch dark. And it happened so quickly. The whole thing was over in a matter of seconds.'

'So nothing? No glimpse of a face? No touch of a body?'

'Well, as a matter of fact, as I tried to defend myself, I got hold of his or her coat. And it felt like waxed fabric.'

'A Barbour?'

'That kind of thing, yes.'

Jude nodded thoughtfully. 'Oh, well, no doubt the police will catch the culprit.'

'I doubt it.'

'Why not?'

'Well, it was probably a drifter, who just broke into the Drama Studio in hope of finding some equipment he could sell to buy drugs.'

'That's nonsense, Andy. Too much of a coincidence. My view would be that your attacker was very definitely targeting you. You said as much yourself. It was someone who knew your habits very well, knew

309

that you frequently went into the Drama Studio without switching on the working lights.'

'I'm sure it wasn't.'

This was said with such intensity that Jude suddenly understood. Andy Constant thought he knew precisely who had attacked him. And at that moment Jude reckoned she did too.

'Andy, was it Sophia who stabbed you last night?'

'No. Of course it wasn't.'

But he didn't sound convincing, so Jude pressed on. 'I think it was. And I think that's why you're going to push your theory about the perpetrator being some nameless drifter. You're afraid that if the police get on to Sophia, Esther will find out about the affair you've been having with her.'

'No, Jude. I'm sure it wasn't Sophia. It wouldn't be in her nature to do something like that.'

'You don't think so? "Hell hath no fury" . . . et cetera.'

'I'm sure it wasn't her.' But now he sounded as though he were trying to convince himself.

'It could have been, though,' Jude persisted. His silence was more eloquent than an admission. 'Come on, Andy, tell me what it was made you think it was Sophia?'

'Well,' he said feebly, 'it's just an impression I got, split-second thing. But there's a very distinctive scent she wears. I thought I got a whiff of that last night.'

Chapter Thirty-six

It was nearly nine o'clock when Jude left the hospital. Her route back to Clincham Station took her past the university campus. Which meant that she also passed by the Bull, from which emanated the sound of music and weak applause.

Of course. Friday night. She had witnessed the workings of synchronicity too often to be surprised by its magic. Friday night was the night the Bull hosted 'Clincham Uni's Number One Folk/Rock Band.' Magic Dragon, the band fronted by Sophia Urquhart. Who were actually playing in the pub at that moment. Now that was magic.

She called Carole on the mobile. 'Look, I haven't got time to explain the details, but could you come to Clincham straight away? Meet me in the Bull. And could you check at Woodside Cottage to see if Zofia's there? If so, could you bring her too?'

Magic Dragon didn't seem to be much of a Friday night draw. Maybe the University of Clincham students went further afield for their weekend entertainment, to the clubs of Brighton or Portsmouth. Or maybe they wanted a more up-to-date musical repertoire than the band provided.

There had been so many sixties revivals, but Jude was still surprised to hear the songs that Magic Dragon had chosen. It was mostly the Joan Baez back catalogue. Given Sophia Urquhart's voice, this made sense. The songs suited her pure soprano. But they seemed an odd choice for a student group in the early twenty-first century.

'Farewell Angelina', 'Banks of the Ohio', 'Go 'Way from My Window', 'There But for Fortune', 'With God on Our Side' . . . they all brought back Jude's youth and she loved hearing them, but she wondered who had made the selection. Was one of the band members an enthusiastic researcher of the period? Had there been some influence from Tadek, with his love of sixties music? Or from Andy Constant, who seemed never to have left the sixties? Maybe Jude would find out when she finally spoke to Sophia. Though she had more serious things to discuss with the girl than her musical tastes.

Carole and Zofia arrived in the pub at about twenty to ten. Which was good timing – more synchronicity, thought Jude – as Magic Dragon took a break, after their first set, at nine forty-five. So she was up at the bar buying drinks when the thirsty band approached.

'Sophia!' she cried. She was aware once again of the girl's expensive perfume, the smell that Andy Constant had detected on his attacker. 'I'm Jude – remember?'

'Yes, of course.'

'Wanted to hear your band. Your father was telling

me how good you were. Wonderful stuff! Can I get you a drink by way of congratulation?'

'Well, erm . . .'

'Go on, what would you like?'

Like most students, the girl didn't prevaricate long over the offer of a free drink. 'Pint of Stella, please. I get very thirsty singing.'

'I'm sure you do.' Jude added it to her order. 'Do come and join us. I've got a couple of friends who'd love to meet you.'

'Well, I . . .' She didn't want to, she wanted to be with her mates, but Sophia Urquhart was a well-brought-up girl and knew that accepting a drink from someone did involve certain social responsibilities. 'Yes, fine. But I'd better not be long, because we don't get much of a break before the next set.'

Sophia helped Jude carry the drinks across to her table, where she was introduced to Carole and Zofia. By first names only.

'Excellent music.' Carole had only heard one number, but she knew it was the appropriate thing to say.

'Not much of a turn-out tonight, though.' Sophia Urquhart looked round the room with disappointment. Now she had a chance to study the girl, Jude could see that she looked stressed and tired. The gold-red hair didn't quite have its usual lustre, and there was a redness around the eyes.

'Our type of music's not very popular, I'm afraid. Most of the people at uni want stuff they can dance to. Think this could be the last gig we do here.'

'Oh?'

'Landlord said, if we didn't pull in a bigger crowd, that'd be it.'

'Well, hopefully you'll be able to get booked in somewhere else.'

'Maybe.' The girl sounded listless, as though the fate of Magic Dragon didn't matter one way or the other.

Jude decided it was time to move into investigation mode. 'Sophia, Zofia is the sister of Tadeusz Jankowski.'

The shock took their suspect's breath away. She looked at the Polish girl with a mixture of incredulity and fear.

'I think you knew him,' said Jude.

'No. I . . . don't know what you're talking about.' Sophia Urquhart's hastily scrambled-together defence didn't sound convincing.

'You met at a music festival in Leipzig last summer.'

In the face of the facts, her resistance crumbled. 'Yes,' she admitted apathetically.

Zofia took over the interrogation. 'We know you play music together. Pavel has sent me recordings.'

'Pavel,' came the echo.

'I have come from Warsaw to England to find out what happened to Tadek . . . to my brother.'

'He was killed.'

'I know that. I want to know why he was killed. And who killed him.'

The English girl slumped like a rag doll. Her spirit was broken. 'Everyone wants to know that. Everyone always asks the same questions.'

'When you say everyone,' asked Carole, 'do you mean the police as well?'

Sophia looked puzzled. 'Presumably the police will be asking questions, if they're investigating Tadek's death.' She was now making no pretence of not having known the murder victim.

'But have the police questioned you?'

'About Tadek's death? Why should they?'

'Didn't they know about him being in love with you?'

'I don't think so. Nobody knew.'

'We managed to find out about it,' said Carole. 'It's pretty difficult to keep a love affair a complete secret. The participants may think nobody knows, but that's very rarely true.'

'Where did you meet after he came to England?' asked Jude more gently.

'We went to his room in Littlehampton. First he found me at the college. He had been texting and calling me and sending me songs ever since we met in Leipzig. He kept saying that he would come to England, and I didn't believe him. Then one day, early in the term, there he was on the campus. And he's telling me he loves me.'

'Were you pleased?'

'Yes. But it was difficult. I didn't want people to know about him.'

Zofia was offended by this apparent slight on her brother. 'Why you not want people to know about him?'

'Because . . .' The English girl looked confused. 'Because things were more complicated than he thought. Tadek thought if we loved each other, everything would be fine. That was all that mattered. We wouldn't have to think about practical things. He wanted me to drop out of uni, travel Europe with him, play music. I told him life could not be as simple as that. You have to get qualifications, make a living, get on with things. You can't just drift.'

As her brother had, Sophia Urquhart sounded as though she were parroting her father's sentiments. No relationship between the idealistic Pole and this conventional product of the Home Counties could ever have had a long-term future. But would Sophia have regarded the young man as enough of an inconvenience to murder him?

'Tadek thought that was possible,' responded Zofia sadly. 'All he wanted to do was just drift. Write his songs, play music and drift.'

'Well, that's no way to go through life.' Sophia Urquhart was once again her father's daughter.

'Did you love him?' asked Jude.

'Maybe for a while. I liked him, certainly. In Leipzig it was very romantic. Yes, I think I was in love with him then. It was a kind of unreal time, I was away from home and . . . yes. But that was an exotic dream, and it's difficult to recapture that kind of dream in somewhere like Fethering or Clincham. So the relationship had to end.'

'But he still loved you?'

'Probably.' She spoke as though the boy's continuing adoration had been a minor irritant. 'He kept phoning and texting me, and writing the songs. I got sick of it. Every time I heard his voice, saying, "Fee this, Fee that".'

'"Fee"?'

'It was his nickname for me. He could never pronounce "So-fie-ah". He always said "So-fee-ah". So he called me "Fee".'

'Ah.' Finally Jude had her explanation for Tadeusz Jankowski's dying words. But she didn't pursue it at that moment. Who knew how the girl might react on hearing that the boy had died with her name on his lips? Anyway, there were more urgent questions to be asked. 'You say you didn't want anyone to know about the connection between you. Is that why all of his music had to be taken from his room?'

Sophia Urquhart hesitated before replying, as though she needed to prepare her answer. 'Yes. Once he'd died, there was bound to be a police investigation. I didn't want to get involved in anything like that.'

'So what did you do with the CDs and things?'

'I put them in a litter bin on the street.'

'But not the guitar?'

'No, it wouldn't fit. I was looking for a skip to dump it in on my way to uni the day after Tadek died. But then I met one of my friends from the Drama set and she asked me what I was doing with the guitar. I remembered that Andy had asked us to bring instruments in, so that's how I explained it away. I thought it would be safely hidden in the Drama Studio. The police investigation wouldn't go as far as uni.'

'You mentioned Andy Constant,' said Jude.

'So?' The girl looked defiant, but a blush was spreading up from her neck.

'Might he have been another reason why your relationship with Tadek had to end?'

'I don't know what you're talking about.'

'I've just come from the hospital where Andy Constant is recovering from being stabbed.'

There was a silence around the table. The raucousness of a small group of students round the bar was suddenly loud.

'Andy told me about the affair that you and he had been having,' Jude went on. 'He told me about using the nickname "Joan" for you.'

'Which is the name Tadek used,' said Zofia.

'I didn't know . . . Andy . . . had been stabbed.' Sophia spoke haltingly, with great difficulty.

'No?' asked Carole sceptically.

'I thought it possible that someone might have attacked him . . . but I didn't know he had been . . . stabbed,' she said again. 'You say he's in hospital. Is he badly hurt?'

'He'll survive. Though he was lucky that his attacker was frightened off before more damage could be done.'

'Good,' said Sophia Urquhart softly.

'Andy also said,' Jude went on inexorably, 'that he recognized the perfume his attacker was wearing.'

'Perfume?' Sophia mouthed, uncomprehending.

'Yes. Andy Constant said his attacker smelt of the perfume that you use.'

The girl looked bewildered, but whether her bewilderment was genuine Carole and Jude could not guess.

Then suddenly a memory came to her, and her hand went up to her mouth. 'Oh, my God. My Barbour!'

'What?'

'My Barbour jacket. I couldn't find it last night. That would smell of my perfume.'

Carole thought this sudden recollection was too neat. She felt sure the girl was just play-acting. 'And what time did you go out last night?'

'About eight. I went to meet Daddy in a restaurant for dinner.' Sophia Urquhart caught sight of the other members of Magic Dragon, who were gesturing that they should start playing again. She half-rose from her seat.

'No, you can't go yet.' Carole said this so fiercely that the girl sat back down again. 'Tell me, were you at home before you went out to meet your father?'

'Yes, I'd left uni early. I wasn't feeling too good. So I got back to Fethering at about four.'

'And didn't go out again till eight?'

'No, I didn't.' If that were true, then Sophia Urquhart couldn't have been in the Drama Studio at the University of Clincham at six, stabbing her lecturer and former lover. 'It was when I went out to meet Daddy that I couldn't find my Barbour.'

'I don't suppose,' asked Carole cynically, 'that anyone could vouch for the fact that you were at home yesterday at the times you say you were?'

'As a matter of fact,' the girl replied almost smugly, 'there's someone who can. It was fairly slack in the office yesterday, so my brother Hamish was home by five. And he was still there when I left.'

With that and a curt nod, Sophia Urquhart went across to join the rest of Magic Dragon. The moment she arrived, the guitars and fiddle started the intro to 'All My Trials', and, whatever emotions were going through her mind, they were suppressed as her pure voice took up the song.

> *Hush little baby don't you cry,*
> *You know your mama was born to die.*
> *All my trials, Lord, soon be over.*

Just like Joan.

Carole and Jude looked at each other. And the identical logical progress was going through both their minds.

Chapter Thirty-seven

There was no difficulty the next morning in making an appointment with Ewan Urquhart. Though it was a Saturday, business in the offices of Urquhart & Pease remained slack. 'Won't really pick up again till the spring, when the sun comes out,' he had told Jude when she rang through. He sounded, as ever, urbane, the Old Carthusian to the last polished vowel.

If he thought it strange that Jude arrived with a friend to discuss the valuation of Woodside Cottage, he was too well bred to articulate his feelings. He and Hamish were both in the outer office when the women arrived. The younger man sat at a desk, looking blank. Despite the potential seriousness of the situation, Jude couldn't help being reminded of the old joke:

Why don't estate agents look out of the window in the morning?

Because it gives them nothing to do in the afternoon.

There appeared to be no other staff on duty that morning. Maybe 'in the spring, when the sun comes out', there would be more. Ewan Urquhart offered them coffee, but Carole and Jude said they'd just had some. He then invited them to join him in his back office. 'You hold the fort out here, Hamish. Fight off the hordes of eager purchasers, eh?'

His office gave the impression of the library of a gentlemen's club. There were shelves showing the leather spines of unopened books, and the intervening areas of wall were dark green, with a couple of framed sporting prints. In pride of place was an etching of the neo-Gothic splendour of Charterhouse school. The desk was reproduction mahogany, the chairs were reproduction leather. And Ewan Urquhart's vowels were reproduction upper-class.

He gestured them to chairs and said, 'Now do tell me what I can do for you, ladies? I didn't gather, Mrs Seddon, do you actually live at Woodside Cottage with, er . . . Jude?'

'Good heavens, no.' She didn't know whether he actually was making a suggestion of lesbianism, but it was a notion she wanted to dispel as quickly as possible. 'I live next door. High Tor.'

'I know it well. Part of my business to know the names of all the houses in the immediate vicinity. Never know when one might come up for sale, and one likes to keep a step ahead of the opposition. A highly competitive business, ours, you know.'

'I'm sure it is.' There was a silence. Having built themselves up to the confrontation, neither of the women was sure how next to proceed. They should have planned what to say.

'So, Mrs Seddon, am I to gather that you are also thinking of putting High Tor on the market? I would be more than happy to arrange a valuation for you too if—'

'No, no. I'm quite settled there at the moment, thank you.'

'Good.' As another silence extended itself, Ewan Urquhart pushed his fingers through the greying hair of his temples. 'So, please tell me. What can I do for you?'

Jude had had enough of prevarication.

'We've come to talk to you about Tadeusz Jankowski.' He looked surprised. 'Don't pretend you don't know the name.'

'I am making no such pretence. I read the news-papers and watch television. I know that Tadeusz Jankowski was the name of the young man stabbed here in Fethering a couple of weeks ago. But I don't know what he has to do with me.'

'He has to do with you the fact that he was in love with your daughter Sophia.'

Ewan Urquhart chuckled lightly. 'My dear Jude, I'm sure there are a lot of young men who have been in love with my daughter. She is an exceptionally beauti-ful and talented young woman. It is inevitable that she attracts the interest of the opposite sex. Whether she would give any encouragement to a Polish immi-grant, though, is another matter.'

'Your daughter met Tadeusz Jankowski at a music festival in Leipzig last summer,' Carole announced. 'While she was InterRailing in Europe.'

He did look shaken by this revelation, but they couldn't tell why. It could have been new information to him, or he could have been surprised by how much detail they knew of his daughter's life.

'They had an affair out in Germany,' Carole went on, 'and then Tadeusz Jankowski came over to England to look for her.'

For the first time Ewan Urquhart began to lose his cool. 'My daughter would not have a relationship with a foreigner!'

'What you mean, Ewan,' said Jude, 'is that you wouldn't like your daughter to have a relationship with a foreigner. I don't have children, but I've seen often enough that they do not always turn out as their parents want them to.'

'Sophia is an intelligent girl. She wouldn't mix with people who're unworthy of her.'

'And what makes you think Tadeusz Jankowski was unworthy of her?'

'His nationality, apart from anything else. All right, I know we have reason to thank some Polish airmen for the help they gave us against Hitler, but as a race they're not to be trusted. Sophia has been brought up to keep foreigners at a healthy distance.'

'Didn't it occur to you,' asked Carole, 'that if she went InterRailing round Europe, she might meet some foreigners?'

'Yes. I wasn't keen on the whole idea of a gap year, but Sophia managed to persuade me. She went against my better judgement. But I can assure you you've got the wrong end of the stick if you think she's been having affairs with foreigners. When Sophia does get to the

point of having affairs, I'm sure she will be very selec-
tive in her choice of men.'

'"When she gets to the point of having affairs"?'
Jude echoed. 'How old is your daughter, Ewan?'

'Nineteen, nearly twenty.'

'Well, surely you know from the media that these
days most young women of nearly twenty have been
sexually active for some years.'

'Most young women, maybe,' he snapped. 'Not
Sophia!'

For the first time they realized the depth of his
obsession with his daughter, and his obsession with her
purity. In her father's eyes, no man would ever be good
enough for Sophia Urquhart. He had built up an image
of her as untouchable, and what he might do to anyone
who threatened that image was terrifying.

'If you claim not to know about her affair with
Tadeusz Jankowski, then presumably the same goes for
her relationship with Andy Constant.'

'Andy Constant?'

'You know the name?'

'Of course. I've met the man. He's Sophia's Drama
tutor at the university.' He was now very angry. 'Look,
what is this? What are you two up to? I don't have to listen to malicious slander of my daughter from small-
town gossips.'

'It is not malicious slander. It is the truth. Andy
Constant was, until recently, your daughter's lover.'

'No! He couldn't . . . Sophia wouldn't . . . Not with a
man of that age . . . She's not like her mother. Her
mother was little better than a tart, who'd open her legs

325

for any man who offered her a smile and a kind word.' Gifts of which, both women imagined, she hadn't received many at home. 'Sophia's not like that. She wouldn't . . . She hasn't been brought up like that!' Now he was really losing control. His face was growing red and congested. 'God, if I thought a man like that Andy Constant had touched my daughter, I'd kill him!'

He seemed then to realize what he'd said, and opened and closed his mouth, as if trying to take the words back.

'Which,' said Carole calmly, 'is what you failed to do last night.'

'What?'

'You stabbed Andy Constant,' said Jude, 'but you didn't kill him.'

'I'm sorry? Where is this supposed to have happened?'

'In the Drama Studio at Clincham College. You waited for Andy Constant in the lighting box. When he came in, you stabbed him. You would have stabbed him more than once, but you heard someone arriving. It was me, actually. You passed me in the lobby, I think, when you made your escape.'

'You're saying I stabbed Andy Constant?' His eyes were wild now, darting about from one of the women to the other.

'Yes. For some reason – maybe to disguise yourself – you wore your daughter's Barbour when you committed the crime. You couldn't stand the thought of anyone touching Sophia, so you tried to kill Andy Constant – just as you had killed Tadeusz Jankowski.'

He shook his head wordlessly, a pathetic figure now. His urbanity had deserted him, leaving a shell of a man, a husk wearing an Old Carthusian tie.

'Maybe you stabbed the young man here in this office,' said Carole. 'It was somewhere near the betting shop, somewhere along this parade probably. Or maybe the attack took place in your car. You'd managed to get him into it on some pretext.'

'I can't stand this,' Ewan Urquhart moaned feebly. 'What on earth is going on?'

'Don't worry, Dad. I'll deal with it.'

They hadn't heard the door from the outer office open. Carole and Jude both looked round at the same time to the source of the new voice.

And saw Hamish Urquhart standing in the doorway. With a long kitchen knife in his hand.

Chapter Thirty-eight

'Hamish, call the police,' said Ewan Urquhart. 'These two women are mad and dangerous.'

'They're certainly dangerous,' his son agreed, 'but I don't think the police are the right people to deal with them.'

'I don't understand. I've hardly understood anything that's happened for the last half-hour.'

'Don't worry about it, Dad. I'm in control of the situation.' And, for the first time in Jude's dealings with him, Hamish Urquhart did seem to be in control. There was now a dignity about him which she had not seen before. She was aware of the power in his stocky body and the cold menace in his eyes.

Both women made as if to stand up, but were stilled by a wave of the knife.

'I'll sort this out, Dad,' said Hamish. 'Just as I sorted out your other problems.'

'What other problems?'

'I know how you feel about Soph, Dad. I know how you'd feel about her getting into the wrong company. Particularly the wrong male company. So I sorted things out for you.'

'What do you mean, Hamish? I don't know what you've been doing.'

'No, I know you don't.' There was a quiet smile of pride on the young man's face. 'You didn't need to know. I did things the way you've always said they should be done. The British way. No fuss. No showing off. Not standing up and saying "Aren't I wonderful?" But that quiet British pride of doing the right thing without crowing about it.'

It was chilling to hear the young man echoing his father's words. Ewan Urquhart cleared his throat uneasily and said, 'What do you mean by doing the right thing, Hamish?'

'Getting rid of the wrong sort of people. People who threaten us Urquharts. I knew what you'd think about Soph going around with a foreigner, so I . . . dealt with the problem. Never wanted you to know anything about it, but these two busybodies have told you, so you may as well have the details. Soph told me about this chap she was seeing, this Pole, and I knew you'd disapprove. So I thought, "No need to get the old man worried about this. Time for me to show a bit of Urquhart initiative and sort the problem out for him."

'So I got his address from Soph and went round to see him. He wasn't in, but the door to his room was open. Inside I found . . . He had written songs about her, songs about Soph. There were tapes, CDs, a guitar. I took them all. I didn't want any connection ever to be made between my sister and . . . *that foreigner*!'

'Sophia implied that *she*'d taken the guitar and things,' said Carole.

329

'Did she? No, I got them, then I gave them to her to dispose of as she thought fit.'

'So your sister knew what you had done?' asked Jude. 'She knew it was you who stabbed Tadek?'

Hamish Urquhart smiled a patronizing smile. 'I didn't tell her. There was no need for her to be involved in anything distasteful. I've always tried to protect Sophia from the nasty things in life.'

Just as your father has, thought Jude. She looked across at Ewan Urquhart, whose face registered growing shock and disbelief as Hamish continued to describe his actions.

'Anyway I had just started driving back here, when I saw the Pole walking back to his room. I stopped the car, told him that I was Sophia's brother and that she was back at the office and wanted to see him. He was over the moon about that and got into the car without a hint of suspicion. So I drove him back here. Knew you'd be off for a couple of hours doing a valuation, Dad, knew it was unlikely there'd be much trade on a Thursday afternoon.

'Anyway, soon as we get back here, his first question is: where's Sophia? I tell him she must have just slipped out for a minute. Said she was probably shopping along the parade.'

Finally Carole and Jude had the explanation for Tadek's appearance in the betting shop on the afternoon of his death. He had been looking for Sophia. His last moments of life had been spent looking for the woman he loved. Though whether they would ever be able to pass the information on to anyone else looked, at that moment, unlikely.

Hamish smiled in self-congratulation. 'I thought that was rather clever. Thinking she was nearby and would be back in a minute, he relaxed. I asked him to take his coat off, and then revealed the real purpose of his visit. I told the sneaky bastard we took a pretty dim view of his interest in Soph and . . .' He made an eloquent gesture with his knife.

Ewan Urquhart was having difficulty in believing what he was hearing. 'You stabbed him?'

'Yes. In the chest.' Hamish grinned with self-satisfaction. 'Worked out rather well, really. I hadn't decided what I was going to do with the body, but then he put his coat on and went out. Luck was on my side, of course – it always is for people who dare to be bold. The weather suddenly turned, and that hailstorm meant nobody saw him leaving the office. Then he went to the betting shop and . . .' He spread his hands wide. They all knew what had happened next. 'I think I can be said to have used the Urquhart initiative.'

'And Sophia's lecturer?' asked Ewan Urquhart, his eyes wide with terror.

'Yes. Andy Constant,' said Hamish in a self-congratulatory tone. 'Soph had mentioned him to me, but I didn't know until recently that he'd been coming on to her.' He grinned triumphantly at Jude. 'In fact I had my suspicions confirmed when I was doing the valuation of your cottage. There was some writing in a notebook on your kitchen table which linked Andy Constant's name to Soph's.

331

'Well, I knew what your views would be about that, Dad – the idea of someone nearly your own age messing around with your daughter. And I was right, because I just heard you telling these ladies what you thought about that. So again I thought, no need to bother you about it. I took things into my own hands. Soph had told me a bit about Andy Constant's habits, and I worked out that the Drama Studio would be the best place to get him. I borrowed Soph's Barbour because I thought it'd make me look more like one of the students, you know, pass unnoticed on the campus. And I told Soph, if anyone asked, she should say I was at home with her yesterday evening. Oh, I thought the whole thing through. And I would have killed the lecturer too, if I hadn't been disturbed. By you, I gather,' he said, turning with sudden vindictiveness towards Jude.

She said nothing. The knife was dangerously close, and Hamish Urquhart's eyes showed that he was way beyond responding to logical argument.

'So what are you going to do now?' asked his father, very quietly.

Hamish gestured with the knife. 'Deal with these two,' he said airily. 'I'll put their bodies in the van and dispose of them after dark.'

'Where?'

'I don't need to bother you with the details, Dad. Trust me, it's all in hand.' He still sounded like a parody of Ewan Urquhart. Hamish was relishing the reversal. For once, he was patronizing his father, he was the one making the decisions. 'We need never talk about it again. And don't you worry. If I find any more unsuitable men sniffing round Soph, trust me to deal with them.'

'Are you telling me, Hamish, that you killed Tadeusz Jankowski and nearly killed Andy Constant because you didn't think they were suitable men to mix with your sister?'

'Yes, Dad. Of course. Come on, you're not usually so slow on the uptake.' The boy guffawed. 'Usually I'm the one in that role.'

'But, Hamish, don't you realize, killing someone because they're having a relationship you disapprove of, well . . . that's no different from an "honour killing", the kind of thing Asian immigrants get involved in?'

'Nonsense. Totally different. I'm just upholding the honour of the Urquharts, that's all.' He looked around the room, then turned to his father and said compassionately, 'Look, I'll sort this out, Dad. No need for you to be involved. Why don't you nip out to Polly's for a coffee and a teacake? Come back in half an hour and the whole thing'll be sorted.'

He spoke so airily that Carole and Jude had to remind themselves that what he was proposing to 'sort' was their deaths. To their dismay, Ewan Urquhart rose, zombie-like, from behind his desk and said, 'Yes, Hamish. Maybe that's a good idea.'

When his father reached the door, the son stopped him with an arm on his sleeve. 'One thing you haven't said, Dad . . .'

'What?'

'You haven't said you're proud of me for what I've

333

done.' The appeal in the young man's face was naked and pathetic.

'No, I haven't,' said his father dully.

'Well, please. Say you're proud of me.'

The two generations looked at each other. In Hamish Urquhart's eyes was abject pleading, asking his father at last to give him a ration of praise. The expression in Ewan Urquhart's eyes was harder to read.

The older man moved very quickly. With his left hand he snatched the knife from his son's grasp. His right, bunched in a fist, crashed up into the young man's chin.

Hamish Urquhart went down like a dead weight, thumping the back of his head on a shelf as he fell. He lay immobile. As ever, his father had proved stronger than he was.

Carole and Jude breathed out, letting the accumulated tension twitch out of their bodies.

Chapter Thirty-nine

Hamish Urquhart was taken in for questioning by the police later that Saturday morning. Their suspicions had been moving towards him for some time, and these were confirmed by their interview with Andy Constant in the hospital. He had also been identified by CCTV camera footage on the campus of the University of Clincham. Soon after, the Maiden Avenue entrance to the campus was bricked up.

In police custody Hamish Urquhart made no attempt to deny his crimes and was quickly charged with the murder of Tadeusz Jankowski and the attempted murder of Andy Constant. His defence team were in a quandary as to whether they should put in a plea of insanity. He showed no remorse about his actions, and kept telling them that he had finally done something that would make his father proud of him.

While he was on remand, his sister Sophia visited him as often as she could. Their father didn't. In Ewan Urquhart's view, his son had always been unsatisfactory. Now he was no longer on the scene, the older man found it easier and more convenient to forget that he had ever had a son.

And, once her brother had been sentenced to life, Sophia's visits to him ceased.

She dropped out of the University of Clincham before the end of that academic year and went to join her father in the offices of Urquhart & Pease. She learnt the business quickly and her good looks went down well with the male clients. There were plenty of admirers around, but none of her relationships lasted for more than a few months. All of the aspiring swains failed for the same reason. They couldn't match the impossibly high standards set by Ewan Urquhart for 'the kind of man worthy of my little Soph'.

Magic Dragon broke up even before Sophia left the university and she didn't sing much after that. The gold of her hair faded and her face and neck thickened out, as she reconciled herself to her fate of looking after her father until he died. Which, of course, suited Ewan Urquhart perfectly. And everyone appreciated the sterling work Sophia put in making teas at Old Carthusian cricket matches. Maybe after her father's death she might be able to carve out a life for herself, but nobody was putting bets on it.

Bets continued, however, to be put on horses at the betting shop (though most of the shop's income continued to come from the fixed-price gaming machines). Sonny 'Perfectly' Frank continued to ask 'Know anything?' to everyone who came in. The waiters from the Golden Palace regularly abandoned serving sweet and sour pork for the quick fix of a bet and kept up their high-pitched wind-chime banter. Pauline continued to enjoy the warm, while Wes and Vic continued to neglect their decorating work. They still shouted at every race, surprised like circling goldfish every time their latest brilliant fancy turned out to be a failure.

One regular ceased to attend. After his flu Harold Peskett had resumed going to the betting shop with his elaborate scribbled permutations of doubles and trebles. Then finally one day the results worked for him, and he won over a thousand pounds. So great was the shock that he died of a heart attack right there in the betting shop. Though it was rather inconvenient for Ryan and Nikki, there was a general view that it would have been the way he wanted to go.

Melanie Newton never went back into a betting shop. She didn't need to. Her laptop offered everything she required. She could play the virtual casinos and roulette wheels twenty-four hours a day. Which she did. And as her credit card debts grew, she kept taking up offers of new credit cards. And kept moving to ever more dingy accommodation, one step ahead of her creditors.

Andy Constant was not the kind of man to change. He recovered completely from his stab-wound, and the scar became another part of his seduction technique. He told wide-eyed female freshers how a woman had once been so desolated by his ending their relationship that she had persuaded her brother to attack him. He continued to entice women into his little kingdom of the Drama Studio. And his wife Esther continued to think that they had a happy marriage, though Andy's workload did mean he often had to stay late at the university.

Whenever Jude thought of Andy Constant, she felt very sheepish and shamefaced. She realized how near she had come to making a complete fool of herself. But she knew that, if the same circumstances were to arise, she might again prove susceptible.

So she continued to do some good by her healing. And to wonder whether she really ought at some point to move on from Fethering.

Zofia Jankowska stayed there, though, moving after a few weeks out of Woodside Cottage to a flat of her own. She enrolled in a journalism course at the University of Clincham, and subsidized her studies by continuing to work at the Crown and Anchor. Ted Crisp grudgingly admitted that she was the best bar manager he'd ever had, 'even though she is foreign'.

Carole Seddon watched the miracle of her grand-daughter Lily's development with growing awe. The child's existence brought her closer to Stephen and Gaby, but she resisted their ongoing attempts to include David in family encounters.

And she appreciated increasingly the sedate friend-ship of Gerald Hume. They didn't often go out for meals or anything like that. Such activities would have had too much of the flavour of a 'date' about them. But they did quite often meet in the betting shop.

Carole became very quickly convinced that Gerald's 'system' for applying his accountancy skills to gambling was just as ineffectual as every other 'system' that had been invented since mankind had first bet on horses. But logic did occasionally work, and she drew